THE WRATH of HEROES

DAVID BENEM

THE WRATH of HEROES

A REQUIEM FOR HEROES
BOOK TWO

The Wrath of Heroes
A Requiem for Heroes, Book Two
© 2017 David Benem. All rights reserved.
ISBN: 978-0-9961939-2-4

Cover and formatting by Damonza.com
Map by Dan Martin (http://www.wondrousworks.art)

ACKNOWLEDGEMENTS

I CAN'T DO this alone and I've realized I wouldn't want to. I've had plenty of excellent help from plenty of excellent people and that's made the journey all the more worthwhile. Thanks first and foremost to my most patient and loving wife, who's always the first to give me praise even when I'm not certain it's deserved. Thanks to my amazing kids, whose many talents and many smiles remind me every day there is real joy in this world. Thanks to my dear mom and dear sister. Thanks to my many fine friends who read the words nearly as quickly as I wrote them—you helped me feel good about the first book and even better about the second. And thanks to the fabulous Laura M. Hughes for the insightful edits and inspiring comments.

Special thanks also to the indie fantasy community, particularly the Terrible Ten and the SPFBO crowd. Long live the writers!

And, most of all, thanks to those many supportive readers who've been willing to take a chance on my work, for taking the time to leave reviews and mention it to friends and online. Word of mouth is everything for an author, and I can't thank you enough. I hope you enjoy this next step in the journey as much as I have.

To Dad,
I miss you.

The Waters of World's End
Xallorath
GHUNT
The Highlands
THE FIRST FOREST
Pryam's Bay
Farwatch
TYRENE
STORMFALL
Beldin
IRONMOOR
N
Rune
RELLIC
Silverflow
Drimrill
RIVERWEAVE
The Sea of Thieves
TREEMARK
RAVEN'S ROOST
THE TEETH
Trader's Pass
The Ghostwood
The Sullen Sea
The Southwalls
KHAL
Khaldisia
Arranan
ZYN
A'DUAB
The Bowl of Fire
The Ebony Sea
SHACKLESPORT
Rimgald

1
BACK IN THE SADDLE

THIS WOULD BE a lot easier if I were drunk.

Lannick eased back in the saddle and scratched at his scarred face, grimacing crookedly as he did. His destination, Kevlin's farm, stood only another day's ride distant. There a motley bunch of old soldiers awaited, a fair number of whom either thought him dead these last nine years or at least wished he'd been.

A gull squawked in the afternoon sky, a rumor of Ironmoor and the Sullen Sea two days behind them. The place dragged at his thoughts still, with murky, wine-blurred memories of too many years spent draining too many tankards. Too many years spent blaming himself for the murder of his family at the hands of General Fane.

He sighed. Part of him worried he wasn't fit to leave that place, like he belonged to its seedy taverns the same way a corpse belonged to a tomb. But another part of him—an increasingly louder part—hoped leaving meant a sort of liberation, like he'd buried that bloated carcass of shameful mistakes and left it behind.

He looked to the landscape aside the dusty road. Low hills with thin trees and tall grasses rolled languidly about, dotted by the occasional farmhouse or mill of piled stones.

Lannick grimaced again.

And nary a tavern in sight.

"Now there, Captain," said Brugan beside him, the barkeep's thick form looking as though it might cause the scrawny, piebald horse beneath him to snap in two. "I'm seeing that old look, that sad scowl you'd wear when you'd skulk into my tavern after making an ass of yourself the night before."

"You needn't worry, Brugan. I won't be turning back to *that*."

"But Lannick," Brugan rumbled on, acting as though Lannick hadn't spoken, "you needn't feel that way. You gave your speech to these lads. They agreed to join this effort and follow you, remember?"

Lannick remembered well his "speech." He'd managed precisely one word: *vengeance*. His heart had trembled that day much as his hands would the morning after a bad drunk. He knew the men harbored ill feelings toward him for what had transpired after the Battle of Pryam's Bay, almost a decade before. After Fane branded Lannick a traitor, every last one of his men was decommissioned. Those who'd voiced objections were tossed into the brig.

First a parade of proud heroes, then a march of shackled prisoners.

He looked to Brugan. "I reckon most of those men blame me for what happened after the war."

"Don't fret, Lannick. The lads will come round. They respected you. All of them did, and they will again."

"That was a long time ago. When you gathered them up in Ironmoor a couple of weeks back, all I saw was doubt and anger. They think I betrayed and abandoned them and I reckon it won't be easy convincing them otherwise."

Brugan clapped a hand against Lannick's shoulder. "You've changed these past months. You've changed into something closer to your old self and the lads will see that. Hell, you even look like your old self again, if the eyes can forgive a crooked jaw and twisted nose!" He chuckled. "Even with your new dents and divots, you look less the scoundrel than that shaggy-haired, stubble-faced drunk I got too used to seeing at *The Wanton Vicar*."

Lannick scratched at the salt-and-pepper hair he'd been keeping cut short in soldier's fashion. "I always was the handsome sort," he said with a smirk.

"You and me both!" Brugan laughed, patting his flat, nubby face. "But you need to trust me, Lannick," he said, sounding serious once more. "The lads will notice the way you've changed, and I know it won't take them long. Let your deeds speak for you and the lads will listen."

Lannick nodded, eyes dropping to hands looped by the leather reins of his horse. His palms were yellow with callouses, his knuckles striated by small scabs and scars. They seemed different hands than what they'd been months before, when they'd seemed most suited to drawing a tankard to the lips over and again.

Now they seemed hands most fit for hefting a sword, and that notion carried with it the thought of the man for

whom that sword was intended. That mad, vicious bastard who'd taken from him all he held dear.

General Fane.

Lannick bunched his hands into fists, a sudden anger
swelling within him. "Aye."

"Lannick, all you need do to make this happen is keep
from slipping into those old habits again. Stay away from
the drink. You need to—"

"I know," Lannick said firmly, his hatred of Fane chasing doubt to the far corners of his head. "There's no need
to worry."

"Better not be. I'm happy to be your sergeant again,
but I'm through being your nursemaid."

"Enough, Brugan."

Brugan regarded him with a cocked brow, his lumpy
face puckering in odd places. "Oh?"

Lannick was rankled by the challenge in his friend's
tone. "Dead gods, man! I don't need such talk from you!"

"Really? You need such talk *most* of all from me. You
don't think I recognize that look in your eyes? That look
when you waver from old hero to old drunk? I have every
right to remind you, to keep you in line. How can you
expect the men to keep from doubting you so long as you
doubt yourself?"

Lannick stared straight ahead. His will faltered
at times, sure, but he remained determined to see
this through.

"I shouldn't make sure you're staying true to this?"
Brugan asked. "I shouldn't make certain the resolve hasn't
fled your heart?"

"No," Lannick said, voice steady. "You think I don't

want a drink now and then? Of course I do. But I've stopped blaming myself for the death of my family, and realize now their blood has not stained my hands. It's Fane. It was always Fane, and it took me far too long to realize that. Don't worry, Brugan. I'll not let my thirst—or any other weakness—keep me from vengeance."

"That's it, Lannick," Brugan said, his tone softening. "You can't be forgetting that, no matter how hard it is. We can win this thing, but we'll need every bit of venom and vigor within us all. Keep your edges sharp, lad. Even if it means reopening those old wounds now and again."

Near evening they caught sight of other riders kicking up yellow dust far ahead. The glint of metal shone upon the riders in the waning sunlight, weapons likely. Crows cawed from a skinny tree then scattered, as though racing to warn the local farmers of strangers on the road.

"Perhaps a few more lads riding to join our cause," Brugan said, pride lifting his voice. "Cudgen said he'd passed along word to his relations. Not former soldiers, but a few capable lads whose father commanded a garrison near the Southwalls. The fellow died at the front because Fane refused to send reinforcements. We can expect them and perhaps more."

Lannick didn't answer, studying the figures. Two on horseback, two others atop a horse-drawn cart. They were well distant but it seemed clear they were riding toward them, not away. What was more, Lannick spied red sashes on their shirts. *The High King's men. Men under Fane's command.*

"More of our lads," Brugan said, a smile creeping across his face.

"No," Lannick said, finding the hilt of his sword. "Fane's men. Keep your weapon ready in case this gets complicated."

Brugan shaded his eyes with a hand and squinted. After a moment his wide face paled. "Dead gods. There are a couple of lads in the bed of that wagon. I heard rumors of conscriptions, especially after the thanes got word of the desertions at the front. They'd never try that sort of thing in Ironmoor where it'd draw notice, but out here in the countryside I reckon it's a different matter. We should leave the road and make for cover."

Lannick shook his head. "They've seen us already and they'll track us down if that's what they're after. Best to take our chances and try talking our way around any questions."

"And hope they find no use for a couple of old soldiers?"

"I'd suggest only admitting to being a barkeep and his favorite drunk," Lannick said through his crooked grin.

Brugan smiled anew. "I can play that part, and have an idea or two. Don't say a word. Pretend you can't hear and can't speak. Leave the talking to me."

"I usually do."

The distance between them was closing. Soon Lannick could see the figures wore not only the red sashes of the High King's armies but leather armor and plenty of weapons, as well. The wagon held two young men with hands bound, though it seemed big enough to hold half a dozen or so more. Lannick reckoned the soldiers were itching to fill it.

"These soldiers aren't likely to be the hardest of men," Lannick said. "Regulars, perhaps, but not the sort needed at the front. Probably old dogs or lame ones." He frowned and rubbed at his aching jaw. "But then we're not exactly at our best anymore, either."

"Speak for yourself," Brugan said with a huff. He loosened the straps holding his hammer to his saddle. "I can still crack heads with the best of 'em. I was always gentle with you when I had to toss you from my tavern but most other louts weren't so lucky."

Lannick studied the soldiers as they approached. They were much as he expected: two with bellies broad as their horses, two others with faces pinched from age. Nevertheless, they were well-armed and armored, while Lannick and Brugan had merely a sword and hammer between them.

"Halt, by order of Chamberlain Alamis," said the fattest one, a man on horseback with a sour sneer twisting his pimply face. He raised a hand and pulled his miserable-looking horse to a stop.

"The *chamberlain*?" Brugan chuckled. "Since when is he—"

"Since High King Deragol died two nights back," the soldier said with an annoyed tone. "Died without an heir, he did."

A terrible weight fell upon Lannick's mind and his hand moved to his Coda. *The High King? Dead without an heir?* His thoughts were pulled along an old and almost forgotten course, a feverish curiosity coupled with a driving purpose.

Most regarded the High King as a blithering idiot, but

Lannick knew the man and his forebears carried a divine blessing. Illienne the Light Eternal had blessed the High King's line with the grace to rule Rune, and the ability to touch the Godswell where Illienne and Yrghul descended into oblivion a thousand years before. It was said only those of that bloodline could touch that eternal gate.

Without the High King, could another open the Godswell? Lannick gripped the box holding his Coda, seized by fear and desperate for the information the Variden were certain to be trading.

"Hadn't heard that," Brugan said, shaking Lannick from his thoughts. "Troubling news."

"Needn't trouble you fellas," said another mounted soldier, an old one near the wagon with pale eyes and half an ear missing. He had three yellow stripes on his red sash, marking him a sergeant and the leader of this contingent. "We're still at war and the army needs sword-arms all the same," the man continued. "You fellas look like you'd make fine fodder for the front."

Lannick did his best to appear unmoved. The problem was the more he tried to look like he wasn't troubled the more troubled he became. He felt sweat beading on his forehead and it wasn't overly hot.

"Sorry, lads," said Brugan. "My friend there is deaf. Dumb, too. Can't hear, can't talk. I'm a cousin of his—alas, with a trick knee and a few other infirmities myself—taking him back to the family farm so he's no longer a burden to the good folk of Ironmoor. He can milk a cow, maybe, but he's not good for much else."

"That so?" said the half-eared sergeant, matter-of-factly. "I reckon I've heard worse lies along this road, but a lie's a lie all the same. You boys look familiar…" He stared to Lannick. "You ever serve?"

Brugan puffed his chest a bit. "I did, and proudly at that. That is until my knee took a hard blow from a hammer in the last war. Sadly, my cousin's afflictions kept him from taking up arms for the Crown."

"That so," the sergeant said again, pale eyes narrowing. "I guess my sight must be failing me, 'cause he looks real familiar. Clagger, see whether this 'deaf' idiot minds a wee whisper in his ear."

Clagger, the fat one who'd stopped them, clicked his tongue and eased his horse forward. He came even with Lannick and looked to him with a nasty smile. He pulled uncomfortably close, tilting in his saddle until Lannick could see the purple veins on the bulb of his nose and smell his fetid breath.

"Now, lads," Brugan said, holding his hands out. "We don't want no trouble, least of all from honorable soldiers of Rune. As I said I served honorably myself many years ago! Men like us—old soldiers—needn't disagree."

The sergeant sneered. "Clagger?"

Clagger grabbed Lannick's chin between plump fingers and drew even closer, bringing his mouth just beside Lannick's ear. Lannick felt sweat trickle down his brow, wishing very much Brugan had told a very different lie. With his far hand he found the hilt of his sword again.

"Good day, lad," Clagger said softly.

Lannick blinked but did not otherwise move, keeping his eyes straight ahead and playing the role of deaf mute.

"I said…" Clagger's voice rose, its volume becoming painful.

He's going to shout. Shout as loud as he can.

Lannick wasn't about to have his ear ruined. *Damn it, Brugan!*

He heard Clagger's deep inhalation. Then Lannick gave the fellow a hard pop in the gut with his elbow followed by a fierce whack to the throat with the back of his fist. Clagger reeled backward, struggling for balance with flailing arms. He teetered and fell from his horse with a heavy thud.

"To arms!" screamed the half-eared sergeant, struggling for his sword as his horse wheeled beneath him. The soldiers driving the wagon followed suit while Clagger kicked at the dirt, hands pressed against his throat as he gasped.

Brugan freed his hammer from its straps. He pulled his horse close to one of the soldiers seated atop the wagon. Brugan twisted the hammer back and made ready to swing.

Lannick ripped his sword from its scabbard and dropped from his horse. He moved straight at Clagger. The man's eyes bulged as Lannick closed upon him. He struggled upon his back, waving hands frantically. Lannick noticed the man's sword in a scabbard on his horse but the beast meandered a dozen or so yards away.

Lannick felt a hint of mercy stir within him. Then the nearby crack of Brugan's hammer against bone forced such notions from his head.

There can be no half-measures now. No turning back.

He plunged his blade into the man, through a pleading hand, a layer of hardened leather and into the chest beneath.

Lannick pried his blade from the corpse and looked about. The soldier Brugan had struck twitched on the dirt beside the wagon, half his head turned into a bloody crater by Brugan's hammer.

Only two soldiers remained, the two older ones. The veterans. The half-eared sergeant with a dented blade in hand and a hooded, squint-eyed codger standing in the wagon's bed with a bow drawn.

Lannick focused on the bowman, knowing the half-eared sergeant was too far away to do him harm. This man with the arrow nocked was the man who could kill him now.

The bowstring twanged.

Lannick lurched forward and arched his back, contorting as an arrow whistled behind him. He rushed ahead and pressed near Clagger's wayward horse, keeping its mass between him and the archer. He snatched the horse's reins and tried guiding it along. He cooed in its ear and scratched its shoulder but the horse fought and stamped its hooves.

There were grunts and the clang of metal. Lannick knew Brugan had engaged the sergeant. With any luck the big barkeep would avoid the blade long enough to whack it from its wielder's hands.

The bowstring sang again. Lannick ducked behind the horse as a shaft whizzed overhead. "Move, beast!" he urged, seizing its mane in a fist and pushing forward. At last the horse yielded and began prancing along a round-about course toward the archer.

Lannick chanced a look over the saddle. He saw Brugan and the sergeant grappling, both atop their mounts but in peril of being unhorsed. Each held the arm of the other, their weapons swaying overhead but incapable of being put to use. Black blood colored Brugan's sleeve. Lannick guessed that if not for the wound the barkeep would have overpowered his opponent by now.

Twang!

Lannick ducked behind the horse just before hearing the *thunk* of an arrow sinking into flesh. He hissed as the horse beside him shuddered.

The beast reared clumsily and then fell. Lannick barely managed to dance away before the falling steed could crush his legs. A shaft protruded from the horse's neck, the wood still quivering.

Not more than twenty feet away the squint-eyed archer stood atop the cart. He drew another arrow from his quiver.

Lannick saw his moment and ran. There was no cover between him and the bow but the distance was short and the archer unready. Lannick drew back his blade, roaring as his did.

The archer nocked the arrow but wasn't quick enough. Lannick leapt over the cart's edge between the wide-eyed conscripts and dove headlong into the man, knocking him from the wagon. They fell in a tangled heap, Lannick barely managing to avoid the arrowhead meeting his neck.

The archer flailed but couldn't stop Lannick's sword from piercing his ribs. He clawed at Lannick with empty hands, then fell still as Lannick twisted the blade and drove it deeper. Lannick rolled away and rubbed sweat and blood from his eyes.

He sucked in a breath and lay still. He listened, but

there were no grunts or shuffles or clashes of steel. He exhaled. It seemed Brugan had managed to smash his hammer into the sergeant's skull.

"So," came a deadpan voice, "seems you're not much of a soldier after all."

Lannick jerked upward. There, just half a dozen yards away, the half-eared sergeant sat on his horse, leering triumphantly over Brugan. The big barkeep struggled to his knees, his sleeve soaked through with blood and another spot welling on the opposite shoulder. He reached for his hammer with shaking hands but it was too far for him to grasp.

Lannick tugged at his own weapon but it wouldn't move, the blade stuck between the fallen archer's ribs. He scrambled about and found the archer's bow and an arrow nearby. He grabbed both then fumbled to fit the arrow against the string.

"No need to stand," the half-eared man said to Brugan. "You'll die just as well on your knees."

Lannick drew the bow, aimed for the man's head, and loosed the arrow. It flew toward him but Lannick had been too hasty. The shaft sailed just wide of its mark.

The sergeant looked away from Brugan, startled. His pale eyes narrowed and he bared his teeth ferociously.

Lannick searched about and spied the archer's quiver. Another chance. He seized a shaft and nocked it.

The sergeant had returned his attention to Brugan who was suddenly out of reach of his blade. The big barkeep had collapsed, whether by wit or weakness Lannick couldn't guess.

"Bah!" the sergeant cursed. But then he hesitated,

seemingly trying to decide whether to dismount and finish Brugan or make a move toward Lannick.

Lannick used the moment to aim carefully. He was no marksman, but at this short distance and with this time he could shoot true. He breathed, made certain of his shot, and released the string.

The arrow found its target, sinking into the shoulder of the sergeant's sword-arm. The man grunted and his weapon fell from his hand. "Bah!" he said again.

Lannick snatched another arrow.

The sergeant kicked his horse's flanks. The beast leapt forward, past Brugan and onto the road. The sergeant looked back to Lannick with a glower, then charged down the road at a gallop.

Lannick loosed the arrow. It smacked into the horse's haunch. The mount stumbled and clumsily fell, pitching the sergeant from atop it. The horse rolled over the sergeant then struggled upright. The sergeant, though, remained face down on the road a hundred feet away, immobile.

"Dead gods," Lannick spat. He knew they needed to get clear of the place, and fast. He dropped the bow and rushed toward his friend. "Brugan!"

Brugan groaned and rolled onto his back, a pained grimace on his face. "Bastard fought dirty," he said with a wince. "Kicked my horse and the dumb beast dropped me. Then he stabbed my shoulder when I rushed him. A lucky poke is all. I'll live."

"Lucky," said Lannick in agreement, though he wondered how much of it had been rust and age.

Brugan pulled himself up and stared at his arm, the

brown sleeve slick with blood and stuck to the skin. "I don't think it's too deep but I'll need to stitch it. You hiding anything to drink? Any strong spirits?"

Lannick's hand found his satchel and then the outline of his flask. He paused for an instant. *No half-measures, and no turning back.* He slapped open the flap and handed the flask to Brugan. "Use all you need, then toss the flask aside. I'll not be needing it any longer."

"Very well, lad." He pressed himself to his feet, swaying slightly and steadying himself against Lannick.

"You shouldn't ride."

"No. I reckon not."

"Get in the cart. We'll take it and their horses and head off the road."

"And what of us?" came a timid voice.

Lannick looked to the cart where the bound conscripts still sat. They were skinny fellows, barely older than boys and clad in little more than rags. "Are you lads alright?"

They nodded in unison, grubby faces easing with apparent relief.

Lannick moved back to the corpse that trapped his sword and, with some effort, yanked the blade loose. He cleaned the blood and gristle from the weapon then strode to the wagon.

The boys held gangly arms toward him, thin hands squeezed together by thick rope. Lannick set about sawing through the cords to free their bruised and bloodied wrists.

"You can walk?" he asked. "You can ride?"

They stumbled away from the wagon, both rubbing their hands. "Aye," they answered.

"Very well," Lannick said. "Take two of the horses and ride away from here as swiftly as you can. There'll be trouble coming soon," he said, thinking again of the death of High King Deragol. "Trouble for us all."

Near nightfall they made camp far from the road, beside a tumble of stones that looked to be an ancient cairn marking some forgotten death or battle. Brugan sat by a small fire, wincing as he wrapped new bandages about his wounds. He wore a weary look, his wide face showing no hint of the smile that usually warmed it.

Lannick paced farther away, allowing the silence to settle upon them. He studied the land about, the setting sun drawing long shadows across the hillsides. He pulled his green cloak—the cloak of the Variden—about his shoulders, worrying over threats drawing near.

He worried not over conscripting soldiers, though. His head could manage swinging steel and violent men. He worried of threats far graver. These were near-forgotten thoughts, things he'd not considered in a long time. But now they troubled him once again—old worries of ancient evils. Worries of a dark lord thought vanquished a millennium ago and of the vile necromancers who'd persisted in his wake.

The Necrists. With High King Deragol dead and heirless, could the power of the Godswell open to them?

He considered General Fane. The fact that the man had struck some black bargain with these creatures, a bargain that initially demanded the general's daughter and later Lannick, the fallen disciple of the Sentinel Valis.

Lannick had not thought long on this before—his

head had been too sullied by drink and grief and shame. Besides, he'd always known Fane to be a viciously ambitious man, and so even some compact with the Necrists seemed something of which he was capable. A bargain, perhaps? Some deal for ill-gotten influence, the answer to some imponderable question, or maybe the perverse return of a loved one long dead…

A shiver seized Lannick as he thought on that last possibility, his head filling with images of the stitched faces of his own wife and children worn by the Necrists who'd hunted him.

He shook it aside as best he could and focused.

Fane had bargained with the Necrists. In light of the warnings of his former Variden brethren that the Spider King had allied with the Necrists—coupled with the news of the death of High King Deragol—Lannick wondered just how treacherous Fane's dealings really were. The general had lost battle upon battle to the Spider King's armies, casting his men to the enemy like stones to the sea.

Could he have bargained with the Spider King as well?

He wondered if the Variden had underestimated the general's role in things and the danger he posed. He wondered if Fane's ambitions stretched so far as to compel the ultimate treachery.

Could he be losing this war by design?

Suddenly, Lannick knew his quest for vengeance had become all the more desperate, all the more vital. The stakes had grown immensely greater, and Lannick knew what would happen if he failed.

His hand found his purse and the outline of his Coda. He reckoned he'd need the thing far sooner than he'd like.

He remembered when the Coda had *chosen* him. He was a much younger man, only a year past twenty, back when his motives and ideals were still untainted by the corruptions and compromises of age. He'd been traveling from Ironmoor to his father's farm when he stumbled upon an old man, perhaps sixty years of age and wearing a cloak of green. The man's wagon had lost a wheel and the fellow fumbled about trying to refit it to the axle. Lannick offered to help but upon seeing him the man succumbed to some sort of swoon and collapsed beside the wagon.

"It is yours to bear!" the man had gasped when he awoke. With shaking hands he'd seized Lannick's wrist, then threw upon it a heavy bracelet of black iron.

The Coda had snapped shut on his arm like the maw of some terrible beast. Lannick was horrified, and his head flooded then with an agonizing torrent of visions. He'd seen then—through the Sentinel Valis's eyes—the form of Yrghul the Lord of Nightmares, a monstrosity of bone and swirling shadows, standing triumphant upon the ruins of Ironmoor. Lannick's eyes had burned as Illienne illuminated the darkness, and he'd watched in awe as she diminished while divesting her divine power. He'd felt the surge of that power as a part of Illienne's divinity filled Valis, forcing his mind to burn and his limbs to tremble. He'd felt Valis's confusion when Illienne told the Sentinels she needed to descend to oblivion with her dark twin in order to defeat him. And he'd felt a cold fury in his heart as Valis and the other Sentinels rushed to Illienne's side in her final struggle, falling upon Yrghul with vicious blades and sending both gods to oblivion.

He'd felt Valis's disgust upon being banished from

Rune, and his steely resolve to hold true to his oath while he and the other Sentinels were led in chains over the Southwalls. And, lastly, he'd felt the sharp point of the knife—wielded by Valis's own hand—against Valis's throat as he'd made ready to pour his power into the Codas he'd forged, thereby carrying out his oath through his followers, the Variden.

Then the cascade of the Variden's voices had struck Lannick. They'd assailed him with a barrage of welcomes and warnings, followed by whispers of history's secrets. Ominous accounts of a war in the shadows of the world, a desperate battle against those foul necromancers who'd remained true to Yrghul. Tales of an eternal vigil, a watch against the Necrists and other enemies in Rune and foreign lands.

His world had changed that day. It had expanded to a vast realm of uncertainty and peril, a place stalked by foes who'd not rest until their vile master had risen from death and laid waste to the living.

He'd agreed to take the oath of the Variden, and keep at bay those forces lurking in the dark.

Lannick felt again the weight of that oath. He'd sworn to remain ever watchful against Rune's most ancient and powerful enemies, those forces common folk were either merrily ignorant of or thought of as villains in fairy tales. For most, the truth of the enemy's existence had faded from memory and into myth as the world moved on from the dead gods.

But the Variden are sworn to remember. And in the nine years after my family's murder I permitted myself to forget.

He paced farther from the camp, holding his Coda in

his hands. He drew it close, studying in the fading light the lines etched across its dull surface—words of power in the very language of gods.

The weapon with which to fight the shadows.

A notion struck him, and he exhaled with a whistle through his chipped tooth. Codas left their bearers when those men and women died or grew infirm or useless. Just as his Coda had chosen Lannick, it could have chosen another after he'd hammered it from his wrist those many years ago. It would have sensed his thoughts, his failure and despair, and would have compelled him to give it to another more suited to carry on the fight.

Yet it didn't, even when I abandoned the others.

As they had many times of late, his thoughts turned to Fane. This time, though, those thoughts carried a new urgency. If Fane was in league with the enemy, then the man *needed* to be slain. His leadership had brought nothing but ruin, and had allowed the Spider King to march nearly undeterred through Rune's southern reaches with only an illusion of resistance. Rune's armies needed to be freed from his deception or they'd have no chance at all of beating back the Arranese.

Lannick knew, then, this was why his Coda remained his and his alone. His purpose—vengeance—was now intertwined with that of the Variden.

He sniffed. He'd not be lashing the Coda to his wrist anytime soon—he didn't fancy the idea of old comrades poking about in his head.

No. My grief and regrets are mine alone to possess.

He looked outward, across the darkening landscape fading beneath the blanket of night. He was very likely headed to his death, as were a good many folk finer than he. The task would be as great a one as the kingdom had ever faced. There'd be horrors unimaginable ahead.

There seemed an inevitability to that. An impending doom that inspired even as it frightened, for it left no room for half-measures or turning back.

This was his path.

This was his purpose.

This was how he'd avenge those he'd loved.

He would kill Fane. And after Fane's death, he'd wage war with Fane's army against the Spider King and his Necrist allies. And in doing so, perhaps he'd save the kingdom.

A crooked smile crept to his face.

Captain Lannick deVeers, he thought. *Protector of Ironmoor, indeed.*

2

DOUBT

ZANDRACHUS BALE SHUDDERED and
pulled his robes close. The fire would not warm
him, nor would the light of the sun setting over
the barren steppe beyond. It wasn't a cold evening—rare
indeed was such a thing in Arranan—but then, this was
no chill of the body.

It is one borne by doubt alone.

He wondered if he'd have the strength to see his task
to its end, and shuddered once more. He was so very far
from his home, so far from the sheltered nooks of the
Abbey, and there would come no assurances. He was on
a quest to summon another Sentinel, and the last he'd
encountered had been none too pleasant. The thought
of Lyan the Just looming over him in the cavern beneath
Cirak still unnerved him, her eerie gold skin shimmering
in the cavern's light and her ominous sword at the ready.

There were so many uncertainties, so many awful ends
he could meet in this place. If there were anywhere in

all the world that would seem most perilous for an acolyte of the Ancient Sanctum it was Arranan, the nation of marauders presently warring with Rune. Bale pulled strands of graying hair from before his eyes to behind his ears and scanned the far horizon. It seemed at least they were alone here, though Bale wondered whether such was a good thing in this stark land.

Lorra grunted, drawing Bale's gaze. The woman sat across the fire, poking a bent stick into a foul-smelling pot of misshapen roots. Firelight danced about her sharp nose, thin lips, and green eyes. She was not a beautiful woman in the classical sense fancied by painters and poets. Yet there was a prettiness about her. It was one set with many rough edges, but it was a prettiness nonetheless.

I would never have made it this far without her.

He studied her for a moment longer then sighed, pulling his eyes from her face and back to the wasteland before him. Stunted trees clung near broken boulders, drawing crooked shadows across the yellow dirt. Ragged-winged vultures circled on hot breezes in the distance, and Bale guessed some strange beast was dying somewhere beneath their spiral. There were no signs of proper civilization in this hard land, and the sudden, dry wind carried naught but the reek of desolation.

Arranan.

Bale had studied much during his time in the Abbey. Indeed, rare was the day he'd spent away from a musty book in the sputtering candlelight of its library. He'd read of this place, known as a hard land with hard people. Brave merchants were said to travel to its ancient capital of Zyn, though otherwise the realm had remained largely isolated for centuries. It was often described as a nation of violent tribes ever at war with one another, with no ambition beyond avenging ancestral grudges.

But then came Arranan's Spider King. If the whispered rumors were true, the Spider King had quelled the tribal infighting within a matter of months, completing a stunning rise to power by being crowned the very first ruler of a unified Arranan. It was said that, during his coronation three years ago in Zyn, Arranan's tribal chieftains prostrated bare before his throne, which had been built from the bones of those who'd opposed him. He seemed a most terrifying figure.

And it is his realm I encroach upon now. Can I do this thing?

"Hungry?" Lorra grumbled from across the small fire.

Bale breathed deeply and pulled himself from his thoughts. He looked again to the pot she tended. Floating in a greasy broth were several lumpy roots she'd pulled from beneath a bush a league or so back. The concoction smelled none too pleasant, a scent not so different from that of his feet when he'd gone too long without removing his boots. He smiled weakly. "A little."

She huffed and pulled a wooden cup from her pack. She dunked the cup in the pot then handed it and a spoon to Bale. "You're quiet," she said. "I'm usually more annoyed with you by this time of day. What's bothering you?"

Bale cleared his throat. "Just far from home, is all."

"Must be a pleasant thing," she said in a low voice. "Having a home you miss, I mean."

Bale's heart sank with pity. "I'm sorry," he said sincerely.

"It's nothing for you to worry about," she whispered, eyes tilting skyward.

The light of early evening was a tricky thing, but Bale thought tears fell upon her cheeks. His father's apathy and rejection, as much as they'd hurt him, were far lesser crimes than the violations Lorra had suffered. "I'm sorry," he said again, then shifted about the fire to sit next to her.

"Eat your stew," she said gruffly, wiping her nose with her sleeve.

Bale looked at her a moment longer before turning his attention to his cup. He pressed at the ugly root and it crumbled easily. He ate a spoonful and found it tasted less like stinky feet and more like potato. He was hungry and ate the rest quickly. "Thank you," he said through his last mouthful. "You are quite the cook. I'd never have guessed those roots were edible."

She chewed and shrugged. "It's nothing."

"Nothing? It's quite a skill. I have knowledge of herbs and certain minerals and other such compounds, certainly. Things my order uses in alchemy, for the healing arts and our other works. Those things I can find and identify and use. But the food we've eaten? I would have never—"

"I said it's nothing. As long as you know the difference between what you can eat and what can poison you, you can find something to fill your belly."

"But it is real knowledge, a true talent, a—"

"There you are," she said, eyes squinted and brow bent. "Now you're back to being annoying."

Bale's shoulders slumped. For a time he sat aimlessly trolling his spoon about his empty cup, looking into the campfire's flame.

And then Lorra placed a hand on his knee.

"Bale," she said. Her eyes were wider and kinder now and her tears had dried.

"Y-yes?" he stammered, startled.

"I know I said I'd be your courage, but sometimes it's you who makes me feel safe."

Bale smiled widely, and for an instant his doubt disappeared.

"But let's talk no more of it," she said, and scooted away from him.

"So where are we going?" Lorra asked, squinting at the horizon in the morning light.

Bale placed the last of his things in his pack and stood, groaning at the pain in his knees. He shielded his eyes from the sun and looked about. The landscape consisted of yellow dirt and claw-like trees and scrubby brush, with no features to mark the progress of their journey aside from the receding silhouette of the Southwalls behind them. In the far distance a white-robed shepherd tended a herd of what appeared to be goats.

"You *do* know, don't you?" Lorra asked, her tone impatient.

"I do," Bale said slowly. "The seeking stone I used, the one Lyan held. It points southwest, so that's where we're headed. The pull is quite intense."

Lorra snorted. "Southwest isn't a *place*, spooker. Do you know where? How far?"

"Zyn. I think Kressan the Kind may be there."

"Think?" she said with a wrinkled scowl.

Bale threw out his hands, pleading. "I wish I had better

answers to offer, Lorra, but much of what guides me is written in old books I read some time ago, and even those books sometimes disagree with each other. The ancient accounts claim that High King Derganfel, the one who banished the Seven Sentinels from Rune, had his army escort them to the Southwalls, where they were forced into exile. Exiled and never to return."

A vulture croaked harshly. It stood on a small rise nearby, wings twitching as it tugged at the red flesh of some rodent.

Bale rubbed his overlarge nose and continued. "One forbidden account I read claimed Kressan came upon a starving acolyte in this very wasteland, roughly eighty years ago. The acolyte had been on a pilgrimage to the Temple at Cirak, and afterward was inspired to venture farther south to see if these lands held any sign of the Sentinels' passage. He became lost, exhausted his provisions, and was close to death. The account claimed Kressan carried him to a shanty in one of Zyn's vast slums, where his health slowly returned."

"Eighty years? And you think she's still there?"

"It's where the stone points."

"You and your magic rock." She kicked at the dirt with a boot that had lost much of its stitching. "I'm trusting you, Bale. Don't disappoint me." She shouldered her satchel and set off southwest.

Bale hefted his pack and stumbled after her, finding the dusty, uneven ground difficult to traverse. They'd found a road the day before, one moving southwest to Zyn, but he thought it best to avoid it. He didn't fancy the notion of encountering a group of Arranese warriors headed toward Rune.

"So this Sentinel is real nice, or something?" Lorra asked. "Kressan the Kind, isn't it? She won't be like that last one?"

Bale shrugged. "'Kind' is a lazy translation of the word that was used in the ancient tongue. The old accounts instruct that she had profound empathy, a deep sensitivity to the feelings of others. It may not mean she'll be nice to us."

Lorra huffed, her expression sour. "And just how far is this place?"

Bale scratched his nose. "If my recollection of the maps is accurate, I'd guess sixty leagues. Perhaps less. If we don't wander too far off course we should make it in a week or so."

"A week? On these scraps?" Lorra said, jabbing a skinny thumb toward her pack. "I have only a few turnips and potatoes, and too many of those smelly roots I cooked last night will make a body sick. Watery craps and worse. Can't eat them raw, and we don't have much water for boiling. Or drinking, for that matter."

"Worry not. My order was gifted with ways of finding water, drawing it from earth and plants and such. A little, at least. Enough to survive." He enjoyed the woman's practicality and admired the dogged determination of her stride. And then his thoughts turned to the idea of eating those foul-smelling roots for an entire week or more and he giggled. The odors his body would produce were sure to be most foul.

"I'm trusting you with an awful lot, Bale," she said through a frown. "With my life."

Bale nodded, his mirth fleeting. "And mine, as well," he whispered.

"And just what is Zyn? Like Cirak, all wicked and abandoned?"

"Most certainly not," Bale said. "Zyn is one of the oldest cities in all the world. The historians say it had the only clean water in all of Arranan, and after much fighting the tribes agreed it'd be something of a sanctuary, a safe haven. With the tribesmen being such rovers, Zyn became the only permanent city in the entire land. It grew into a place for trade with other nations and meetings among the tribes. It was said to be a truly grand city, a great bazaar for things and peoples both odd and wonderful. And then," he cleared his throat nervously, "it became the place where Arranan's Spider King set his throne."

They walked in silence for a long time, over broken earth, through dry creek beds, and through the jutting teeth of splintered boulders. They spied in the distance a collection of a few dozen rounded tents and gave it a wide berth. At other times they caught sight of riders on horseback and huddled low against the ground until they vanished in the distance.

Doubt haunted Bale as they trudged along. Lorra had been justified with her questions. He was relying upon a decades-old tale discounted by scholars and upon a stone that revealed only the direction in which he could find a Sentinel.

Perhaps not even the one I'm seeking, and perhaps one who'll prove to be less welcoming than the last.

"Bale!" came a sharp hiss.

Bale sucked in a mouthful of the night's hot air and his eyes fluttered open. A starry, cloudless sky above. He felt about. Rocks and dirt and scratchy weeds beneath his hands. "What?" he moaned, his tongue thick with sleep.

"Quiet!" came the hiss again, along with a sharp jab against his shoulder.

His eyes fluttered again. The voice was Lorra's, of course. *But why such a tone?* He pulled himself upward and peered ahead.

There was only darkness. A vast and impenetrable darkness untouched by the moonlight above.

"What?" he asked again, but much more quietly this time. "I don't see anything."

"That's just it," said Lorra, her voice shaking. "Can't see anything at all over there."

Bale swiveled his head about. Behind and to his sides was a moonlit landscape, a wasteland palely illuminated in places and full of shadow in most others. Ahead, though, beyond a hundred or so yards of broken stones and cracked earth, there was nothingness. Only a curtain of deep black that stretched from the earth to the sky above.

What strange necromancy is this?

He narrowed his eyes and peered hard into the void of purple and ebony. As he looked, a coldness settled upon him, an icy, unnerving sensation that felt like fear given form. It felt familiar, somehow. His brow wrinkled and he struggled with memories held in his sleep-fogged head.

I have sensed this before.

The darkness appeared a physical thing, a blanket of

tangible shadows gathered in the distance. It seemed to shimmer and shift though not from any reflection of the sky above. It was as though it was *moving*, slithering slowly northward upon the steppe.

The cold fell upon him again and then he remembered it: that sensation he'd felt in the governor's mansion in Riverweave. When he'd overheard General Fane's disturbing insinuations of betrayal to that thing he spoke with. That thing with the stitched face.

The Necrist.

He fumbled for the satchel he'd used as a pillow and withdrew from it his leather sleeve of reagents. He undid its clasp, unfurled it before him, and felt the various pouches and pockets, recognizing the compounds by shape and texture. He knew he'd packed spit-thistle—a weed named for the usual reaction to its vinegary flavor—and after a few moments he located it.

He cupped a sprig of spit-thistle in his hands and thought of the words that would awaken the hidden power within the plant, powers granted to it and many other living things by the Elder God when the world was wrought.

"What are you doing?" Lorra whispered.

"Something that will lend me sight in the darkness."

He calmed himself and mouthed words without speaking, words taught to him by Lector Erlorn, the Sentinel Castor himself. He paused and thought of that, how what seemed a simple lesson from a caring teacher was in fact knowledge from a man who held within him the very essence of godliness. For that instant, Bale's fear subsided and a power surged within him, a spark of courage that told him these terrible tasks could be overcome.

He concentrated deeply and uttered the sacred, divine phrase. *"Ea sparos,"* he whispered, *"abralide y ganode vira." Spirits of the gods, awaken and grant me sight.*

The sprig burned in his hands, but it was not overly hot and the burning incited neither ember nor flame. Rather, the weed dissolved, changing from a stiff, prickly shoot to a viscous paste. When the transformation was complete, Bale raised his cupped hands to his face and the substance dripped like thick phlegm into his mouth.

He chewed with a pucker. It tasted much like vinegar though many degrees stronger. He fought back the urge to expel the stuff and instead forced it down his throat.

The effect of the weed took time to manifest. Bale waited and watched. In time, the night glowed, the whole world set alight with a bluish hue in his eyes. Soon, the black curtain became translucent.

And what was beyond it was terrifying.

Bale sucked in a shuddering breath, rubbed his eyes, then breathed again.

"What is it?" Lorra whispered.

He could only shake his head and stare. Before him, along the road he and Lorra had avoided, walked a long line of black-robed Necrists. Three score or more, slinking in dead silence through the night. Their stitched skin glimmered in Bale's augmented vision. Pallid flesh wriggled and writhed against the stitches, forming faces cobbled together from corpses.

Bale rubbed his eyes again, almost hoping the effect of the spit-thistle would subside.

In the Necrists' trail trudged the twisted creations of their dark sorcery. Dwarfs hobbled crookedly, gnarled things with stunted limbs and humped spines. They tittered and rubbed knotted hands together, possessing what seemed the faces of slain children. And there too lumbered giants twice the size of men, tethered by great chains. Hands like shovels dragged against the earth and eyes too large even for their massive heads lolled miserably about.

These were things wrought in the deep shadows and the old hells. Half-made things, clumsy and unnatural.

Things not meant to be.

"What is it?" whispered Lorra again.

Bale could not manage an answer. His mind reeled, searching for any minutiae he'd encountered in his studies, any hint of the Necrists and their powers. The Necrists cloaked themselves in secrecy, so much so they'd become an almost mythical enemy. Precious little was known of their ways and methods, for such knowledge had been buried beneath the dust of ages.

But Bale had studied much—more than most—and had often pursued subjects frowned upon by his brethren. Perversions, forbidden histories, even the macabre. As he filtered frantically through the memories of his frightened mind, he recalled weathered scrolls reciting accounts of Necric practices. Blood rites, rituals of speaking with the dead god Yrghul through the pooled blood of sacrifices. The manipulation of shadows into something tangible, and moving unseen among the black paths of shadows cast.

He surmised this was what he saw now, only different. The eerie caravan moved not along the jagged weave of the shadows cast by stones and stunted trees, but behind and beneath a veritable wall of them. He wondered for an instant if a collection of many Necrists could work their powers in concert, amplifying them to *forge* a path of shadow.

He'd read, too, of their reworking the flesh of their sacrifices, using it to cover their sinews and bones after necromancy had rotted their own skin. And there were also rumors of how they used what was left of the dead. These things, these dwarfs and giants, seemed the products of such foul industry. Beings assembled from the leftover bits and bones of those who'd died in terror.

At the train's rear walked a tall Necrist, its head lost in a black hood. It wielded a barbed whip, lashing the giants' knotty shoulders and sloped backs. The sound did not penetrate the black curtain, but Bale sensed the whip's crack in the wide, cow-like eyes of the monstrosities.

Then the tall Necrist halted and the whip fell slack at its feet. It stood immobile for a long moment, the caravan of Necrists and their abominations trudging away. Slowly it cocked its cloaked head and the opening of its hood drooped, a black abyss revealing nothing.

Bale shivered, sensing unwelcome eyes upon him. *Does it see me?*

"Bale," Lorra hissed, "you're scaring me. What is it you see?"

Bale sat speechless, gripped by fear and doubt.

The Necrist squared to him, the hundred yards between them feeling no more than an arm's length. It turned its whip in a lazy circle that stirred eddies of dust. It moved its other arm upward, sleeve falling away to reveal an ashen, skeletal hand. Then it pulled aside its hood to display a sickening visage.

It seemed to glow in Bale's enhanced sight, a hairless,

pale head of messy, mismatched flesh. The skin squirmed as though trying to escape the gnarled bands of black stitch binding it. The Necrist smiled, a grotesque gash of yellow teeth dripping from purple gums. Obsidian eyes glittered from sunken sockets.

Bale's mind whirled as he frantically sifted his memory for any incantation that could be of use against a Necrist. Lector Erlorn had taught him many things, including means of summoning light. Erlorn had also taught him divine spells to subdue wicked spirits. He remembered these, vaguely, and surmised they'd prove effective. Yet he'd never performed a true exorcism nor confronted a wraith, and thought this a poor time to try.

The smiling Necrist glided forward, pressing against the curtain of shadow. Its mouth moved with apparent commands and its hands worked upon the wall of shadow, thin fingers with bony knuckles seeming to search for a seam. Two of the misshapen dwarfs hurried clumsily back from the caravan to join the tall Necrist. They poked stunted fingers against the curtain and its surface warped and swayed.

Bale found himself creeping backward across the dirt. *I am too weak an instrument!* "Run," he whispered.

"What is it?" Lorra demanded.

"Run!" he commanded, tugging his boots on. He scrambled to his feet, snatched his pack, and took several quick steps from their campsite. He turned back and saw Lorra still gathering her provisions and cookware. "Run! Now!"

He plunged into the night, stumbling over toe-stubbing rocks and clawing brush. Lorra moved swiftly beside and then ahead of him, seizing his hand as she passed. She ran with certainty, leading Bale along and away from obstacles that surely would have toppled him.

After many strides he chanced a look back, but discerned no sign of the tall Necrist or the black wall of night. Yet a chill remained, an icy touch that prickled the skin.

"Where do we go?" Lorra said.

"Away! Just away!" He sniffled and wiped away a dribble of snot with a trembling hand.

They hurtled through the dark. The effects of the spit-thistle waned and Bale had only a vague sense of direction—he'd rarely touched on the positions of the stars in his studies. He hoped they were moving southwest but all that mattered was that their bearing led them away from the Necrists and their horrors.

They ran. Bale's body screamed with pain, his feet loudest of all. He groaned as Lorra dragged him across the waste, fear the only fuel for his legs. They clambered up a hill, a clatter of loose stone falling behind them, then tumbled down its opposite slope.

"Ah!" Bale shrieked. He fell, grasping an ankle that'd painfully turned. The joint burned like fire. He rolled into a heap against a thorny bush at the hill's base.

"Bale!" Lorra said, rushing to kneel at his side. The moon, nearly full, framed her face. Her sharp features caught the moonlight and silver highlighted her shoulder-length hair and glinted in her green eyes. "Are you hurt?"

"My ankle," he grunted through gritted teeth. He twisted his foot, testing the joint, and groaned again. "I'll need time to work with my reagents before I can run again."

Lorra darted her eyes about. "I don't see that shadow anymore. We may be safe."

Bale tested his ankle again and frowned, then sank back against the hard earth. He stared at the night sky and breathed deeply, realizing he sensed none of the earlier chill upon the air. "We are safe," he heaved. "For now."

He sat and found his thoughts turning to the Abbey, to Prefect Gamghast. *Should I turn back? Should I get a warning to him, somehow?*

He looked to the bleak night and thought on this. After a moment, though, he knew he needed to take the risk of continuing his journey, of continuing the mission of Lector Erlorn. He would just need to have faith that Gamghast and the others could deal with the threats descending upon them.

Sweet Illienne, please spare your loyal servants...

Lorra caressed his shoulder. She eased toward him, her hair drooping and brushing against his bow. "I'll watch for anything unnatural," she said. You tend to your wound, then get some rest. Just as I've said, Bale, I'll be your courage." She bent near and kissed his forehead.

Bale shut his eyes. Lorra's lips were the only ones to have touched his face other than his mother's, many years before. He smiled, then winced as the pain in his ankle flared again.

3
A CURSE UPON THE WORLD

FENCRESS FALLCROW GLANCED back nervously, emotions wavering somewhere between relief and revulsion. There, behind her, Drenj and Paddyn slogged along the rugged trail dug between the thin trees, pulling a rickety two-wheeled wagon. Within that wagon rested the source of Fencress's unease: the killer Karnag Mak Ragg.

The massive highlander sat upright, broad back turned to them with his gaze fixed upon the path stretching behind. He was draped in wool blankets despite the summer afternoon's heat. Flies buzzed about the thick, black braids that fell from his head, but he made no effort to shoo them.

Almost as though they buzz about a corpse, Fencress thought.

She'd been relieved when Karnag awoke—if one could

use such a word for his apparent return from near-death—two nights before. They'd been nearing Ironmoor's North Gate when he'd started from his slumber and tossed about in a lather of sweat. His fits had helped Fencress sell her story of infectious disease to the guards, even as her friend's state alarmed her.

And then came the words. Those strange, broken-sounding things that fell from Karnag's tongue in a chant that made her skin crawl. She'd heard them enough by now to realize he was repeating himself, gurgling out some kind of long, awful curse upon the world. He uttered them even now.

She exhaled and turned her gaze back to the trail ahead. She worried over her friend's state, over the dark struggle that seemed to rage within him. She'd never been one for prayers, and was loath to plead to the dead gods for Karnag's sanity when it seemed those same dead gods had meddled with it in the first place.

No, I place my hopes in turns of chance instead.

She knew—she hoped—there had to be some chance her old friend could be saved from his madness, and wagered that without such a chance the man was good as dead.

She knotted her hands into fists, black leather gloves creaking as she did. She had no idea how this would end, but she owed it to him to at least try the odds. Being at his side discomforted her, but she'd stay there so long as there was hope.

So long as there's a chance.

They were a dozen or so leagues south of Ironmoor, and the rolling hills and brackish breezes near the sea had given way to sparse copses, tall grasses, and air thick with moisture and mosquitoes. She scolded herself for giving up their horses, realizing the deal had made an already troubling journey all the more arduous.

Ahead of them, many days away to the south, crossed the Silverflow and the Drimrill rivers, a few days west of that crouched Raven's Roost. From what they'd seen of the Arranese, Fencress reckoned the army was marching straight to Riverweave and then Ironmoor. She guessed Raven's Roost was too wretched a place to warrant attention, and aside from that it was home. It seemed the best place to take Karnag, as perhaps some familiar things would help shake his head enough that he'd be back to being himself.

After a time, she realized Karnag's chant had ceased. She steeled herself, wondering whether the silence meant something more terrible than the chant. She turned, fearing what she'd find.

Karnag remained seated in the wagon but faced her now. His face was haggard, cheeks sallow and sunken. His black braids formed a heavy mantle upon his head. And his eyes were just as she'd remembered, dark and lifeless.

"Fencress Fallcrow," he said, his voice the roll of thunder.

Drenj and Paddyn dropped the handles of the wagon and dashed from its sides. The wagon pitched forward, tilting as the handles fell to the ground.

But Karnag did not tumble. He moved smoothly forward, stepping from the wagon to stand. He'd snatched *Gravemaker* from the wagon and held it now. He stood tall and broad and fearsome, even absent some kind of demonic possession.

"You recovered my sword," he said, eying the massive blade. He sounded almost touched. "I thank you for that."

"You…" Fencress said, "are welcome, Karnag."

His dark brow knotted. "I had not foreseen a need for your help, but help me you did. I thank you for that, as well. You are my friend."

"Till the end, Karnag," she said and she felt she meant it. The man she'd known as Karnag would ever be dear to her, though at times like this she wagered much of that man had died the night they killed the Lector. She swallowed hard. *Is there a chance to get him back?*

"You intend to take me to Raven's Roost."

Fencress nodded and forced a smile to her lips. "I figured since we're finished with the Lector and you're all hale and hearty again, we'd best head home."

Karnag's face seemed a stone, unreadable. "We will head south, though Raven's Roost is not my destination. My task has only begun."

His task. Fencress let the words hang, turning over the odds of whether now was a decent time to ask Karnag the many questions she had. For a moment she held his eyes—those eyes of the dead—and decided it was not.

Karnag looked to Drenj and Paddyn. "You need pull me in the wagon no longer. The walk will strengthen me."

Fencress nodded to the boys and tried to quell the doubt in her voice. "Best get walking, boys. I don't wager the road will come walking to us."

Karnag walked at the group's lead, his stride tireless and

inevitable. He uttered occasional nonsense, misplaced observations of things unseen interspersed with phrases in some strange tongue. Drenj and Paddyn spoke to him not at all, and Fencress only when necessary.

She walked a dozen or so yards behind her old friend so she could just hear his words but would not be expected to respond. She'd held hope he'd be different—more *human*—after Merek and those spookers worked their tricks on him. But if anything, it seemed he was worse.

"The dying will fill this place," Karnag said, sweeping an arm across the landscape. "The plague of the Necrists will drive them here, from their cities and villages. The stink of it fills my nose even now, and their cries resound in my ears. Thaydorne will laugh at this. Though..." He paused, looking upward. "Though the atlas of fate shifts and shimmers even now, and will tremble all the more when I force my hand upon it. Behold! The futures I foretell can be changed according to my will, and Thaydorne's laughter will squelch to silence in his throat. All these possibilities... Great change will come if my blade severs his head."

As she listened Fencress thought over the chances posed by the days and weeks ahead. If whatever consumed Karnag remained so obsessed with death, he'd insist on dragging them right into the teeth of battle. She needed to sway him, somehow. He wouldn't listen to reason— not if he was still the same creature who'd constructed that great pile of bones and bits on that hillside south of Riverweave. But perhaps whatever the Sanctum and that bastard Merek had done to him had changed him.

Perhaps there was a chance they'd changed his course for the better.

The trail widened as they trekked southwest. The earth became flat and the soil soft and dark. Tall foxtail grasses swayed in the summer breeze. Slatted farmhouses squatted in the distance and rag-clad farmers paused their plowing to eye them suspiciously as they passed.

And for damned good reason.

"Ahem," came a soft sound from behind her. It was Drenj, his kohl-lined eyes narrow with meaning.

Fencress slackened her pace, allowing the Khaldisian to pull even. "What?" she whispered, gaze remaining upon Karnag.

He leaned close. "How long must we bear this?" he whispered.

"As long as it takes."

Drenj shook his head. "I have no heart for this, Fencress. I have been too long from my family, too long in the presence of wickedness. We should go our own way. Walking in his wake invites only evil."

Fencress knew there was truth in the Khaldisian's words, but she knew she couldn't show it. She needed to bluff a play bolder than the dice in her cup suggested. Tugging her black cowl, she looked to Drenj with an icy glare. "I am in this to the very end. If you'd like to flee, friend, that is fine. I've no quarrel with it, but I'm not so sure about him," she said, nodding toward Karnag.

Paddyn pulled near. The youth looked shabby as ever, skin caked with dirt and limbs too lean for his clothes. "Drenj is right, Fencress," he said, words whistling through the space left by his missing tooth. "We didn't agree to this sort of thing. This has gone far beyond gutting some old holy man in the woods. We're cursed, especially at *his* side."

"Cursed?" came Karnag's resounding voice, followed by a deep chuckle.

Fencress winced, worried they faced some awful retribution from Karnag. But the imposing man continued walking steadily forward, his gaze not upon them but upon the trail ahead.

"You are not cursed," Karnag said. "The only curse fate can conjure is my wrath. My blade is the father of fear, and woe to any man I find deserving of it."

They made camp on the road. Paddyn prodded the fire again though it blazed well enough. Fencress knew it was a rote exercise meant only to excuse his eyes from Karnag's. Sitting about the evening campfire would normally have been a thing to invite bold talk and ribald comments, but Karnag's presence chased the humor from the company.

"A mad thing, that," Fencress ventured, doing her best to distract the boys from the dead-eyed highlander seated at the fire's edge. "Rune's king, heirless at death for the first time in history. You sure one of you bastards isn't really *his* bastard? There'd be some damned good coin coming to you, not to mention a castle filled with servants eager to lick your royal ass."

"No," said Karnag, the joke obviously lost on him. "There are secrets yet to be revealed."

Drenj looked up from the fire, his gaze catching Fencress's. He cocked a dark brow and in return Fencress narrowed her eyes as a warning.

"Many secrets," Karnag continued. "Secrets open to me. The High King sired a son, but the child's birth remains an uncertainty. Many possible fates must converge for the child to arrive."

Drenj turned to Karnag. "And how is it you know such things?"

"As I said, these secrets are open to me."

"And what other mystical secrets do you know?" Drenj persisted, his tone mocking and dangerous.

"*Drenj…*" Fencress hissed, knowing it unwise for the young man to challenge Karnag.

Drenj persisted. "What other secrets?"

Karnag looked skyward, the firelight falling from his face so that his countenance was cloaked in darkness. He remained quiet for a long moment before speaking. "Your youngest daughter will not live to see the fullness of her second year. She will die of plague, her skin weeping blood from many lesions. She will shudder and at last fall still while your wife wails her name in agony. 'Ryaza,' your wife will cry, for days heaped upon days after your daughter dies."

A whimper fell from Drenj's mouth and tears dripped from his kohl-stained eyes. He whimpered again, stood, then stormed into the waist-high grass lining the road. A moment later Paddyn followed the Khaldisian into the dark.

Fencress sat in slack-jawed silence, finding the notion of a witty rejoinder terribly inappropriate, even from her sharp tongue.

Karnag looked back to Fencress. "The man in green," he said matter-of-factly.

She rubbed her head, trying to get her thoughts past the prior comment. "Merek."

"He was the one who followed us from Raven's Roost, yes? The one you saw on the road?"

Fencress nodded.

"Strange. I could not sense him, nor could I foresee his actions. He was concealed from me, somehow."

Fencress grabbed the stick Paddyn had used and stirred the campfire. "He was some kind of witch," she said softly. "Said he belonged to some old order that dealt with things like the dead gods."

"Ah," Karnag said, his tone one of genuine surprise. "A Variden. I see that now. Valis was a powerful Sentinel. His disciples have methods of hiding themselves, even from my divine inquisition."

She held his gaze, discomforting as it was, and readied herself to ask hard questions. "I don't know what you mean, Karnag. Are you possessed, as Merek said?"

"Possessed?" Karnag spat out the word like bad meat. "Possession implies I *belong* to another. No, I belong to no one. Rather, I have *taken* something. When I took the Lector's life, I took something else from him as well. Something very old, eternal even. The Lector housed a spirit, a spirit that tried to bend me to its purpose," he said, eyes not dead but piercing. "Lesser men have bent to that spirit's will, but I do not bend."

"And what is it you've become?"

Karnag looked to the fire. "I have become more than I was. Much more. I see things, not in your manner of seeing but in a manner in which time and purpose are aspects visible to me. I see past and present, but even more I see what is to come, or can be. Ripples stir from my hand and the hands of others as actions occur, and I see how these ripples shift the vast array of probable fates. I see all men, women, and children, their beginnings and their possible ends."

Fencress's brow raised. "You've become a soothsayer?"

Karnag laughed, a low rumble like a distant storm. "I am no fortune teller or circus freak."

Fencress's mouth tilted with a slight smile despite her discomfort. The humor seemed a rare hint of humanity. She awaited more, but Karnag's visage remained dark, his stare a black void.

"Not a soothsayer," he said. "An eternal force."

The words were uttered with disturbing certainty and Fencress looked askance. Now she found need to stoke the fire. She said nothing, setting about stirring the sticks and embers as though the task held profound importance.

Karnag remained quiet for a long while. He studied the fire with a strange intensity, flames dancing upon his hard features. He did not blink. As she stared at him she grew increasingly uneasy, wondering when Drenj and Paddyn would return, if at all.

"Fencress," he said at last, "I am pleased you came for me at the Sanctum's Abbey. You are my friend and you saved my life. I foresee you have a part to play in things, still. I did not perceive that when we last parted ways."

Fencress swallowed, weighing the sort of obligations her old friend seemed to be placing upon her. She tugged at her cowl. "And what is that, Karnag? What part do I play?"

"There are many yet to die by my hand. Foes innumerable. And you, my friend, will accompany me."

Fencress felt a cold sinkhole form in her stomach and she thought of the ways in which she'd seen Karnag kill after the murder of the Lector. Of the horse trader in Raven's Roost, split from cock to crown with guts slopping over his sides like an overfilled bowl of stew. Of Tream, begging for his life in that bloody creek and then beheaded by Karnag's *hands*.

She gave brief thought to joining Drenj and Paddyn far from the fire, but knew she could not. Then she thought of partnering with Karnag on his quest to slaughter countless victims. It sounded awful—beyond awful—but there remained within her the hope her old friend could be saved from this madness. Some hope he'd return to what he'd been.

And some hope I will, as well.

"What..." she whispered. "What is it you need of me?"

Karnag stood and circled the fire, his broad form shifting the shadows the fire cast. All the while his face stayed fixed on the flames. "War is upon my realm," he said, voice resonant with unyielding conviction.

"*Your* realm, Karnag? Forgive me, friend, but these things you say and the way you say them do not sound like things that'd come from the mouth of the Karnag I know."

Or knew.

The flames blazed in his flint-colored eyes, somehow seeming brighter than the firelight they reflected. "We will not travel to Raven's Roost, for a war awaits me. Their so-called Spider King... Ha! He clothes himself with the titles and trappings of power, but he rots from within. He dares bring death to my door? He dares lay claim to *my* instrument? No. He will be made to understand that *mine* is the hand that delivers the ending of all things. Mine and mine alone."

"Karnag…"

Karnag turned from the fire and seized his massive sword. He moved it slowly over the tongues of the campfire, fanning the flames. "I will deliver a maelstrom of blood and broken bone. The Spider King will hear my song, a great song of woe, and he will cower. The Spider King will see all the deaths he has written to be a mere verse beside my song, and he will shiver."

Fencress sighed. *Is he lost forever to this madness?*

Karnag hoisted his sword skyward. His massive chest heaved and his sinews flexed. "I come for you, Thaydorne!" he screamed, shattering the night. "You will learn death is mine alone to wield!"

Fencress retreated from the fire and wiped aside a rare tear with her gloved hand. She looked again to the tall grasses, wondering where Drenj and Paddyn had fled. "And what of them?" she asked, gesturing. "What of Paddyn and Drenj?"

Karnag looked skyward once more, quiet for a disturbing moment. "They may leave if they wish."

Fencress smirked, at once happy for her companions' reprieve but heartbroken at the thought of being left alone at Karnag's side. "They'll be glad to return home," she whispered, her gaze finding the fire.

"I do not need them, but they will die if they stray from me. All of you will."

"By *your* hand?"

"Not mine, but those of others. I cannot choose what I see, and know not all possible fates, but I know we are hunted. Retribution is sought for the deaths in the Sanctum's Abbey, and for what I have taken from them. I know not all who hunt us or when we will be found, for forces cloud my vision. I do know I will possess the strength to defeat these hunters, but you will not. If you wander, you will be slain."

"You are sure of this?"

Karnag's heavy brow arched. "Only truth is upon my tongue. Deception is a tool of the weak."

Fencress looked again to the vast field of tall grasses swaying beneath the moonlight. "I must tell them."

"Tell them we ride tomorrow," Karnag said. "I will have horses. Be ready at dawn. We will ride to war, and death will be visited upon all deserving."

He said no more, then sank into the black of night.

Fencress spotted Paddyn and Drenj beneath the heavy eaves of a lone oak. The massive tree stood silver in the moonlight and her companions seemed silhouettes of dis-embodied heads floating amongst the foxtails. She tugged at her cowl, finding the image disconcerting with Karnag undoubtedly stalking about in the night.

She kept low and silent, hoping to steal a few moments beyond Karnag's dead stare. The boys showed no sign of having heard her approach so she rustled the grass with a gloved hand. Paddyn tensed and turned. His eyes found Fencess and his frightened expression seemed to shift to one of pensive dread.

Fencress slipped into the tight clearing beneath the

tree and sank between her companions. "Boys," she said, forcing humor to her tone. "Lovely evening, eh? All quiet beneath the twinkling stars with nary a care in our hearts?"

Paddyn scratched at his short hair, his dreary look unmoved. "I've known Karnag a while, now. Not nearly so long as you have, Fencress, but a while nonetheless. He's become a demon."

"You see that look in his eyes," Drenj said, drawing close to Fencress. "He's mad. And more, he's cursed." He stared out into the night, dark eyes stained with tears. "I saw a man, once. In Khaldisia, in my youth. A trader from my village sailed the Ebony Sea to the jungles of Rimgald, seeking rare gems. When he returned, he carried a purse full of glittering rubies and he boasted of having looted them from a wizard's tomb. That very night, though, he ran screaming though the village and collapsed, weeping, in the market square. We all gathered about and the elders tried to soothe him. But he would not be soothed. He wailed of the wizard cursing him in a nightmare, and claimed the wizard's form took shape in the shadows of his dwelling. The elders told him he merely dreamed this, but I saw a look in his eyes. An *emptiness*. The trader shook with sobs, then pulled a dagger across his own throat." Drenj shuddered. "He was cursed, Fencress. Cursed from the grave, just as Karnag is."

Fencress gave a rueful smile. "A most heartwarming story."

"There's the same kind of evil at work here," Drenj said quietly. "Evil in its purest form." He looked to her. "Don't tell me you don't fear him."

She pressed a stray curl of hair back into her cowl and

then sat quietly. "I *am* afraid of him," she said after a time. "I've been afraid of him ever since we killed the Lector. I've been afraid, and I wager I fear him more than the both of you together."

"So we leave him, then?" Drenj whispered, an eager look in his eyes. "We could leave now. There's no need to endure another moment!"

Fencress swallowed back the sour spit filling her mouth. "I'm staying by his side so long as I think there's the slimmest chance of saving him." Her voice softened to a near whisper. "I have to trust in chance."

"But what of me?" Drenj asked. "What of me and Paddyn?"

She shrugged. "You are free to go, but he claims we'll die if we leave."

"What?" the Khaldisian squealed, his long-fingered hands upraised. "He'll hunt us down?"

"No, not him. Someone else. He says we're being hunted for what happened at the Sanctum."

Paddyn's jaw sagged. "How could he know this?"

Fencress shook her head. "I don't know that he does, but I fear odds are he can foretell some things yet to be. I'd not bet against him. Not with my life, anyway."

"But I didn't kill *anyone* at the Sanctum!" Drenj pleaded. "I killed no one!"

Fencress regarded them glumly. "It doesn't matter whose hand killed them. We were there, we were a part of it all. The Lector, Tream, the Dictorian, Merek, all of it. It's just as they've always said. Dark work brings dark rewards."

4
THAT HINT OF DANGER

THE SUN SAGGED toward evening when Lannick first caught sight of Kevlin's farm. A stone farmhouse and a wide barn lorded over a hill squeezed by pens of scrawny livestock. Two dozen or more horses wandered inside a corral, and a matching number of men drifted about the structures.

"Looks like a good many of the lads made it," said Brugan from the creaking cart, blood-soaked bandages wrapped around his shoulders. He'd not been feverish and the wounds appeared clean, though his wide face seemed drained of its usual cheer.

Lannick nodded, feeling for an instant like he'd rather tug the horses' reins and turn the cart around. As much as he relished the notion of exacting revenge, a sense of uneasiness gnawed at him over facing so many certain to think so little of him. He shook his head and urged the horses forward. "How are the shoulders?"

Brugan worked his arms about, wincing as he did. "They've been better but I've had worse." He smiled. "I'll soon be cracking skulls with the best of 'em again."

"Fane's Scarlet Swords will no doubt tremble before your hammer, my friend," Lannick said, though he suspected it false. They were older, now, and old bones didn't heal in the way of young ones. Lannick felt aches of his own, the occasional twinge in his hip from Silas's blade, the grind and crack of his jaw from his beatings at the hands of Fane's men. His will and wits might have sharpened but the burdens of age had dulled just about everything else.

And while they'd grown older the weight of their task had grown heavier. The High King had died and there were revelations from Lannick's erstwhile Variden companions that Arranan's Spider King kept the counsel of Necrists. Lannick added to that his increasing certainty that General Fane *intended* to lose this war.

The task had indeed grown heavier, and it seemed it'd be one borne upon backs bowed by time and infirmity. He sighed and drew his hands into fists.

Bear it we must, though, for there can be no failure.

"Ah!" said Brugan, his bright tone stirring Lannick from his thoughts. "It warms the soul to see so many familiar faces! Ulder, Cudgen, Hanner, Arleigh... I never dared hope so many would join us. You've stirred something in these men, Captain! This is how great victories are born!"

Lannick grimaced and looked to the men milling

about the farm, their features now discernible in the dying light. Many had grown too fat or too thin in the years since Pryam's Bay. None seemed younger than a few dozen years, and most looked to be a number of years older with graying hair painted white by the fading rays of the sun.

From this distance they had the look of farmers or craftsmen, like common folk accustomed to the toil of labor rather than battle. But as they neared there could be seen that hint of danger lurking beneath the veneer of practical purpose. The odd scar or missing part whispering a familiarity with violence, a cold glint in the eye that told of having borne witness to death.

Lannick knew these men, though youthful eagerness had long given way to age and cynicism. He spied Cudgen Ashworn, a thin man with sunken cheeks and a neatly-trimmed beard who'd proven a most deadly archer at Pryam's Bay. Beside him Kevlin deKray, a square-jawed brute who'd killed three men with just his shield. Arleigh Lay leaned against the barn, his mess of black hair darkening a face curled in what seemed a permanent scowl. His one remaining hand fingered an ebony jerkin that surely hid a long dagger. There were many others, too, all members of the cohort Lannick had commanded.

Lannick smiled weakly, remembering for an instant how they'd looked before Pryam's Bay those years before. "*Captain!*" they'd hailed, clad in oiled mail with swords held high.

They would look to him differently, now, he knew. After seeing a number of them a few weeks back, he knew their faces would no longer alight with admiration or confidence, as they once had, but rather would dim with disdain. They were eyes he didn't fancy facing, but his task left him no other choice.

No half-measures and no turning back, he told himself, trying to give the phrase the ring of truth in his head.

Lannick guided the horses and cart between a couple of fenced corrals and up the easy slope. The men on the hilltop started shuffling toward them, taking notice of their arrival. Sour grimaces wound into grins.

"Brugan!" several called. None shouted Lannick's name.

Brugan shifted about the cart, grunting as he did. "Well met, lads!" he said, his big bellow undiminished. He gingerly hauled himself over the cart's side once Lannick drew it to a halt, then lumbered toward the top of the hill and the growing throng of old soldiers.

"Me ol' friend!" roared Kevlin, striding over to Brugan. A wide grin stretched across his square face as he grabbed Brugan in a hearty embrace. Kevlin had always been known more for his brawn than his brain, and furthered that reputation by smacking Brugan squarely upon his bandaged shoulders.

"Oof!" Brugan flinched and moved his shoulders in a slow shrug. "Go easy on me, lad! Seems I've taken the first wounds of our new war. Soldiers conscripting along the road."

"Sorry to hear," came Cudgen Ashworn's voice. His beady eyes grew beadier as they found Lannick. "You wounded on account of protecting our esteemed *captain*?" The last word sounded soaked with sarcasm.

Lannick's felt his heart quail with that awful unease.

He kept his eyes level, though, knowing that letting those feelings show would only worsen matters.

Brugan turned his lumpy face to Lannick, his smile falling to a look more thoughtful. "Hardly," he said, voice steady and earnest and kind. "Captain Lannick there saved my skin. I'm ashamed to say it but I got unhorsed and some bastard of a soldier had me on the tip of his blade. Captain put an arrow in him and killed two others. They were hard-edged soldiers—fine warriors—but Lannick bested them all the same and with little help from me. As fine a swordsman as he ever was."

Lannick winced at his friend's puffery, even thankful as he was for the man's kind words to a crowd certain to carry a hearty share of skepticism. There'd be no undoing his mistakes, Lannick knew, but he was determined to fill the other side of the scales with deeds both righteous and overdue.

Cudgen's narrow face eased somewhat, but after a moment his thin mouth curled disdainfully. "Sounds like he might have been sober. For once."

Brugan turned to Cudgen, his big, bandaged form appearing to grow to an even more imposing size. "Captain Lannick saved my life, Cudgen, and he's a changed man from what he'd been. I've witnessed it myself. If any man wants to claim something otherwise," he said to the gathering, "he'll be having a hard talk with me."

Cudgen's sneer diminished, though scorn lingered in his eyes. A few of the others—dark-browed Arleigh Lay the most obvious—held on to their scowls and murmured unheard words with gazes fixed on Lannick.

Lannick shifted on the cart's seat, doing what he could

to keep his eyes from falling from those who mocked him. He focused his thoughts on his purpose. First on the grinning skulls of his wife and children, faces torn from the bones beneath them. Next upon that smug, scarred face and those demented eyes that reveled in the pain he inflicted.

On General Fane and his hatred for the man.

On the hope of stilling his black heart with my sword.

The thought steeled him and he straightened his spine, his expression daring the doubters to challenge him. His heart thundered as he did, though for a moment at least he felt his shame cower before his resolve.

He refused to be that dog that'd skulk away to a corner when kicked.

Not this time.

Not anymore.

After a time some unheard jest brought snickers and smiles to a clutch of the men. Soon the company seemed themselves again, sharing old tales and old boasts in the manner of old friends. They smiled and spoke with each other, and most seemed content to leave Lannick entirely alone.

For now, perhaps that's just as well.

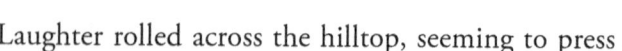

Laughter rolled across the hilltop, seeming to press away the night's heavy darkness.

"And you lads remember what came next!" Brugan bellowed from atop a stump at the group's center. Wounded though he was, his good humor rose undiminished on his broad face. "Hanner was chased from that whorehouse by two women twice his size! They said his cock was so small they had to do all the work—so he owed 'em double on account of it!"

"Not true!" shouted Hanner Hale, a barrel-chested fellow with a salt-and-pepper beard. His face flushed crimson in the light of the flickering fires.

The men laughed ever louder.

Lannick felt a slight smile stray to his face. Brugan had told the story many times before, though the lads laughed all the same.

The laughter settled at last. The men resumed their talk about the several fires, grins greasy from the pig Kevlin had roasted. They downed their supper with tankards of ale.

Lannick sat alone—without the ale—atop the splintering fence of a corral a dozen or so yards from the gathering. He didn't enjoy the thought of facing those dubious stares in such abundance, and a rare moment to himself with his supper seemed a fine thing. Yet he'd cleaned the meat from the ribs he'd taken and now his task's urgency loomed over him.

He knew he needed to take hold of this thing. He needed to explain to these men that the whole fate of the realm now rested upon their unsuspecting shoulders, that General Fane and the Spider King were very likely working in concert with Rune's most ancient enemy.

That this wasn't simply about revenge, but about saving all they held dear.

He flicked the bones to the corral and looked about. After a time, his eyes strayed to the shadows dancing across the hilltop, those stretching from every man gathered about the fires. He watched as those dark swaths painted their way across the farm before becoming lost in the night, weaving together into an impenetrable black.

He thought of the Necrists and reckoned they hunted him still. He was Fane's promised currency in his bargain with the Necrists and they knew him now. They knew him by the scent of his flesh and the cast of his shadow, as it was said.

He wondered what they had in store for him next.

He felt it best to move. He pushed himself off the fence and began making his way toward the throng of old soldiers. As much as he dreaded the doubting stares he dreaded the shadows all the more.

"Alright lads," Brugan barked, standing tall. He waited as the chatter faded. "About our business, then. Word is thousands of soldiers have deserted the army, with most sticking together rather than making their way home. They've gathered along the Silverflow not fifty leagues from the fight. Tomorrow we begin our ride to their camp to see if they'll follow us to victory."

"You're certain these are true deserters, Brugan?" Cudgen Ashworn called. "Not just some ruse of General Fane? You sure they'll not gut us on arrival?"

The big barkeep pinched his lumpy face in apparent thought. "I've heard a fair bit, some of it nonsense but much with the taste of truth. These are lads who've seen their brothers fall. They've seen them fall on account of those same mad choices we all know Fane capable of making. These lads have witnessed what is supposed to be the finest army in the world lose battle after battle to a bunch of wild horse thieves."

"And yet they've fled the front?" grunted Arleigh Lay,

slouched in the shadows beneath the thatched eaves of the farmhouse. "Why? To stand aside and watch Rune burn?"

"Think of it, Arleigh," Brugan said. "These lads left the front but not the war. I've heard nothing of large numbers returning home, just word of soldiers leaving the ranks and heading west along the Silverflow. If they'd a mind to leave the fighting they'd have broken up and wandered home long ago. Sounds to me as though they're willing to fight for Rune. Just not so long as Fane's in command."

Lannick eased closer, through the men ringing the crowd's edge. Old soldiers looked to him sidelong as he passed, some faces that'd once been friendly but were no longer. Suspicious gazes greeted him, along with a few possessing outright derision. A sharp elbow jarred him.

"So what makes you think they'll follow us?" Cudgen said.

Brugan smirked. "There are certain to be some veterans among them. Soldiers who respect experience, and soldiers who've heard of Captain Lannick there."

Cudgen snorted. "Let's hope they haven't heard anything about the last decade," he muttered.

A smattering of snickers sounded and Lannick felt blood color his cheeks. Self-doubt shook him but he pressed on, shifting his crooked jaw. He knew the challenges ahead of him—ahead of them all—were weighty enough without him feeling as though he were wilting within.

"That's a wet mess there along the Silverflow," said Hanner Hale. "If the deserters are encamped there then they're starved or sick or worse by now. Perhaps they haven't moved from there because they can't."

Brugan raised a thick hand. "Rumor is they're ready and being supplied from somewhere."

"From *someone*," blurted Ulder Prane, his freckled face aglow beneath his red shock of hair. His skinny frame swelled as he looked about the company. "My brother's a smuggler. For years he and I ran boats along the Silverflow and he keeps after it still. He hears a fair bit of gossip in his trade, and told me a few weeks back that Thane Vandyl's sending them provisions from his hold of Rellic."

Lannick paused as old memories nearly forgotten crept into his head. *Thane Vandyl?*

Brugan's brow knotted. "I'd not heard that."

"He swears it's so," said Ulder.

Lannick's head swirled, spinning through a mire of memory muddied by old mistakes. He'd met the thane, once. They'd been seated beside each other at a banquet in the Bastion's great hall. Vandyl—a serious, stubborn man—had expressed his admiration for Lannick's actions in the battle that decided the war, and whispered outrage over Fane's blunders that nearly lost it. He'd confided his opinion that Lannick rightly deserved to command Rune's armies rather than the general.

Will he remember that? It was so very long ago…

He shook his head.

Or was it?

"If these soldiers deserted the front," squealed Cudgen, "aren't you worried General Fane will send a column of men to drag them back? I'm with you, Brugan, but my head tells me some of this doesn't make sense. The thanes are calling for conscriptions when there are thousands of trained soldiers just sitting there that close to the front? Are we sure we want to risk joining those lads?"

A number of men murmured agreement, mostly those whose faces held the most doubt when looking upon Lannick.

"Besides," Cudgen continued, "Fane's a vicious bastard. Worst there is. You remember how he enjoyed making examples of men. Why's he not dragging those lads back to the front by their ears then forcing them to be first to fall on Arranese swords?"

Lannick's hand fell to his Coda and his thoughts turned again to that certainty he'd settled upon. That certainty that General Fane *meant* to lose this war.

His heart flooded with purpose and he pushed his way through a barrier of heavy forms.

Brugan was nodding. "Just as you said, Hanner, it's a wet mess along that river. Perhaps Fane doesn't want to risk sending soldiers away on some slog through the marshes. Perhaps—"

"I'll tell you why!" Lannick shouted, moving to stand beside Brugan at the group's center. "Fane doesn't march on those deserters because he doesn't *need* them. Because he doesn't *want* them."

Arleigh Lay chuckled. "You been drinking again?" His wry smile shone from the shadows.

Lannick stared him down. "He doesn't need those men because he intends to lose this war."

The men quieted, confusion drawn on faces striated with scars and wrinkles.

Arleigh smacked his knee with his one remaining hand. "He *has* been drinking again! I told you lads!"

The laughter rose again and the sound of it fired Lannick's anger. "Shut your mouth, Arleigh," he growled.

"Or what, *Captain*? You'll burp up your last drink on me?"

The laughter grew louder.

Lannick looked hard at him. Fear and doubt chewed his innards but he'd not let it show. Not to these men, not now. "Or I'll toss your ass off this hilltop right now."

"C'mon, lads!" said Brugan.

Arleigh's face twisted in a nasty smirk and he sauntered from the shadows of the farmhouse's eaves. His fingers moved just beneath the neck of his black jerkin to where his knife likely rested. "Will you, now?"

The men nearest Arleigh cleared away and he took a few swaggering steps forward. He came within arm's reach of Lannick and glared up at him with danger in his eyes. He slid the handle of his dagger from his jerkin and grinned.

"Easy, lads!" Brugan said with a forced laugh. "Fane's the enemy, not each other! We here are brothers!"

"Brothers?" Arleigh huffed. "I fought the same war he fought, yet he ended up with an honorary title while I rotted in a prison cell. Is that any way to treat a brother? What do you think, Cudgen? Or you, Ulder? Or any of you others who were there with me, taking our lashes? I was in there a whole fucking year after our *captain* received a special pardon from the High King himself!"

Brugan lifted his hands upward. "We know, Arleigh. You needn't remind any of us. We all—"

"We all what?" Arleigh snapped. "They locked our good captain in there, too? Funny. I don't recall seeing him in the brig, but I do recall hearing he spent his days shitting himself in tavern after tavern."

"My wife and children were murdered, Arleigh," Lannick said, trembling inside. "That was my punishment."

"My son was killed! The Tallorrath put the torch to my farmhouse, with him barred inside. Was my loss any less than yours?"

"No, it wasn't. But at least you had a measure of vengeance against his killers, spilling as much Tallorrathian blood as any man. My family's killer remains very much alive." His voice strengthened. "Since murdering my family he's been lauded with every manner of glory. He's lived lavishly on hoards *we* plundered. He's danced at the Bastion with the most beautiful women in the whole of Rune, all while having his ass licked by Rune's thanes. He's ascended to great power and now commands Rune's armies, sending young soldiers to their deaths. All this achieved atop a heap of atrocities committed upon the lot of us."

Arleigh's scowl did not waver. "No one's here on account of what happened to you, Lannick. We were all wronged by Fane, and every last one of us wants to stick a knife through that bastard's throat. You've no right to lay claim to vengeance alone."

Brugan moved to stand beside Lannick, placing a hand on his shoulder but addressing the whole group. "This lad's suffered as much as any, and more than most. I've witnessed it myself. Have any of us made all the right choices? I know I've not—would've married if I had. We all have regrets, things we could've done different. Most of those bad choices we can't make right, not ever. But this one we can. All the captain's asking for is a second chance with us, so we can all right that wrong of years ago."

Lannick nodded. "And I've no right to ask more from you," he said, voice low. "Any of you. I'm ashamed of what I allowed myself to become, and ashamed we didn't right those old wrongs long before now. I know you doubt me, and you've reason to." His voice trailed and his gaze fell from theirs.

"Go on, lad," said Brugan.

Lannick's hand felt the outline of his Coda and he looked to the men once more. "I just beg you listen to what I say here, for *everything* depends on it." He paused, letting silence take hold. "All of Fane's evil deeds are nothing when weighed against what he has planned. He is a madman, lusting for power. But he doesn't seek the power of this world. He seeks the dark power of old, power over death and darkness. And to gain that power he's allied himself with Rune's gravest enemy, the Necrists. They seek—"

"Aw, c'mon!" blurted Cudgen Ashworn. "Fairy tales, now?"

A number of the men laughed, Arleigh loudest of all.

"He speaks truth!" scolded Brugan. "Like any of you, I've never been one to believe in ghosts or demons or other such silliness. But back in Ironmoor, just a few days ago, I saw these *things*. Two things, and they commanded the shadows. What's more—"

Cudgen spat. "A good many of us have left our families to join this endeavor. We risk our lives. We know that already. No need to try and spook us with falsehoods."

Brugan took a heavy stride toward Cudgen, his good

nature giving way to menace. "What's more," he growled, "is that they were covered in the faces of Lannick's dead wife and son. These were not natural things, Cudgen."

Lannick nodded. "These things are what await your families with blood rites and perversions. They are what your families will face if we fail. I assure you, there is something dark and powerful afoot in all this."

Cudgen fell silent, though his brow curled with skepticism. Many others wore similar expressions.

"These things are real, Cudgen," Lannick said. "You must prepare yourselves to confront worse than warring soldiers. Fane may have surrounded himself with far fouler allies."

"You ask us to believe a good many things," Arleigh Lay said, his scowl undiminished. "The very worst may be that you're fit to lead the lot of us to war once more. The way I see things, you're not fit to lead us anywhere but a tavern. You're bound to fail us again, Lannick, and when you do it could cost us our lives. Rune has no king anymore, so why should we? I say let a man prove his worth. Nothing that happened at Pryam's Bay should count for us here."

Many heads bobbed in agreement.

"Well enough," said Lannick. "But I promise I'll not fail you. I know you don't have much faith in me now, but I swear to every one of you I'll die before I let you down. I fight for vengeance. *We* fight for vengeance. We fight for vengeance and we fight for far more. We will not—*must* not—lose." He looked to each man in turn, challenging the doubt still lingering on their faces. "Fane will die. I swear it."

Lannick sat in Kevlin's stone farmhouse, studying the map on the table before him. Firelight thrown from the hearth played across the yellowed parchment, lighting all but the deepest furrows of the map's folds, and shadows shifted across the faces of the three old soldiers seated about him.

Lannick placed a finger on what he reckoned was the general location of Kevlin's farm then traced it south. Across the sketch of rolling hills, past occasional hamlets, then at last to black line of the Silverflow. Somewhere along its banks, west of Riverweave, stood what Lannick guessed was his best hope of winning this thing. An encampment of soldiers who'd fled Fane's madness, deserters who risked execution for treason rather than serve the general.

Thousands, Brugan had said. Thousands massed and ready.

An army.

Brugan sat across from him. "We're not far from the hold of Thane Vandyl. Two days' ride, maybe, and the deserters' camp is but a few days beyond that. It'd not be out of our way."

Lannick's brow curled. "You really think he might be supplying the deserters?"

"Ulder says so," Brugan said, "and he's always been a reliable sort. What's more, folk say Vandyl holds the kingdom's old traditions most sacred, and there were rumors of a rift with Chamberlain Alamis after High King Deragol's troubles began."

Lannick nodded. "He seemed no friend to General Fane after Pryam's Bay. Perhaps he's an ally in waiting…

We could pay him a visit on our way to the encampment. If he lends his support that will send a powerful message."

"Aye," Brugan said. "Sounds to me it'd be well worth the effort, Captain."

Cudgen shifted in his creaky chair beside Brugan, the firelight making his narrow face seem skeletal. "Is it? You think a thane will open his gates for the like of us? For the likes of the renowned drunkard Lannick deVeers? Ha!"

Brugan straightened and stared at Cudgen. "Mind your tongue, Cudgen. I for one know what Lannick is. What he can be and what he can accomplish."

Cudgen huffed and began tapping a thin finger on the table.

"Hmm," rolled Kevlin's gravelly voice as the man scratched his heavy chin. He seemed nearly as imposing as he'd been with his broadsword a decade before, his now-balding head like a polished stone. "Cudgen might be right. It's risky asking a thane for help. He might send us in chains to Ironmoor. Maybe worse."

Brugan shook his head. "If what Ulder said is true—and I trust Ulder—then Thane Vandyl's not standing on the general's side of things. Besides, Vandyl's the sort to honor a Protector of Ironmoor. He'll remember Lannick."

"He will," said Lannick.

Cudgen snorted. "And you think that's a good thing? You were branded a traitor after the war."

"And pardoned by the High King himself," said Brugan sternly, folding meaty arms across his broad chest.

"We'll call on him," said Lannick firmly, holding Cudgen's gaze. "We'll see if we can learn where he's placed his loyalties. Just a small group so we don't seem a threat or a burden. After that, we'll rejoin the others and together make our way to the deserters' camp. Hopefully with the thane's endorsement."

Brugan nodded in agreement, and after a moment Cudgen's sneer faded.

For a time they were quiet, the only sounds the fire's crackle and the din of the old soldiers outside. A number had taken up a song, drunken voices lilting off-key.

On wagons borne they be
Free at last of misery
Their pain forgot
Their vict'ry not
On wagons borne they be!

Lannick frowned, not fancying an old tune about carrying the dead from the battlefield. They'd be seeing all too much of that in the coming months.

Kevlin cleared his throat behind a square fist. "What you said before," he said. "That thing about Fane meaning to lose. If that's true, why's he not been yanked from command already?"

"Because he's a deceitful snake," Brugan said, the fire-light drawing odd shadows upon his lumpy face. "Fane has spent years courting favor, years forging loyalties in the highest circles. Chamberlain Alamis has thrown his support behind the general, and he's the very man who's managed to slip his skinny ass onto the throne. Meanwhile the thanes bicker amongst themselves over their own merits to the crown. Between those political disagreements and Alamis's position the general will have a long leash."

"That's why we must prevail," said Lannick, "and quickly. If Fane can hold out long enough then Rune will be lost. We have to remove him before he's had time to make real whatever plan he has in his sick head."

Cudgen grunted. "Any word on where he is? That general was always a cowardly sort. My guess is he's nowhere near the fighting."

Brugan planted a thick finger on the square marking Riverweave. "Agreed, and that's why he's likely there. Riverweave. Somewhere secure, deep in the sprawl of the city and far from the front. Fane always wanted to stay safe until he thought the battle was nearly done. Likely he's somewhere real comfortable, and with a fast ship at the ready."

Lannick looked to the map's dark lines marking Rune's great rivers—the Silverflow and the Drimrill—as they tumbled toward the Sullen Sea. Toward Riverweave.

Toward Fane.

Cudgen leaned near the map. "So we mean to drag those deserters to Riverweave? You think they'll follow the likes of us? The likes of Lannick?"

Lannick looked to him for a moment then shrugged. "It doesn't matter what they think of me. As long as they remain willing to take up their swords for Rune and rally against the general, it doesn't matter who's in charge. As long as they can get us within reach of Fane they'll be serving our purpose."

Kevlin tilted his head, the hairless peak of it catching

the yellow glow of the fire. "Right-thinking folk respect experience. I'd guess they'll give you a listen, Captain."

"Let's say we get these deserters to march on Riverweave," said Cudgen as he scratched at his neatly-trimmed beard. "What then? We attack Rune's army? Wouldn't we be doing Fane's work for him?"

Lannick looked again to the map, to Riverweave sitting at the convergence of the Silverflow and Drimrill and sprawled upon the shore of the Sullen Sea. "No. If I have my say, we'll approach Riverweave from the north." He moved his finger along the line of the river, then round to the north of the city. "With any luck we can pass ourselves off as reinforcements from one of the columns in Ironmoor. If that doesn't work, the city's northern gates are likely to have the weakest defenses and the fewest soldiers. Once we're in the city we'll hunt down Fane. We'll kill him and every last one of his Scarlet Swords. Then, hopefully, this war will be free of his treachery, and we can keep the Arranese from advancing to Ironmoor."

Cudgen snorted. "So that's your plan. Sounds to me like an awful lot of hoping."

Lannick looked to him, quiet for a moment and with a pit in his chest. "You're damned right," he said at last. "For nearly a decade I forgot what a valuable thing hope can be. But now I have it again. *We* have it again. Be glad we have it still."

5
FRIENDS

BALE TURNED TO his side, uncomfortable on a bedroll that did little to dull the edges of the sharp stones of the Arranese steppe beneath it. What was more, the thin sheet he'd propped overhead with a stick did nothing to blunt the blaze of the rising sun. The sight of the Necrists a few nights before unnerved him still and his ankle throbbed with pain, but he was tired and stubborn and not about to surrender to the day's toil.

He squeezed shut his eyes, determined to send the sun back beyond the horizon and return the sky to night. Then, as if in answer, darkness pressed aside the light glowing through his eyelids, blotting the sun's brightest beams. He smiled wanly, glad to give his aching ankle and blistered feet more time to heal.

A sharp kick struck him.

"Ouch!" he screeched.

"Quiet, Bale," grumbled Lorra from nearby.

"Then stop kicking me!"

Another kick. Sharper this time.

"Get up," said a woman's voice.

But that's not Lorra.

Bale pried his eyes to a squint and beheld a black silhouette framed against the harsh Arranese sun. He yelped, threw aside his makeshift tent and scooted back along the rocky ground. *A Necrist!*

"Easy," said the figure, the voice a touch softer. "I'm a friend."

Lorra growled beside him and darted upward, dust puffing in yellow plumes from her rough-hewn clothes. She brandished her wooden cooking spoon in an angry hand. "You're no friend of mine! Are you some kind of thief?"

Bale rubbed at his eyes as they adjusted to the sun and the figure resolved in his vision. It was a woman, short-haired with wide brown eyes and a cloak of forest green. She wore a scabbarded short sword and had a practical look about her.

This is no Necrist.

"I am no thief," the woman said.

Lorra thrust the spoon outward like a dagger, her face wrinkled and suspicious. "Then what do you want? You've been following us?"

The woman turned her eyes to Bale. "I'm here to learn what an acolyte of the Ancient Sanctum of Illienne the Light Eternal is doing in Arranan, so far from his quiet Abbey in Ironmoor."

Bale pinched his loose nightshirt about his skinny form then reached for the bundle of his brown robes.

"And who are you to want to know?" he asked, tugging the robes over his head. He looked nervously to her sheathed blade.

"My name is Alisa," she said, bowing. "Like you, a loyal servant of Rune. And I suspect our purposes in this wretched land are intertwined."

Bale squinted, as much from the sunlight as distrust. "And what is your purpose here?"

"I was tracking something. Something moving through the night. Something you saw just three nights ago, Acolyte. You know of what I speak."

Bale cocked a brow and rubbed at his overlarge nose. He didn't know yet whether to trust this stranger, but knew he was a poor liar. *I'll ask more questions, not give answers.* "How is it you know we saw anything?"

A smile danced across the woman's lips. "The two of you blunder through this land like blind bumpkins. I could smell those rotten roots you were cooking a league away. That," she said, her expression becoming somber, "and my order has ways of detecting spellcraft."

"You insult my cooking?" Lorra growled.

"Your order?" Bale said.

Alisa dropped to a knee before him. "Do you know who keeps watch? Who fights the enemies lurking along the shadow's edge? Do you know of the Vigilant?"

Bale pressed a finger to his lips, dredging the depths of his knowledge, those esoteric things he'd studied in the books buried deepest in the Abbey's library. Those books laughed at by scholars, some even forbidden. There'd been a book on Lector Erlorn's—the Sentinel Castor's—private bookshelf, which the Lector had suggested he read only a few months before his death. The Variden were described therein. "Variden..." he murmured. "The descendants of Valis..."

The smile returned to Alisa's face. "You know secrets well kept, Acolyte. I am impressed. Then you know what it is you saw that night?"

"Necrists," he said quietly, giving up on his questions. "Necrists and their creations."

"Yes," she said. "I located their lair in Zyn and tracked them across this very waste."

"You know their destination?"

"Rune," Alisa said. "Likely to join the Spider King's army. I followed them to the foothills of the Southwalls then left my watch to another of my order. I returned to find you, to see what you know—and how I can be of help."

Lorra squinted at the woman, wooden spoon drooping. "We let her stay with us?"

"For now," Bale said, looking timidly at Lorra.

Lorra's apprehension remained etched upon her hard face. She paced at a wary distance.

Alisa gestured for Lorra to come near. "Please," she said, her tone earnest. "You will find we need each other."

"Bale?" Lorra asked.

Bale nodded. "We'll listen to what she has to say."

"Good," Alisa said. "I found food before coming to you." She presented a small satchel and revealed a number of small, greenish eggs. "Breakfast?"

"A welcome treat," Bale said, gulping down a mouthful of scrambled eggs. "Delicious."

Nearby, Lorra grumbled something that didn't sound as complimentary. "I'll forage for stouter food while the two of you talk of how tasty these tiny eggs are." She dropped her bowl with a clatter and rose, flashing Bale an angry grimace.

Bale looked to her with pleading eyes, but that didn't stop her from stomping away from their campsite.

"She seems quite the character," Alisa said once Lorra was a few dozen yards away.

"She's a loyal friend," Bale snapped.

"I am sure she is," Alisa answered, brown eyes staring meaningfully at Bale. "You may find I am, as well."

"We'll see," he said slowly. He knew but little of the Variden. The books he'd read instructed that Valis vested his power in physical devices upon his death, devices used by his disciples to carry on his vigil over Rune. Bale surmised he'd trust the woman in better circumstances, but surrendering that trust in the wastes of Arranan seemed a different matter.

Alisa scraped the last of her eggs from her shallow bowl. "Zandrachus—"

"Just Bale, if you would. My father called me Zandrachus." His contempt for the man rang sharply on his voice.

"Very well, Bale. Circumstances are dire, and we must speak directly. There is no time to do otherwise."

Bale placed his bowl on the hardpan dirt beside him and smoothed his robes.

"If you know of the Variden you can guess my purpose in this place," she said. "Rune has been invaded by the Arranese, and, as you've seen, the Necrists have a role in this. As a Variden I'm sworn to watch over Rune, to keep an eye on her enemies. I have scouted this land to see just how grave our problems are and the scale of the Necrists' involvement."

"And how grave are those problems?"

She sat quietly for a moment, eyes downcast. "The gravest, I fear. We know not for certain, but from what I've learned things are far worse than we suspected. The Necrists are *many*, Bale. They are many, and their hive is beneath Zyn. They are entwined with the Spider King. He receives their counsel. Worse, he may be a Necrist himself, though none of our number has managed to get close enough to determine that with certainty. But we do know the Necrists mingle with his army, even performing rituals on soldiers dead and dying." She looked back to the sun, as though seeking solace in the light.

"I saw one in Riverweave," Bale said. "A Necrist. Conferring with General Fane and speaking of some black bargain. They talked of an 'Auruch.' I know little else, for I traveled south thereafter."

Alisa's eyes widened. "We knew of some contact, but nothing of that nature. We've focused our efforts on the Spider King and the Necrists, though it seems Fane deserves more... scrutiny. One of our number— or, at least, one we *used* to count among us—has set out for Fane's head. I'll send word to my order that he requires assistance."

"From *here*?"

"We have methods of speaking, even at great distance, by virtue of the gifts Valis bestowed. But," she said, pulling closer. "I have said much, and you very little. Why are you here, Bale? You learned of General Fane bargaining for an Auruch yet you continued here, into this barren land. Why? What drives a man such as you so deep into the land of our foe? You don't strike me as a traitor, nor one particularly accustomed to the rigors of travel."

The sun's glare had grown intense and Bale felt sweat beading on his brow. "I am no traitor."

She edged closer still. "You observed a small army of Necrists, a direct threat to Rune. And still you continued your trek. Why? What is of such importance?"

Bale noticed the woman's left hand caressing a bracelet of iron worn just above her right. He suspected it was one of the devices passed on by Valis.

"I can *help* you, Bale. I serve Rune above all, as you do." Her large brown eyes were suddenly difficult to avoid. "You know of your Lector's true nature, don't you?"

He felt as though the answer crept along his tongue, drawn out by this stranger. Sweat dripped on his face and his heart pounded. *I am too weak an instrument!* "Yes!" he squeaked.

"You know he was something more than a man, don't you?"

He tore his gaze away from hers. *She knows.* He tugged in a breath, trying to calm himself. "Castor," he whispered.

"Then we each serve a Sentinel. As I said, our purposes are conjoined. Did you find the site of his murder?"

"My superiors at the Sanctum tasked me with finding that, and with seeking answers."

Alisa eased back, her hand dropping from the black bracelet. "We discovered who killed him. A man who carries his spirit still." She sighed. "I hate to bring news of more tragedy, but both our orders have been beset by it and I fear more will come. One of my brothers, Merek, captured Castor's killer. He's a vicious highlander, an assassin who was retained by the Necrists to slay your Lector. Merek captured him and took him to your Abbey, and there they tried to tear Castor's spirit from the highlander's flesh. In the process, the highlander slew your Dictorian, and my brother Merek died as well. We know not where the highlander is now."

Bale sat slack-jawed.

"What's more," Alisa continued, "High King Deragol passed, less than a week ago. There are rumors Queen Reyis is with child, but only rumors. She's said to have disappeared from the Bastion, and the castle's halls are fraught with chaos and whispers of betrayal—"

"The Last King, indeed."

"I needn't tell you what trouble this portends."

Bale tucked a dangling strand of hair behind his ear. "Such is the nature of troubled times."

"Another of my brothers—also slain—accompanied Castor on his quest. We knew the purpose of his mission. You know of that purpose as well?"

He nodded, finding his earlier distrust had vanished. "To summon the Sentinels to Rune in defiance of the banishment."

"I see now that Castor anticipated these events." Alisa fixed him with her gaze. "And so I am led back to my original query. What is *your* purpose here?"

"I continue Castor's quest, to find Kressan the Kind in Zyn. Then I am to bring her to the Sacred Place beneath Cirak."

"Then you'll have my help in doing so. There's another friend of ours there and he's certain to aid us, as well. Nevertheless," she said, rising and extending a hand, "we have a most arduous task ahead. Get up, Acolyte. We've no time to waste."

They walked in the dying light of evening through a valley between flat-topped hills. Fires dotted the hilltops, and Bale guessed they marked camps of roving Arranese. He wondered whether they, like the Necrists, were headed for Rune and war.

"Make camp now?" muttered Lorra from several yards ahead of them. She'd spoken only rarely but ever gruffly since the morning.

"Not yet," said Alisa. "We need to get clear of these hills. We're safer from the Arranese at night than we are during the day. But as you are coming to know, Acolyte, the darkness gives us things to worry over besides the Arranese."

Bale pulled his robes close. With every breeze he felt a chill—real or imagined he could not be sure. Whichever, he knew he'd not be comfortable during any night spent on this steppe after witnessing the march of the Necrists and their abominations.

"Another mile or so," Alisa said, "but no fire at our camp this night."

Bale nodded and tried turning his mind from the image of the Necrists. "Your order," he said. "How many Variden are there? The accounts I read were unclear."

Alisa's eyes glinted with the light of the fading sun. She paused, seeming to consider whether to answer.

"There are but twenty, twenty-one if I count Lannick… If I count the one who abandoned us."

"So few?" he asked, his curiosity kindled.

"Valis divided his power among us, just as Illienne did among the Sentinels. Had Valis divided that power any further it would have been diminished, leaving us too weak to combat our enemy."

"And what of the other Sentinels? The histories are unclear and some of the Sentinels unaccounted for. Did they divide their power or retain it? What is it you know of them?" He stopped, knowing he spoke too quickly. "Nothing?"

"The occasional rumor. Rumors infrequent and fleeting and rarely confirmed. There were rumors a hundred years ago of Thaydorne venturing into the Bowl of Fire in search of one of the old hells left by the Elder God. Another that Sienne served as a trusted advisor to the last Sage-Emperor of Harkane. Lyan the Just was allegedly spotted just a decade ago, stopping the execution of a traitor at a watchtower along the western shores. Pastine is thought to have vanished and been survived by but a handful of disciples. All considered, it is such that we wonder if many of the Sentinels abandoned this world long ago. I hope your Lector was correct in thinking they could be summoned back. I hope there is meaning to your quest."

"There is, Alisa. We spoke with Lyan the Just in Cirak, just weeks ago."

Alisa turned sharply to him, eyes wide and glittering in the fading light. "You were in the presence of a Sentinel?"

Bale sniffed in a breath of the dry, dusty air. "It was… uncomfortable."

"You have seen a rare thing, Acolyte. Tell me of this."

Bale rubbed at his nose and trudged along. "It wasn't what I expected. She was majestic and intimidating and seemed to fill the entire room when she spoke. She was more than mortal, certainly, and I felt the presence of divinity. But there was an anger, too. Some deep-seeded hatred for Rune that I imagine has festered in her heart for a thousand years." He tucked long strands of gray hair behind his ears. "She said she'd wait for us to complete our quest and then speak with the other Sentinels. However, I have much doubt she and the others will be persuaded to come to Rune's aid." He looked to her. "Do we have other friends who share our cause? Others who might help us?"

Alisa smiled slightly. "We have friends, Bale, but few. Most have forgotten the evils of old, or would rather think nothing of them. Your order has stood with us. The heads of your order always shared with us those portents and omens they felt necessary to our task. I mentioned Pastine, who is survived by disciples who may help as well. I know one for certain who may assist us."

"Pastine…" Bale said, recalling the Sentinel was known as 'nurturing' but recalling little else. "Are we enough? Are we enough to defeat the enemy?"

Alisa took a long, even breath. "Rune has weathered many storms without Lyan and the others, but I worry what comes now is too fierce a thing without the aid of all the Sentinels. Let us pray Castor foresaw things that we cannot."

Bale nodded and turned tired eyes overhead, to stars struggling to light the sky in the wake of the waning sun.

Prefect Gamghast sat at the table in his small quarters, old eyes trained to his solitary window. Raindrops spattered against the glass from an angry sky, a thunderstorm darkening the summer day. And there, not far from the Abbey, stood the foreboding silhouette of the Bastion, erstwhile home of the High King of Rune.

He looked upon the brooding mass of leaden stone, a cold pit forming in his belly. Somewhere within—upon the throne most likely—was Chamberlain Alamis. Gamghast's mouth sank to a bitter frown beneath the wisps of his beard as he thought of the man's treachery.

His attention turned to the frayed note upon his table, the note the now-dead scullery maid had given to Bale shortly before the acolyte's departure. *"The King is being poisoned,"* the note began. *"That's why he's gone mad and why he's making no babies. He is in grave danger. Beware of the chamberlain. He speaks much with a man whose face is made of stitches."*

It seemed a certainty that Alamis had forged a relationship with the Necrists, and had played some role in causing the High King's troubles with conceiving an heir. It seemed a distinct possibility—nay, probability—that the chamberlain had hastened the High King's demise, as well.

Rage seized Gamghast and he slammed a gnarled fist against the table.

How could we have been so blind? How could our old enemy have worked beneath our very noses for so long?

He looked back to the window.

Because we've holed up within these damned walls for too long, poring over old books while our enemy courted an alliance with the chamberlain himself...

They'd permitted the old order of their world to crumble about them, its foundations corroded by arrogance and ignorance and neglect. They'd raised only faint protest when formerly routine audiences with the High King were refused. After all, the royal staff still called upon the Sanctum regularly for the treatment of ailments and matters of faith. But they never encountered the High King during such visits, and after a time only the Lector was permitted an annual, ceremonial audience with the man.

Their connection to the Crown withered while they busied themselves with dusty tomes and tedious prayers to a dead god. They'd allowed the walls of their Abbey to constrain them like a prison. All the while, their ancient, near-forgotten foe worked its way inside the Bastion itself.

They'd disregarded warnings from the Variden as nonsense, even though they'd worked closely with Valis's order in the centuries before. They'd puzzled over the news of Queen Reyis's first miscarriage, considering it an oddity but not an alarm. By her fourth, they were mildly concerned, but the platitudes of their faith soothed them still. They prayed, believing no ill could befall the Crown. The order of things would continue undisturbed, they'd thought, so long as they observed the tenets of their faith.

And thus our very faith blinded us to the workings of our enemy!

He thought of Castor, and of the ragged highlander who held his divine spirit. Despite the man's vicious appearance and the violent acts attributed to him, Gamghast remained convinced the highlander was Castor's chosen vessel. The man had uttered what had to be the confession, but the spirit had refused to be dislodged in spite of the Dictorian's most potent incantations. Gamghast *knew* Castor had chosen the instrument most suited to his purpose.

And yet there was Kreer. Prefect Kreer, his tall, droopnosed counterpart at the Sanctum. The man—blinded by self-righteous ambition—had vowed some mad crusade to hunt down the highlander Karnag and tear Castor's spirit from him.

And perhaps, in the process, doom what little hope remains.

Gamghast smacked the table again.

It seems our faith blinds us not only to the workings of our enemy, but also to whom that enemy really is.

The notion of sitting for a moment longer in his cramped quarters beneath the pile of rocks known as the Abbey angered him. He needed to throw open the shutters of his senses, to consult something other than old books holding accounts of faith-blind, long-dead scholars. He needed to clear his head of the cobwebs that draped this place.

With a pained groan he pressed himself to stand. He grimaced as he struggled to straighten his crooked back, then pulled a cloak over his robes and snatched his walking staff. He left his quarters and limped his way through the dark, stagnant corridors of the Abbey.

Gamghast trudged across the rain-sodden cobbles,

clumsily picking his way through the foggy gloom. Rain hammered upon him and trickled from the brown brim of his hood through the white thatch of his beard.

People hurried past him. He overheard many cursing the weather and others worrying over the war with Arranan. Only a scant few troubled themselves with the recent news of the passing of High King Deragol.

He slogged along and soon left the old haunts of the Nearer Ward behind. He passed the estates of minor nobles, the comfortable homes of merchants and the gilded shops of artisans. He then ventured into the lower areas of Ironmoor, closer to the Sullen Sea. Places he'd not visited in what had to have been years. More modest places, those upon which Illienne's blessing did not seem to so brightly shine.

The cobblestones of the road gave way to gravel and mud. The masonry of prouder structures gave way as well, and here buildings of warped and weathered wood leaned precariously against one another, looking as though a sharp push could send them all tumbling in succession.

A clutch of rag-clad urchins splashed across the wet street before him, hefting between them a wheel of cheese and a few loaves of bread. A shopkeep howled somewhere in the distance. Meanwhile, the urchins leapt into an alleyway, disappearing in the manner of practiced thieves.

Gamghast snorted and walked onward, managing at last to reach a tight grouping of houses. He studied them for a time, uncertain which was his intended destination. Then he spied it, a simple, two-storied home of gray wood, candlelight glowing behind its fogged windows.

He approached and thumped the door with the head of his staff.

After the fifth thump the door drew open to a crack, presenting Gamghast with a solitary, twitchy eye. The eye flicked up and down the length of his form. After a moment the opening widened, revealing a tiny, ancient man seemingly made of barely more than bone.

"G—" the small man stammered, thin hand pressed against a skull holding only a hint of hair. His bulging eyes zigzagged about. "Gamghast?"

"Tolem," Gamghast said with a nod.

"Dead gods," Tolem grumbled. "Whatever is it you want with me? I left for a reason, as you well know."

Gamghast looked to the heavy sky and raindrops splattered upon his worn face. "For now," he said, "a simple respite."

"Dead gods," the little man said again as he pulled the door wide. "If you must."

Gamghast slipped inside the small house, into a cramped room. In the room's center stood a table stacked with books and aglow with candles, about which were pressed two chairs.

Gamghast pulled away his wet cloak and hung it upon a peg beside the door. "May I?" He gestured to a chair.

Tolem looked nervously about the ill-lit room, fidgeting, but then nodded toward the table.

Gamghast set aside his staff and eased himself into a seat. The chair's wood creaked and complained but seemed sturdy enough. "Thank you, Tolem."

Tolem stood nearby, picking at his fingertips. "Wine?" he said eventually. "I have a couple of bottles stashed away.

I imagine a visit from such a *venerated* guest warrants the opening of one."

Gamghast recognized the sarcasm, but the notion of wine after limping through such weather appealed to him. "That sounds most excellent."

Tolem grunted and rummaged through a cupboard. He emerged with a dusty bottle and two wooden cups, then settled across the table from Gamghast. "Whatever is it you want?" he asked flatly as he yanked the cork from the bottle.

Gamghast waited until his cup was filled, then took a hearty sip of the red liquid. It wasn't as fine a drink as what was generally available in the Abbey, but then he reckoned he and his whole order had grown too used to the comforts of luxury.

"And I ask again," said Tolem, irritation in his tone, "whatever is it you want?"

Gamghast took another sip of his wine, eyes wandering across the room's many smoldering candles and dusty books. "Why did you leave?"

"Why?" Tolem asked, his voice shrill. "You visit me to ask me *that*? To ask me why I left the Sanctum? I gave you that answer years ago."

"You said your faith had faltered. You said you couldn't serve as a prefect if you didn't fully believe in the truth of our faith."

Thunder cracked outside, rattling the home's thin walls.

Tolem's eyes twitched. "And you're expecting a different answer now?"

"No," Gamghast said tiredly. "It's just that I find myself feeling much the same way."

"Oh," Tolem said, his pinched face slackening.

"Did your faith ever strengthen after you left?"

Tolem shook his head. "No. If anything, it's left me completely."

Gamghast stared at his wine, its deep red impenetrable. "Tell me, then, how is it you find hope in a life that lacks faith?"

Tolem shrugged his bony shoulders. "The sun rises in the morning and I still draw breath."

"That is hardly a reason for *hope*. As old as you and I are, that breath could give out any time."

"Is it *not* hope?" Tolem said. He took a long drink of his wine. "If one doesn't believe the Elder God's heavens await us beyond this life, then every new day—what is *here* and what is *real*—is cause for hope. Life becomes everything, if after it there is nothing. Hope rests in the desire for more moments, and in the anticipation of what those moments could hold."

Gamghast shifted in his chair, his back aching. "And," he said as he stifled a groan, "what if one knows those moments will hold only misery? How can one have hope then?"

Tolem sat for a time, a frown upon his face. Rain hissed and thunder rolled again. "Then," he said, after the thunder quieted, "one would hope to meet one's end with dignity."

Gamghast took a swallow of wine, a droplet of it falling from his mouth to stain an edge of his white beard.

"You have found a workable logic, at least. I, however, find myself struggling to answer a slightly different question."

"And that is?"

"How can I have faith in the absence of hope?"

Tolem huffed. "You are so shaken by the death of High King Deragol? If so, it seems you had only scant hope in the first place."

"No," Gamghast said, "not just that. Our old enemy has been hard at work. They—"

"*They?*" he exclaimed. "You speak of Necrists?"

"I do," he grumbled. "We were blind to them, made too comfortable by centuries of near-silence, lulled into inaction by an arrogant belief that they were too weak to rise against us again. But while we slept they accomplished much, and now they have wormed their way within the shadows of this very city."

Tolem slurped from his cup, then grinned to reveal a mouth of few teeth. "And the great Lector never spoke of these things? Our mighty Sentinel, guarding us from all things evil? *He* never warned you? Ha."

"Perhaps they blinded even him. He—Lector Erlorn— was murdered, you know. Murdered by a barbarian from the north, a man I am convinced now possesses the spirit. That man spoke the confession, warning of the return of the Necrists and the need to summon the other Sentinels. And now Prefect Kreer has set out to stop him. He seeks to pry the spirit from him and command it himself."

"Kreer? That pompous peacock?"

Gamghast nodded. "The very same. He's not changed since you knew him, still the ever pious and righteous man who alone privy to all the great truths… If he succeeds in displacing Castor, what then? And even if he does not, why would the Sentinels return to save the likes of *us*?"

"So what little hope you have rests in these Sentinels? In these petty gods? These so-called aspects of divinity? Not me, Gamghast. My faith in them—in their so-called righteousness—failed long ago. They may be *powers*, but they are not gods. They serve their own ends, as did the High King and his whole line before him. Cursed be the day Illienne and Yrghul descended upon this realm. They were naught but tyrants, and we have always been used as pieces in their game. You should remove yourself from that contest, my old friend."

Gamghast tapped his bent fingers against his cup, watching the liquid shudder. "It is too late for that, Tolem. I cannot abandon this 'game' as you call it, for I am too invested in it and there is too much at stake. The Necrists have gotten to the chamberlain. The war with Arranan is being lost. Our Variden brethren claim the Spider King is in league with the Necrists and may be one himself. Meanwhile, those left to fight for Rune are few and flawed and weary."

"So what do you intend to do?"

Gamghast rose with a muted groan. "I will fight on. It is not within me to surrender though I know the battle to be a losing one. Perhaps I'll assume your philosophy, and endeavor to face my end with dignity."

6
TROUBLE

ENCRESS FALLCROW SAT in *The Mewling Mutton's* low-raftered common room, absently peering out the bleary window as she fingered the dice in her gloved hand. The sad street outside seemed little more than mud and the gray sky above wept a steady rain.

"Another round?" grated the white-haired hag preening over her table.

"More of your finest, of course!" Fencress said with a nod of her ale-warmed head, watching as the wench limped across the empty tavern to the sagging bar at its end.

"As bad a place as this is," said Paddyn with his whistling voice, "it's a damn sight better than sleeping in the fucking wild again." He tilted his wooden mug to his lips, brown ale dripping from the corners of his mouth. "I'm sick of scratching at bugs on my ass."

The old wench returned with a pitcher. She dumped

ale into their mugs until foam swelled over the mugs' lips and tumbled in caramel ribbons down their sides. "Damn lot of drinking for breakfast," she huffed. "Innkeep's not even finished frying your eggs and hash."

Paddyn roared with a burp and Fencress couldn't help but giggle. The hag retreated, whispering something about drunkenness being akin to blasphemy.

"My friend," Fencress said, "a belch of that magnificence would be an eloquent curse in any tongue."

Paddyn smiled his gap-toothed smile then glanced toward the window. "Any idea where we are?"

Fencress flicked the dice upward then snatched them from the air with a practiced hand. "This is Shank's Hollow, or Shit's Hollow as I've always thought of it. I took a job to steal something from someone here once, ten or so years ago when Rune was last at war. Some rich fuck—the crack-brained brother of some thane—lives in this town, probably still sleeping with all the cross-eyed, inbred whores of this shithole when he's not counting his coin." She laughed. "We're not far from the Sullen Sea. Perhaps a week's ride shy of Riverweave. The war's likely just south of that city, if it's not made the gates already." She took a swig of ale. "War's a time of profit for the likes of us. Especially with Karnag taking the heads of all before us."

Paddyn grimaced and dragged another long sip from his tankard.

A creak sounded nearby and Fencress saw Drenj stepping lightly down stairs that seemed little more than a ladder in the room's center. The dusky-skinned Khaldisian was wrapped in loose clothes that fell from his increasingly thin frame.

"By the dead gods, come eat something!" Fencress said with a smile and a gesture of her mug. "The two of you are starting to look frailer than ghosts. At least young Paddyn here is trying to fatten himself up with some ale."

Drenj fumbled with a rickety chair close by, shuddering as he pulled it near. At last he sat and slumped against their small table with what seemed utter exhaustion.

"Drenj?" asked Paddyn.

"I haven't slept…" Drenj sighed.

Fencress tried her grin again. "Have you and Karnag been up to something? Planning a surprise, perhaps? You know my birthday falls in but a few days…"

Drenj sighed and rested his face in his long-fingered hands. "He was still mumbling on when I left the room."

Fencress's smile faded and she took another pull of ale. "He's troubled by some kind of spirit. Seems to me most times he can master it, but there are times when the two of them rage in a struggle for his sanity."

"Dead gods," Paddyn said. "Could he be worse if he loses that struggle?"

Fencress stared to the dice in her glove, a pair with edges rounded from age. She'd found them left on a table in the tavern's common room the night before, after they'd arrived near midnight. Each had shown just a single pip—a good start in deadman's dice. Fencress had taken it as an omen and had slipped them in her pocket right then.

We need all the luck we can find.

Drenj laughed, pulling his hands from his face to

reveal eyes wet with tears. He laughed again, high-pitched and with a touch of madness. "*Worse?*" he cackled. "What could be worse? Him dragging us into the old hells of the Elder God?"

Fencress looked to her ale and smiled slightly. "I thought Khaldisians weren't much for gods, yet now you speak of the old hells and the Elder God? Amazing how folk find religion in desperation."

Drenj's laughter turned to a stifled sob. He swiped tears from his eyes, smearing black kohl in uneven streaks. "No… No. You misunderstand us—or what I was taught to fear, at least."

"Do I?" Fencress said, trying to keep her tone jovial. "Remember, I've seen your greed, Drenj. You place gold over gods—and I respect that—but now you've found faith?"

Drenj shook his head, his expression dour. "No. Khaldisians don't worship the dead gods, or any others for that matter. But Khaldisian children are taught there was an Elder God, a creator, and that when He abandoned this place a darkness swept into the void. And in that darkness demons live, demons sucked from the old hells and into this world by the pull of the Elder God's wake."

The wench returned, dropping plates of steaming food on the table with a clatter. "You need something?" she grunted at Drenj.

"Tea, please," he said weakly.

She grunted and left.

Fencress drew her wooden plate closer, inspecting for a moment the clump of yellow eggs flecked with brown from the shells, as well as the greasy glob of what she wagered was last night's—or last week's—meat minced and mixed with potatoes and onions and bits of who knew what else. She seized her spoon and shoveled in a massive bite.

It was delicious. She savored the mouthful, the black pepper and garlic and juicy meat, finding it a feast after weeks of mostly chewy, stringy things foraged in the wild. She gulped it down, washed her gullet with a swig of ale, and returned her gaze to Drenj.

The young man's eyes were trained on her plate, not in a hungry sense but in a way that seemed to crave something else.

Perhaps normalcy.

"So," she said, venturing a return to their earlier discussion, "Khaldisians have religion after all, eh?"

Drenj's eyes, vacant and tired, remained fixed. "Not precisely. As a child I was warned there were demons, demons in the worst parts of the dark. I just wasn't told about gods who could save me from them."

Fencress ate quietly, the only sounds at the table those of Paddyn's noisy chomping and barely-stifled belches. The bar hag returned with Drenj's tea, though the young man only stared at the cup, dark eyes following the wisps of steams as they drifted from the liquid and vanished into nothing.

After a time Fencress hoisted her tankard and tugged down the remaining ale. She slammed it on the table, shaking Drenj from his trance and drawing a grin from Paddyn.

"Boys," she said, flashing her most winsome smile, "we need something to lighten your moods. Trouble.

Mischief, perhaps…" she said, remembering again the wealthy crackpot who called Shank's Hollow his home. "Yes, mischief. The visceral excitement of thievery is what's needed to return those smiles to your handsome faces. The thrill of seizing things chance has failed to hand you! The fact is, you both look like ragamuffins and could use new clothes, and one can never have enough coin. I'll retrieve your cloaks and we'll set out to make our fortune!"

Fencress tiptoed up the final steps of the steep stairwell to the inn's low-ceilinged second floor. She straightened her black clothing and tugged tight her leather cowl. Then she crept forward, slowly and silently through the short hallway—a squeeze of thin wood—to the doorway a few yards ahead. There were cracks in the door's uneven planks and a hole in a large knot near its middle. Fencress peered through.

The meager inn had no private rooms, only a drafty attic with a dozen or so bunks. She smirked ruefully, noticing all the beds were empty. She remembered there'd been several others sleeping in the room when they'd arrived the previous night, all of whom had scurried out upon catching sight of Karnag.

And there he was, kneeling on the planked floor in the room's center, his broad, dirty back to the door. He murmured something unintelligible, something that made her skin prickle.

Fencress pulled away from the door, steeling herself against the unnerving presence her friend had become. She felt uneven. Her head kept summoning thoughts of when she'd first met Karnag, years before, aside some filthy canal in Riverweave. She'd had too much Khaldisian spiced wine that night, and three rough bastards tried taking advantage after she'd taken their coin in deadman's dice. Karnag happened upon them just before they could harm her, and all three were floating dead in the canal before they knew he was there. She'd never expressed her gratitude—she'd been too angry with herself for not playing things smart—but then he'd never asked for it nor did she wager he needed it.

Besides, she'd saved his skin a few times in return.

In the years that followed, rare was the job they'd not taken on together. She'd been mostly a gambler and petty thief before meeting Karnag, but quickly discovered the coin was a fair bit better with assassinations. She had some misgivings about the darker deeds at first, but always reminded herself that a price had been placed on her life, too, when she'd been sold among slavers.

She'd vowed never to be counted less than any other.

Between them, she and Karnag were damned good at killing folk—Karnag especially so, though at times he lacked the subtlety some jobs required. She provided that, and they split many a pile of coin over tankards of ale at *The Dead Messenger* in Raven's Roost. Karnag's slow nod and tilt of his mug were usually the only compliments he'd offer after a job, though those were enough to earn her the lasting respect of every crook in the city.

She smiled at the thought, fleeting though it was.

But she thought also of the danger he'd become, an unpredictable force possessed by some sort of horrid thing. Of his warning that she and the lads would die if they strayed from his side.

She swallowed hard, turned the knob, and eased the door open. She walked gingerly about him, mindful of the sound of her footfalls upon the creaky planks. Karnag seemed not to notice, remaining an implacable and imposing pillar of menace.

"There," Karnag grated, voice low and seemingly addressed to none. "The spearhead of the war is there, scattering the cranes and dragonflies of the marshes. War rages along the winding coastline, those wetlands where armor is anchor and invaders can ambush with deadly speed. Brutal, it is. A suitable prelude for what comes. Infection festers in many wounds, that sickly-sweet scent drawing the spawn of Yrghul to beset the wailing wounded. The unblemished flesh and red blood of the still-living are their spoils…

"And Thaydorne? Ha. He must cower far from the clash of blades. He'd rather search the shadows, yearning for the fulfillment of promises spoken through a mouth of lies. He seeks answers in blood and darkness, but he cannot comprehend those scant things he's discovered. There are far deeper truths. Those truths—the truths I foretell—are understood only through death."

Fencress settled upon a plank. A groan escaped the wood and she grimaced, unnerved at the thought of drawing Karnag's attention while he remained in this trance. She waited, but he said nothing to her, continuing instead with his strange soliloquy.

"But where is he? I see him not, and Yrghul's spawn obscure my vision more than all the whimsies of men. Something of Yrghul's power lingers within them. No matter. I will draw him out. I will proclaim my challenge with all the bellow and bluster of the great war-horns of Gannock Ghunt. Does he remember the sound of those horns as they pealed across the Waters of World's End? Does he remember the tremble of mountains?" Karnag smiled, his mouth stretching to reveal filthy teeth. "No, but through death he will be made to."

She tried closing her ears to his voice and swept over to the beds to seize what she needed: rope, her lock-picks, and Drenj and Paddyn's threadbare cloaks. She looked to Karnag one more time—finding his dark eyes as dead as ever as he droned on—and slipped out the door.

The common room of *The Mewling Mutton* now held a small clutch of other customers, grayish farm-folk worn to the nub and grasping tankards with weary hands. Drenj and Paddyn still sat by the window, silent with eyes downcast and speaking little.

Fencress donned her cheeriest look, trying to summon a sparkle to her blue eyes. She sauntered over and tossed them their cloaks. "Let's find some mischief, boys."

Paddyn sucked down the rest of his ale while Drenj sighed and took a last sip of his tea. After a moment, both rose from the table.

"Can't say I'm up for much," Drenj said, "though I'm certainly willing to get clear of Karnag for a while."

Fencress pinched his cheek teasingly. "That's the spirit! Now, let's go make believe it's months ago, like we're back in Raven's Roost and none of this ever happened. Let's go score some coin and fancy clothing from the coffers of a wealthy son of a whore."

Paddyn grinned, showing the gap left by his missing tooth. "Something easy, then? Easy with a good payoff?"

"Nothing like our last job?" Drenj asked, eyes sunken. "I tell you, Fencress, all the coin in the world isn't worth the trouble that's brought us."

Fencress placed a gloved hand on their shoulders and looked to them with lips curled in a smirk. "Trust me."

They made for the door. Fencress tugged her cowl overhead and gripped the rusty knob, then turned with a smile to her companions. They looked to her with a mixture of frazzled nerves and youthful eagerness, shifting ragged cloaks upon thin shoulders.

"Let's go." She turned the knob and pulled the door wide.

"Your bill!" crowed the bar hag.

Fencress grinned and dashed into the rain, onto a muddy street that sucked at her boots. She plunged across the slop and slowed to a halt beneath the leaky eaves of an abandoned smithy, waiting for the boys to catch her.

"What an awful mess of a place this is," said Drenj.

Fencress stared about and had to agree. Sad folk trudged along sad streets, between sagging homes and shops and mills, and many of those structures appeared to have been hastily boarded up. Shank's Hollow was a bit more than a hamlet, though the word 'town' seemed generous. Fencress guessed a few hundred or so people were unlucky enough to call the place home in peaceful times, and now there seemed far fewer.

"Any guards about?" Paddyn asked.

She squinted to sharpen her vision, ale still tickling her head. "I didn't spot any red sashes last night and I see none now. It seems likely they were either summoned to the front or wise enough to flee north." She spotted the home she'd burgled those many years before, a strange three-story thing with a gaudy tower of white stone that seemed woefully out of place among the town's hovels. She pointed a gloved finger. "There. That's where that rich bastard lives, that thane's brother. With him having his share of coin, there's a fair chance he left this place at the first rumor of war. This'll be an easy score, boys. Just what our dastardly little threesome needs."

The three-story home appeared in fine condition, a stark contrast to the weary structures crowded near it. It was a tall house of stained wood peaked with a pitched roof of many pointed gables. After waiting for the muddy street to empty, Fencress stalked over and looked about for a suitable entrance.

They found the oaken front door had been barred from within, a lock not breakable with the tools they had without making a ruckus. They searched the exterior and found every window of the first floor boarded over with fresh planks. Many on the second and third stories, though, remained unsecured.

"Up there." Fencress gestured to a window less than ten feet up the silly stone tower built against the house's side. "The fool must've been in a hurry to leave town or at least too foolish to expect the likes of us. A little help from one of you fine young men and I'll be through."

Paddyn obliged, holding his hands outward and knotted together. Fencress placed her boot upon the improvised step and thrust herself up, coming even with the rectangular window. It was locked from inside, albeit lazily. She produced a lock-pick, slipped it between the shutters, and with a deft flick of her wrist felt the latch give way.

"Welcome home, my friends," she said through a grin. "Let's see if we can brighten your sad faces with some stealing and skullduggery." She hefted herself through the window, into the tower, and onto a spiral stairway of stone.

The stairwell was dimly lit and musty. Dust fell in a fading curtain from the parts of the window she'd disturbed. Fencress crinkled her nose. The place held the faint stink of shit. She reckoned the bastard who owned it hadn't bothered to empty his chamberpot before skipping town.

She kept still, listening. The rain-muted barking of a dog outside. Groans of the house's wood with the wind. The patter of rain on the roof's shingles. A distant dripping sound from up the stairwell.

But nothing that sounded like a person inhabiting the place.

She turned back to the window and signaled her companions. Drenj hoisted Paddyn through then acknowledged Fencress's sign to keep watch.

"The place seems empty but for the treasures awaiting us," she whispered to Paddyn now crouched at her side. "Let's inspect the top floors first. Follow me."

She crept upward, rounding the stairwell and coming upon a sitting room lined with plush chairs and faded tapestries. Closed doors stood in the middle of each of three other walls. Within the room itself several empty wine bottles lay tumbled about, as well as dinner plates speckled with crumbs. The dripping sound seemed just louder and Fencress guessed the house's roof had a leak the owner had been too lazy to repair.

"The man lives well," Paddyn muttered. "This plate is real silver."

Fencress nodded. "Family money is a fine thing if you can come by it. Keep the plate. It'll fetch us a handful of crowns."

She moved to a nearby door and opened it, finding a library filled with leather-bound tomes. A desk squatted in the room's center, a thing with curving legs of expensive wood. She didn't fancy the thane's brother a scholar so wagered the desk and shelves contained more than just books.

A lock bound the desk's single drawer but Fencress quickly opened it with one of her picks. She slid the drawer wide and smiled. There were scattered coins, a gold signet ring, a silver spyglass, and a few scattered gems. She swept them all from the drawer with a gloved hand and tucked them neatly in her pocket.

"What do you think of this?" came Paddyn's voice from the doorway. He was draped in a long cloak of oiled leather trimmed with fur. Against the pauper's clothes that hung from the rest of him, it looked positively ridiculous.

"Most elegant," Fencress said. "Most elegant, indeed, my young friend. You found our little lordling's wardrobe, I take it?"

Paddyn nodded with a wide, gap-toothed smile. "That door just there. A whole *room* of clothes. Just clothes!

Shirts and trousers and boots and such. I've never seen such a thing!"

"Well, have at it. Treat yourself to things more befitting a man of your substance, and grab Drenj a few fashionable items, as well."

Paddyn returned to the wardrobe, a spring in his step.

Fencress shook her head and followed Paddyn from the room. She looked about the sitting room's chairs and tapestries. All seemed rather expensive, though she figured she had neither the time nor the means to remove them. There were large vases of crystal and painted porcelain, as well, but she knew they'd never manage to get them to a suitable buyer without breaking them first.

An unfortunately useless fortune.

She turned next to the one door that remained unopened, guessing it to be that of the owner's bedchamber. She placed a hand upon the knob, sniffing as she noticed the stink of excrement hanging stronger in the air.

"What of these?" Paddyn asked from behind her. The lad was now festooned with a foppish hat and upon his feet were black boots that shone from much polish, the leather folded over just below the knees. He had a new satchel slung about his shoulder, as well.

Fencress smirked. "Dead gods! Dead gods, indeed! I daresay every last strumpet in Raven's Roost will be vying for your affections!"

"Don't know about the hat," he said, removing it, "though the boots fit me well. Too bad the fellow's trousers are too large. Drenj and I could both fit into a single pair."

"Perhaps the two of you should give that a go," she laughed, then pressed the door open and stepped within.

And froze.

In the ill-lit room before her stood a bed upon which was splayed a fat corpse. She'd seen countless corpses, of course, but this was no ordinary corpse. This one had no face. Just sinew and bone stuck in a sickening grin, complete with lifeless eyeballs bulging from their sockets and staring gleefully at nothing.

She steeled herself, leveling her breathing. The smell of shit had grown noticeably worse and she knew now the source: the man's bowels had emptied at the moment of death. Watery shit mingled with blood and dripped in a puddle upon the wood floor—the dripping she'd heard. She rubbed at her face and willed her stomach not to spill.

A hoot sounded from outside.

Then again.

A signal?

"Fencress?" came Paddyn's voice. "Fencress, I think that's Drenj. Did—" A guttural sound followed. "Dead gods."

Fencress shook her head. "Hardly a dead *god*, but most certainly dead, yes."

"That's the rich fellow who owns this house?"

"Hard to tell without the face, don't you think? But I'd wager it is. It'd be terribly rude of someone to shit all over another's bed, and I like to think better of people."

Paddyn groaned. "Who would do such a thing? Take his face?"

"A revenge killing, most likely. Perhaps an assassin hired by a former lover or someone holding his debt." She winked at Paddyn. "The world is full of sick bastards who do that kind of thing for coin."

Another hoot.

"We'd best go," Paddyn said.

Fencress looked about the room's heavy shadows for anything of value but found nothing. She moved toward Paddyn and the two of them found the stairs.

Drenj stood in the gray haze outside, near the window. He appeared wet and miserable, and his nervous-seeming eyes were fixed upon some point farther along the street.

"We have trouble?" Fencress asked, poking her head into the rain.

Drenj's gaze didn't stray from the street. "I-I... I don't know. I saw..."

"These are not excellent answers, my friend. There are plenty of things in here worth taking. Is there cause to leave?"

"Five men approaching. Two had green cloaks like the one Merek wore, the others were robed like wise men. They were coming this way but something distracted them. There were shadows at the street's far end. Shadows that moved. The men ran that way and the shadows fled. The shadows moved..."

"Lots of folk wear green, Drenj—it is quite fashionable. You'd learn that if you took just a peek at this little lordling's closets. And moving shadows? This rainy haze is playing tricks on your eyes. You're talking nonsense."

He turned sharply to her, his kohl-lined eyes narrow. "Am I? After the things we've seen, you question me?"

Fencress opened her mouth to speak but promptly snapped it shut. She thought of the structure of severed heads and hands and whatever else Karnag had assembled from the Arranese he'd killed. Of Merek and the strange sorceries he'd worked upon Karnag when he'd captured him. Of the awful words Karnag now spoke.

And of the faceless corpse she'd just stumbled upon.

No. Drenj tells the truth. Something follows us.

She looked to him kindly. "Sorry, Drenj. You're wise to worry. Let's rouse Karnag and get clear of this town."

Fencress and Paddyn slipped from the dead man's home, hauling a score that seemed paltry considering the relative riches they'd discovered. They found Drenj huddled against the structure's stones, shying from the rain with eyes darting about the surroundings. Fear seemed to widen the young man's face.

"Over that way," the Khaldisian hissed, gesturing around the home's corner and toward the street. "There were lights a moment ago. Lights and shadows."

Fencress tugged at her cowl and motioned for the boys to stay put. She skulked along the side of the house toward the street, hearing nothing but the drum of the rain. She reached the corner of the home then peered around it.

The street was a stretch of muck lined with shabby shacks, just as they'd first found it. She spied a few locals plodding along, another guiding a cart drawn by a droop-eared donkey that seemed near death.

Then there was *something*. Something just at the edge of her vision—a flash or flicker that drew her eyes. She stared to a point fifty or so yards away on the street's opposite side. There seemed an alleyway or narrow side street between a pair of two-story homes, choked by the same gray gloom as everything else.

She held her eyes upon that point, waiting.

Nothing. She breathed easier.

"Whatever you saw," she said, turning, "seems long gone. There are a few more things in the house worth taking, and—"

The sky brightened for an instant with brilliant light. *Lightning?*

A faint scream sounded from somewhere behind her. *Or…*

She spun round and looked again to that spot down the road.

Just then a red-haired, brown-robed man stumbled from the alleyway and fell into the muddy street. He sobbed and shivered.

Another man—a lanky one clad in a green cloak that looked an awful lot like Merek's—emerged and retreated to stand near the fallen fellow. He shouted back toward the alley, brandishing a sword that gleamed with a distinct greenish hue.

Two others spilled into the street from the alley, one in a green cloak, another a young, chubby fellow in brown robes.

Shadows—or what appeared to be shadows— stretched from the alleyway like the tentacles of some sea beast. The man with the sword hacked at them as though they were physical things. The shadows reeled back, gathered, then lashed at the group.

A tall, gnarled codger in heavy robes wobbled across the street from its opposite side, hefting a staff. He shouted something in an odd tongue. A pure, white light blazed from the staff's head.

There came a shriek, a hideously pained sound that pierced Fencress's ears even at this distance. Someone—or some *thing*—staggered into view, a bald and black-garbed thing. It fell, clawing at its pale skin and wailing in a high-pitched sound that seemed incapable of being produced by a human throat. It wailed and twitched with unnatural quickness, quivering in the street's slop.

The sight of it made Fencress's small hairs rise.

She felt almost relieved when she watched one of the green-cloaked men thrust his glowing sword into the thing, at which point it gave a final shudder and fell still.

"Two more!" shouted the old man. "Kill them! Kill them so we can seek our true quarry!"

The odd group looked about, seeming to regain their bearings. One of the green cloaks helped the robed fellow up from the street and after a moment the five of them set off at a brisk trot, away from Fencress and her companions.

Fencress didn't realize she'd been holding her breath but found herself giving a long exhale. "Let's get out of here. Now."

They found Karnag waiting beside *The Mewling Mutton*, just beneath its peeling shingle depicting a sheep impaled upon a spear. He stood with horses already fitted with tack and strapped with stuffed saddlebags. His torso was bare and as the rain fell upon him the bloodstains wept like wounds freshly opened. His eyes carried the look of death.

Fencress tried to repress the fear she felt, not

permitting her swift stride to falter upon catching sight of her old friend. She heard Drenj whimper, though, and sensed the boys flagging on the muddy road behind her.

"Ready for a pleasant morning ride, Karnag?" she asked, donning a bold grin.

Karnag nodded. "Mount your steeds," he rumbled. "We ride at once."

Fencress turned to Drenj and Paddyn and kept her voice low. "Do as he says, or be left to face whatever it is you saw back there."

The young men seemed to give genuine thought to the options, but after a moment spurred their pace and made for the horses.

Karnag—now atop his black steed—stared past them with dead eyes. "Hurry," he said in an eerily even tone. "Our pursuers have found us. They… and others. Shifting things that lurk just beyond the edges of my visions." He looked to them. "You will be slain if you stray from my side. We ride. Now."

Fencress doubled her pace, boots splashing upon the road. She yanked herself atop her waiting horse with as much grace as the muck would allow. "Boys?" she said with pretended cheer.

Drenj and Paddyn looked to Fencress with worried eyes as they slogged across the street. They pulled themselves atop their mounts and regarded Karnag with what seemed profound fear.

"Ride!" Karnag roared, digging his heels into his horse. The black steed reared and Karnag threw a fist to the sky. "Ride!" he roared again, then set off at a gallop.

They followed after him, their horses unsteady upon

the muddy ground though rushing ahead with seeming desperation. Fencress wondered if they feared Karnag's wrath as much as she did.

They fled the town's ramshackle outskirts and followed Karnag as he left the road, charging up a low hill aside it.

We're headed straight toward Riverweave.

Straight toward the war.

"Ride!" Karnag bellowed once more.

Thunder cracked overhead and the world trembled beneath it.

7
THE PAST'S LONG FINGERS

⟡

LANNICK GUIDED HIS horse through the rain, the beast's hooves slurping their way along the muddy road. It was a gloomy evening, clouds casting a heavy shade upon the plain. He studied every shadow's stretch, wary eyes lingering upon the dark.

The coming of night held a dread, one which Lannick worried would cling to him always. Shadows covered the land, and he wondered how many of them reflected a shadowpath below.

"There," said Brugan beside him. "Another mile at most."

Lannick pulled his eyes from the dark and looked ahead. He spotted a rise, a deeper black against the bruised sky.

"Last chance to turn back," grumbled Cudgen Ashworn. "You're sure this is a good idea? Five strangers paying a visit to a thane during wartime?"

"As much rumor as ale flows in my tavern," Brugan said. "It's known Thane Vandyl didn't support the Crown's war strategy, and that was before High King Deragol died. Now, with Chamberlain Alamis setting claim to the throne, he's likely to be opposed outright. If Vandyl's supplying the deserters as Ulder says, I'd say he has plans similar to our own. He's a man who'd not see Rune fall."

Arleigh Lay chortled. "And so you think five old soldiers the thane knows nothing of will be granted an audience with him? And if we are, you think he'll gladly confess he's committing treason and invite us to join in?"

Lannick shifted his crooked jaw. Cudgen and Arleigh's presence in this endeavor troubled him, but Brugan insisted that bringing them was the best way of overcoming their doubts. *"You need to let them see how you've changed, Lannick,"* the big barkeep had said. *"Hearts aren't changed by words alone."* Lannick knew the truth of his friend's statement, though that did little to quell the quiver in his guts whenever they questioned him.

"Do you, Lannick?" Cudgen asked shrilly.

Lannick turned his horse. Arleigh and Cudgen regarded him with suspicious stares beneath their dripping hoods, Kevlin with an impassive glare, and Brugan with what seemed close to, but not quite, a steadfast trust. Years before these men had been his closest advisors and finest soldiers, and had looked to him a hero. Now, aside from Brugan, they viewed him as something far less.

"I've met this man," Lannick said, steeling his tone with what confidence he could. "I met him after being named Protector of Ironmoor. The title is the greatest honor a common man can achieve. The thanes are bound by tradition to open their holds to me, to offer provisions in times of need, and to assist my cause of defending the kingdom. Vandyl will honor that, even if his memory has faded."

Arleigh's gaze darkened beneath his hood. "You served as Protector for, what, a few months before disappearing into a drunken haze? Ha. You're not that man any more. Word is you've not protected more than a tankard of ale these past many years."

Lannick drew a slow breath. He knew no matter how far he dragged himself from the taverns of Ironmoor—no matter how much he'd changed—the past's long fingers would claw at his heels. Regret, shame and despair. They'd always try keeping their grasp.

"And where is your prized sword?" said Cudgen. "How will he even know you are who you claim to be without it?"

"Fane stole my sword," Lannick said, eyes falling. "But even without it… I've met Thane Vandyl. He'll know."

Brugan pressed close. "The captain's right. Thane Vandyl will know him in spite of the years. I was there that day, and Lannick drew the thane's admiration."

"Hope so," said Arleigh. "Else it's our heads."

Lannick nodded, as much an assurance for himself as the others. "He'll know," he said with feigned certainty. "His ancestors were some of Rune's greatest heroes in fighting our enemies."

Ahead, Thane Vandyl's hold of Rellic appeared an imposing thing in the evening's murk, a fortress of black stone glowering atop a hill about which huddled a modest township. A wall of stained wood taller than two men encircled the town and the obsidian barriers of the fortress above stretched thirty feet or more to the sky. Torches sputtered all about from a good many guards pacing in the spitting rain.

They came nearer the outer wall. Guards stalked battlements atop it, where the stained and fired timbers had been hewn to spiked points. Two men in mail hauberks and cloaks of brown and red stood beside the main gate.

"They wear the thane's colors," said Kevlin in his low, level tone, "but they wear the red sash as well."

"Aye," rumbled Brugan, "though that only means they're loyal to Rune. Not that they're loyal to Fane."

Arleigh grunted. "Doesn't mean they stand against the man, either."

"Keep your hands from your weapons," said Lannick. "Remember it's wartime and they'll be wanting no sign of trouble."

They were perhaps fifty feet distant when the guards spotted them. The two men stepped from the gate, hands moving to the hilts of their longswords. The larger of the two, a man whose thick head barely squeezed into his round helm, raised a hand.

"You'll stop there," the guard said, "and come no closer. We've no refuge here."

Lannick nudged his horse a slow step forward. "We call upon Thane Vandyl."

"We are at war, stranger. Who are you to call upon Thane Vandyl and on such a night?"

Lannick cleared his throat, remembering the old words he'd hardly had occasion to use before. Once, maybe, and as he recalled that'd been with a Khaldisian prostitute. He grimaced sourly, tasting a hefty amount of self-disgust. After a hard swallow, he announced himself.

"I'm Lannick deVeers, seventy-fourth Protector of Ironmoor, and I demand entry."

The ironbound portcullis of Thane Vandyl's keep squealed upward. Hard-eyed soldiers glared from the torch-lit passage behind it then parted to reveal a smallish, stiff-postured man in a tailored tunic of brown and red. The man approached the rising gate and appraised Lannick and his company with narrow eyes.

The man gave a slight tilt of his spine. "I am Loryn, steward of Thane Vandyl. *You* are a Protector of Ironmoor, and ask to speak with Thane Vandyl as such?" he asked, though whether his tone was one of sarcasm or genuine curiosity Lannick could not be sure.

Lannick returned the bow. "I do. I am Lannick deVeers, seventy-fourth Protector and so named after the Battle of Pryam's Bay. Your lord and I shared the same table to celebrate the war's end. I ask to speak with the thane. I must share with him news of our enemy."

Loryn's expression did not change. "Very well. Thane Vandyl honors tradition and will grant you a brief audience. I trust our guards were accommodating? They stabled your horses? Good. And your weapons? Remove them. Our guards will return them to you after you've spoken with Thane Vandyl."

Lannick untied his scabbard from his belt and offered it to a nearby guard. Brugan and the others did likewise, though Arleigh grumbled a good deal when parting with his long dagger and two more knives.

Loryn gestured down the passage. "This way."

Lannick nodded to his companions and they followed

the steward, the smallish man's hands clasped behind his back as he walked. Lannick's eyes drifted to the ceiling's many gaping murder-holes for hot oil, acid, or whatever else. Vandyl's keep seemed ready for war, and Lannick felt himself bracing for the rushing sound of the keep's defenses as he strode ahead.

At the passage's end Loryn pressed open a double door beneath a second raised portcullis. They followed him through and found themselves in a wide courtyard. Wooden scaffolds lined the inner walls and barrels and boxes stood in tall stacks all about. Rain-soaked soldiers hurried from one corner of the keep to another or practiced with weapons in a muddy training circle.

"Thane Vandyl is well prepared," Lannick said.

"War is at our doorstep," said the steward as he led them onward.

"Yet the thane has yet to commit his oath-bound?"

Loryn glanced back over his shoulder, leading them toward a square tower at the courtyard's far end. "The thane's oath-bound are needed here. One never knows if the Arranese plan to widen their attack, especially if General Fane holds them at Riverweave. It is the thane's sworn duty to protect his lands and those north of here."

Lannick looked to Brugan and the big man shrugged. The steward's answer seemed reasonable enough, even though Brugan's rumors claimed it to be in defiance of the Crown's command. Lannick wondered over the truth of his friend's tavern talk and felt his boots growing heavy.

How much dare we reveal of our intentions?

They reached the tower's broad base. A red-sashed soldier opened a door and the small steward strode through.

Lannick and his companions exchanged a brief look, then ducked under the doorframe and followed Loryn inside.

They moved through a cramped foyer into a room furnished with a long table lined with tall chairs. Bearskin rugs covered the floor and torches burned in sconces upon soot-stained walls of stone.

"Thane Vandyl will receive you here," the steward said. He strode through another door at the room's far end.

Lannick glanced to the others. Nervous gazes met his own.

"Take care, lad," Brugan said. "We need his help, but try not to say too much. Politics is a twisted, slippery mess. Careful where you step."

"We need his help," Lannick said, settling into a chair along the table's side. "His support would give us a far better chance of winning over the deserters—and a far better chance of winning the war."

Arleigh plopped into a chair with a grunt. "Just mind your damned tongue and don't get us killed."

"I know how to handle this," said Lannick.

At least I hope so…

The door at the room's end creaked open and the steward returned. He bowed and gestured. "Rise for Thane Vandyl of Rellic."

Through the door stepped an old man, his broad but sagging shoulders draped by a brown bearskin matching those piled upon the floor. He wore no adornment upon his white-haired head, and the only outward mark of nobility seemed to be the signet ring upon his right hand. He regarded them with shrewd, gray eyes beneath bushy brows, and motioned them to sit.

The thane assumed his seat at the table's head and nodded to Lannick. "You," he said in a scratchy voice. "We've met. Remind me of the occasion."

Lannick suppressed a relieved smile at the recognition. "After Pryam's Bay, Thane Vandyl. We celebrated our victory at a feast in the Bastion's great hall."

Thane Vandyl coughed wetly. "Hmm," he said, followed by an audible swallow. "My steward Loryn tells me you are here with news of our enemy, the Arranese. The hour is late and war rages too near my keep. Waste neither time nor words. Speak."

Lannick shifted in his seat, feeling the eyes of his companions upon him. He focused his thoughts on his task and the dangers facing them all. They'd need all the help they could find.

No half-measures and no turning back.

"The Arranese," he said in a measured tone, "may not be the kingdom's most pressing concern in this war."

Arleigh grumbled something from across the table. Lannick glanced over to see the man scowling as he scratched the shiny stump where his left hand had been.

"Go on," Thane Vandyl said. "I didn't receive you to solve your riddles."

Lannick's gaze darted to Brugan, who winked in a show of what seemed confidence. "*Go on,*" the big man mouthed.

Lannick turned back to the aged thane. He knew this was a terrible risk though his instincts instructed it was one worth taking. He reminded himself those very instincts had always been sharp—when not dulled by alcohol at least—and he drew an even breath.

"Go on," the thane said impatiently.

Lannick shifted his crooked jaw. "Do you remember our discussion the last time we met? At the Bastion, after the war?"

"No. Remind me."

Lannick found the old man's eyes told nothing. "You confided," Lannick said after a long breath, "you thought General Fane unfit for command."

Vandyl's stare remained fixed on Lannick. "Pryam's Bay was a complicated battle, and many believe General Fane learned much from any mistakes made. This, now, is a complicated war. Are you suggesting General Fane should not be commanding Rune's armies?"

No half-measures…

Lannick straightened in his chair and returned the gaze, sensing some agreement behind the man's gray eyes. "He's lost battle after battle already."

"The old forests of the south would have been difficult ground for Rune's soldiers. It was wise strategy for the general to surrender those lands while offering just enough resistance to slow the enemy's advance."

"His losses extend far beyond the old forests and have cost this kingdom thousands upon thousands of lives."

The thane sat quietly for a moment then arched his brow. "And you think he should be removed from command? This is why you call upon me?"

No turning back.

Lannick nodded. "I call upon you not just because I think he should be removed from command, but because I think he should be hanged for treason."

Cudgen grumbled noisily then Arleigh smacked the table with his one remaining hand.

Thane Vandyl coughed again, a hard, long hack that rang of illness. "It seems your companions may disagree."

Lannick steadied himself. He felt moved by his hatred of the general and his certainty of the man's treachery, but at the same time old doubts nagged at him. He gritted his crackling jaw, knowing he had to press on. "General Fane is a madman," he said. "You know of the deserters? You must know why these men have done this, why thousands— *thousands!*—have fled the front, yet not made their way home? It's because of the general. You know this."

Thane Vandyl suppressed a cough then sat quietly, eyes downcast. His steward shifted behind him, smoothing an unseen wrinkle on his black tunic.

"You know this," Lannick persisted. "You most of all."

"*Lannick*," Arleigh hissed.

Lannick ignored him.

"The council stands by their choice of commander," the thane said, though to Lannick the man's eyes said something else. "Our foe has been an unexpectedly daunting one and some soldiers simply lack the nerve to face that enemy. The general cannot be faulted for the cowardice of some in his charge."

Lannick dragged in the smoke-filled air. "Those men are not cowards. They are Rune's best hope. Besides, why would Thane Vandyl provision a gathering of cowards?"

Thane Vandyl's keen eyes pierced Lannick's. "I..." he muttered, his lower lip stiffening. "I do not provision cowards."

"No," Lannick said, daring to leave himself no room for retreat, "you do not. You provision a great gathering of soldiers who stand ready to save Rune. Soldiers who can topple Fane from his pedestal and set this war aright. You provision them because you know Fane cannot continue to lead Rune's soldiers to defeat after defeat, and you know that someone must stop him. We," he said, certainty swelling in his throat, "are here to help that cause. We are old soldiers ourselves, soldiers who managed to win Rune's last war by overcoming this general's madness."

The room was quiet, the only sound that of the snapping torches in their sconces. Lannick sat still, feeling the weight of his companions' eyes and refusing to meet them. He kept his gaze steady upon the thane as the old man shifted beneath his bearskin cloak.

"Hmm," the thane said at last. "But our enemy is dangerous... More dangerous than anyone suspected. Why would I not want a gathering of armed men nearby? Why would I not want such a gathering precisely where they are, standing between the enemy and my gate?"

"Because," Lannick said, "you are a great thane who honors the greatness of Rune, and you would not suffer seeing your kingdom fall to our most ancient enemy. You would not suffer the return of Yrghul the Lord of Nightmares."

Vandyl sniffed sharply. "Those old tales?"

Arleigh chuckled. "We don't believe them, either, Thane Vandyl. Sorry to trouble you." He began to push his chair away from the table.

Lannick felt old furies fire within him. He stood and leveled a finger at the thane. "You are the twenty-seventh thane of Rellic! You know the accounts of your forefathers! Do you deem them liars, now?"

The steward took a stride forward. "Sir! You will not address the thane in this fashion!"

Thane Vandyl twisted his gnarled hands into fists. "Nor will you dishonor my forebears in this place. Loryn—"

"I do *not* dishonor them!" Lannick said. "I am one who knows they fought the foes their histories claim. I am one who knows they braved the deepest darks, and they kept those foes at bay when needed. I am one who knows they provided aid to those who wage war in the shadows of this realm."

"And what," Vandyl said, coughing, "does that have to do with the foes marching upon us now?"

"Everything. Everything, because the foe we face is the very same faced by your forefathers. The Spider King has allied himself with the Necrists, as has General Fane. This is no mere war for land or wealth. This war is for the very dearest of stakes. If men such as we do not take action now, all will be lost."

Thane Vandyl's glare softened and he took a long breath. His knobby hands unclenched. "You believe this, don't you?"

Lannick nodded. "I do, Thane Vandyl. I do with all my heart."

The thane pushed himself upward. "Precious few of us do, anymore. I'll give you an escort of twenty of my oath-bound. Take coats of mail, weapons, supplies. Whatever you require. Tomorrow you'll set out for the deserters' encampment and my oath-bound will let those in charge know you are there with my blessing. They'll also let those men know to listen to you and share with you their confidences. They'll be made to know that I for one believe you're the man most qualified to lead the assault on General Fane." He coughed. "Those men will listen."

Lannick exhaled heavily, shoulders drooping and his legs suddenly so weak he nearly collapsed. He nodded again and looked to his companions. All regarded him with slack-jawed expressions.

Lannick almost laughed aloud.

I could really use a drink.

"Well I didn't expect *that*," Cudgen Ashworn said, sounding dumbstruck.

Me neither, Lannick thought, gaze drifting about the torch-lit mess hall of Thane Vandyl's oath-bound. Soldiers—all in the thane's colors of brown and red—hefted tankards of ale at tables about them, carousing into the night's wee hours.

"You knew the thane would help us?" asked Kevlin, scratching his square chin.

Lannick gave a slow, thoughtful, and utterly false nod. "I've always known the thane's heart," he lied, "and knew for certain he'd stand on the right side of things when pushed."

"Have to say," said Arleigh, slurping a foam-capped tankard across the cramped table, "you did a decent job of not getting us killed, Captain."

Brugan puffed out his chest. "The captain here did a hell of a lot more than that. I told you lads Lannick's the same hero who led us to victory at Pryam's Bay, and I meant it. Well done, Captain."

Cudgen sniffed. "Didn't think you still had it in you."

Lannick felt a grin stretch his mouth and forced it away. It stirred his heart to hear such things from these men, though he knew better than to wear that satisfaction on his face. He distracted himself with his new longsword from the thane's armory, pretending to inspect the quality of the steel.

A heavy, apron-clad woman came near and touched Lannick's shoulder. "You sure I can't fetch you an ale, dear?"

Brugan smiled wide. "You've earned it, Lannick. I'm proud to say you've earned it."

Perhaps just the whole barrel? Lannick thought, slipping the sword into its scabbard. "Dead gods, yes," he said cheerily. "A tankard of your very finest, m'lady."

Brugan grinned and nodded. "No man's earned it more than you."

The serving woman soon returned with a tall, handled tankard, golden foam crowning its contents. Lannick had always preferred wine and the stronger spirits, though nowadays knew better than to risk dancing with those demons.

So ale it is, he thought, his crooked face curling with a genuine smile. He drew the mug close and slurped the foam off its top.

Arleigh raised his tankard. "To the captain," he said, his tone ringing with what seemed almost sincerity.

Lannick hoisted his own. "A lot of hard work ahead."

"Aye," said Brugan, "but these first few strides have been strong ones. We're marching with the support of one of Rune's most revered thanes. All thanks to you, lad. Now we win this war!"

Cudgen saluted with his mug. "Never thought I'd drink to those words, but glad to be doing so now."

Lannick tipped the mug and took a deep draw. It was dark, bitter stuff, though with a smooth finish. He took another drink and set the tankard down, savoring the ale's flavor and watching with familiar bemusement as the oath-bound soldiers crowed and joked and laughed, spittle spraying from their lips as they did.

A group of soldiers in the hall's far corner—visibly drunk—began swaying their tankards and singing some bawdy song.

The drafty, dreary Hole You're Inn,
Its piss-stained ale and sailors' gin,
Made me head sway east to west.

That rotten, horrid Hole You're Inn,
The crooks the crooked 'keep let in,
Picked clean the pockets of me vest.

That ugly, awful Hole You're Inn,
The moldy cheese and bad mutt'n,
Left me cot a filthy mess.

But pretty Rosie's sly and fetching grin,
And the lovely little dress she's in,
Are sure to get me there again!

Cheers sounded. The performers raised tankards, tossed the contents down their gullets, then belched and stammered back to tables with wide smiles on their faces.

"Hadn't heard that one before," chuckled Arleigh Lay, turning back to the table.

"Sounds like a terrible, disreputable place if you ask me," said Brugan, shaking his head. "I hope folk don't speak of *The Wanton Vicar* that way."

Lannick tugged down another mouthful of ale. "Why would anyone *ever* talk that way about your tavern, my friend?" He gave an expression of outrage. "I daresay *The Wanton Vicar* has the best lamb stew in all of Ironmoor, if not the whole of Rune."

Brugan looked to him, brow cocked. "Damned right it does."

"Indeed, Brugan," Lannick continued, knowing well his friend's fondness for flattery. "I swear I heard that stew's praises sung at a dozen taverns, both in and out of Ironmoor. Legendary stuff, it is. The very, very best."

Brugan sank back in his chair, a sheepish grin pinching his lumpy face. "It *is* delicious. I just hope Lacy hasn't changed the recipe. Fresh rosemary can be hard to come by at times and forgetting that could ruin my reputation."

Lannick tipped his mug toward his friend. "And a fine reputation that is, Brugan."

"Speaking of reputations," said Cudgen, "seems you still have something of the better of yours, Captain." He shook his narrow head. "*Captain*," he repeated. "So what's our next move? What do we do from here?"

Lannick took a slow sip of ale. "With the thane's men marching among us the deserters should listen. They should listen to what we know of General Fane. If they do, and if they're willing to march soon, we'll march on Fane.

If we kill him quickly enough there might be time to save Riverweave and turn back the enemy there."

Brugan raised his tankard. "Aye, Captain. Those deserters will rally to—"

The door to the mess flew open and smacked against the wall with a loud crack. A mail-clad sergeant took several hard steps in, breathless and red-faced. "To arms…" he wheezed through ragged breaths. "To arms!"

The room fell utterly quiet for a long moment, expressions turning from mirth to confusion.

"What's happened?" demanded one of the revelers, slamming his tankard upon a table. He squared his pot-bellied form to the man at the doorway.

The red-faced sergeant rubbed at his eyes. "Two lads atop the ramparts. I couldn't tell who they were by the looks of them." He shook his head and his lips trembled. "Their faces… Something's in the keep."

Lannick tensed.

Faces?

Necrists?

"Well, what in the old hells is it?" the reveler asked, hand moving to the pommel of his sword. "Arranese?"

"I… I don't think so. Something in the dark. The shadows moved…"

Lannick's hand found his Coda and he stood tall. "I'll go with you," he said boldly. "I know what stalks the night."

The pot-bellied oath-bound looked to Lannick. "What is it, stranger?"

Lannick straightened his spine and regarded all in the room, trying to stifle the doubts creeping in his head. "There are things stalking Rune far more dangerous than the warriors of Arranan," he said. "Old forces are at work in our kingdom, wicked things that work the shadows. Grab torches and oil, and lead me to them."

"This nonsense again?" grated Arleigh.

"With you, lad," Brugan said, giving Arleigh an angry glare. He rose to stand beside Lannick.

The red-faced soldier stared to Lannick with eyes wide beneath a knotted brow. "What I saw wasn't natural, and the shadows shifted about it." He nodded. "Torches and oil, you say?"

"As much as you can find," Lannick said, hefting the scabbard of his new sword and walking toward the door. "Now."

"You heard him, soldiers!" shouted the man. "Move!"

A clamor arose as the soldiers set aside tankards and readied their weapons. Beneath the din there came the murmur of voices, soft-spoken words quavering with what seemed an edge of fear.

Lannick stopped at the open doorway and gritted his teeth, achy jaw cracking as he did. He looked out upon the night beyond, the heavy black that had settled upon the courtyard and smothered the frail torches and lanterns lit within. Oath-bound soldiers moved haltingly about, eyes straining against the dark. The air seemed still, stagnant, but a chill crept upon it.

Lannick tugged in a deep breath, knowing precisely what it meant.

Lannick pressed into the darkened courtyard. Footsteps crunched behind him as the men from the mess filed into the keep's ward. More torches sparked to life, a dozen or more, though the night yielded nothing.

"Careful," Lannick said, scanning the dark. The night's chill tickled the nape of his neck and he shivered. "They are among us," he said, suppressing the tremble in his throat. He turned to the red-faced sergeant. "Where are your fallen men?"

"Atop the southern rampart," the sergeant said quietly, eyes darting here and there. He pointed. "Up that tower there."

Lannick nodded and began walking, determined to make his strides stoke his courage. "This way. Bring the torches and keep them moving. Don't allow the shadows to settle. Make certain the oil's handy."

Arleigh and Cudgen jogged to his side. "This is a load of shit, Lannick," Arleigh hissed. "You'll not gain any man's confidence by telling him a bunch of lies meant for children. You risk the thane withdrawing his support on account of these delusions!"

Lannick shot Arleigh a baleful look. "Come with me, then. Come bear witness yourself, but be prepared to risk your life if you do."

Arleigh spat and pulled loose his long dagger. "I fear no man."

"These are not men," Lannick said. "Not anymore."

"Captain?" called Brugan, lumbering just behind them. "I've one torch lit and a few more at the ready, and managed to grab a jug of oil as well. I'll await your orders."

"Good, Brugan," Lannick said, noticing the big man's uncomfortable wince as he hefted the brands and oil with still-wounded shoulders. "You all right?"

"I'm fine, lad. I remember what to do from… the last time round. Outside my tavern."

Lannick nodded. He neared the base of the tower and slowed. Ahead stood the tower's entrance, an arched wooden door resting ajar with only darkness beyond it. The air felt cold despite the warmth of summer.

He turned, seeing a dozen or so of Thane Vandyl's men standing behind him. The red-faced sergeant stood closest though the rest kept a healthy distance, holding torches high and fingering weapons as their eyes searched the ramparts above.

"Keep hold of the torches," Lannick said firmly, "and follow me up the tower. Leave some men with torches in the courtyard, though, and make certain they move the flames about."

"You're sure of this?" said the oath-bound sergeant. "You're sure we aren't just making ourselves all the more visible and vulnerable to whatever's in here? You sure we're not just running headlong into an ambush?"

Brugan turned to the oath-bound soldier. "The captain knows what we're dealing with, sergeant. He knows what he's doing." He returned his gaze to Lannick and lowered his voice. "You *do* know, don't you?"

Lannick nodded. "All too well. Keep your wits sharp and follow me." He stretched his shoulders and rubbed his neck, trying to shake off the chill. He gritted his teeth, squeezed the hilt of his sheathed sword with one hand and stretched out his other against the door's splintered surface. He pushed forward. The hinges groaned and the cold from within rushed out to seep into his very bones.

"Torches!" he shouted.

He waited for the light to grow behind him then entered the tower's base. Though more torches had been fired, their yellow flicker flailed weakly against the darkness ahead. Lannick looked down to his own shadow, stretched and shifting upon the stone floor and winding stairwell ahead. Beyond, just up the spiral staircase, the darkness seemed impenetrable.

He paused and listened, noticing how the night's sounds had muted to a whisper. Brugan and a couple of others stood just behind him, though the crackle of their torches and shuffle of their boots seemed barely audible. It was as though the shadows drowned everything in nothingness.

He reached into the satchel strapped upon his belt and found again the box of his Coda. There were enough armed, trained men in tow that he'd not likely need to call upon its power—so long as the Necrists were few. Yet two soldiers had died already and without the Coda he'd probably not be swift enough to prevent the death of at least a few more. He shifted his jaw and studied the dark.

Can I trust these men with the secrets of the Variden?

Do those secrets even matter in such times?

He took a hesitant step toward the dark, his boot scraping against the rough stone of the tower's first stair. He could count the edges of only three more of the winding stairs, as though everything after had been swallowed by the dark. The light behind him failed against whatever stood beyond.

"Lad?" whispered Brugan. "You're certain of this?"

He sucked in a shuddering breath. His heart thundered. The Necrists' presence seemed a distinctly physical thing, like the chill of a fever that left one shivering and slicked with sweat. As much as he wanted to avoid it he knew it folly to shun his Coda, one of the most powerful weapons against the enemy. His fingers found the box's seam and drew it open, touching the cool metal of the object inside. He clutched it, feeling the sketched iron to be a strange and nearly forgotten comfort.

Perhaps I have no choice.

He held still, one hand about his Coda and the other gripping his sword. He readied himself. The shadows ahead were heavy and something even darker seemed to dim those thin margins where light still dared to wander. The cold wrapped about him like a noose.

Lannick drew the blade, the sword scraping against the scabbard's iron lip with a jarring squeal. He stood upon the tower's first stair, watching.

He turned his gaze about but there was nothing but blackness. He knew they were here, though. He could feel them. *The Necrists know men by the scent of their flesh and the shadows they cast*, his fellow Variden had warned.

"*Lannick...*" The whispered word came from what seemed nowhere.

He froze, fearful.

"They call to you?" came Brugan's voice just behind him.

"*Lannick, my love...*"

Lannick snatched his Coda from his purse. He used his sword hand to ease open the iron then worked clumsily, holding both sword and Coda in one hand and making ready to snap the Coda upon his wrist. *No half-measures*, he thought.

A piercing scream shattered the darkness, an awful, ear-searing sound that shook Lannick to his core.

"Dead gods!" Brugan shouted, then lurched into Lannick's side.

The blow caused Lannick's hands to fumble. His Coda fell and tumbled across the floor with a terrible clanging. He dropped to a knee, hands sweeping over the stone in search of the instrument. Brugan and the others stumbled about, kicking Lannick as they did. "Move back!" Lannick spat.

Another scream tore from the tower's reaches. Boots shuffled back toward the door.

"What is that?" said Arleigh Lay, voice tinged with a rare hint of fear.

A mad chitter fell from the stairwell, an insect-like ticking.

"Move back!" Lannick shouted. "Out of the tower!"

The men did as ordered, drawing back with fear written on their faces. The light drew away with them and Lannick was left on his knees in an utter darkness. He shifted hurriedly, pressing his hands this way and that. The sound grew louder and he heard with it the intonations of sorcery. Spiteful, broken-sounding words that seemed to summon a greater chill to the air. The weight of the darkness crushed him.

Sweat beaded upon his brow in spite of the cold. He eyes darted about. *Where is my Coda?*

"*Lannick…*"

The word was intoned with sick familiarity, a perverse affection. Lannick's guts twisted. He lunged about, fingers splayed wide and seeking the cool iron of his Coda. He glanced toward the door and saw Brugan and the men outside, just yards away though it might as well have been as many leagues. Their burning torches seemed distant as starlight.

"Old hells!" he hissed, finding nothing upon the tower floor. "Where is it?"

"You seek this?" said a slithering voice from the stairwell. "Your trinket?"

Lannick wheeled about, forcing down the sudden rise of bile in his throat. He arose, brandishing his blade against the darkness and retreating toward the door. "Brugan!" he roared. "Torches and oil!"

"General Fane promised you to us," the Necrist said, its voice a serpent's hiss. "You were promised as his part of a special bargain, Variden. Now we have come to collect the general's debt."

Lannick tugged his cloak—the green cloak of the Variden—tightly about his shoulders, remembering it offered some protections against the night. His head spun as he tried to recall old wards and invocations, but in this moment he could remember nothing. Those old prayers seemed buried too deeply beneath the fog of forgetfulness. He needed his Coda.

"Brugan!" he shouted and spun toward the doorway. He could see Brugan and the others standing just where they'd been, ten yards distant and staring dumbly about. It seemed they'd heard nothing of his commands.

"Brugan!" he shouted again, though the big man's lumpy face shifted not at all. "Now!"

Thick fingers of shadow stretched across the faint light of the doorway and began knitting together.

"Your family loved you," the Necrist said. "Memories

linger in the flesh, and those of your family have become known to us. Death is not the end. Come…"

"No!" he screamed. He cleaved the shadow with his sword. The darkness retreated for an instant then reformed.

A hand caressed his neck. A cold, clammy hand. *"Lannick, my love…"*

No, he thought. *Not again!*

"Brugan!" he cried. He thrust his hand outward, through the icy shadows obscuring the doorway. "Brugan!"

He jabbed his sword behind him but caught nothing. The hand had left his neck and he felt cold tendrils wrapping about him, about his legs and waist and forearm. He hacked his sword about, feeling resistance as the blade dug against the darkness. The shadows were thick, almost tar-like in consistency. His sword stuck and seemed in danger of being sucked away as he thrust.

He tore through to the outside and shouted again. "Brugan! Torches!"

The tentacles yanked him back into darkness, turning him about to face the Necrist. The shadowy things lifted him from his feet and drew him toward a pale circle now just visible along the stairwell. Not a circle, but a face. A pallid countenance set eerily aglow by no visible light. A chalk-colored face divided into neat quarters by a crisscross of thick stitches stretching from chin to crown and ear to ear. It wasn't a face Lannick knew, though that made it no less grotesque. Black eyes glimmered in deep sockets.

"Lannick," the Necrist said, its black tongue rolling indulgently in its mouth.

"No!" he screamed, jerking about. His sword arm was

pressed against his side though he managed to work it upward, slicing through the darkness as he did.

"Captain?" he heard from somewhere.

Brugan?

"Lannick," the Necrist whispered, its voice carrying some awful parody of comfort. "Be still... Be quiet... We have you now. Come learn all that the dead take with them. Embrace the gentle dark beyond this world. Embrace it, and yield to us your secrets."

He shivered and shook, struggling against the sorcerous bonds. His sword cut through the shadow though there remained many more restraining him. He felt their grip slacken but soon they held him fast again. He looked to the stairwell and saw two more pale, stitched faces descending toward him.

"Lannick," they said in unison.

"No!" came Brugan's bellow from behind him. "Back to the old hells with you!"

Fire came from everywhere. Men shouted curses and threw torches that smashed against the stairs, sending showers of sparks and flames into the dark. A ceramic jug banged into Lannick's shoulder then tumbled over it, shattering against the stairwell before him and spreading a mess of oil. A vase followed it. Flames erupted and engulfed the Necrists. A clanking sound came from the stairwell.

My Coda!

The shadowy tendrils vanished and Lannick dropped to the stone floor. The Necrist that had held him convulsed about, smacking pasty hands upon its black garments and the flames that covered them. The fire swept up the stairs and consumed the other two creatures.

Lannick searched about in the fire's orange blaze and found the dull metal of his Coda. "Illienne the Light Eternal!" he roared, rising. He snapped the instrument upon his wrist. "Banish this darkness!"

Green fire dripped down the length of his blade. An assault of images flooded his head though he silenced them with old training and hard resolve. "Cut them down! Now, while the flames still burn!"

He charged toward the closest Necrist with sword held high and Brugan and others followed him. A cascade of steel rained upon the Necrist as it twitched on the stone. At last, with a horrid shriek, it fell still.

Lannick leapt over the corpse to the next creature, the vile thing flailing just two stairs ahead. Its patchwork face twisted in agony as bright fire surrounded its still-standing form. Lannick reared to strike but just then a dagger struck the creature square between its black eyes, sinking halfway into its skull. Its arms fell slack against its sides, the crackling flames upon it rising anew. It snarled with yellow teeth and ugly gums, as if making ready to speak. Then a fist rushed over Lannick's shoulder, cracking into the butt of the dagger's hilt. The Necrist's eyes rolled and it collapsed in a lifeless heap.

"Fucking devils!" Arleigh cursed from beside him, shaking his hand. "I didn't dare believe you!"

Lannick turned to see the third Necrist bolting up the stairs, the smoldering tatters of its robes just visible in the firelight. "Hurry!" he called, leaping up the stairwell. "They are weak in the light but fearsome in the dark! We must kill it while we still have fire!"

He bounded up the stairs. Shadows cloaked the tower's

interior, though the remaining torches of the men who followed him seemed able to penetrate the gloom at last. What was more, these shadows somehow seemed more natural than those at the structure's base.

Lannick at last came to another doorway, this one thrown open to the night. Beyond it stretched the rampart, a walkway only a few feet wide and lined with waist-high walls capped by merlons. The rampart ran perhaps eighty feet to another tower, and about halfway down its length slumped two corpses in a bloody tangle.

The Necrist was nowhere to be seen.

"Where?" huffed Brugan from the stairwell behind him, hefting his sledge with obvious discomfort. "Where'd that thing go?"

Lannick looked about and caressed the cool iron of his Coda. "Stay here, Brugan," he said, worrying over his friend's injuries. "You and a few of the oath-bound."

"Captain," Brugan grumbled. "I'll not shy away from a fight."

"Of course not," Lannick said softly. "It's just that you're the one man I can trust to keep a watch on this stairwell. We're not sure if the one we're chasing is the last of them."

"Very well," Brugan said. He shifted his eyes about and gingerly rested his hammer upon his shoulder. "I'll have your back, Lannick."

"Just as you always have," Lannick said with a quick grin, "and I'll never forget it." He slipped out onto the rampart.

Though the heavier darkness seemed to have diminished and the moon now lit the keep, a chill lingered upon the air.

It's here, somewhere, Lannick thought.

"Lannick, I'm with you," whispered an unwelcome voice within his head. *"I can help."*

Lannick whipped his head about, then realized the voice's source.

My Coda.

Alisa.

For an instant his mind was drawn to her and he could see through her eyes. A vast, barren landscape of dust and scrub beneath a starry sky. A campfire burned near, about which huddled a frail-looking man in heavy robes and a rough, dirt-crusted woman.

"We toil each of us in secret," came Alisa's voice, *"but we are never alone."*

Lannick shook his head and pulled his thoughts to a tight focus. To the present, and to the night about him. He sucked in the cool air and took an uneasy step along the walkway, his sword raised. He heard the boots of others scrape upon the stone behind.

Several torches still burned. Between their light and that of the moon, Lannick could discern the pitiful dead. Two armed, armored men whose scabbards still held their blades but whose bodies no longer held their flesh. Their hands were all bone and sinew, their faces sickening masks of red tendons and bulging, sightless eyeballs.

Lannick bent low, pressing a hand upon one of the blood-soaked oath-bound. *Cold*, he thought, withdrawing his hand.

Cold as newly fallen snow.

"Dead gods!" Arleigh spat. "What could do this?"

Lannick rose, shifting his jaw and studying the night. "I've told you."

A hideous shriek pierced the air. Lannick spun back to see the Necrist leap from the shingled roof of the tower they'd exited, its black robes reduced to rags and blown open to reveal a gangly, pallid body crossed with the same stitches as those knitted across its head. "Variden!" it screeched.

Counting his companions and the oath-bound there stood at least a dozen men upon the rampart between Lannick and the Necrist. The soldiers braced themselves as the creature rushed toward them. Two threw torches but the fires sailed well wide. Another did the same and the Necrist ducked nimbly beneath it. The thing wailed a sickly wail as it ran, its whole form shifting and shaking from some vile sorcery.

In the moonlight Lannick could see the Necrist gathering shadows to its hands, tugging black curtains from cracks in the stones and dark corners where walls met the walkway.

Lannick gripped his Coda and willed his head to some semblance of calm. In a moment his mind swirled with those old words, those old spells. Those divine enchantments that'd not filled his thoughts in a decade.

"Lannick!" Arleigh barked, looking back to him with wide, terrified eyes. "We're out of torches!"

Lannick struggled with the torrent of power filling his head and the mad scene before him. "W-weapons," he stammered.

The Necrist charged the closest of the oath-bound. Thick tangles of shadow whipped from its hands like striking serpents. The soldier fell to the walkway, writhing on the stone with a sad gurgle. The shadowy tendrils curled back to the Necrist then bolted forward to strike another.

"Weapons!" Lannick screamed, his head finding some sense of order.

The oath-bound brandished their blades and jostled for position. The walkway, though, left room for only two men to stand abreast so they could not assail the Necrist with numbers.

His head spun and panic seized him. *They'll be ripped apart like this...*

"Attack!" Brugan bellowed from the tower's doorframe. The big man twisted his sledge about with a flinch and lumbered forth, charging the Necrist from behind with two of Vandyl's oath-bound in tow. "To the old hells!"

Lannick bared his teeth and his green-hued blade. He focused on his Coda's power and clambered to the wall's crest. He tilted precariously on that edge, fearing the fall to the keep's courtyard some twenty feet below.

But the power filled him, whispering through his head and coursing through his limbs. His feet found a firm balance. He turned and he ran, leaping across the merlons toward the Necrist.

He closed the distance. The Necrist had cloaked itself behind an amorphous mass of shadow, its features invisible. Lannick leapt, hurling himself toward the thing and cleaving away at the swirling tendrils that bit his skin like ice. He cleaved with great swings of his blade and the shadows retreated, freeing the trembling oath-bound soldier they'd seized. The man collapsed, dead, upon the rampart. But the mass of shadows remained, the Necrist indiscernible within.

"Lannick!" cried Brugan from somewhere on the other side of the dark.

Lannick hacked again with his blade but could see nothing. He pulled himself atop the wall again and jumped ahead. He spotted his friend flailing weakly with his hammer. Sweat shone on his lumpy face and a serpentine shadow wound about his midsection. The oath-bound accompanying the big barkeep thrust their blades blindly.

"Brugan!" Lannick screamed. He darted past the black mass then dropped near his friend. He swung his sword at the thick braid of shadow wrapped about the big man then cleaved his glowing blade into the gathered dark. Ancient words of divine spellcraft resounded in his head. His mouth moved with their utterance.

The shadows diminished. There stood the Necrist, its maw of yellow teeth chattering and spitting out incantations of necromancy. Its nearly naked frame of sickly skin shook with impossible speed. Its arms became a blur. It dodged swinging blades from the oath-bound behind it and managed to lunge toward Lannick an instant later. Long-nailed and pale fingers shot toward Lannick's throat. He spun sideways but the dagger-like nails found the back of his neck, rending flesh. Pain seared him and he staggered back.

"I have your back, Captain!" Brugan groaned, lurching past Lannick. He hoisted his heavy sledge with a pained look then brought it down toward the Necrist.

"Brugan!" Lannick yelled. "No!"

The Necrist was swift and Brugan too slow. The creature shivered and shook away from the labored blow and the drone of vile necromancy filled the air. Shadows simmered and swelled in its hands then sprang to loop about the old barkeep.

"No!" Lannick roared, rushing forward. He reared his blade and prepared a killing blow, divine and powerful words upon his tongue.

The Necrist looked to him. Its body shook and flailed and tentacles of shadow whipped about it, but look to him it did. It giggled. "Dada," it cooed, its black tongue lolling about its mouth and its voice sounding very much like that of Lannick's eldest child.

My son. My dead son.

Lannick stopped, slack-jawed. His sword-arm lowered. He hesitated.

Brugan screamed.

Lannick looked to his friend to see a long finger of shadow pressed into his mouth. The big barkeep stiffened and his eyes rolled back in his head and his hammer fell to the stones with a great *clang*. The tendril withdrew, pulling with it what appeared to be a large chunk of Brugan's brain.

Brugan stood twitching for a moment before slumping against the low wall and then toppling over it.

"Dada," the Necrist said again, its lips curled in a wicked smile.

Anguish seized Lannick and he howled. He heaved his weapon in a wide and desperate arc, green fire trailing the blade. The sword found the Necrist's arm and cut it in two. The creature screeched and the shadows about it vanished. It chattered and gnashed its teeth and clawed at Lannick with its remaining arm.

Words of power thundered through Lannick's head. His sword-arm burned. He thrust his blade toward the creature's mouth and the point found its black tongue and then the back of its skull. "To the old hells!" he cried.

The Necrist shrieked despite the blade splitting its tongue, the divided organ still wriggling madly about in its maw. The high-pitched wail sounded like something sucked away rather than given voice, and it lasted but an instant. Then the abomination fell slack.

Lannick jerked his sword free and the Necrist tumbled over the wall. It dropped to the ground with a dull thump, coming to rest alongside Brugan's corpse.

Lannick whimpered and blinked back burning tears. All the men about him remained silent.

They buried the dead at dawn.

The graveyard—a place of honor for dead thanes and brave folk who'd died in their service—rested at the town's eastern end, a swath of swaying grass encircled by tall oaks. The bodies of the three dead oath-bound had been wrapped in white linens and placed in a row near the ring of trees, Brugan's covered corpse just beside them. The thane had insisted the old barkeep be buried among his most honored soldiers after hearing the circumstances of his demise. *"He deserves a hero's place,"* the thane had said. *"You have no idea,"* Lannick had replied.

Thane Vandyl himself presided over the ceremony, a solemn affair attended by nearly two hundred of his oath-bound as well as the grieving families of the fallen. Vandyl coughed through old prayers to Illienne the Light Eternal and warned of ancient foes returning to the world. He spoke of the need to be vigilant—a call that brought Lannick's hand to his Coda—and urged that even the worst of evils could be overcome by virtue in the end. He offered well-practiced words of comfort to the weeping families, and worn platitudes about lives sacrificed for the greater good.

Lannick stood beneath a creaking oak at the graveyard's edge, listening less and less to Vandyl's sermon. Instead, he drew long, shuddering breaths and did his best to keep his tears at bay. He felt that cold hollow in his gut, that all-too-familiar feeling of a profound loss. He wanted to cry out, to give voice to his agony, to scream to the dead gods that Brugan did not deserve this fate.

But he knew they'd pay no heed.

He'd learned that long ago.

The silence of the dead gods was the echo of the emptiness in his heart. That sense of terrible sadness he'd never be able to remedy. That reminder he'd never be able to bring back his family.

Or my only friend.

He thought of the wide smile that often stretched Brugan's ugly, lumpy face, and the laughter that rolled from his broad belly. He thought of the man's resolute faith in him, his belief that Lannick could be something more than what he'd allowed himself to become. And he thought of the man's generosity, of all the times he'd helped Lannick in a pinch.

And how he died trying to save me from a Necrist coming to collect on Fane's sick bargain.

He looked to the big man's body, stiff and motionless beside the black pit dug for it, and did all he could not to vomit. He thought of his own weakness in Brugan's final moments, how grief had stilled his hand when the Necrist summoned the voice of his dead son. And he thought, too, of how a stronger man—a man less *broken*—could have continued to fight without hesitation and spared the life of his friend.

He could dam his tears no longer and they spilled upon his cheeks.

Vandyl finished his eulogy and a pair of mail-clad soldiers began placing the dead in their graves. They hefted the corpses one by one and eased them into the ground. Brugan proved too wide for the hole dug for him, and the soldiers set about working with shovels to wedge his form into its hole. The body dropped with a thud.

Lannick's chest wracked with a sob, a cry escaping him. "*Keep your edges sharp, lad,*" he remembered Brugan telling him. He drew a deep breath, trying to steel himself. He turned his ears to Vandyl's words, hoping the routine of ceremony would dull his thoughts of guilt and grief.

Thane Vandyl shifted beneath his great bearskin cloak and walked to the first grave. He coughed wetly against his fist. "Worren served me for twenty years," he said through a rough-sounding throat. "He was courageous and wise and steadfast. A rare man, and I lament his passing. His family?" he said, eyes searching the crowd.

A portly, weeping woman of perhaps forty years stepped forward, two sons just shy of manhood trailing just behind. They shared an embrace with the thane, then each grabbed a handful of the upturned dirt and tossed it across the body.

"May this earth pave your path to the Elder God's heavens," Thane Vandyl said.

Vandyl offered words to the remaining two of his fallen oath-bound, and with both the respective families threw clumps of dirt upon the bodies.

At last Vandyl came to Brugan. He looked to Lannick. "Captain?" he said through a wheeze. "This is your man. I've not the right to speak for you or for others who knew him best. You and your men should say your farewells."

Lannick sniffled and swept tears from his face. He tried to summon some semblance of composure but was unable to speak. Inside he trembled as he watched his companions move near the grave.

Kevlin stooped to grab a handful of the upturned soil. He rose and tossed it across Brugan's corpse. "We're not the same without you," he said, swiping the rest from his big hands. "Not the same at all."

"No," grumbled Arleigh Lay, reaching out his one remaining hand to throw a fistful of dirt. "Goodbye, Brugan. I'd have liked to march with you one last time."

"One of our very best," said Cudgen, repeating the ritual. "We'll miss you, Brugan."

The three turned and looked to Lannick, the weight of their gazes causing him to tremble all the more. After a moment, he trudged toward the grave.

He came to stand at the foot of the pit, Brugan's thick body resting slightly cockeyed at its bottom. He tugged in a ragged breath. His legs felt weak and his head flooded with so much sadness it seemed ready to crush him.

My only friend.

He blinked and stared through bleary eyes. He thought of how Brugan was the person—the only person—who'd remained a friend to him even during his awful descent into those dark depths. For nine long years Brugan stood steadfast while he wallowed and wasted away. Lannick knew he'd given his friend little in return during that time, not even those few silver crowns he'd left unpaid at *The Wanton Vicar*.

"I owe you much, old friend," he said, voice quavering. "Far more than my bill at the *Vicar*. You were a friend when no one else was, and you never gave up on me. You were a fierce fighter and a welcome advisor. I owe you for all that remains of me." He thumbed a tear from his cheek and after a moment continued. "We will miss you as the Elder God welcomes you to his distant heavens, but I know you'll bring him laughter." He snatched three silver crowns from his purse and tossed them into the grave. "Farewell."

"What the fuck is that for?" Arleigh hissed, staring at the coins.

"Brugan would know," Lannick said with a sob, stooping to the loose soil to throw it over the body. "He would know."

He rose and used a sleeve to rub tears from his cheeks and snot from his nose. He heaved a shuddering sigh and straightened his spine.

Thane Vandyl addressed the crowd. "Let the bodies rest and the souls set upon their journey," he called. "Those who grieve may come to the keep for a feast of remembrance."

The oath-bound soldiers and families of the dead shuffled from the graveyard, through the ring of oak trees. Thane Vandyl, though, lingered, then came close to Lannick.

"Three of my men," the thane said, looking to the graves. "Three of my men dead and another of yours. The one wounded sits gibbering madness in my infirmary."

Lannick swallowed hard. "I'm sorry for your losses."

"And I for yours," Vandyl said, squinting toward the rising sun. "Upon hearing of the deaths of these men I considered withdrawing my offer of twenty oath-bound. The danger of these vile creatures of the dark—these *Necrists*—concerns me. But I know such beasts will never be defeated by me holing up and making some sad, last stand in this keep. I know they'll only be stopped by winning the fight against General Fane. By ripping away that tumor festering in Rune's army, and giving those soldiers the chance to defend this kingdom against this so-called Spider King and his foul allies. Only with that sort of victory can we put an end to tragedies like those that befell these brave men."

"I'll do my best, Thane Vandyl," Lannick said.

Vandyl coughed wetly, bringing a fist to his mouth as he did. Dark blood speckled his hand as he removed it. "You'd better do nothing less. I'm dying, Lannick. I'll not live to see the end of this war."

Lannick tried to think of some comforting words but his emotions left little room for another's troubles. "It saddens me to hear this."

"Nonsense. All men die. Every last one of us—pauper and nobleman alike—finds the dirt in the end. Most do so quietly, withering away before passing from this world and from memory." He paused and stiffened, eyes bright in the sun's glow. "Children, for a time at least, may remember a parent's stubbornness when faced with a dire illness, how that parent labored on and on before finally surrendering to death. But others won't remember that, won't even care. Such aren't the tales passed along to others." He cleared a wet throat. "The tales passed along are those of heroes, those rare folk who dare the greatest odds for reasons beyond mere survival. Those are the tales whose echoes will be heard by generations to come."

Lannick nodded, eyes falling to Brugan's corpse.

Vandyl grasped Lannick's shoulder with his blood-flecked hand. "You have that rare chance to be *remembered*, Lannick. Go and win this war for all those you've lost, for all those who are certain to fall. Honor your dead and mine, and let my great-grandchildren hear your tale."

8

THE GODSWELL

PREFECT GAMGHAST DRUMMED the butt of his walking staff against the dusty stone floor of the corridor. "A moment!" he groaned, straightening and rubbing his aching spine. "A moment, please."

The tall, sturdily built man ahead—Tannin, the queen's bodyguard—halted and turned. His face was square and clean but for the pitted ruin where his left eye had been. He shifted his cloak, adjusted the shutters on his lantern, and waited.

"Just a moment," Gamghast wheezed, leaning heavily on his staff. "My bones have weathered many more years than your own."

"We cannot delay, Prefect," Tannin said, shining his lantern into the dark of the musty passage before them. "We risk our lives returning to the Bastion, and the closer we come to dawn the greater that risk becomes. Every corner of the place is closely watched by the chamberlain's men."

"You're certain we can gain entrance?"

Tannin nodded. "Chamberlain Alamis has seized the throne, but there are still some in the Bastion who quietly object. We have some friends yet within those walls."

Gamghast sighed and looked ahead. The catacombs had wound beneath Ironmoor for centuries, originally constructed after the War of Fates, after Yrghul and his forces razed the city. They were intended as a defensive measure, to store provisions and house citizens in the event of siege. Later, the myriad tunnels were used as a tomb, a convenient place to dispose of the bodies of beggars and orphans. Now, many claimed the ghosts of the dead haunted the stagnant passageways. They were avoided and abandoned, traversed only by the desperate or the insane.

Such as a certain mad prefect seeking answers to questions likely too dangerous for him to be asking. He grunted and smoothed the wild wisps of his white beard.

"Prefect," Tannin said firmly.

"Very well," Gamghast huffed, and trudged onward. After a deep breath he paused again to speak. "Has anyone else tried visiting the Godswell? Any of my brothers from the Sanctum? Prefect Kreer? Perhaps several weeks ago? Him, or others?"

Tannin slowed slightly and looked back. "No, not that I've heard. But wouldn't you know such a thing? Is there distrust even within the Sanctum?"

"Distrust permeates all places in such times. Good men are mixed among bad. Worse, good and bad are mixed within the hearts of us all."

Tannin stopped, and the glare he gave through his

one remaining eye seemed not at all forgiving. "I serve no ill purpose. I serve only the kingdom of Rune and the glory of Illienne the Light Eternal."

"Yes, yes, yes," Gamghast said, waving a hand dismissively. *Simple minds are ever less murky.* "I've no doubt you do."

Tannin nodded curtly and resumed his tireless stride through the murk, lantern held high before him. The flame burned brightly enough, though the light seemed to fail as it tried to penetrate the gloom. The wind blew oddly in the catacombs, shifting strangely about and carrying with it the stink of decay. An occasional, distant shriek from somewhere echoed across the stone, though whether from the mouth of man or beast or something else entirely remained uncertain.

Gamghast peered over Tannin's shoulder and thought he sensed a dim flicker far ahead. "How much farther?"

"We're close."

"To think," Gamghast said with a hint of disgust, "a prefect of the Sanctum forced to use such gutters to gain entrance to the Bastion."

"We do what we must, Prefect. We do what is necessary."

Gamghast smiled a rare smile, finding Tannin's practicality a mirror of his own. "Then lead the way, Tannin."

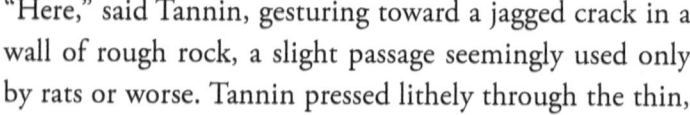

"Here," said Tannin, gesturing toward a jagged crack in a wall of rough rock, a slight passage seemingly used only by rats or worse. Tannin pressed lithely through the thin, twisting space, his large form surprisingly agile.

"Through there?" Gamghast asked, puzzling over the contortions that moving through the crack would require.

Tannin nodded, and held his hand out through the crack as though greeting a maiden descending from a carriage.

Gamghast angrily brushed aside Tannin's hand and forced his way through the narrow opening, leaning his head and neck as far back as his bones would bend and angling his knees just so. Pain filled his form. "I require—" he began, but then moaned as the rough stone bit at his frail chest. He sucked in a deep breath in order to press through the deeper dark just beyond. "I require," he wheezed, "no such assistance."

He stumbled through, and in the faint light of the lantern found himself before a tall door of hardened wood and bound iron.

Tannin rattled the door's hefty handle, seemingly finding it locked. "Beyond this is a passageway leading to an old storage chamber that once served the castle. Dug into the wall of that chamber is a secret doorway—for which Queen Reyis has given me one of only two keys—that leads to the Bastion's cellars. From there it is but a short distance to the Godswell."

"You do have a key for *this* door, then?"

Tannin shook his head. "There are no keyholes on this side. The locks can only be opened from the door's other end. But as soon as the belfries toll the morning's fourth hour, those locks will be undone. I've made arrangements."

Gamghast nodded, impressed with Tannin's thoroughness. The appointed time could not be far away, for they'd left the Abbey shortly after three in the morning.

He suppressed a yawn, finding that thinking of the early hour brought to mind his lack of sleep, both on this night and many others since the Lector's death.

And since Castor's most unusual transition...

Just then there came the sound of heavy tumblers turning, then a squeal like a large bolt sliding. The door creaked open, pressed ahead by thin, withered fingers.

"Hurry," said a frail, wavering voice. "You've not much time. Chamberlain Alamis stirs early these days."

Tannin moved inside. "Many thanks, old friend. You risk much by doing this, and you have my lasting gratitude."

Gamghast came behind, looking at the old man as he passed. He was old, his face withered and his bald head covered with liver spots. Thick, milky cataracts marred his eyes—eyes very clearly blind. Once they'd passed through the door, the man grabbed a long switch and began tapping it before him.

"This way," the old man said over the tip-tap of his switch, walking into the dark passage of stone.

Gamghast followed, recognizing the man. "I'm relieved to see there are some here who yet serve the High King."

"May his soul find rest," the man said, head sagging briefly before rising sharply. "I know your voice."

"Prefect Gamghast of the Sanctum. And I know your face. You were attending Queen Reyis when last I came to the Bastion."

"I am Jalim," he said with a stiff bow. "Simply Jalim, and I have held the queen's counsel since her youth."

Worry pinched his heavily wrinkled face. "Things are well with the pregnancy? There's been no mishap?"

"Fine, fine, fine," Gamghast said, nervous eyes searching the corridor for eavesdroppers. "But we will speak no more of this within these walls. How are things in the Bastion?"

Jalim continued his sightless march through the passage, clicking his switch before him but feet seemingly confident of their path. Gamghast reckoned the man knew every inch of the castle, considering how long as he'd served. The old man remained silent, prompting Gamghast to ask his question again.

"Anxious," Jalim answered after a moment, his tone thoughtful.

Tannin sniffed. "That would seem an improvement from when I departed." He touched the nasty mess of scabs and scars where his left eye had been. "Alamis's lackeys left me half as blind as you."

Jalim nodded. "A frightful night, that. But the violence subsided thereafter, likely because there remained no one left to stand up to Alamis directly. There has been little discussion of Queen Reyis, and none at all of the Sanctum. The chamberlain seems more concerned with consolidating his own power than with those he believes deposed."

"Troubling…" Gamghast mumbled. "Perhaps we've wilted to such weakness that our enemies no longer need give us regard."

The old man gave no answer.

"Herein," Jalim heralded in his frail voice, "is Rune's

greatest treasure. I have a dear memory of beholding it once—only once—before losing my sight."

"Stay here, both of you," Gamghast said. "Tannin, watch for any unwanted eyes."

Tannin nodded. "Do as you must, Prefect, but do it quickly."

Gamghast moved into the circular chamber constructed deep beneath the earth. It was vast, a hundred feet or more across and the ceiling nearly as tall. Eight massive pillars in a ring supported the dome-shaped ceiling above, a rare allusion to the Sentinels being counted with the High King in the number of Illienne's divine fragmentation.

Perhaps one symbol the High Kings hadn't the courage to alter...

The room seemed to vibrate with a low hum, and a radiance emanated from the chamber's center to illuminate the domed ceiling above. Magnificent, glittering mosaics decorated the ceiling, though Gamghast took only scant notice of them, so focused was he on the source of the light.

The Godswell. His eyes widened at the sight of it, a shimmering pool, roughly round in shape and several yards in diameter. The very hole torn into the earth when the gods Illienne and Yrghul descended to oblivion.

The Faith held that, in order to be crowned king, a prince needed to prove his worthiness—and divinity—by touching the waters of the Godswell. The Faith held also that the king was the only person capable of touching the well's waters, and that any other would be destroyed by the fury of the dead gods.

The Faith charged the Sanctum with two primary duties: tending the High King's body and praying over the Godswell. Gamghast was well-versed in the healing arts, but his experience with the Godswell had been rather limited. He had seen it only once, twenty-nine years before, just prior to the coronation of High King Deragol. Prefects weren't permitted to attend the Lector's annual ceremonies at the well.

And now we have no Lector, no idea what such prayers entailed, nor why they were necessary in the first place. He chuckled at a sudden thought. *Perhaps Karnag the murderous highlander will say a few reverent words for the pool.*

He walked with tentative, shuffling steps toward the well, oblivious to the pains still nagging his back, knees and hip. The hum grew stronger as he approached, his bones trembling. He'd never been this close, and curiosity consumed him. Intense light shone from the waters, the illumination nearly blinding. There seemed a pull, also, a force that seized the body and drew it near. Gamghast wondered for an instant if he could tear free, but knew he had no desire to turn from such a wonder.

The very grave of the dead gods. A grave still alive with their divine energy.

Though the gods were far distant, the well held *power*. It contained the most fundamental element of divinity: the power of the infinite. The power over endings and limits, the eternal defiance of death and decay. The Faith claimed the well held echoes of Illienne's wisdom and righteousness, and Yrghul's ambition and mastery of the dark…

He came to the pool's edge, pressing quivering hands

outward. The water—utterly still—glowed with a silvery hue, and there seemed no way to plumb its depths. A seemingly bottomless well tunneled through earth and stone, to a place where time and space ceased to exist, a place from which even gods could not escape.

Gamghast gazed intently into the well, mesmerized. The waters were crystalline, luminescent. Yet, there seemed at their deepest point a dark mote, a distant object.

And then there was movement, a shadow sweeping across the well's depths. The distant portions of the well darkened, and the darkness pressed upward. Fingers of shadow clawed along the radiant walls of the well, darkening the waters as they rose.

He furrowed his brow and strained his old eyes, hoping to see more clearly.

The water flashed brilliantly, blindingly, a great plume of light that spewed from the well to illuminate the golden mosaics adorning the domed ceiling. The massive chamber glowed for a brief moment with the very light of midday, every nook brightening as though the sun blazed within the expanse.

But in the light's wake followed an ever-deepening shadow. The radiance faltered and dimmed, and the great room darkened.

Within the well's shadow he saw something, something that caused his heart to stammer. The skeletal head of some great beast crowned with a tangle of twisting horns. It roared through a maw of fangs, its eyes blazed with fury. Its body was a mass of swirling shadow, slithering about the well's waters like a massive, black serpent.

Yrghul.

Gamghast's hands found the hood of his robes and he tugged the cowl overhead. Terror gripped him and he sucked in a desperate breath.

"Prefect!" sounded a voice behind him, distant as though from a dream.

"This cannot…" he said, eyes fixed upon the horrifying creature within the depths.

"Now!" came a hiss in his ear. It was Tannin, the one-eyed guard yanking Gamghast by his shoulders from the well.

Gamghast staggered to his feet, stumbling backward as Tannin pulled him away. "No…" he breathed, utterly confused.

"Someone approaches," Tannin growled, dragging Gamghast toward the deep shadows of the chamber's edge.

Gamghast stammered wordlessly, eyes searching the cavernous space.

"Listen," Tannin whispered, pulling Gamghast behind one of the gargantuan pillars rounding the room.

Gamghast steadied his breathing and tried to focus his senses. At first he heard nothing but the well's hum. After a moment, though, he detected the echo of voices and the sound of boots upon stone. He looked to Tannin, who gestured with a shift of his head toward the chamber's opposite side.

Gamghast nodded, then noticed Jalim hunkering beside him, his dimensions so thin he'd be hardly noticed. The older man's face was blank, his milky eyes twitching about.

"It's the chamberlain," Jalim whispered. "I know the sound of his stride."

Gamghast studied the chamber with a deeper sense of dread. An opening was carved into the far wall of the chamber, opposite where they'd entered. Gamghast knew this to be the chamber's formal entrance, a short tunnel at the base of a tall stairway that descended from the Bastion above.

"There are others with him," Jalim continued. "A number who walk with soft steps."

Gamghast drew back behind the pillar, peeking around it with just one eye. He pressed down his beard and steadied himself. *Now, Alamis, let your true friends and allies be revealed.*

Six figures emerged from the opening, one tall and well-groomed and clad in an elegant robe of blue silk.

Alamis.

The others were far more unsettling. Five hunched figures draped by black robes, their heads sickening checkers of sallow flesh joined by braided stitches. An aura of shadow surrounded them, flowing from thin fingers and shifting slowly about their frames. A chill settled upon the air as Gamghast stared.

Necrists. Here, at the most sacred place in all of Rune.

"Dead gods!" Tannin hissed. "What are those things?"

"Our oldest enemy," Gamghast said, anger staining his tone, "escorted here by our dear chamberlain. Escorted here no doubt to try to draw their dead god's power from the grave."

Chamberlain Alamis and the Necrists approached the Godswell, though Alamis stopped several yards short of its edge. He gestured with a graceful sweep of his arm and the Necrists moved ahead. They crept in unison to the pool's lip and stared together into the depths. The waters set aglow their faces, revealing mismatched skin stretching against the stitched bonds and quivering grotesquely.

The Necrist at the group's center dug within its robes and withdrew a stoppered wineskin made of some pale leather. The Necrist uttered a long series of jagged-sounding words in a strange tongue, then opened the wineskin and poured into the well a crimson liquid Gamghast felt certain was human blood.

The blood of High King Deragol?

"Great Yrghul!" the Necrist screamed in a voice shrill and shrieking. It threw its arms outward, the sleeves of its black robes falling away to reveal arms covered with the same piecemeal skin as its face. "Forger of night and sculptor of shadow, conqueror of kings and defier of death! Behold your servants!"

Gamghast trembled, gripping his walking staff while his mind sifted through the various spells Erlorn—Castor—had taught him, seeking something to strike down these abominations. There were incantations, words that could bring divine light and dispel dark spirits, but nothing he was certain could destroy all of these things, and nothing that could repel the many guards who'd likely respond to the chamberlain's call. Gamghast was a practical man, and reckoned it best to choose a different moment for any confrontation.

The well's hum intensified, shaking the very stone of the chamber. The room quaked and suddenly the pool shot forth a great plume, a spray of silvery water erupting toward the apex of the chamber's dome. The five Necrists quickly withdrew, sinking to their knees and pressing their heads reverently upon the floor.

Gamghast shivered, a deep cold biting his bones. *What is this?*

In the water's wake came a column of shadow, a twisting spire of black that swelled as it spun. At first it seemed comprised of thick smoke, but it soon resolved into hundreds of wispy shapes roughly humanoid in form, elongated wraiths with drawn-out faces marked only by gaping hollows for mouths. Hundreds of apparitions formed the spire's spinning surface, no doubt heaped upon a core of many more.

Dead gods.

The black column wound upward until it reached a height of more than thirty feet. The chamber's glow flagged and faltered, its silvery incandescence surrendering to an oppressive dark.

"Children," came a great, booming voice from everywhere and nowhere at once.

Gamghast ducked behind the massive pillar, suddenly seized by an overwhelming fear. He saw Jalim and Tannin pressed against the stone with similar terror. He knelt upon the chamber's floor with complaining knees, fighting back a flood of tears.

"My children," the all-present voice continued, bellowing through the hall. "Those many sacrifices have fed me *life*. I am *becoming*, children. Form will forever rest beyond my reach, but the day soon approaches when my power shall return to this realm. With it the light will fail and the descendants of Illienne will be forever lost in darkness—*my* darkness—as what I have prophesied to you in blood will come to pass in your world. The night will belong to you and to my son. Send word to him that I regret I possess no eyes to set upon him when he returns here, but remind him I will give then my power as my gift."

Gamghast cowered, making his arthritic form as small as he could in the shadow of the pillar. Tears spilled across his face and his body shook. He drew his creaking knees as close as he could to his heaving chest, and did his best to slow his frantic breaths.

"I *am*," said the voice, the entire chamber shuddering, "and he shall be! Bring me my newborn son!"

The words thundered through the chamber, but then darkness yielded to light and the shadows shrank away. Slowly, the great space became illuminated once again by the light of the Godswell.

Gamghast wept with more tears than he knew his eyes contained. His entire body quaked, and he found it impossible to rise until several minutes had passed. When at last he could stand, he peeked around the stout pillar and saw that the chamberlain and the Necrists were gone.

He squeezed his staff, shaking his head and quelling at last his emotions. He gestured to Tannin. "Get up," he said, bringing a certainty to his voice that his heart no longer possessed. "We have fewer moments than we have friends. Much falls upon us and those others still loyal to Rune."

Yrghul comes, as does some other horrid thing. The highlander did indeed speak Castor's confession. What will become of us?

9

NIGHTMARES

"FENCRESS," SAID DRENJ, a solitary tear wetting the olive skin of his cheek, "please tell me this isn't so. Please tell me this nightmare will shortly end. Tell me I'll soon wake beside my wife and daughters, all safe in our home in Raven's Roost."

Fencress tugged at her cowl with a gloved hand and looked to the young man. "I wish I could, Drenj. I truly do."

Drenj slumped in his saddle, the bright light of morning unable to chase the gloom from his face.

Fencress tightened her grip on the pommel of her horse's saddle. "It sounds to me we're headed to war..." She smiled. "But think of the possibilities! We've a chance to be real soldiers now, killing folk in epic battles rather than skulking in the shadows. Imagine the honor and glory! I'm Death's Dancing Mistress, remember? What plaudits and poems might celebrate my heroics? Perhaps even you, Drenj, will finally be able to kill a man!" She laughed and shook her head. "So long as Karnag doesn't get to all of them first."

Karnag rode well ahead, ranging a couple hundred yards down the dusty path that wandered amidst the tall grasses. He listed atop a massive black stallion, a magnificent beast that would've fetched a fine price at market. Fencress, though, knew Karnag had paid no coin for the animal, and wagered its former owner had paid the dearest of prices trying to keep it.

"We're not soldiers, Fencress," said Drenj, leaning toward her from his saddle such that his loose clothing seemed ready to drip away from his thin frame. "The furthest thing from. We've no business in battle."

"You boys know I feel the same. I've no wish to work along the front line of a war. I've no quarrel with blood, so long as there's coin in it, but blood spilled for faith or fealty seems like blood wasted in my eyes. But war brings opportunities for the likes of us, ways we can find profit." She looked ahead. "And besides, this is friendship."

Drenj pulled closer, wiping away another tear. "You spoke of a tiger, once. Before we saved Karnag from the Abbey. You told a story warning one not to tempt the most dangerous beast. Will we not be doing just that? Will we not be stretching our necks inside the tiger's cage? This is *war*, Fencress. Even the best killers get killed when enough blades swing their way."

Fencress gritted her teeth. "You have a choice, Drenj! Ride now. Ride away. He'll not hunt you down. Take the chance he's mistaken about folk hunting us. Take the chance those witches and whatnot we saw back in Shank's Hollow won't track you down and kill you."

Drenj stifled a sob. "Will my daughter die, just as he says? Would I reach Raven's Roost to see her if I left? Would I see her before I'm slain?"

Fencress exhaled slowly. She was tired, and her usual cheer faded at Drenj's words. "I don't know," she said, staring down at the fancy reins looped about her gloved hands, the leather straps decorated with tiny inlaid gems. "We take a gamble no matter what we do, and there are no safe choices anymore."

Drenj's thin form trembled. "Every choice I have is fraught with fear. If I leave him, I fear I'll be hunted down and slain. If I stay at his side, I fear I'll see things worse than death…"

Fencress nodded. "There are only nightmares."

Fencress awoke in the dead of night, ears ringing from the echoes of a horrid scream.

The scream sounded again, far across a rolling field drenched in moonlight.

She looked hard into the dark, eyes finding nothing at first. Low hills of tall grass, shoots swaying gently beneath the moon and stars. A copse of thin trees. A deer feeding nearby.

She thought for an instant of rousing Paddyn to fell the deer for food, but the scream sounded once more and the beast darted from sight.

She looked back to their small encampment. Paddyn and Drenj were both awake, squatting on their bedrolls and scanning the same dark as she. But Karnag's bedroll was empty, his sword gone.

"Shit," she spat, then tugged on her boots and cloak and grabbed her twin swords. She darted upright.

"You're going out *there*?" Paddyn asked, mouth agape and eyes wide.

"Our pursuers!" Drenj hissed. "Those wizards we saw in Shank's Hollow! We should flee!"

"I don't know," Fencress said. "Whoever it is, it sounds as though Karnag might be killing them off in the worst of ways. I mean to find out what is happening. I'm heading into the dark."

Paddyn and Drenj looked to each other, confusion written across their young faces.

Fencress smirked in spite of her fear. "You can always just sit here and shiver, wondering which of you will be the first to piss himself." She winked. "The smart bet would seem to be a tie."

The young men cursed in unison and fumbled for their weapons. Drenj looked to her meaningfully. "Just promise we'll not get too close to danger."

She held out a hand and helped Drenj to his feet. "If there's danger," she said, "you stay clear. I'd like it much if you were able to see your daughter again."

They moved in near silence through the night, their only sound the rustle of the tall grass. The screams, though, persisted, growing louder as they approached the source. Fifty or so yards ahead cowered what appeared to be a man shrieking beneath a tree.

A dread settled upon her as Fencress wondered what parts Karnag had removed from his latest victim. From the shrill howls she knew the lungs remained intact, as well as the mouth and throat. *Perhaps he's taken the liver? Or the thumbs or the jingles?*

The man shuddered and screamed. He fell back against the tree's trunk, then slumped to the ground and became lost among the grasses. The shrieks softened to an awful, mournful whimper.

Sounds like the jingles.

"That doesn't have the sound of danger for us," Fencress whispered to her companions. "Sounds to me like utter desperation."

Drenj and Paddyn nodded but showed no intention of going nearer.

"Very well," she said. "Stay here but stay alert. There might be others lurking about."

The young men's faces tightened with tension.

Fencress turned ahead and crept closer, ears pricked and eyes searching the dark. She instinctively found the quiet parts of the earth, her footfalls making no sound. The man continued to sob, the wail punctuated by painful groans. Fencress quickened her pace, feeling a need to discover what had happened before whoever lay ahead bled his last.

What have you done, Karnag?

She came close enough to see the hollow of depressed grasses formed by the man's fallen shape. A terrified moan escaped the man and his breath rattled. Fencress had heard such cries before, after unlucky folk had slid off the points of her blades.

Closer still, such that she could see the man's heaving chest, bare and muscled and slick with a dark wetness.

Then close enough to see the face, a silver mask of agony in the moonlight.

She knew it instantly.

"Karnag!" she shouted. She darted her keen eyes about but spied no one else nearby. She dropped to her friend's side and placed a gloved hand upon a brow beaded with sweat.

His gaze was fixed upon the night sky, eyes not lifeless but filled with panic and tears. He threw a hand upward, as though warding away some unseen terror, but then withdrew it and trembled. He seemed to notice Fencress not at all and appeared but a frail shadow of the fearsome killer she knew him to be.

She noticed his mouth moving, sputtering half-formed words in an anguished wheeze. Her eyes drifted to his chest where a dozen or more long, shallow lacerations welled with blood. She saw also his hands, broken nails crammed with dark, wet gunk. She wagered the wounds were self-inflicted.

"They are dead," whispered Karnag. "All but the children…"

Fencress placed her hand upon his brow. "Karnag," she pleaded, "you have to wake from this nightmare."

Karnag's eyelids fluttered and at last he seemed aware of her presence. He raised up and shivered, his head seeming to clear after a moment. "There are so many yet to perish," he said, his voice finding again its strength. "I can see them all, every one, and those who tell tales of such things will not be able to count the number. Tomorrow will be but a brief verse of a terrifying song."

Fencress shuddered. "What happens tomorrow, Karnag?"

"The Gravemaker sings."

Karnag roused them at dawn, though Fencress hardly required the effort. She'd barely slept, her thoughts haunted by imaginings of whatever grisly task Karnag had planned.

"Get to the road," he commanded, directing them to horses he'd readied. He'd not donned a shirt, wearing only stained leather trousers and weathered boots. Dried blood and long scabs decorated his massive torso and his giant sword rested across his back. "We ride."

"To those who follow us?" Fenress ventured. "Those witches we saw a few days back?"

"No," Karnag said. "They will meet their fate at the appointed time, but not now."

Fencress's head soured, though she kept the cheer to her tone. "Who, then, will be the beneficiaries of our particular talents?"

"We ride for heads unsuspecting. Death will visit itself upon many this day."

Drenj and Paddyn moved haltingly, eyeing Fencress as though asking for answers. She returned their pleading gazes with a sigh and a heavy shrug. She felt their fear. She'd spent years as a thief and assassin, but had no taste for wanton slaughter. She didn't have a tender heart—no one could after killing so many—but the notion of killing for killing's sake chilled her. And she worried this was about to be just that.

She thought of asking Karnag about the night before.

She soon thought better of it, though, noticing the menacing look that darkened his face. She'd seen it before—many times recently and less often in the years before they'd killed the Lector—and knew his mind would not be moved. She settled instead for silence, avoiding Drenj and Paddyn's nervous gazes as she gathered the last of her possessions and trudged to her horse.

"Mount your steeds!" Karnag shouted. "Follow me!"

They all obliged, fear a fire licking at their backs. They rode, driving toward the blinding orb of the rising sun. They galloped over low hills of tall grass and fields of fallow farmland. At a seemingly random point, Karnag wheeled his mount in a new direction and they followed, trampling across a furrowed field. They had no grasp of Karnag's destination but it was clear he traveled with purpose. None of them possessed the courage to question him.

A terrible unease haunted Fencress as they rode. The previous night had unnerved her, with Karnag reduced to no more than a sobbing whelp at one moment then becoming an eerie soothsayer the next. She wondered what nightmares worked through his head to cause such a man to rend his chest and weep, but supposed that was something she'd rather not know.

Karnag crested a grassy rise ahead of them and reined his stallion to a stamping halt. Fencress noticed smoke hanging low upon the sky beyond. She slowed as she rode up the hill to approach him, Drenj and Paddyn quiet behind her, and used old gamblers' tricks to keep the emotion from her face.

Karnag spun his horse about and regarded them

grimly, the dead look once again present in his flint-colored eyes. "Thaydorne has sent war bands away from the front to scout north and west. Those men have become hot with bloodlust, their heads stained by the same corruption as his. There stands a village over the next rise where one such war band engages in rape and slaughter. They laugh—laugh!—while death approaches them. I will use them to send my brother a greeting."

My brother? Fencress shifted uncomfortably upon her horse. She feared Karnag, but knew she could not allow that fear to drive her from him. If there came a chance to save him she needed to be present to seize it.

But does that chance exist anymore?

Karnag studied them with lifeless eyes. "There are fourteen Arranese warriors."

Fencress frowned. "That's too many for the four of us during daylight, especially if they're trained soldiers."

Karnag cocked his brow, a strange, puzzled look upon his hard face. "I will slay ten. You will kill two. You," he said, nodding to Paddyn, "will take one with your bow. And you," he said to Drenj, "will cower at a distance and then become useful only at the end. The one man I let live will be sent back to his Spider King with my missive. It will happen thus."

With that, Karnag spurred his horse onward, moving it to a brisk trot down the slope of the hill's far side. They followed wordlessly, Fencress ahead of Drenj and Paddyn. She glanced back to the young men as they rode, pity creeping within her. She'd been hardened by years of dark work, but knew these two hadn't developed the stomach for blood.

They descended to the tall grasses in the valley between the hills then rode upward, Karnag silent and stoic as he rode. He came to the top of the hill and stopped his horse, studying whatever lay below with his heavy jaw set and his gaze a warrant of death. He seemed an inevitability now, a great force of fate forging his way toward some unknown but invariable end.

Fencress neared Karnag upon the hilltop and beheld the scene before her. At the slope's bottom stood a smoldering hamlet of no more than ten structures, all small, decrepit hovels of burned and burning wood. About the meager buildings lay the bodies of what Fencress guessed had been their residents, humble folk with guts spilled and limbs hacked. An infant wailed as it clutched the corpse of what seemed its mother, the woman's throat a bloody gash. Near the narrow stream at the village's center, close to a collection of horses, stood a rough gathering of Arranese warriors, angular-featured with pointed ears and almond-shaped eyes. They whooped as they passed among them two girls, barely even teens, who wept and flailed helplessly as they were tossed about.

Fencress's fear gave way to anger. She took her hands from her horse's reins and placed them upon the hilts of her twin blades. She remembered her childhood home, some backwater hellhole near the Southwalls. It, too, had been raided years ago by brigands, and she was sold thereafter into slavery. She tugged her black cowl overhead.

"Ready, Karnag," she said, squeezing the swords' handles. "Let's kill them all."

"We will," he said, his voice the certainty of truth. "All

save one." He then fell eerily quiet, closing his eyes for a time.

Fencress exchanged tilted glances with Drenj and Paddyn. "Karnag?" she asked.

His eyes opened. "It will happen thus." He then howled some arcane battle cry and charged on his black mount down the hill, barreling toward the ruined village. They rode in his wake.

The Arranese seemed slow to notice them over their own screams and those of the children left alive. They were halfway down the hill when one long-haired warrior spotted them, paused, then stammered and shouted to his comrades. The Arranese dropped the girls to the dirt and drew weapons, mostly curved swords but a number of spears as well. Then the Arranese rushed forward to meet them.

Karnag galloped on, nearing the village's outermost buildings. He unsheathed his great blade, the steel shining in the morning sun. "Gravemaker!" he roared, rising in the saddle.

Almond-shaped eyes widened in apparent disbelief and the Arranese stuttered to a halt. A group of perhaps six bolted onward, clustered together and pressing ahead in a knot between two of the burning homes.

Karnag yanked his horse's reins and moved straight at them. Twenty-five yards, fifteen. He pressed himself upward to a squat upon his saddle. He came close to the gang of soldiers then jumped, flying through the air and raising his sword as he did. The Arranese shrank away from the charging horse. Karnag fell upon them with a mighty swing of his sword. His blade took the heads of two and the better part of a third's.

Drenj and Paddyn lingered but Fencress rode just behind Karnag. She swept a blade toward one of the remaining warriors, finding his neck with the edge. The sharp-featured soldier fell to his knees, clutching at a fount of blood.

Karnag threw himself against the other two soldiers near them, shoving them through the wall of a burning house and into the flames. They writhed madly and screamed as the fire engulfed them.

Karnag left them and dropped his sword low, dragging it against the dry dirt of the town's empty spaces with an awful scraping. Somehow the sound seemed louder than the wailing of the girls and the infant.

The two girls ran into the stream, leaving the remaining eight Arranese warriors shouldered together at the stream's bank. They appeared to be hard men, dusky skin broken by scars and lean bodies knotted with sinews. Cowardice, though, seemed to wilt them as Karnag approached and their weapons shook in their hands.

"*I am the Gravemaker!*" Karnag screamed, the sound of it a thunderclap. "I am your fate! I am your ending!"

A warrior on the far side of the group lunged and attacked with his sword. Karnag cleaved the man's arm from his torso before the blow reached him.

Fencress heard the whistle of an arrow and watched as a shaft whirled past her and plunged into the chest of the tall Arranese warrior at the line's center. The man, shaven-headed, clutched the arrow in shock then fell back into the stream behind him. The faces of the soldiers about him filled with panic, wide eyes shifting between Karnag, Fencress, and the hillside where Paddyn nocked another arrow.

Karnag became a crashing wave of violence, screaming as he tore his great sword across and through the leather-clad warrior nearest him. Then the next. His precision was perfect, the strikes finding their mark just before any counter, just prior to any defense being raised. He slipped and slid about, his blade ripping through the line of men. It seemed a storm of blood, Karnag killing the Arranese each in turn with sickening quickness and efficiency.

One warrior tumbled forward then around, his back toward Fencress. She raised a sword and plunged it through the base of the man's skull. She yanked it back and watched as the raven-haired man slumped near her horse's hooves.

There remained alive just one Arranese warrior, a nervous-eyed man of perhaps thirty years with black-and-gray hair tied in a knot. He held a spear with trembling hands. His mouth formed silent curses and his angled eyes darted tearfully about his fallen countrymen.

Karnag came before him, his massive sword upraised and a fearsome snarl upon his face. "You," he growled, "you I allow to live so that you may deliver my message to your Spider King."

Fencress heard footsteps behind her and spun her horse about. She sighed in relief when she saw Drenj and Paddyn walking their horses into the village, dour looks on their faces. Drenj seemed particularly affected, his eyes turned to where Fencress guessed the crying baby hugged its dead mother.

"Come," called Karnag. "Drenj and Paddyn. Guard this man while I work. Make certain he does not flee."

The lone warrior stood at the stream's edge, clearly shaken by what he'd witnessed. Paddyn and Drenj moved to his sides, weapons drawn and wary eyes upon him.

Karnag went to one of the dead soldiers and stripped him of his clothes. He retrieved the man's knife then flipped the body over, turning it face down in the bloodied mud. Fencress winced as Karnag set about skinning the man's back as he would game he prepared to cook. He sliced away a thick rectangle of skin, nearly two feet long and a foot across. After making the final cuts, he laid out the flesh upon the ground.

Karnag smoothed and flattened the swath of skin with careful hands. He then dipped the point of his dagger into the bloody mass of muscle left upon the body. He moved the dagger to the skin and shifted it about in some precise pattern. Again he dipped the dagger in the corpse then etched something upon the skin. Over and again he did this before Fencress realized he was *writing* something in blood upon the swath, the dagger his quill and the flesh his parchment.

At last Karnag sank back and beheld his work. Words of some strange tongue were dug deeply into the skin and stained crimson. Seemingly satisfied, Karnag pressed himself close to the skin and blew as though drying ink.

"This scroll is my missive," Karnag said, rising from the ground and holding the skin. He strode to the Arranese warrior and stood before him, brandishing the flesh. "You will give this to your king. You will tell him that I, the Gravemaker, gave this to you. You understand my words?"

The man nodded, shaking more than ever as Karnag loomed over him.

"Very well. Paddyn, fetch two of their horses. One for this man to ride and one upon which to rest my message."

Paddyn obliged, walking quickly to the collection of horses still loitering just upstream.

"What does it say?" Drenj asked, almost as much fear in his voice as was drawn across the Arranese warrior's face.

"It is the elder tongue," Karnag said. "The old and secret language of the gods. It means 'I come for you, Brother. Death is mine alone to wield.'"

Fencress found the wailing infant, a girl at most a year old, still clutching the corpse. She was thin, underfed, with pale skin and red hair like her mother. Both the babe and the dead woman were clothed in rags.

Fencress pulled her cowl from her head to let her black hair fall and pressed a gloved hand outward, hesitantly. The baby screamed, snot and tears mixing on her round face and dripping in a string to the dead woman whose eyes remained fixed skyward.

Fencress withdrew her hand and removed her gloves. She reached again for the little girl, the strand of tears and snot breaking as she pulled the baby from the corpse. She pressed the child against her black shirt still wet in places with blood. The embrace felt awkward and did nothing to soothe the baby's cries. Fencress had no gift with children and couldn't recall ever holding one before.

She'd not known much of her own mother and felt a sharp pang at knowing this girl's life would have a similar absence. She hid the baby's eyes from the corpse and tried rocking her as she'd seen mothers do. The girl's cries softened.

Fencress reckoned she'd left many children without fathers and some without mothers, though she refused to let herself regret the deaths of bad people. This child's mother seemed a simple sort, not the sort to have owed a bad debt, to have killed another's relative, or to have risen to ill-gotten power. Not the sort of person an assassin would have been hired to kill, but rather a loving mother who'd had the bad luck of living in the wrong village at the wrong time.

The woman's daughter had just lost all she knew. Fencress clutched her closer, swaying from side to side. "Don't remember this, child," she said softly. "Your mother will be waiting for you in the Elder God's heavens, if there is such a place. Say goodbye and forget seeing her like this."

She walked with the baby toward the stream. Drenj and Paddyn moved about what was left of the village's homes, salvaging provisions. She spotted Karnag near the stream's edge, scraping a whetstone down his sword. On the stream's far bank, aside a frail tree, cowered the two older girls who'd been tossed about by the Arranese, wet and weeping. They glanced nervously to Karnag, seemingly wondering what to think of the man who'd just slain the slayers.

Fencress waved to the two, trying to summon them over. They caught sight of her and drew near each other, speaking hurriedly while studying Fencress with wide, tearful eyes.

Fencress pointed to the baby, then to the girls. Between their shaking sobs they seemed to be arguing. They looked very much alike, with ginger hair, freckles, and gawky frames in simple dresses of simple cloth. Fencress guessed they were sisters.

"Come!" she called. "No one here will harm you. I swear it."

After another frantic exchange they arose. They walked with halting steps, eyes shifting from Fencress to Karnag. Soon, though, they stopped, seeming too afraid to come nearer.

Fencress shook her head and spat. She balanced awkwardly, grasping the baby while removing her boots. She then forged through the stream toward the girls, hoisting the baby overhead as she did. She danced her way barefoot across the stream's rocky bed, through knee-high waters while keeping the infant dry. She bounded up the bank beyond and pulled the baby to her breast once more.

The girls had crept closer, worried looks on their sad, drawn faces. Fencress regarded them with all the kindness she could find within. She tried to appear nothing like the killer she knew herself to be.

They remained cautious, the shock of the day's horrors still full upon them. Yet they did not flee when Fencress approached.

"You know this child?"

They nodded, the smear of tears shining on faces still red from blubbering.

"Take her," Fencress said, holding the baby outward.

"Take her and take care of her. She is your sister now. Grab whatever food and clothing you can find, take a couple of good horses and leave this place."

The taller of the two girls took the baby in a nervous embrace and began bawling. "Where do we go?" she stammered.

"Do you have any relations? An aunt or cousins or something?"

"All were here," she whined, "and all are dead."

Fencress dug in her purse, grabbed a dozen silver crowns, and handed them over. It seemed a paltry sum compared to what chance had taken from the two sisters and the baby, so she seized another handful and gave it to them. "That's enough coin to feed and shelter you for a good long while, months if you're smart about it."

"But we have nowhere to go…"

Fencress paused, realizing she didn't have much to tell them that wouldn't lead them to dark deeds and likely even greater despair. "Head north or west and get clear of the war that's coming. Find your way to a large town," she said, trying to sound comforting. "Find someone kind and charitable, like a healer or an acolyte of the Sanctum or something. See if they'll take you in, even pay them if you must. Offer to work, to help them. Don't get in with people like us. You'll find your way. Just be brave, and know life has more for you than these nightmares."

She turned and walked away, wondering if there could be any truth at all in what she'd said.

10
A SLIVER OF HOPE

━━━━━◅❦▻━━━━━

LANNICK SWAYED GLUMLY atop his chestnut stallion, his mail hauberk heavy on his shoulders and his heart heavy in his chest. He stared to the meandering mass of mail-clad men about him, their armor cast a sullen gray. There rode Thane Vandyl's twenty oath-bound, sullen-eyed veterans with brown and red cloaks and weapons drawn. At his flank were Cudgen and Arleigh, speaking together in hushed tones. Just ahead was Kevlin deKray, eyes fixed dead on the ground just as they'd been since the moment they departed Rellic.

They rode slowly, horses spurred to barely more than a walk across rolling hills painted a dark hue by stretches of shadow. Above, the late afternoon sun struggled behind swollen clouds and thunder rolled in the distance.

It seemed to Lannick that somber thoughts weighed upon them all, an apprehension of what stood ahead and a shock and sadness over what lay behind. He tugged in a breath then heaved it out with a sigh.

He missed his friend. He desperately, dearly missed his friend.

His head filled with memories of Brugan, each causing that pang of sorrow to sharpen all the more. He thought of the old barkeep's good humor, loud laughter, and big, kind heart. He thought too of the man's dogged friendship, even when concealed behind tough words meant to drag Lannick from the hole he'd occupied.

Lannick wondered if he'd have left behind his sordid life in Ironmoor if not for his friend. If he'd have ultimately succumbed to old weaknesses if Brugan hadn't insisted on this mad venture. If he'd be sitting now upon that all-too-comfortable stool in the darkest corner of *The Wanton Vicar* if Brugan hadn't possessed that hope that Lannick could be a better man.

Lannick turned that word over in his head.

Hope.

Brugan had seemed so very full of hope whenever he'd spoken of this endeavor. He'd wistfully recalled their old triumphs to the point he gave little regard to those terrible obstacles before them. He so hoped for that sense of redemption he was sure could be their prize, and seemed so certain they could make it so.

It was a sense of hope Lannick hadn't possessed during those many long years after the slaughter of his family. It seemed to him he'd lost all sense of that notion—of *hope*—while wallowing in wine and regret.

Except a hope for death, perhaps.

But things were different, now. Through all the self-doubt that still nagged him, Lannick had allowed Brugan's hope to convince him. He'd found himself *believing* there was a chance this task could be accomplished despite all the enemies and evils set before them. Even with all the horrors he'd seen at Vandyl's keep, even with the terrible losses he'd suffered, there was now some part of him that refused to allow that newfound sense of hope to slip away.

He thought of it as something Brugan had gifted to him, some part of the man that remained alive in spite of his passing.

Hope.

Lannick looked again to the men ahead, faces dour and gazes twitching about. Most eyes raked across the shadows rather than looked toward the coming storm, and brave men who'd known war and its dear costs seemed as nervous as new recruits. An oppressive silence hung upon them all.

Lannick knew their world had changed. He remembered how he'd long scoffed at the notion of dead gods and old powers and demons in the night. How he'd dismissed rumors of things lurking in the deepest dark.

And how all those old tales had become a stark and harrowing reality the moment his Coda had been lashed upon his wrist.

He rubbed his arm where the Coda had been. He'd removed it—again—just after they'd departed Thane Vandyl's keep. As much as he valued its protections against the enemy, he'd not fancied hearing the thoughts of others in his head nor others sensing some of his own. It was yet another rejection of his old oath, he knew, but he knew all the more that any victory required vengeance upon Fane first of all.

He shifted his crooked jaw. The task ahead seemed

more fraught with peril than ever, and even with an army marching with him there'd be no assurance of victory. Only a thin sliver of hope. Their prospects were far less than promising, and those small hopes were all they had.

Yet hope I have.

"Captain." The voice sounded like stones scraping together. "May I have a word?"

Lannick stirred and saw Randyn—the pock-faced and thin-haired sergeant who served as the leader of Vandyl's oath-bound—alongside him. "Of course, Sergeant."

"I remember you," he said.

Lannick frowned, worried the man meant to level some sort of accusation. Lannick certainly had no memory of *him*, and there were plenty of unsavory things he'd done over the previous decade he only faintly recalled.

"I remember you," Randyn said again. "I fought at Pryam's Bay, part of Rune's Second Column. My company got hemmed in on a frozen salt marsh by Tallorrathian raiders. We watched as General Fane and his men rode right past us. Left us for dead. We fought on through the day and lost more than half our number."

"Too many good men were lost that day," Lannick said.

He shook his head. "I thought for sure we'd be cut down to the last. Then you led your charge and set fire to the enemy ships. The raiders who'd trapped us were forced to flee back to the shore and we were saved. You saved us, Captain. I wanted to thank you."

Lannick blinked. "You… You are most welcome."

Randyn thrust out his hand. "Thank you. Thane Vandyl knew of this, and that's why he allowed me to ride with you. It's an honor."

Lannick shook Randyn's hand and smiled. "The honor's mine, Sergeant."

Randyn bowed his head. "Sir." He spurred his horse and rode back to a group of his men.

Lannick watched him, his heart warmed by old glories and new hope.

Just then a wind whipped, wailing a long, low howl, sounding much like the Necrists at Thane Vandyl's keep. Much like their vile words offering the promise of the dark, their horrid wails as they burned, and the piercing shrieks of the foul creature that killed Brugan.

Lannick's smile drooped. There were many more deaths certain to come. There were a thousand hardships still to face.

Yet there remained that sliver of hope. As bleak as the path ahead seemed, that sense of hope clung to him.

His hands found the hilt of his sword and the shape of his Coda.

And I cling to it.

They came upon the village of Fool's Leap by early evening, just after the winds rose and the clouds opened to hurl a hard rain upon them. The town—a few dozen buildings of stout wood with peaked, shingled roofs— stood on either side of a swollen creek crossed by a bridge of stone. A tangle of horses had been tied about several carts beneath a thicket at the town's edge.

"The men are sure to be at the tavern, Captain," rolled Kevlin's deep voice from Lannick's side. "Ulder Prane said there's a tavern near the town's center, just beside the bridge. Owned by some relation of his."

Lannick nodded and tugged tight his cloak. "We'll get inside and wait out the rain at least. How much farther is the deserters' encampment?"

"Another day of riding. Two or more if this weather holds."

"We shouldn't tarry long. We need to make that camp."

"Lannick," said Cudgen Ashworn, swiping raindrops from his sunken cheeks, "I'm no coward, but an evening spent in a tavern might be a good thing. A good thing for us all. The night's a little darker these days. Some ale in the belly and a fire in the hearth would help lift the spirits."

Lannick looked to Cudgen and caught a whisper of fear on his thin face. He could see Arleigh Lay just behind the man and he appeared no bolder. "Alright, then," Lannick said. "We'll stay the night but depart first thing in the morning."

Arleigh wiped his brow with the shiny stump that used to be his left hand. "There won't be too many wenches where we're headed," he said, voice swelling with what struck Lannick as false bravado. "I'd sure as hell have a night with one of them instead of the lot of you. To the tavern, boys!" he shouted, turning to the rest of the men. "One last night of women and ale before we head to war!"

A weak cheer came from the rest of the company. Even Thane Vandyl's oath-bound seemed cowed by the coming of night and their faces slackened in apparent relief at Arleigh's words.

"Thank you, Lannick," Cudgen said quietly. "I'd never have thought all those things you said were true. It's a mad thing, that."

Lannick nodded. "An awful thing, and no one wishes those old tales were false more than I. A world where the only wickedness is what's in the hearts of men is a world wicked enough."

"Now that's the damned truth. A good thing we're heading off to kill the wickedest of them all."

Lannick grimaced and spurred his horse onward. He took the company's lead and soon they entered the village proper. They crunched across gravel roads crowded by well-built homes and shops and smithies. Most of the structures were shuttered, though candlelight still shone from some.

"Just there," rumbled Kevlin, pointing. "*The Unclaimed Crowns* is the tavern Ulder spoke of. Said a cousin of his owns the place."

The tavern bore a shingle adorned with the image of five gold coins. Yellow light and the din of loud voices poured from the round windows lining its two stories. Through them Lannick spied many patrons, a fair number of them familiar.

He fastened the reins of his horse to a tie post at the tavern's side and made his way to the door, pausing once he reached it. Loud laughter rolled from within. Lannick knew the mood would change once the men heard of Brugan's demise, and he dreaded delivering the news.

He squeezed the knob, swallowed hard and pressed open the door.

The interior of *The Unclaimed Crowns* roiled with a chorus of voices and the heavy smell of pipe smoke. It was an impressive space aglow with candles, a great two-storied room of dark walnut with a stout bar at its center.

Behind the bar a thin rail of a man darted about, filling tankard after tankard and handing them to the patrons crowded about him. A good number of those gathered were strangers, though mingled amongst them were the old soldiers of Pryam's Bay.

Lannick shook the rain from his cloak, drawing several gazes from the old soldiers. Their eyes narrowed with seeming skepticism, but widened as soon as Thane Vandyl's oath-bound began tramping their way inside. Those eyes then returned to Lannick and grew all the wider.

Lannick reckoned he'd have otherwise felt a swell of pride at the gazes but dread dragged at his heart.

A clutch of old soldiers pulled away from the bar and tumbled toward him. "It worked?" asked Hanner Hale, pressing his burly form forward. "Your plan *worked?*"

"Told you so!" said the skinny, red-haired Ulder Prane through a smug smile. "Never thought Vandyl'd send along some of his oath-bound, though. You must've done some clever talking, Captain."

"Upstairs," Lannick said, spying empty tables along the railing of the second floor.

Ulder threw out his hands. "Nonsense! We're closer to the ale here and there are many toasts to be made!"

"Upstairs," grumbled Arleigh Lay, coming to stand near Lannick. "We need a word."

Hanner scratched his salt-and-pepper beard and looked about. "Alright, but we should wait for Brugan at least. He's the one who brought this whole thing together."

Arleigh grunted. "You'll be waiting a long fucking time for that."

"Upstairs," Lannick said, disregarding the remark. "Now."

"Well enough," said Ulder with an irritated tone. "Cousin!" he howled toward the bar. "Some ale up top? Seems our captain has *ordered* us to head there for now."

The barkeep gave a long look then an exasperated nod in reply. He huffed and summoned a serving girl with a thin finger.

"Up the stairs, soldiers," Arleigh said flatly. "We've many things to tell, and not a one of them good."

<hr>

The loft of *The Unclaimed Crowns* stank with the smoke of many pipes and much spilled ale. The old soldiers of Pryam's Bay and Vandyl's oath-bound had filled the circular tables and now sat fingering tankards and shifting in their chairs. Their chatter had dimmed to a whisper and a good number of them glanced to Lannick with furrowed brows.

Lannick leaned against the rail surrounding the opening to the floor below, a pit in his guts and his tongue thick in his mouth. There was a part of him that had always felt out of place among these men, even before all that happened after Pryam's Bay. He was no speech-maker nor did he possess that sort of easy camaraderie often shared among brothers-in-arms. Brugan had been the bridge between him and the men, and now the big barkeep was gone forever.

Bile crept up his throat. He seized his tankard from the table before him and took a long draw and then another and another still.

"Easy," grated Arleigh beside him.

Lannick gave him a sidelong glance and put down the tankard. He looked out to the mass of dubious eyes, his stomach churning.

Things are bound to be a good deal harder without you, my old friend.

"Well?" yelped Ulder. "What is it? And where's Brugan?"

Lannick gritted his teeth, vainly hoping that doing so could stifle the word in his mouth and make it less true. He hung his head and took a weak step forward. "Dead," he said at last, the word feeling heavy as a hammer as it fell from his tongue. "Brugan is dead."

"Dead?" someone shouted.

Lannick nodded and shuddered inside.

The old soldiers sat in silence, mouths agape. After a long moment the news seemed to seep through them. Many slammed fists or spat curses. A few choked back sobs. Slowly there rose a din of laments.

"To Brugan!" someone shouted, raising his mug. "May he find his way to the heavens of the Elder God!"

"To Brugan!" the men roared in unison, knocking their tankards together.

Lannick lifted his tankard from the table. "To Brugan," he said quietly, then took a sip.

The men swallowed back their ale and raised their mugs to those about them. They chewed at their lips and nodded at remembrances told.

Hanner Hale stood from a table near the room's rear. "How?" he asked. "How'd he die?" Others echoed him.

Lannick's eyes fell to the floor. "At the hands of the vilest of creatures," he said, voice low. "We came upon the ancient enemies of Rune, the Necrists. We took them down, but they managed to slay several good men before we could. Brugan died fighting."

The men whispered and heads shook.

"*Necrists?*" asked Ulder Prane, his tone incredulous. "But those things are for stories! That couldn't—"

"They exist," Lannick said, his voice softer than he'd have liked. "They exist, and they wield the darkness facing us all."

"That can't be!" said Hanner. "Don't tell us that, Captain. What really—"

Arleigh Lay pressed ahead of Lannick, pushing him back with the stump of his left arm. "They tore Brugan's brains out!" he shouted. "Ripped them right out through his fucking mouth! We were there to see it, and any man who doubts our words can go straight to the old hells. Fuck you if you don't believe me!"

The gathered men fell dead quiet, almost as though Brugan's corpse had been dropped on one of their tables.

Lannick winced at the image of his friend's awful end. He staggered back, bracing against the railing once more. He reached for his tankard and held it, trying to find some shred of comfort. There was none, and the silence seemed crushing.

The floorboards sighed as Cudgen Ashworn moved to stand beside Arleigh. "It's true," he said. "No one's doubted Captain Lannick and his tales as much as Arleigh and I. But it's fact. A sad, terrible fact. We've a rough task ahead, even rougher than we thought."

"We saw it too," came a harsh voice from the loft's opposite end. It was Randyn, the pock-faced sergeant of

Thane Vandyl's oath-bound. He stood, his chainmail hauberk giving a faint hiss. He paced with loud steps amongst the men. "We saw it too, and those devils took three of my friends and left another in the throes of madness."

The loft remained quiet, the jovial sounds rising from the floor below a discomforting contrast. All the old soldiers—every one—wore expressions that shifted somewhere between fear and disbelief.

"They…" said Ulder Prane. "They're real? Those demons?"

Arleigh spat. "Dammit, Ulder! We saw what we saw!"

Ulder pressed a hand through the red mess of his hair. "May the dead gods save us all."

The company appeared dour and depressed, heads no doubt doubly troubled. Lannick thought of his dear friend, determined to keep his thoughts on the man's many fine qualities rather than his terrible end. He drew in a deep breath and looked upon the men, wondering what words Brugan would have for them. His heart lifted at that, and after a moment he pulled himself away from the wall and toward Arleigh and Cudgen.

"Hope," he said, his voice strong and clear. "Brugan gave all of us—perhaps me most of all—the hope that we could do this thing, the hope that we could conquer all those things set before us and set aright all the hardships behind. That hope didn't die with Brugan. Instead it's the part of him that lives on for so long as we hold it within us. Don't fear what foes stand ahead. With hope we will overcome them all. We will not allow Brugan's life, or his *hope*, to have been in vain. Rather we will make all those things he hoped for come to pass." He hoisted his tankard high. "Once more, to Brugan!"

The men sat silently for a moment, but soon boots stomped and hands clapped. "To Brugan!" they hollered. "To Brugan!"

Lannick joined their shouting, blinking back tears. "To Brugan!"

How I miss you, my friend.

Lannick sank onto a stool at the bar of *The Unclaimed Crowns,* the rest of the men still occupying the loft upstairs. The evening had grown late and the crowd on the main floor consisted of only a few townsfolk grumbling over slow trade, slim crops and a war raging not nearly far enough away.

The barkeep—Ulder's skinny cousin—was merely a third Brugan's size, though Lannick soon gathered he possessed almost as restless a tongue. "Ale?" the man said. "I brew it myself, of course, and folk come from miles around to drink it. In more peaceful times, a fair number of other tavern owners and innkeeps buy casks to pour in their own establishments. Best in the midlands, they say, one and all. But with all the rumors of Arranese war bands afoot there's likely no having the stuff outside these walls, least for a while."

Lannick nodded, looking past the man's thin frame to the array of libations behind him. Beside the casks of ale there stood several varieties of wines and whiskeys, each of them appearing more tempting and delicious than the last.

My dear friends. At last we meet again.

"So, ale it is?" the barkeep persisted.

"Ah, no," Lannick said through a grimace.

"What'll it be? Ulder says you boys have been riding for days. I got just about anything to cure a thirst. You have your pick."

Lannick chewed at his lip, savoring the word and eager to taste what it'd bring. "Whiskey," he said.

The man cocked his brow. "Whiskey it is. Any preference? I've a rare bottle from near the Waters of World's End, another from Pyrene. They're a tad pricey and full of peat, though gentlemen of discriminating taste usually fancy that sort of thing."

Lannick chuckled. "Gentlemen? I'm hardly one of those. Your cheapest will do just fine."

"Nah," the barkeep said, snatching a dusty bottle and pouring its honey-brown liquid into a metal cup. "You're no refined merchant or such. But Ulder's told me about you fellows, about where you're headed and what you intend. It's a brave and bold thing, and I'm hoping you succeed. This one's on me."

Lannick smiled. "Thank you kindly," he said, placing his elbows on the bar and letting his head droop. He took a sniff of the whiskey and savored its stinging scent, a smell that conjured memories of his time spent at *The Wanton Vicar*. As much as he regretted that time lost to despair, it was time spent with his best friend nonetheless. He thought of Brugan's lumpy face pressed near and speaking words of comfort or caution. He closed his eyes and exhaled, realizing he'd never heeded the latter and only rarely listened to the former.

He lifted the cup and took a small sip, catching the

flavor on his tongue. He held it there before swallowing, recalling—*vaguely* recalling in some cases—those many times Brugan had tried to set him straight.

There was a sadness there, and Lannick regretted it much. He so wished Brugan could have lived to see him become a better man, to see him seize some measure of redemption. He wished Brugan could have lived to see that his hopes weren't all in vain.

I'll not let you down again, he thought, then set down the cup and pushed it away.

"You don't care for it?" asked the barkeep.

"Quite the contrary. I rather enjoy the stuff *too* much, if I'm being honest."

The barkeep's mouth bent with a knowing smile. "I used to drink too much myself as well. After a time, though, I learned to start dealing with my troubles instead of running from them."

Lannick nodded. "I reckon I'm finally doing the same."

"That's good to hear, because from what I gather you have enough trouble ahead of you. No need to drag along more of your own. Ah," he said, eyes looking past Lannick. "It seems another of your band has arrived."

"Who—" Lannick said, twisting about to see the door behind him.

A thick figure stood in the doorframe, lost in shadow but for the outline of a green, knee-length cloak. The newcomer brushed raindrops from the shoulders of the cloak, a garment identical to Lannick's own. He took a long stride into the tavern's golden candlelight, revealing a squint-eyed face squatting atop a nearly non-existent neck.

"Lannick," the thickly-built Variden said in a low, hoarse voice. He moved with quiet steps to Lannick's side.

"Uh…" Lannick said with utter surprise. His hand moved to his sword, worried the man had come to exact punishment for the perceived betrayal. "Ogrund?"

The man nodded, studying Lannick with eyes that seemed almost closed.

"A drink, friend?" asked the barkeep.

"No," Ogrund said firmly. "Just a private word with my… old comrade."

"Very well," the barkeep said, darting away to attend to others.

"Hmm," Ogrund grumbled. "A new coat of armor, a new sword, and, from what I understand, a small army. Yet here you are, sitting on a stool at a bar with a cup of whiskey before you. It seems you've not changed at all."

Lannick felt heat upon his cheeks. He wound his hand about the hilt of his weapon. "It's not what it appears, Ogrund."

"Is it not? I see no Coda upon your wrist, and we've heard nothing from you aside from a brief moment in Ironmoor and another in Rellic. On both occasions you used Valis's great gift, his sacrifice, to protect yourself. Do you not remember your oath? Your Coda is meant to be used to protect the whole of Rune, not to serve the purpose of a single man. Perhaps it should have found another more worthy of its divine blessing?"

Lannick stood, meeting Ogrund's narrow stare. "Yet it didn't. Just why do you think that is? It's because I serve a greater purpose than myself, in spite of what you and the others presume. And the whiskey? A last toast to a man I watched die at the hands of a Necrist just two nights ago. He was a dear friend, and deserved a far better death."

"Alas," the Variden said, "such are the wages of this war. In spite of all our efforts, many more will die. Only by holding true to our eternal cause can we hope to light the darkness."

Lannick looked to the man and his thick, impassive features, and wondered if there burned the scantest ember of emotion within him. He knew Ogrund to be a fearless guardian of Rune, though every word he uttered seemed a practiced, hollow platitude. "You should leave, Ogrund," Lannick grated, squeezing the hilt of his sword.

"I cannot, Lannick. Not until we have seen this through."

"Seen what, exactly?"

Ogrund made a swift movement, twisting as his hands sought something within the shadows of his cloak. Lannick started to pull his sword free of its scabbard but soon stopped short.

Ogrund bowed stiffly, a shining blade resting upon his upraised palms. Lannick knew the sword—his old prize. The trophy presented to him by High King Deragol himself after Pryam's Bay. The sword marking him Protector of Ironmoor.

The very sword Fane stole from me after his bastards beat me down.

"Your old sword," Ogrund said in his gravelly voice. "Wil remembered you said that General Fane took it, so he burgled his way into the general's manor at Ironmoor to regain it. I thought it both unscrupulous and unnecessary, but he insisted. It is at his request I deliver it to you here."

"Wil?" Lannick asked incredulously as he studied the weapon. The longsword shone as it ever did, honed to a deadly precision. Runic marks ran down the center space between the twin edges, ancient words reading 'Protector of Ironmoor.' The crossguard, a shiny brass that contrasted the blade's silver hue, was etched with the image of a dragon with wings extended outward to the guard's ends.

"He believed in you," Ogrund said, his expression flat. "He believed in you, even when others doubted, even when you broke your oath and left the order. Perhaps... Perhaps that is why he seemed the most bitter after we rescued you."

Lannick took the sword, a long breath escaping his lips. "Send him my thanks, Ogrund."

Ogrund eyed the sword. "There is no need. You'll be able to thank him yourself. Once he's accomplished his present mission he intends to accompany us to war."

"Us? You have no place among these men. Nor does he. You told me I was set upon some misguided revenge, that I was a prideful fool, that—"

Ogrund raised a hand. "We were mistaken. You foresaw evils we did not. We will help you destroy General Fane, and after that you will help us win the war against Arranan's Spider King."

Lannick fought off a smile as unexpected joy swelled within him. "I will, Ogrund. I swear to you I will."

11
ONLY MEN

ZANDRACHUS BALE TRUDGED onward, shuffling footsteps dragging across the slate of hard earth. The sun tilted just past midday but exhaustion had already set heavily upon him. He burned as though he baked in his brown robes and his face was slicked with a curtain of sweat.

He squinted, seeing naught but a bleak canvas of yellow dotted by stones that seemed like bleached bones poking from a shallow grave. Shimmering heat rose from the surface of everything, a spiteful illusion of water. Bale fumbled with the cap of his wineskin then sucked in a sip of warm water that did no more than taunt his swollen tongue.

There were no features to mark their location, no quaint signs telling distance as there were in many parts of Rune. Only Alisa's assurance they were getting nearer to Zyn. That, and the firm point of the seeking stone held in his hand.

"Keep up," Alisa barked from a dozen yards ahead. "There are eyes on the horizon." She gestured with a nod. "We must find cover."

Bale shaded his gaze and stared across the featureless landscape. He saw nothing but an endless waste. "Where?" he croaked through dry lips.

"There," said Lorra from beside him as she jabbed a finger, pointing to something Bale's eyes failed to perceive. "A village, and a group of riders leaving it. Six or seven of them."

"Seven," Alisa said firmly. "Seven is a sacred number to the Arranese. It is a war band, seven riders strong. They are moving quickly."

Bale strained his eyes in the direction of still-indiscernible riders. Waves of heat, yellow dirt, outcroppings of jagged rocks, some scrubby brush, and... And then he spotted them. Small, dark motes shifting in the heat and marring the barren plain, creeping across the steppe like insects. Panic swept over him. "Are they coming this way?" he said, words tumbling over themselves.

"In this direction generally," Alisa said, "though not precisely toward us. I don't think they've seen us, but if they have keen eyes they most certainly will soon. There. Make for those rocks. I can conceal us there."

Bale's heart thumped and he quickened his pace, keeping low just as Alisa did ahead of them. Stinging sweat dripped from his brow and blurred his vision. He rubbed madly at his eyes and tumbled, falling hard against the earth.

I am too weak an instrument!

Lorra dropped to a knee beside him and placed a

hand upon his shoulder. "They are still far away," she said gently. "We'll be safe."

Bale lay still for a moment, blinking, worried he'd sustained injury. He quickly realized there was nothing beyond his usual arthritic aches. He took Lorra's hand and shuffled upward, then rushed ahead on clumsy legs.

Alisa crouched behind a formation of white rock just taller than her huddled form. She had her green cloak wrapped about her and gestured them over, a stern look upon her face.

Bale and Lorra closed the distance quickly then stumbled to a stop beside Alisa. They drew close together, collapsing in a tight knot behind the rock, holding hands and bowing their heads. Bale trembled, and as he did Lorra rubbed him with rough encouragement.

"Shh, Bale," Lorra whispered. "I am your courage."

Bale cowered near her, shuddering. His overlarge nose caught the stink she carried from many days of travel. He breathed deeply and took comfort in it, knowing it was *hers*.

They waited long minutes pressed against the rock, Bale quivering and Lorra soothing him. Alisa seemed eerily calm, caressing the strange bracelet of dull iron clasped about her wrist.

"You are not worried?" Bale asked, his voice shrill.

Alisa looked to him, a cryptic look in her wide, brown eyes. "My order has secrets, Bale, as does yours. These appear to be mere men riding upon the plain, none possessing any understanding of arcana. We will remain hidden to their eyes. Be still, and you will look no more than a stone to them."

Bale shook his head. He heard the drumming of approaching horses and shook, squeezing against Lorra's bony frame.

"Be still…" Alisa said softly.

Bale drew a deep breath and held it. He shut his eyes, listening as the sound of hooves on hard earth grew steadily louder. His heart was a staggering hammer in his chest, the sound of its uneven beats a dreadful echo of the horses. Seconds seem to draw into minutes and the horses' gallop became a thunderclap in his ears.

He eased an eyelid open, his vision hazy from the sun's glare. Giant shapes of black moved before him and the ground shook. Bale's vision adjusted, and he saw seven Arranese warriors riding away on massive horses. They were draped in oiled leather and from the horses beneath them many weapons—long bows and longer spears—dangled and clacked.

The Arranese seemed lean and hard and fearsome, but they did not look back. Indeed, they took no notice at all of Bale and his companions, instead riding onward upon the steppe. Soon they were nearly a hundred yards distant and showed no signs of slowing.

Bale drew a relieved breath and then another, trying to calm his stuttering heart. He found his wineskin and took a long drink. His breathing eased a bit, his head finding reassurance in the fact that these Arranese, though known to be fierce warriors, were only men made of the same flesh and bone as he. They were not undead horrors like the chattering hobblers in Cirak, nor practitioners of the foulest arts of the dark like the Necrists. They were men, suffering from the same limitations as any other, perhaps capable of feeling the same fear and uncertainty.

He took comfort in this notion and sighed.

Only men.

Bale slouched wearily aside the fire, watching Lorra cook in the waning sunlight. She sat stirring a steaming pot of beaten metal, sprinkling into it various crumbs that would seem no more than dirt had Bale not tasted her concoctions before. His face lifted to a wan smile and his slouch deepened.

He saw Alisa sitting far from the fire on a slight rise. She seemed to have her eyes closed and her hand was wrapped about the iron bracelet she wore—a "*Coda*" he thought it was called. He heard the sound of whispered words slipping from her mouth.

He shifted and upon doing so felt a sharp pain in his feet, the sting from the bends in his boots and a good distance walked. He winced and removed his boots and threadbare socks, then rubbed feet that had always seemed to him too skinny with toes too long. He found the swell of new blisters and the painful patches where others had popped and the skin had rubbed away.

He retrieved his traveling pack and fished from it his sleeve of reagents. He undid the clasp and unfurled the sleeve, eyes darting across the many pockets in the faltering light. He found it quickly, the herb he needed, and snatched a few pinches of the dried leaves from the pocket.

He held the crumbled leaves, dripped some water from his wineskin across them, then rubbed his hands together until he felt a thick liquid form. He applied the balm to his feet, in between his toes and over the blisters. The substance cooled the skin and the wounds felt mended soon after contact.

He breathed deeply and wiggled his toes. "Much better. All ready for another stroll at sunrise!"

Lorra regarded him with a disdainful squint. "Your feet stink. Keep them away from the food."

Bale nodded meekly and pulled his socks back on. "Sorry."

She grunted and set about stirring the pot's contents. "I don't know what kind of rat your new friend Alisa caught, but it smells less foul than your feet. It'll make a decent stew."

Bale sighed and settled back, heaving his traveling pack behind him and lying against it. The heat had abated, with the sun almost beneath the far horizon and the sky a deepening purple. He gathered his robes about his thin form and allowed his gaze to wander.

The steppe seemed a barren land of dust and scrub, darkened by long shadows stretched by the sinking sun. Faint pinpricks of yellow colored a distant rise, no doubt an Arranese village with fires to chase away the coming night. It was miles away, and, after troubling over the distance a moment, Bale decided there was no cause to worry.

He looked skyward and watched as the stars blinked to life. It was a sight he'd not often seen in the many years he'd spent sequestered in the Abbey, where most of his evening hours had been spent poring over a candlelit book in the deep bowels of the library. The Arranese sky seemed tremendous when compared to the sliver he'd peeked at from the Abbey's windows, a vast and daunting gulf of *nothing* that surrounded the whole of the world and was unbothered by the tiny stars flickering within it. It seemed an ominous darkness, a great shadow surrounding all things.

Bale thought on this, but then recalled the gentler tales. He remembered the ancient writings of the Old Faith, those that told of the creation of the world and the sky above. The tales claimed the stars were the torchlights of guardians of the gates the Elder God's heavens. He imagined the guardians to be kind-eyed, looking down upon him from innumerable, unassailable towers about the heavens. He eased against his traveling pack and curled upon the hardpan dirt, suddenly thinking he could find it almost as comfortable as his lumpy bed at the Abbey.

Lorra shoved a steaming bowl toward him. "Eat."

"Thank you," Bale said, rising on an elbow. He looked at the shallow bowl and sniffed at it with his overlarge nose, smelling strange but appetizing scents mingling with what smelled vaguely like rabbit. He trolled his spoon through the thin stew of stringy meat and lumpy vegetables, then took a bite. It seemed as delicious as anything he'd eaten since leaving Ironmoor those many weeks before.

Lorra looked to him, her gaze expectant as he ate. "I enjoy cooking for you, Bale."

Bale smiled. "Thank you, again." He dragged his spoon about the bottom of the bowl then paused as he noticed an odd look in Lorra's eyes. He settled his spoon against the bowl's rim. "But why?" he asked.

She averted her gaze and was quiet for a time, her face sad and for a brief instant enraged. "Because..." she said, her tone carrying an edge. She tugged in a breath and her features slowly eased. "Because."

"Oh. Well, your efforts are much appreciated. I suppose I'd be a good deal thinner now if it weren't for your talents. I know incantations that can draw water from even the scrawniest desert bush, and I have reagents that can prevent starvation for a time, but—"

"Because," she interrupted. "Because the only men I'd known before you were all vicious, selfish bastards." She paused, her thin lips trembling. She spat and seemed to compose herself. "You're all the things they were not. You are weak and frightened and unsure of yourself."

Bale's waxing smile drooped, finding the words far from the compliment he'd expected. "No, perhaps not physically strong, but I like to think—"

"You are weak and scared and yet you are here. What's more, you are kind and caring and... Bale, I am with you because you give me hope. You give me hope that there is some good that refuses to be crushed beneath all the bad things in life."

His smile returned, wide and toothy. "Lorra, I'm finding you make me feel much the same. I'm glad you're with me."

The slightest of blushes colored her face and a tiny grin played on her lips. "Eat," she said firmly.

He dug into his stew with gusto.

Alisa roused them before dawn, the sky overhead a brightening purple and the eastern horizon warmed with only a faint hint of orange.

Bale rose haltingly on creaky knees, then rubbed at a

back that seemed unable to accustom itself to sleeping on a bed of hard earth. "Why so early?" he groaned.

Alisa looked eastward. "A caravan approaches, no doubt bound for Zyn. We're less likely to encounter trouble when entering the city if we're in the company of others, particularly merchants with an honest purpose there."

"You mean to join a caravan of merchants?"

Alisa nodded as she adjusted her scabbard. "We'll blend in, and won't be viewed with suspicion by the city guards."

"Are these merchants Arranese? Won't they have suspicions of their own?"

"My guess is they're Khaldisian, judging from the looks of them and the build of their wagons. Regardless, they are merchants, driven by profit. Any suspicions they hold will be assuaged by coin." She jingled a small purse that drooped from her belt.

Lorra grunted, rubbing away the sleep from her eyes. "More strangers?"

Bale looked to her and nodded. "I fear Alisa's right. The guards at the city gates are certainly used to merchant caravans entering the city, but likely not visitors from Rune."

Lorra grumbled and began gathering her things. Bale knelt near her and did the same, trying to offer a reassuring look as he did. "We should trust her," he said softly.

"You're the only person I trust, Bale. Everyone has some wickedness inside, some much more than others. There's good reason not to trust strangers."

Bale tucked a long strand of hair behind his ear and sighed, guessing there was little he could say to sway

Lorra's feelings. He double-checked his satchel for his wineskin and sleeve of reagents, drew his robes tighter and tugged on his boots.

"Let's move," Alisa said. "The caravan is drawing near."

They arose and followed Alisa as she set off east. They clambered over shattered ground, the land tilting upward in a long and uneven slope. Bale trailed behind Lorra and Alisa, finding the gravel and stone made for poor footing. He stumbled often, and used his hands nearly as much as his feet to ascend the rise.

At last the ground leveled to a wide plateau of flat rock. Bale rested hands upon his knees and drew heavy breaths. He was relieved to see Lorra waiting for him nearby, and Alisa not far beyond.

"Just there," Alisa said, gesturing, "beyond this hill. A road cuts its way across the steppe, all the way to Zyn."

They strolled across the plateau to its far slope. Soon, the sun broke the horizon and yellow stretches of light painted the landscape before them. All seemed bleak and barren, a canvas of dirt and rock. But there was movement upon it, a train of horse-drawn wagons trundling across the steppe just a hundred yards ahead. The wagons were piled with sacks and crates and cloths of many colors, and driven by men and women wearing robes of bright fabric that shone in the sunlight.

"Follow me," Alisa said, beginning the descent. "They'll mistake us for bandits in this place and at this hour, so let me handle the talking."

They scrambled down the hillside, the loose gravel fleeing their boots in tiny, hissing cascades. The riders of the caravan seemed quick to take notice, and Bale could see them shouting and whipping the reins with urgency.

Alisa ran to the road ahead of the caravan. She dropped to her knees and kept her hands in her lap, caressing her bracelet of dull iron. Bale rubbed at his eyes, seeing that she appeared different, somehow. Meek and less capable, her rich green cloak now a simple garment of rough cloth.

This is no mere trick of the light.

"Please!" she shouted, her voice a hoarse wail. "We are not thieves!"

The lead wagon closed the distance. The man perched on the bench—a lean Khaldisian with eyes lined with heavy charcoal—pulled the horses to a stop just before they could trample Alisa's crouched form.

"Make way," the man said, hefting a curved sword. "We have no food for beggars."

Alisa bowed low to the ground. "Kind sir, we are not beggars. We are mere pilgrims, traveling this land in hopes of seeing the glories of the Spider King at Zyn. But our journey has been beset by peril and I worry we will not reach our destination. May we travel with you, so that we are safe? We will pay good coin for passage."

The man turned to his companions, a collection of ten or so Khaldisians seated atop four dusty wagons. Their olive faces, bearing similar dark linings about the eyes, were implacable.

The man looked to Bale for a moment in seeming appraisal, then to Lorra and at last back to Alisa. He lowered his sword.

Alisa raised her head from the earth and returned the man's gaze expectantly.

He cocked his dark brow. "How much coin?"

Prefect Gamghast sat alone in the Abbey's vast dining hall, the hour well past midnight but still well before dawn. He picked apart what was left of a skinny half-chicken in the dim candlelight, collected a clump of greasy meat, then dipped it in the puddle of gravy on his plate. He dribbled half the gravy or more across his white beard as he drew the morsel to his mouth with a trembling hand.

He cursed, knowing the shakes came from more than just old age and injury. He brushed away the larger dollops that'd fallen into his beard, chewed the dry, over-cooked chicken and swallowed hard.

He sighed and his shoulders slumped. The bare bones and slack skin of the chicken suddenly seemed a wreck of a thing, a carcass sucked of the life that once animated it. His thoughts turned to the Necrists he'd seen at the Godswell, their hideous faces patched with the flesh of the newly dead.

The thought sickened him.

And it angered him. Nearly as much as did his feeling of impotency in the face of such power.

He struggled upright, tired eyes drifting to the rafters. The wooden beams were distinguishable only by virtue of being painted a slightly lighter hue than the shadows surrounding them. He thought then of that horrid swirl of darkness—of Yrghul—defiling the holiest place in all of Rune.

He patted his beard, mind whirling for some way to confront this evil.

He could think of nothing particularly promising.

We are only men. How can we overcome such evil?

He pondered this for a long moment. The enemy's victory would be assured if those capable of action remained paralyzed by fear, lost in worry. Old and broken as he felt, he knew he could still serve to defend Rune, and there were others yet loyal to the cause, as well. Victory seemed a scant hope, but a hope it was.

He grunted, grabbing the table's lone candlestick with one hand and his walking staff with the other. He shuffled along the darkened aisle between the dining hall's long tables and toward the door.

He spotted a tall figure at the door and he stopped, a sudden fright seizing him. He thrust his candlestick forward, though the light failed far short of the doorway and the figure remained cloaked in darkness. "Who comes?" he demanded, the strength of his voice lost in the empty space of the chamber.

"My apologies, Prefect," came a calm yet firm voice— a woman's. "You seemed preoccupied and I thought it best not to disturb."

"Queen Reyis?" he asked uncertainly, eyes straining to make sense of the woman's features in the dark.

"That title seems a bitter taste of irony after being forced to flee my castle, Prefect. But yes, it is I. May we speak privately?"

Gamghast managed a swift, stiff bow in spite of the queen's previous admonitions against formalities. "My queen! Your presence here is still a secret and you must not be seen in these halls! This is not safe, even at this late hour!"

Queen Reyis waved a hand dismissively. "My

attendants scouted ahead for me for precisely the reasons you mention. But again, my question. May we speak privately?"

Gamghast straightened. "To my quarters? There we may speak far from the ears of others."

"Lead the way, Prefect."

Gamghast nodded and shuffled past into the tight, winding hallway beyond. The candlelight struggled against the dark, though Gamghast reckoned after so many years in this place he needed the light not at all.

"You're finding sleep a rare thing as well, my queen?" he asked.

She breathed deeply. "Of course I am. It is all crumbling about us, Prefect. The whole of our world."

He turned his neck—painfully—to Queen Reyis walking near his shoulder. She looked frail in the light's flicker, her face drawn and her flaxen hair revealing many strands of gray. She walked haltingly, her belly swollen with child. She held a hand against the swell and a wince squeezed her delicate features.

"All of it," she continued. "All seems destined for ruin."

"This way," Gamghast said flatly, turning down another dark hallway.

They walked for long moments, the Abbey's corridors quiet but for the rustle of their robes and the clack of Gamghast's walking staff upon the stone tiles. Shifting candlelight crept timidly from beneath occasional doors they passed, no doubt that of acolytes unnerved by recent events.

They arrived at his quarters. He turned the knob and

pressed the head of his staff to move the door open, then bowed stiffly and gestured for the queen to enter.

His quarters were the same as ever, with his simple bed, simple desk, and simple chairs. *Practical*, he thought. However, with Queen Reyis, the queen of all of Rune, standing in the room's center, the place seemed embarrassingly paltry.

"My apologies, Queen Reyis," Gamghast said, rushing to light the stout candle on his table with the one in his hand. "I've never had occasion to entertain a visitor of such stature, and I realize this place must seem—"

"Nonsense," she said, silencing him with an upraised hand. "You need apologize for nothing, Prefect. Your quarters seem a stateroom to me, and your Abbey has been a most welcome and comfortable refuge." She held her belly and eased into a seat, then fixed him with an odd look. "I spent much of my youth in poverty. You didn't know that, did you? Only two men in Ironmoor did, and they're both dead. My husband, and his father before him… One who comes from poverty never forgets that struggle, and never feels fully at ease amidst luxury."

Gamghast smiled. *I like this queen.* He folded himself painfully into the chair opposite her, rubbing his still-aching back.

Queen Reyis looked to the room's small window and the darkness beyond. "Of course, we needn't worry over the comforts of possessions, certainly not at this dire hour. The poor and the wealthy seem destined for the same ending now, do they not?"

Gamghast grunted. "Aren't they ever destined for that same ending, my queen? Death comes to us all, every one."

She nodded with a smile that seemed at once elegant and humble. "That is as I've always thought, despite the bold proclamations one often hears in the company of nobility. Though," she said, her smile faltering, "*this* ending seems terribly imminent, and terribly certain. No matter the wealth or influence or power one has, death seems certain to arrive at the door as quickly as to the doors of all others. Tannin told me what you witnessed at the Godswell, Prefect. Is this the end of all things?"

Gamghast drew a shaky hand across the wisps of his white beard, smearing a droplet of gravy as he did. He pulled in a deep breath. His thoughts turned suddenly to Acolyte Bale, wondering whether he was close to home and whether he'd been able to learn anything that might help their cause.

Or if he's perished along the way...

"Prefect? I ask my question in earnest."

"I'm sorry, my queen. At times my head struggles with the weight of these concerns. You know of the old histories? The War of Fates? Illienne and Yrghul and the Sentinels?"

"I did not spend my days in the Bastion simply fretting over pomp and finery, Prefect."

Gamghast waved his hands in protest. "Of course not, my queen. Again, I apologize and meant no offense. It is just that we in the Abbey spend so much time tucked within these halls of quiet stone, noses drooped over dusty books. When we do venture without it seems those we encounter give no mind to the antiquities we study, and no longer heed the tenets of our faith."

"No offense taken. Life in the Bastion can be equally

secluding. But my answer is yes, I know of Illienne's division and the demise of Yrghul. Tannin described the fearsome creature you saw. Is that what emerged from the Godswell? Yrghul?"

He looked to the night sky outside his window. "I fear so, my queen. Yrghul, or at least some reflection of his power."

"How can that be? He is bound in oblivion, and only a High King can touch the well's waters."

"I do not know. Yrghul has followers, dark sorcerers known as Necrists. They've lurked in the shadowy places of the world since the War of Fates, but recently seem to have grown bolder and more powerful. They were present at the Godswell that night—in the company of the chamberlain—and were able to draw something of their vile master into this world. The Necrists poured blood into the well, my queen, and it seemed to work as a sort of key. I worry the blood was that of your husband."

Queen Reyis stiffened in her chair, her expression stoic. "These things dare defile his body?"

"That is nothing when measured against what they intend."

"And what is that? What are they?"

"I cannot fathom their ultimate aim, though it seems certain whatever that is will entail the death of days, the end of light. Their lord Yrghul gave himself over to darkness more than a thousand years ago, when his kingdom was ruined and became the Bowl of Fire. It was ruined by a fallen star and became the most desolate place in all the world. The departed souls of his land sought the heavens of the Elder God, and Yrghul tried in vain to cling to them, to drag them back. When they refused, he grew mad, choosing as his new realm the black of night, the horror of nightmares, the creep of decay. The old texts say he scoured their corpses for whatever was left and eventually found something there, some dark residue of life that could be shaped to a foul purpose. With that, he empowered new followers. They became his pupils, his acolytes. They are our enemy. They are the Necrists."

"And now they are the companions of the chamberlain, laying claim to the Bastion."

Gamghast nodded, feeling a somber resolve settle upon his heart. "They must be cast out, my queen. They must be excised, along with Chamberlain Alamis. The risk of confronting him—and them—is far outweighed by the risk of failing to do so. Allowing them to fester here unchallenged will only allow them to grow stronger."

Queen Reyis looked to Gamghast with inquisitive eyes. "And how can this be done? How can I help this cause?"

Gamghast raised a shaking hand. "You should not be troubled with such things. The welfare of the Bastion and its denizens has long been the concern of my order."

"Nonsense, Prefect," she said. "The Bastion is *my* home. Its master grows in *my* belly. This cause is as much mine as anyone's and I will not permit that traitor Alamis to desecrate my husband's legacy any more than he already has."

Gamghast met her stern glare. After a moment, he nodded. "Very well, my queen. Let me delve into some of our older texts. We will concoct a cure for what poisons the Bastion."

12
THE HAND THAT SAVED THE WORLD

PREFECT KREER SAT straight in the saddle of his well-built mare. She was an impressive beast, nearly seventeen hands tall with an unblemished white coat and a neatly braided mane of gold that shone in the glow of the late afternoon sun. She struck him as a most suitable mount, a symbol of the righteousness of his purpose.

A purplish smile stretched beneath the old man's long nose. His cause *was* righteous, he knew, and this notion pleased him much. His faith filled him, it drove him.

It always had.

He'd been a fine horseman in his youth, roving his family's estate atop a magnificent ebony stallion. He'd always loved riding, at least until the day his horse killed his youngest brother when its hoof caught the child's head. The beautiful, sandy-haired boy—rosy-cheeked and ever-smiling—had been just five years old at the time. Kreer had wept as he watched his brother twitch upon the straw-covered floor of the stable, bleeding from the hole in his skull and his exposed brain.

Kreer had prayed that day with all the conviction in his heart, certain the dead gods could save the child. However, his faithless father refused the arts of a local acolyte from the Sanctum. The boy died within hours, and his father hanged himself soon thereafter.

Kreer *knew* the Faith could have saved his young brother. After both the boy and his father were laid to rest in graves near the family's manor, Kreer had asked his mother's permission to disclaim any inheritance and join the Sanctum. His faith was pure, he knew, and he wanted nothing more than to devote his life to the Faith and the healing gifts granted to those who served it. Through her tears his mother told him she understood, confessing to him she knew the dead gods had destined him for greater things after having taken the life of his baby brother.

He'd thrown himself into prayer and study for decades at the Sanctum, hoping to find the heart of truth and the fate the dead gods intended for him. Eventually, after years of excelling in all the Sanctum's most sacred disciplines, he was elevated to the rank of prefect. The Sentinel Castor himself—then Lector Erlorn—had disclosed to him the order's deepest secrets, and Kreer's faith told him he'd one day lead the Sanctum. When he'd failed to be elected Dictorian at the Sanctum's last Quorum he'd doubted, though not for long. Now, with the Dictorian dead, Kreer knew Illienne's divine providence rested upon him.

The Faith swelled within him, consuming his every

thought. He was bound to become the purest of instruments, set to a direction dictated by the very gods. He would echo the divine.

His would be the hand that saved the world.

"Any sign yet?" he called to the two green-cloaked Variden riding ahead through the hill's tall grasses. "The seeking stone pointed this very way, and there is no truer means of drawing it to its pole than with the blood of the person sought." He brandished a stoppered vial and shook its scarlet contents. "The highlander cannot be far!"

One of the green-garbed men—Wil, he was called—spun his horse about. He was a middle-aged man with a soft, youthful face, though fierce eyes burned beneath his rounded bowl of brown hair. "The signs of their passage are growing fresher, Prefect," he said. "They have fast horses but they've ridden them hard. They'll soon need to slacken their pace. With any luck we should be upon them within a couple of days at the latest."

Kreer's smile widened. "Very well," he said, waving a hand about. "Ride along, then!"

Wil stared back to Kreer with a cocked brow that seemed to express insult, though he said nothing.

Kreer dismissed the gaze, guessing the man had only a thin grasp of the pure purpose that drove this endeavor. He sniffed the countryside's manure-tinged air and bounced along all the merrier. He patted the saddlebag containing his tome of ancient and holy rites and made ready to meet his destiny.

Soon Castor's spirit would fill him. His faith would reshape it and guide it back to its true path.

He knew this to be true. Faith demanded it.

Prefect Kreer stretched his long bones alongside the evening's fire, then creaked open his leather-bound tome to reread for what seemed the hundredth time the great Rites of Excision, Exorcism, and Unmaking. He studied the yellowed pages by the fire's flicker, making certain his memory of the passages remained true, that there was no word of which he was uncertain.

There could be no mistakes this time, and no hesitation about taking the highlander's life. There could be no holding back. No allotment of mercy that could allow the highlander to retain Castor's spirit.

No.

The man's body and soul needed to be rent asunder so that the spirit could find rest within a proper vessel.

So it can find rest within me, a man unwavering in the Faith.

"I will not be gentle with him," Kreer mumbled.

"I'm sorry, Prefect?" said Lund, one of the two brown-robed acolytes tending his supper nearby. He was a skinny fellow of perhaps twenty years with red hair and freckled cheeks. "You require something, sir?" he asked.

"Nothing, Acolyte. Just be ready when we confront the highlander. Be ready, and be pure in your faith. You will need to join your prayers to mine and not falter."

"Are you certain?" said Barly, the other acolyte. He had a pale, doughy face and a voice pitched too high for Kreer's liking.

"Am I certain of what?" Kreer said sharply, setting aside his book.

Barly shook his fat head. "Sorry. I misspoke. It's

just that with the news of the High King's passing I worry that…"

Kreer's eyes narrowed and he drew nearer to the fire. He glared at the two acolytes until both shrank before his gaze. "I will not tolerate doubt. A faith plagued by doubt is no faith at all. You must believe—you must *know*—that Illienne's great purpose lights our way. If we stay true to the Faith, and act in the way that best serves it, we will overcome this darkness."

The acolytes nodded, eyes straying to the fire they tended.

"Very well. Cast any doubt from your hearts, for doubt is what allowed this highlander to murder our Dictorian and escape from the Abbey. We had him—the very man who slew Lector Erlorn—but he slipped his chains when the faith of one of our prefects wavered."

Damn your arrogance and apprehensions, Gamghast.

Lund looked to him. "How could a mere man do such a thing? Was he possessed by a demon, as the rumors claim?"

"No…" Kreer said, mulling over whether he should tell the young men the Sanctum's secret, that the Lector was in truth the Sentinel Castor and that the highlander now held that spirit. After a moment he sniffed. It seemed to him the rules were different now with the Lector and High King dead and the kingdom at war. What was more, the acolytes needed to understand the stakes if they were to participate with the fervor required of them. "No," Kreer said again. "Not a demon, but a Sentinel."

Their eyes widened, glittering in the firelight. "W-what?" Barly stammered, jowls quivering.

Kreer matched their gazes. "It is true. The Sentinel Castor. It is the Sanctum's most sacred—and most closely guarded—trust, to have among our number a man possessing the immortal spirit of one of Illienne's seven chosen Sentinels. Castor has lived in the form of every Lector the Sanctum has had, and has guided us in all matters of the Faith. Castor refused to abide his banishment, knowing his oath to Illienne to protect Rune to be far more binding than an edict from a jealous king. And so he has lived secretly among us for nearly a millennium."

The acolytes sat slack-jawed.

"The highlander?" Barly squeaked at last. "*He* has Castor's spirit?"

"You doubt?" Kreer asked, steepling his fingers.

After a time the young men shook their heads.

"There can be no such thing as doubt in your hearts," Kreer said. "Doubt erodes purpose. Doubt destroys courage. You cannot doubt anything I say to you, nor can you question my commands."

"We doubt not at all, Prefect," said Lund.

"Good. To answer your question, then, yes, the highlander possesses the spirit. For now. He holds the spirit of a Sentinel, and this possession defiles the Faith. We must regain it or all could be lost."

They nodded again, their expressions earnest.

"Very well," Kreer said. "Now you understand why our quest is so critical. Now you know why we must recapture what this monster has stolen. We will save the world when we do."

Prefect Kreer awoke just after dawn, the day's perfect,

golden light shining brightly upon him. The sun seemed a divine missive, a prophecy of purpose. It filled his old flesh with new vigor, a feeling of imminent possibility and power.

He shut his eyes and soaked it in, drawing his robes aside to allow the light to shine upon his naked body and through to his core. He squirmed upon his bedroll in the sunlight, a grin upon his face. The spirit would be his. It seemed even the heavens knew this to be true.

Yes. I awake this day a mortal man, but soon will offer myself as a vessel for the divine.

"Prefect," came a stern voice. "Clothe yourself."

Kreer snapped his eyes open to the sun's blinding glare. He could make out a shape obstructing the light, perhaps a man in a cloak. "Who dares—"

"I said clothe yourself." The stern voice was that of the Variden, the one called Wil. "Now."

Kreer grumbled an old curse beneath his breath as he pulled his robes to cover himself. He tied the garments together then sat upright, eyes narrowing in anger as much as an effort to dull the sun's blaze.

"The highlander," Wil said. "My brother Stendall scouted ahead and came upon the site of a slaughter. The tracks of the highlander and his companions lead to the place."

Kreer stared at the man for an instant, the weight of this news settling upon him. "Then it was the highlander who did the killing. He violates the spirit so long as he is possessed by it."

Wil nodded. "It seems he may not be far."

Kreer slipped narrow, bony feet into his boots and

arose, stretching to his full height so as to peer at the man from atop the long length of his nose. "Then it seems destiny will soon arrive, and I am glad to have the help of your order in delivering it. Illienne the Light Eternal has anointed us."

"We will need all the favor she can spare. Remember, when my departed brother Merek captured the highlander he had the aid of the man's companions. The highlander was unsuspecting and thus the enchantments more effective. What is more, the man may have grown in strength since then, as he's had more time to develop a bond with the spirit. Stendall and I may only be able to hold him for a short while."

"Worry not. I have been preparing for this moment for nearly all of my life."

Prefect Kreer tilted his chin sharply upward, the stench assaulting his nostrils. Below, at the base of the hill, rested the ruins of a sad hamlet aside a swift stream. Dozens of crows fed upon bloated, discolored corpses, squawking their satisfaction with the meal.

Kreer bowed his head and shut his eyes. *Sweet Illienne, please guide the souls of the faithful to the heavens, then guide my hand with your righteous purpose.*

Wil grunted from atop the horse beside him. "You see the tracks descending this very hill? Four horses. Those of the highlander and his companions."

Kreer took a deep breath of the acrid air as he opened his eyes.

Stendall, the other green-garbed Variden, shifted in his saddle and spat. He was a tall, lanky man with hawkish features and studied the scene with a keen gaze. "Could the highlander have slain all these people?"

"Yes," Kreer said. "I am certain of it. Search about and you will see this to be true."

"A desecration," Wil said, shaking his head. He rubbed the thick bracelet of black iron clasped upon his wrist. "Prefect, we should inspect the scene more closely. The dead often betray the secrets of the living. We'll require every advantage we can obtain when we find the highlander."

Kreer nodded. The beacon of his faith had ever shone brightly within him, and the carnage before him made it shine all the brighter. There could be no question—no doubt—about the truth of his decisions now. Castor had never meant for the highlander to seize his spirit, and less restraint should have been shown during the attempted excision at the Sanctum. The man was no vessel for the Sentinel; he needed to be slain so the spirit could be released.

Wil spurred his horse down the hillside, followed by Stendall. Kreer and his acolytes came after, their horses snorting and stamping in protest as they approached the dead.

"The highlander did this?" Barly squeaked in his high voice.

"He and his murderous companions," said Kreer stoically. "But the highlander most of all. He has twisted Castor's spirit to hideous ends, and we will not permit such defilement."

"Dead gods," Lund muttered. "Even children hacked apart!"

Kreer pursed his lips in disgust, again looking over what was left of the settlement. His eyes brushed across rag-clad bodies in crooked poses, from the very young to the very old. Around them stood a haphazard cluster of shanties, several of which had been reduced to ash with blackened bones resting within. Crows scattered from the corpses as they moved near, though quickly returned to their feasts once the group passed.

He heard Barly retch behind him, and amidst such a scene Kreer could not fault the young acolyte.

Ahead, Wil and Stendall slipped from their horses and tied the steeds to what was left of a tumbledown structure. They moved methodically about the bodies—squatting for quick inspections then moving briskly on—all the while clutching their iron bracelets.

Codas, they call them, Kreer remembered.

He dismounted as well, handing his mare's reins to Lund. He rifled through a saddlebag and retrieved his sleeve of reagents and his weighty tome. He found a spot of reasonably dry ground clear of the dead then knelt and unfurled the sleeve.

The stretch of leather held multitudinous pockets and pouches containing all the necessary components for the Sanctum's most potent incantations. There were powders, roots and herbs, those rarest of substances from the original creation of the Elder God, each bearing echoes of the divine. Illienne had known their potency, and had passed that wisdom to Castor.

And then Castor to me.

Kreer located the tiny pouch of dried dragwitch, a yellow nettle found in the deep jungles of Rimgald and planted by Castor long ago in the gardens of the Abbey. Kreer untied the thin strings and withdrew a pinch, studying the brittle leaves resting against his wrinkled palm.

I will bear witness to the highlander's depravity, and then none will doubt again.

"Acolytes!" he called. "A fire!"

Barly and Lund clambered off their horses, muttering as they trudged between the corpses. At last they snapped wood from the wreckage of a nearby hut and with shaking hands assembled the splinters into a pile beside Kreer. Lund produced flint, steel and some wispy tinder from his robes, and in time the sparks thrown by his scrapes yielded embers, smoke and flame.

Kreer shifted away as he awaited a proper fire. He pulled open his tome and gingerly leafed through it until he found his incantation: the Spell of Remembrance. It was a powerful incantation, one the Sanctum had not often used in the many years of relative peace in Rune. It required a confluence of circumstances, not least of which was a reasonably fresh, intact corpse that had been the victim of extreme violence.

I will stare into your very eyes, Highlander.

The fire crackled, the blaze becoming almost uncomfortably hot. Kreer closed his tome and drew close. "Fetch a corpse," he said, crumbling the dried dragwitch leaves in his palm. "The least mangled you can find."

Barly and Lund sighed and stood. They looked over the bodies nearby then appeared to settle upon one. They stooped and pulled the body across the mud to the fire. It was a dead woman—middle-aged and simply clad with red hair—frozen in a rigor with a pale arm bent as though clutching something no longer there.

A child, perhaps.

Kreer stretched out a hand and caressed the woman's blood-spattered forehead. He closed his eyes and calmed his mind. He focused upon faith and purpose, those purities that defined him. He scooted to the fire's burning edge, pressed out his other hand then tilted it to sprinkle the dragwitch upon the flames.

The fire roared and the dragwitch burned with a sweet scent and a white smoke. Kreer leaned close, nearly singeing his long droop of a nose as he inhaled the weed's citrus-like odor.

"*Illienne abralide y ganode rogo rab corpu!*" he whispered, the ancient words falling from his tongue with the weight of their power.

Illienne awaken and grant me the sight of the dead!

He waited, preparing to see the highlander and his companions. He prepared to bear witness to whatever deviltry the killers employed so as to better counter it with the teachings of the divine.

He inhaled again, drawing within a thick tendril of the dragwitch's smoke.

At once Kreer's consciousness shuddered. His thoughts were crowded by those of another, sights and sounds from some strange source floating upon the current of his mind.

He cried out, alarmed by what felt a sudden loss of self.

He pressed frantic hands about and found the coarse fabric of his robes. His eyes could not see it but it was there. He grasped it tightly; it was real. He breathed in, exhaled, and gave himself over to the vision.

He was swept to the moment just before the violence, just as the hamlet was raided. Shouted warnings sounded. He watched through the woman's eyes as she cracked open the door of her hovel and beheld sharp-featured men in hides and leather armor charging through the hamlet on horseback. They howled in harsh voices and hoisted curved blades and long spears.

The woman's gaze darted about and the sounds of her quickened breaths rushed and wheezed. There seemed no means of escape. She eased shut the door and moved its wooden latch into place.

A child wailed. Her child. Her daughter. She spun about and snatched the rag-swaddled, red-haired babe from her basket. She shushed the infant but the girl wailed all the louder. She drew the child close to her breast, offering softly spoken words of comfort. *"Hush now... It's alright, my little love. Mum's here. It's alright. Quiet..."*

The child's sobs subsided.

A frantic din sounded outside. The woman chanced a peek through the shutters of her small window. One of the mounted strangers—black-eyed and face full of rage—thrust a spear into a peasant's chest, driving him to the ground in a twitching heap.

The woman started to call out but stifled her words with a trembling hand. Clutching her child, she ducked away from the window and sank to the straw floor, into the shadows of the hovel's far corner.

More frenzied screams. The thud of hooves and the

clash of steel. Sounds of bodies falling to the wet ground. Moans of terrible pain.

All of that, yet the child seemed content, at ease. Her tiny mouth tilted upward and her green eyes rested upon her mother's face.

"It's alright, little love…"

Soon all fell quiet beyond the hut but for the squelch of boots and hooves and the utterance of terse commands. *"All are dead,"* came a man's sharply-accented voice. *"All except for a few of the women. Take your spoils!"*

The woman looked to her child, focusing solely upon her in the dark interior of the hut. She caressed the girl's pinkish face. With a shaking hand she soothed the girl's brow and stroked her red hair. Tears welled in the woman's eyes, her sight clouding over.

"Shh…" she whispered, naught visible but the pale circle of her daughter's face. *"It's alright, little love… Stay quiet, now."*

She blinked. Heavy tears dropped from her eyelids, falling to spatter upon the infant's round face.

The girl seemed startled but then smiled wide. She giggled—loudly—her cheeks dimpling. *"Mama!"* she blurted through a gleeful chuckle.

"Shh!" the woman hissed. *"Shh!"*

Footfalls slopped in the mud outside.

An instant later a loud crack and crash.

The woman's gaze jerked from her daughter's smiling face to the sight of a tall, long-haired invader smashing away the remains of the hovel's door. He had a curved sword drawn and a grim look upon his sharp features.

"No!" she shrieked, pressing back against the wall and

standing. She clutched her child with one arm and brandished a thin fist with the other. "*No!*"

The fierce-eyed marauder stormed across the short distance, kicking aside the hovel's flimsy furnishings. He feinted with his sword then thrust out his free hand, seizing the woman by her red hair as she recoiled.

She screamed. She squeezed her daughter close as she was dragged across the straw-covered floor. She flailed with her fist, striking the man's arm.

But to no avail.

She bawled as she was dragged stumbling across the sharp splinters that had been the door to her home. The man yanked her upward then tossed her out into the day's gray haze. She slipped and staggered, holding her daughter close. The child cried, now. Together they tumbled to the ground, a brown muck broken by crimson rivulets.

She scrambled back, away from the man. Away from the point of his weapon. She held out a hand as though it could ward away the blade.

She stopped suddenly. She had backed into something.

She turned and found herself faced with another stranger, this one shaven-headed with dark, almond-shaped eyes. The man grinned toothily. Others sat atop tall horses behind him, wiping wet blood from their blades.

The woman screamed, looking this way and that. Her village was a ruin. All about lay the dead.

She glanced to her daughter once more. *"It's alright, little love,"* she said in a frail, sweet voice.

She ran. Hopelessly she ran through across the muddy earth, holding her daughter close.

It was not long—seconds, perhaps—before a horse thundered aside her.

A shining blade swept across her vision, a silver arc across the gloomy sky.

She fell. She fell upon her side. Her child sobbed in the mud beside her, the girl's pale face now speckled with blood.

The woman reached, her arm twitching with spasms. She clawed at the mud, drawing her arm outward.

At last she found her daughter and pulled her close one last time.

Then all faded to black.

"Prefect Kreer!"

Kreer blinked dumbly, senses still distorted from his trance and his ears ringing with the woman's screams.

"Prefect!" demanded the green-cloaked man standing over him. "Are you awake? Are you with us?"

Wil, Kreer recalled through the fog of his thoughts. *The Variden.*

"I have you, Prefect," said Barly, clasping Kreer beneath the arm and pulling him up and away from the fire. "I have you."

Kreer stood on wobbly legs, eyes nervously flitting about the village for signs of the invaders his vision had revealed. He pulled in a shuddering breath, leaning more than he would have liked against Acolyte Barly.

"Water," he said, voice weak.

Lund, the skinny, freckled acolyte, found a wine-skin and came near. Kreer instinctively withdrew, for a moment finding the youth's red hair unsettling.

"Prefect?" Lund asked, cradling the wineskin.

Kreer shook his head, trying to shake away the remnants of the vision. "Water, please."

Lund tilted the wineskin to Kreer's lips and the water flowed. Kreer swallowed several times before turning his head away, sated and with his thoughts beginning to clear. The reality of his surroundings solidified at last.

"Prefect," came a rougher voice, that of Wil. "May we speak? Stendall and I have found the bodies of Arranese warriors by the stream. The signs indicate the Arranese slaughtered the villagers, then the highlander the Arranese. We should discuss this. Perhaps the highlander and his company are allies of ours, however unlikely?"

"No," Kreer said, waving a hand and drawing a deep breath. "A moment. I need a moment. The spell is quite taxing. I must recover and make sense of what was revealed. I have learned much, much not visible to your eyes."

Kreer shifted from Barly's supportive grasp and smoothed his garments. His hands ached—he realized he must have been gripping the fabric of his robes all the while.

He staggered away from Wil and the acolytes, weaving unsteadily across the wet ground. Crows squawked, still ripping flesh from the corpses. They fluttered their black wings as he neared but did not flee their banquet.

Kreer looked about the ruins and the dead, seeking the child, the pale, red-haired daughter he'd held—*she*, the woman, had held. There seemed no sign of her, no echo of her cries.

He feared the worst and it saddened him.

At last he found the hovel, the home occupied by the woman and her daughter. The door had been kicked through, just as he'd witnessed. He steadied himself against the remains of the doorframe and peered within.

It was a small, pathetic place. Broken furnishings of brittle, ill-carved wood lay strewn across a straw-covered floor of dirt. Kreer wandered inside the cramped space and spied the shadowed corner in which mother and daughter had taken brief solace.

He'd not seen the highlander and his murderous companions commit this slaughter. Rather, he'd seen angular-featured horsemen, men with curved blades and almond eyes.

Raiders from Arranan.

He cursed, feeling—knowing—such could not be true.

He denied the truth of the image. It was contrary to his pure faith, to his pure purpose.

It *had* to have been the highlander Karnag and his vile band of assassins.

Any vision indicating otherwise had to be the highlander's perversion of the spirit, his abuse of Castor's power. His effort to *deceive*.

No, Kreer thought. *The highlander does not fight for Rune. He is an abomination. He seeks death alone, and the spirit of Castor must be ripped from his soul.*

Kreer looked to the small, simple basket that had served as the child's bed. To the shattered remains of a rocking chair. To the clumsy wooden carving of a horse pressed into the hovel's dirt floor.

It cannot be true. Such would be a perversion of the Faith, and the Faith cannot be perverted.

Kreer knew he needed to possess the spirit—control it—so as to bring it in line with the tenets of his order. He knew violence, whether against foe or friend, would never be employed by Castor. Such wanton destruction stood contrary to the Sentinel's divine wisdom.

The highlander deceives us.

"Prefect?" asked Wil from behind.

Kreer sniffed and straightened his long spine, stretching to his full, tall height. "Yes," he said, certainty again filling his voice.

"It seems the highlander and his company hunt the enemy," said Wil. "Are you certain of your cause? Are you certain we should strike down one who seeks to destroy those who wage war upon us?"

Kreer closed his eyes briefly, focusing upon faith and the purpose that drove him. "I *witnessed* what happened here," he said, turning. "You and your brother Stendall are deceived by the highlander's lies—by the manner in which he's twisted Castor's spirit. I saw and felt it all. I witnessed the *truth*. The highlander and his company killed every one. The Arranese arrived only after the slaughter, and were slaughtered themselves in turn." Kreer held their gazes, and none shied away. "We must hunt down this highlander. Then we must destroy him."

13
THE PROMISE OF REDEMPTION

———✦———

ANNICK SAT HIGH in the saddle, craning his neck to take in the whole of the scene before him. In spite of all his losses, all his grief, a crooked smile managed to slip across his face. Suddenly it felt as though he'd sloughed away the weariness of his long journey, the heavy burdens of his past. The promise of redemption, he knew, lifted him.

Below, beyond the sloping hillside, bustled an encampment upon the sun-soaked plain beside the mighty Silverflow. A vast number of men gathered about innumerable tents, wagons, and corrals of horses and other livestock. Steel glinted in the midday sun and smoke rose from many campfires.

An army, he thought.

"An impressive assembly," said Ogrund from beside him. "Well-armed and well-supplied."

"Indeed," said Lannick, glancing to the squint-eyed and green-cloaked Variden. Ogrund had pressed him with only a handful of questions and hadn't scolded him with old proverbs. Yet the man's narrow gaze drew often to Lannick in seeming appraisal, as though he remained unsure whether Lannick met the measure of his task.

"There are many soldiers," Ogrund said, "but are there enough to present any sort of challenge to General Fane's forces?"

"Yes," Lannick said, trying to give his voice the ring of conviction. "They are more than enough if properly led. So long as the right hand wields the sword, as they say."

"Hmm," Ogrund grunted.

Randyn—the pock-faced sergeant of Vandyl's oathbound—spurred his horse beside them. "Captain? It'd be best to allow me to handle introductions. There are some among the deserters who know me. Once we arrive at their camp I'll—"

"We'll not need wait," said Ogrund. "Look there, atop the ridgeline."

Lannick followed the man's stare and spied four soldiers riding the crest of a grassy hill. One raised a lance tipped with yellow cloth that snapped in the breeze. He moved the weapon in a slow circle, an apparent signal to the encampment below.

"Likely not the first time they've seen us," Randyn said. "These soldiers are ever on watch for an assault from General Fane from the east or the Arranese from the south, and have patrols ranging far about these lands."

"Then why have we not been confronted?" asked Lannick. "We have near fifty men."

"They're used to seeing Thane Vandyl's colors ranging these lands," Randyn said, "and know well his… sympathies. I should address them."

Lannick nodded. "By all means, Sergeant."

Randyn bowed his head. "Sir." He turned his horse and spurred it toward the patrol, holding hands upward and away from his weapons as he rode.

The patrolling soldiers rose no alarm as Randyn approached, rather greeting him with brisk salutes as he neared. The group spoke for a time, Randyn gesturing toward Lannick and the others. Randyn handed something to a patrolman—a scroll, perhaps—then turned about and led the patrol back toward them.

"They appear to know the thane's man," Orgund said. "A promising sign."

Arleigh Lay sidled over on his horse, a nasty smirk across his face. "Looks like those old instincts of yours might still be intact, Captain. So long as we can keep you sober, that is." He chuckled and rode away.

Lannick laughed, the gibe failing to trouble him. "Perhaps so."

Ogrund raised a brow, ever so slightly. "I find no humor in this. One's poor behavior in the past sows doubt among others in the present. The example you set now, Lannick, is vitally important precisely because of that past behavior. You *must* lead by example, and must show no failings."

Lannick's grin curdled and he thought of Brugan's words. "*Keep your edges sharp, lad… Even if it means reopening those old wounds now and again.*"

Lannick turned to Ogrund, steel in his eyes. "Lead

by example? These men know I've suffered in the worst of ways, suffered losses that cut so deep you couldn't possibly comprehend. Did I allow those hardships to drive me to drink, to make a miserable hole of my life? Sadly yes, and that's something that shames me. But these old soldiers see me here now. They see that suffering driving me toward revenge. They can say what they will, but I'm determined to make them see every day a man who's crawled out of that hole, who's seen life's worst and fights on still."

Ogrund sniffed, watching as Randyn and the four scouts closed the distance.

A thick-necked man of perhaps thirty years held the lance—still upraised with its yellow sash snapping—and seemed the patrol's leader. His dour face bore the stitch of a recent wound. The others were younger, though they too had hardened looks about them.

"Captain," hailed Randyn as they neared. "The corporal here," he said, gesturing to the rough fellow with the lance, "says they've been awaiting our arrival. He and his men are to escort you to the camp's commander. Immediately."

Lannick shifted his jaw, sensing the weight of the moment. He felt Ogrund's eyes and those of many others upon him. *How I miss Brugan*, he thought. *His comfort and his counsel.*

He knew then he had none to trust, none to lean upon aside from himself.

"Lead the way, Corporal," he said at last.

Keep your edges sharp, lad.

Lannick rode down the long hillside, several yards behind

the corporal and his patrol. He found his hand drifting between the press of his Coda in his purse and the hilt of the prized sword on his hip. He wondered which he'd need first. He'd not known exactly what to expect upon arriving at the camp, but the idea of some kind of interrogation made him uneasy.

His recent successes had granted a new confidence, yet those old ghosts of doubt haunted him still. What was more, the importance of this encounter made things seem at once more daunting, more critical. He worried that without these deserters—this army—he had little hope of seizing his revenge and winning the war that would follow.

He spat. He *needed* this to happen. He needed his revenge, his *victory*. He'd spent far too long languishing in past failures and could not allow himself to fail again. He owed this to his dead family and his dead friend Brugan. He owed this to the old soldiers of Pryam's Bay. He owed them all, and himself, a triumph.

And he owed General Fane his due.

They trotted down the hill's bottom and onto the grassy plain below. Soon the patrol led him to the camp's outermost edge, a makeshift fortification of piled earth only as tall as a man in most spots. A creaky gate of wood opened and they entered the camp.

The encampment held a massive assembly of fighting men that grew ever denser as they made their way through, and the scene struck Lannick with a rush of familiarity. It appeared so very like those military camps he'd been a part of during the war with the Tallorrath a decade before. The air—thick with the odors of sweat and smoke—moved with the ring of blacksmiths' hammers, the drone of nagging insects, and the lilting song of many conversations.

Countless soldiers gathered about, ranging from barely more than boys with the wispy beginnings of beards to gruff veterans with faces like chewed meat. All wore the red sash of Rune, though these fellows had marked theirs with a thick stain of black across the sash's middle.

They sharpened weapons, repaired armor, mended wounds, or lounged upon crates and sacks of supplies. They tended corrals of horses and oxen and mules; others gutted chickens or stirred steaming cauldrons of soup. Some rested on tattered bedrolls in the open air, while those more fortunate reclined within small tents shielding them from the buzzing mosquitos. Thankfully only few made obvious use of the outdoor latrines.

Most of the eyes that found Lannick turned quickly on to something else. A small number, though, lingered, particularly the gazes of some of the older veterans, their heads seeming to struggle with the memory of something nearly forgotten.

"Just there," said the corporal, gesturing ahead.

Lannick turned to see a tall tent standing not more than twenty yards away. A flag moved lazily at its top, a red square of linen bearing a black cross.

He drew a breath and braced himself.

One more step toward redemption.

The entrance to the command tent was flanked by a couple of rough, mail-clad soldiers hefting broadswords. The corporal gave them a curt nod then disappeared inside.

After a couple of minutes he returned, flanked by a short, stout man in an unadorned brown shirt.

"Lannick deVeers?" asked the man, coming close. He tilted his bald head upward to regard Lannick with eyes pinched by crow's feet. "*Captain* Lannick deVeers?"

Lannick gave a halting salute. "The, uh, one and only!"

The man held a rolled parchment Lannick guessed to be the thing Randyn had given the patrol. "Thought you were dead."

A wry smile wandered to Lannick's face. "At times I thought I was."

The man chuckled. "Glad we both were wrong. I'm Black Jon, former lieutenant in General Fane's army and now leader of this band of so-called deserters. I don't ordinarily receive newcomers at the command tent, but it seems to me you deserve a measure of respect. I remember what you did at Pryam's Bay. Come on inside and let's talk for a while. Corporal, you and your men are dismissed."

The tent's interior was a hexagonal space dominated by a flat, four-wheeled cart serving as a makeshift table. Atop it were various maps and markers, and about it were seated two men—veterans, judging from their age—locked in heated discussion. A third, a burly soldier with a long mess of brown hair and a stained tunic, shuffled at the tent's rear with a limp.

Black Jon gestured to a bench at one end of the cart-turned-table. "Have a seat."

Lannick slipped onto the empty bench. The two men halted their discussion and turned to eyeball him with what seemed cool consideration.

"Gentlemen," said Black Jon, walking round to sit in a chair at the table's head, "this here is Captain Lannick deVeers, a genuine hero of the war with the Tallorrath. Bid him welcome."

One of the men, a thin fellow with thinning black hair, scratched a face unremarkable but for its smugness. "The very captain who was charged with treason at the war's end, as I recall."

Lannick cleared his throat. "I... I—"

"And the very same who won that war," said the other in a gruff voice. He was thickly built, with bristly brown hair. "Well met. I'm Sergeant Kaldare, and the idiot opposite me is deMond."

"*Sergeant* deMond," said the other. "And you'll find I'm far from an idiot."

Kaldare smirked. "I was trying to be kind. Captain deVeers, don't mistake this man's arrogance for intelligence. He—"

"How dare you!" barked deMond. "No man has studied military history more than I!"

"And none has fought less," chuckled Kaldare.

"Enough!" said Black Jon, glaring at his sergeants. "The two of you can silence your rivalry for now. Harl," he said with a gesture to the big man limping behind him, "some water for our guest, please. I'm sure the captain's journey has been a long one."

Lannick nodded. *You have no idea.*

"Sir," grunted the man, then lumbered to the tent's far end and set about fumbling over a table. He soon returned cradling a cup in massive hands then smacked it down before Lannick. Half the cup's water slopped onto Lannick's lap.

"Careful, Harl!" Black Jon laughed. "The captain needs a drink, not a bath!"

Lannick smiled and looked to Harl. The man's long hair framed a stern face stretched with many scars. "It's no problem," Lannick said. "I reckon I could probably use both. Thank you." He took a deep drink and looked to the others. "Thank you all. You received word of our coming?"

"We have our scouts," said Black Jon, "as well as contact with certain high-placed people throughout the kingdom."

"Wise decisions both," Lannick said, doing his best to assume an air of capability.

Black Jon's face straightened into a more serious look. "Speaking of those high-placed people," he said, holding up the scroll in his hand, "it seems Thane Vandyl believes you'd make a fine addition to the leadership of our little outfit, and that we'd best listen to you."

Sergeant deMond stiffened, his brow arching. "We know nothing of this man outside of a long-forgotten victory, a descent into treachery, and who knows what else."

Sergeant Kaldare made a loud sputter. "We're all traitors at this point, deMond."

Lannick smiled crookedly, finding comfort in the man's apparent support.

"Aye," chuckled Black Jon, though humor quickly left his face. "I'm happy to listen to you, Captain, but understand that while I trust Thane Vandyl's judgment, I need to trust my own even more. I need to know why you're here, why a bunch of old, retired soldiers would seek to join our ranks. Retired soldiers we've heard nothing of in a decade."

"My men didn't retire," Lannick said. "They were decommissioned. They were loyal fighting men who had no choice in the matter. As for our purpose," he said, his tone filling with the certainty of his words, "we're here because of that madman presently commanding Rune's armies. I've suffered—*we* have suffered—much at the hands of our dear general, and we aim to set things aright. We mean to take down General Fane. First for vengeance and second to give Rune some chance of winning this war."

Black Jon sat with eyes trained on Lannick. "And you think that simply taking out the general turns the tide? That one man has made all the difference? You don't think displacing the general will send the army into chaos?"

"Fane is the very worst of men, a man so twisted by ambition he's lost all sense of sanity. He *means* to lose this war. He's sending good soldiers to their deaths."

Black Jon's gaze did not waver. "Why do you say this? The High King's own council keeps the general in power. Why do you think his defeats are the stuff of treason rather than blunder or bad luck?"

Lannick looked to the man. "If you don't think that then why leave his army? You don't think his 'bad luck' could take a turn for the better?"

Black Jon was quiet for a long moment. "Maybe I left because I thought it wise to sit things out until his luck turns. Or maybe it's because I'm a coward. A sniveling, whimpering coward who shits himself at the merest hint of violence."

Kaldare chortled, smacking the table. "Tell that to those Arranese we routed at Hargrave! As I recall your sword was painted with most of their blood."

"Ah yes," said Black Jon. "The very battle that led our dear General Fane to threaten to string me from a tree." He moved his hands in a choking motion about his neck then shook his head and huffed. "Captain, we know the general's come unhinged. At Hargrave he'd ordered us to stand down but we didn't, and as a result we had a rather unpleasant visit from several of his Scarlet Swordsmen. Then, after, we started hearing similar accounts, word of Fane being quite vengeful when victories won were not according to the very letter of his commands. But the thing was, it seemed the only victories achieved were those where men acted contrary to those commands. I didn't know if it was madness or arrogance or a desire to lose the war, but I reckoned it didn't matter. We knew we'd best leave the ranks before ending up piled among the dead."

"Aye," Kaldare said. "Three hundred of us, gone in the black of night."

"And now you have thousands," Lannick said.

"More than two thousand men," said Black Jon. "As soon as word spread soldiers began following us. There was resistance—harsh resistance—from Fane and his Scarlet Swords at first. Many died, else we might have twice our current number. But I reckon you know well how spiteful a bastard the general can be."

Lannick shifted his crackling jaw. "I do. Better than most."

Black Jon nodded. "That I'd heard. I served in the war against Tallorrath. Not at Pryam's Bay but on the seas, fighting galley to galley and deck to deck against those salty devils. Nevertheless, I heard what you did in that battle, and something of what happened to you afterward. You were wronged, Captain. You and the whole of your lot."

"You're damned right," Lannick said, swallowing hard. "And we've waited long enough for revenge. Revenge, and redemption."

"You'll not need to wait much longer."

"When?" Lannick said, pressing close to the table. "When do we march? You must know Fane's treachery worsens with every passing day. Who knows how many men will die if he's not stopped?"

"Three days," Black Jon said. "Three short days. There are two hundred men riding from the south to join us. Once they do, we head to war. We head to war and we head there with the very same purpose driving you. We head to war to remove General Fane from command. We're glad to have you, Captain."

Lannick reclined against his traveling packs, away from the hot blaze of the campfire. The ground he stretched upon was somewhat damp and lumpy, though he reckoned that wasn't much different from his bed in Ironmoor's Hollows.

And at least this dampness is rainwater rather than, well, something worse.

"Hungry?" grunted Kevlin deKray, looking to Lannick from the fire's opposite side. "We've got plenty of cheese and bread, and the soldiers at that fire there said we could share their soup."

"Thanks, but not just yet," Lannick said, shooing a

mosquito and allowing his eyes to wander the darkened encampment. A multitude of men gathered about tents and low fires, chewing away at their suppers and waxing bravely over deeds yet to be done. Weapons rested against carts and sacks, swords and bows and axes just waiting to be put to their purpose. Horses snorted and whinnied in a nearby corral.

A real army.

His companions, the old soldiers of Pryam's Bay, kept mostly to themselves but a few engaged the deserters about them. Some of the words worked their way through the din, including Arleigh Lay's shouted vow to slice off General Fane's cock. Arleigh left no confusion among his listeners, illustrating the promised deed with a twist of the long dagger gripped in his remaining hand.

Lannick smirked and turned his gaze to a sky full of stars. His father had taught him of the constellations long ago and Lannick found their shapes with practiced ease. He spotted the Spitted Sow and the Three Witches, sketching the forms with his eyes. High above, at the night's apex, burned the bright star known as the Eldest Eye. And there, beside it, stood the starred outline of the Hero of the Heavens, a constellation resembling a warrior with sword upraised.

He remembered his father telling him the tale of that last one when Lannick was barely tall enough to ride a pony. The stars, he'd told Lannick, were torches carried by guardians of the Elder God's heavens, and the Hero was the Elder God's champion. The Hero, brave and strong and pure, battled beyond the heavens' gates, refusing to allow the cold dark to enter. On those nights the stars dimmed, the Hero remained locked in that desperate struggle. The brighter nights that followed signaled her victory.

The stars shone brightly now. They blazed across the blanket of night, thousands upon thousands of fires kindled and crackling and chasing away the darkness surrounding them. Lannick reckoned that if he believed all those things he had as a boy, he'd believe the Hero had bested the dark in a brilliant, decisive battle.

He didn't believe such things anymore. Not as much, anyway. Yet, there was something of it that bolstered him. Something that gave him hope.

Perhaps it was a sign, an omen. A promise that he *could* be the man he once was. Perhaps he could be like the Hero, brave and strong and pure, and could prevail against General Fane and all the foes certain to stand before and after him.

He smiled at that, thinking how proud his father—and his wife and children and only friend—would be.

He shifted upon his traveling packs, no longer holding any regard for the dampness of the earth beneath him. Ironmoor stood far behind him now, and all that stood ahead was the hope of redemption.

He shut his eyes and slept more peacefully than he had in years.

14
ZYN

ZANDRACHUS BALE SWAYED beside Lorra and Alisa in the creaking wagon's bed, crammed between scratchy sacks of pungent spices and piles of colorful silks. He craned his neck about the form of the Khaldisian merchant manning the reins and saw beyond a road of straw-colored dust etched across the steppe of broken stone. Travelers dotted the sun-baked thoroughfare, lean Arranese on horses and a smattering of other merchants hauling wagons heaped with oddities.

Beyond it all lay Zyn, a city much larger than Bale had imagined. It was a massive sprawl—miles across—situated on an otherwise bleak and rocky plain. A pale wall surrounded most of it, though the populace seemed to have spilled beyond its bounds, erecting tents and sandstone buildings outside the confines. Behind the wall, standing watch over a vast myriad of squat structures, dozens of tall minarets gleamed white in the afternoon sun. At the city's center, standing taller than all the towers, rose an obsidian obelisk, a behemoth of black stone.

"What is that?" Lorra asked, pointing with a thin finger.

Bale rubbed the tip of his overlarge nose. "I reckon that's the home of the mysterious Spider King."

"It is," said Alisa. "Precisely as tall as the Tower of Lords in Ironmoor, a mocking reflection of it. It was built in mere weeks, if what I gathered is accurate. The construction was performed entirely at night."

Bale's eyes widened. "All under the cover of darkness…" he whispered. "The Necrists?"

"Their abominations carried every brick," Alisa said. "I told you I'd located their lair. It lies underground, beneath the Spider King's palace. I couldn't get near their sanctuary, but from what I understand it is a sick imitation of the Godswell. Those taken there never return."

"It is their butchery," Bale said with a shudder.

Lorra seized his hand and squeezed it. "Are we safe?"

Alisa turned to them. "I'll not give any false assurances. Zyn is dangerous. Though the Spider King and his army are far away, he's left some of his most powerful allies here until such time as they're needed. We must take utmost care with our every action, and employ every manner of discretion. I can conceal us for a time, but we must reach our destination before nightfall."

"Our destination?"

"A friend. He's remained in this city, observing what he knew were troubling events. Until we reach him, you must allow me to speak with any who confront us, and follow my every lead. Beware the shadows."

"What can we expect?" Bale asked.

"Our darkest foes, performing their darkest acts." She looked askance, brown eyes troubled. "On one night— my last in this city—I watched as a cartload of children entered the gates of the Spider King's palace, just as a cartload of small bones left it."

"The Arranese countenance such things?"

"They see the Spider King as their god, a terrible and fearsome one. None dare question him or his associations, for fear of death or worse. Those who challenge him are taken in the night, and only the dead gods know what he does with them. Terrible things, I'm certain."

"Probably torture and worse," murmured Lorra, voice laden with pain.

Bale looked to her. He nodded and cast his eyes downward, feeling the hard sun hammer upon him.

The sun had dipped to the far horizon by the time they made their way to Zyn's outskirts, the road now a crowded avenue of chalky bricks. The city's edge seemed a confusing jumble of tight streets and squat structures of yellow stone and animal hides. The hot air hung thick with the odor of pack animals and spiced oils. Voices called out in harsh Arranese accents, shopkeepers drawing attention to their wares and mothers scolding unruly children.

A strange beast honked beside them, a heavy-tusked and white-maned thing atop which sat a sinewy Arranese man holding a longbow. Bale drew his hood down to just above his eyes and cowered low against the wagon's side.

The other wayfarers about them were mostly Arranese, sharp-featured with skin bronzed from lives spent upon the sun-beaten steppe. There were smatterings of foreigners, though, including Khaldisian traders and a few small groups of black-skinned Harkanians—legendary warriors from across the sea. Much to Bale's relief, none regarded them with particular suspicion as they sat in the wagon's bed.

They came within sight of the wall, a mass of bleached stone etched with geometric patterns. At the arched gate stood a spear-wielding group of guards interrogating those trying to enter the city. Near the guards loomed another man, robed in white, seeming to preside over the process.

Bale began to sense a *wrongness* about the place, some vague, creeping haunt at the edges of his mind. They rode now in the shade cast by the great spire of the Spider King and the darkness it splayed upon the road felt oppressive. Bale's eyes wandered to the structure's surface and he saw strange glyphs scratched into the jet-black stone. A sick chill slithered up his spine as he looked upon them.

Alisa drew near him. "You feel it, don't you?" she whispered. "All who serve the Sentinels can."

"What is it?" he groaned, trying to shrug off the ill feeling.

"Need I tell you?" she asked, eyes wide with meaning. "We'll need to leave the caravan soon. We risk great peril if we are on these streets when night falls. Hide your fear lest it betray us."

He shook his head and tucked strands of long, graying hair back within his hood and behind his ears.

Lorra seized his hand and pulled him close. "Tell me, Bale."

He looked to her, seeing the worry upon her face.

"Remember the wall of shadows on the steppe?" he whispered. "This city is home to more of such things. We must find shelter before darkness falls, or…"

"Or what? Will they find us? Will they take us to that black tower just like those children she spoke of?" Lorra asked.

Bale rubbed his hands together, afraid of giving voice to what he reckoned was the truthful answer.

Lorra stared at him, seeming to await a response.

His shoulders sagged. "We must follow Alisa's guidance. We should be safe so long as we do."

Lorra's hard features crinkled in a scowl and she looked ahead. "And who is he?" she said, gesturing. "The man in the white robes?"

Bale's eyes followed the point of Lorra's bony finger, spying the cluster of men near the arched gate. The robed man seemed harmless enough, a young Arranese with angular features and skin of light brown. Yet there seemed something *unnatural* about him, something Bale could not place.

"Quiet, now," Alisa said firmly. "Make ready. Do precisely as I say."

"Bale?" Lorra whispered, gripping his hand tightly.

"The enemy watches," he replied, "and listens."

Alisa rose slightly, looking about them and rubbing her bracelet of black iron that glowed now with a greenish hue. She snatched a bolt of blue silk from the goods about them and shoved it toward Bale. "Cover yourselves with this and be ready to move the moment I fetch you."

Bale clutched the silk and looked nervously to the gate. "This will fool no one," he hissed.

Alisa slipped from the wagon. As she had when they'd first come upon the merchant caravan, Alisa seemed to transform her appearance to that of a simple wanderer. She regarded him with a stare that was inescapable. "We are concealed for the moment. Do it now."

Bale nodded and pulled Lorra close. He unfurled the fabric and dragged it over their heads, then pressed a finger upon Lorra's lips. "Say nothing," he whispered.

They waited for tense moments, feeling the slow rock of the wagon as it rolled over the avenue's bricks. Bale dared to shift aside the fabric's edge and peek toward the street. He saw Alisa move to the wagon's lead, toward the Khaldisian merchant guiding the horses. There was some exchange of words, then Alisa gave the man a handful of coins. She returned to the wagon's side as it creaked to a stop.

They were at the gate and he spied the young Arranese man robed in white. At first Bale only had a vague feeling about him, but soon he noticed a gnarled stitch of black at the very edge of the man's dark hairline. He shuddered, ducked under the blue silk and cowered against Lorra. Terror seized him, an icy fear gripping his heart. His lungs churned, frightened breaths sucked through clenched teeth.

He heard deep voices murmuring, the words muffled.

"A pilgrim," came Alisa's voice, yet in a perfect Arranese accent with words harsh and angled. "A pilgrim seeking to witness the glorious city of our Spider King, may the shadows guard him always. I come also with a humble tribute for his coffers."

There was the tinkling of coins. Low voices rumbled but then fell quiet.

Short moments passed, though the time felt immeasurably long. Bale's body shook and he felt tears tumbling down his cheeks. A hand gripped his shoulder—Lorra's—but he was not soothed.

Another voice, clearer. "Leave the tribute and move along."

The cart lurched forward. It wobbled over the bricks and, after a time, Bale's breathing eased.

"We're safe," whispered Lorra beside him in the dark. Her hand slid to his.

Bale clasped her hand tightly, his fear receding somewhat. He sucked in a long and soothing breath, swaying with the movements of the wagon.

Then someone pinched his neck. He stifled a yelp and started, then recoiled as the edge of the fabric was swept away.

"Get out," said Alisa, standing aside the wagon. She looked herself again, framed by the waning light of the sun. "Now."

Bale clambered out of the moving wagon and onto the street, tugging Lorra after him.

"This way," she barked. "Quickly."

They followed Alisa across the wide thoroughfare and down a street that seemed barely more than an alleyway. Alisa gestured for a faster pace and they sped to a jog, slipping through the squeeze of stone and shanties, around strewn refuse and over the swell of a sleeping drunk's round belly.

The tight road intersected another. Alisa stopped and

guided them down it, directing them to a path even narrower. The road bent in odd places and seemed to move away from the wall. "Hurry," Alisa called after them.

Bale ran and as he did he felt something, a tingle on his neck. He halted and turned, and saw the far end of the road behind them had become steeped in a heavy darkness. Fingers of deep black, like shadows bound together, stretched toward them along the street's edges. The tendrils wove swiftly through the zig-zag of paving stones like a torrent of water to within mere feet of Alisa.

Bale trembled. "Alisa! Behind you!"

Alisa caught sight of the dark. She uttered a few sharp words then sprang forward with an unnatural agility. She dashed ahead of the shifting shadows with her green cloak whipping about. She reached Bale's side and shoved him onward.

Bale's feet tangled and he stumbled but Lorra was there to catch him. The three of them sprinted with abandon, not caring for the protests of passersby who were forced to make way.

They ran for several minutes, turning this way and that where roads intersected. Clay pots and tall baskets of wicker cluttered the road and someone shouted at them with accusations of thievery. Down one street then another, through a slum where sad hovels of torn cloth huddled against stone ruins. The hands of beggars clawed at them as they swept past.

The hot air burned and sweat stung Bale's eyes. He wiped his brow with the sleeve of his robe. His lungs felt afire and his achy legs screamed.

Sweet Illienne please spare your loyal servant!

He could run no longer. He wilted against a rough tumble of sandstone and sank to the road's dusty bricks. Alisa and Lorra were several strides ahead before noticing, then both returned to his side.

"Get up," Lorra urged, wrapping a hand under his arm.

"Hurry," said Alisa, an edge on her voice. "We don't have far to go."

Bale struggled upward, knees creaking as he did. "I can't..." he huffed through heaving breaths.

He looked back to the stretch of road behind them, an uneven path between walls of crumbling stone. A few Arranese children played in the street, rolling and then chasing after a round fruit of some kind. There was no sign of the strange shadows.

"Is it gone?" he said weakly, bracing against the stone.

Alisa took a step down the road, a hand rubbing her iron bracelet. "I still sense something."

Bale felt it, too. A faint chill, an eerie coldness that raised his short hairs.

"Bale!" Lorra screamed. She grabbed him and spun him about, toward the street's other end.

There, just more than ten yards away, thick tentacles of murky black poured along the road, darkening the stone as they passed. They seemed shadows possessed of substance, darkness given physical form.

Bale frantically searched the distance between them and the twisting blackness. There were no side streets or other means of escape, only blank walls of broken rock. He whirled to Alisa. "Back the other way?"

"No," she hissed. "The shadows are there as well."

He glanced back and saw the road was empty, the playing children gone. In their place crept more swirls of heavy darkness.

"Bale?" Lorra pleaded, grabbing at his robes with fear upon her face.

Alisa sprang ahead of them, her iron bracelet aglow with a greenish hue. She brandished her short sword, the weapon wrapped in the same luminescence as her bracelet. She charged at the shadows, slashing her sword about. The shadows she struck relented, though others formed and curled about her.

A desperate courage arose then within Bale. He pulled Lorra close with one arm and held the other upward, hand clenched in a thin fist. He drew a deep, calming breath as his mind focused upon the words Lector Erlorn, his Sentinel, had taught him what seemed ages ago.

"*Illienne!*" he said, "*Illienne abralide y ganode allum!*" *Illienne awaken and give me light!*

He opened his hand and from it came a brilliant blaze of white, a great beacon lashing pure light at the shadows in every space about them. The light exploded across the street, engulfing Alisa and the black tendrils about her. The shadows immediately shrank and shriveled and slunk out of sight. Alisa lowered her sword and looked to him, an awed expression on her face as she shielded her eyes from the light.

Bale turned his head and saw only brightness behind him, an empty street awash in blinding light. He exhaled and drew his upraised hand to his side. "They're gone."

"Not gone," Alisa said, "just diminished. Run this way!"

Bale's legs felt unsteady and he slumped exhaustedly against Lorra. He tried to stand and withdraw his arm but she held him tightly, nearly carrying him as she barreled ahead to follow Alisa.

"I have you," she said, tugging him forward.

The light he'd cast began to fade—quickly—and Bale worried the strange shadows were waiting not far ahead. They ran. Slung upon Lorra's gangly form, he provided what effort he could, pained legs churning. They made their way through a confounding maze of narrow streets, following the green swirl of Alisa's cloak.

After a series of manic turns through another slum, Alisa stopped suddenly in the midst of a thin street shouldered by tents of yellow cloth and brown animal hides. Night was drawing near and fires glowed from between the parted flaps of several of the structures. A pair of uneasy eyes stared at them from the entrance of another.

Alisa turned about, studying the tents while caressing her Coda. After a moment she seemed to settle upon one of the drooping hovels and approached it, hands nearing her sheathed blade. She patted the closed hide flap that formed the entrance and took a step back, waiting.

Bale stretched his neck and looked behind, nervously surveying the twisting street behind them. Night was falling and the shadows were deepening, so he couldn't be certain whether any of the darkness seemed somehow unnatural. The uncertainty unsettled him and his heart fluttered.

"Is this wise, Alisa?" said Bale. "Is this safe?"

Alisa waved aside his question and swatted the flap once more.

An eerie quiet hung over the street and the darkness of night seemed to descend with an awful quickness. Alisa looked about, holding her bracelet which once again held a green glow.

"I think—" she said, just as the flap was swept aside.

A ringed hand shot from the tent and hurriedly gestured. Alisa clasped the hand then summoned Bale and Lorra to her side. They moved with furtive glances to the tent, then together they plunged into the dark shelter and away from the night.

A'Sha was a heavy-set Harkanian with brown skin and a bald head that glowed warmly in the light of the fire pit dug into the shelter's floor. He sat at the fire's edge in loose, multicolored robes, thoughtfully stroking a beard of black curls while a gray ferret perched upon his shoulder.

Bale and Lorra huddled on a plush pillow opposite A'Sha, Alisa upon another nearer him. Bale's eyes wandered about the tent, an octagonal space filled with warbling birds, sniffling rodents, and other creatures he could not identify. Many twittered within wicker cages but others roamed free, some approaching Bale with tiny eyes bulging.

It was a menagerie wholly unlike the musty halls of the Abbey where the only creatures of note were the occasional spider, roach or bothersome bookworm. Yet as much as the sight fascinated Bale, he felt his gaze drawn to the tent's flap. He wondered what shadows stalked the night.

"You are safe here," said A'Sha in his ponderous

baritone. "Be at ease. The eyes of those foul sorcerers cannot enter this place."

Bale rubbed at his nose. After a moment he realized he sensed nothing of the sickening chill that had plagued him earlier, just a weighty worry over its return.

A'Sha smiled. "I must say it is delightful to have three visitors from Rune, even during such troubling times." He gathered his robes about him and rose to stand. "Tea?"

"Thank you," Alisa answered. "That is most kind."

A'Sha shooed a hummingbird from a cabinet and retrieved a ceramic teapot. He poured into it water from a pitcher, then hung the pot's handle on a hook dangling from a metal tripod. He lowered the contraption into the pit, suspending the teapot just above the flames.

He grunted as he settled upon his pillow, his ferret scurrying to his shoulder once more. "Alisa, it is a pleasure to have you beneath my roof, though I must say I'd not thought you'd return so quickly. As I recall, you left Zyn to track the enemy to Rune."

Alisa nodded. "I did, but I left that to another once I encountered Bale. It seemed his was a task far more urgent and deserving of my aid—and of yours."

"Oh?" A'Sha said, his dark eyes turning to Bale. "And what task could be graver than determining where our ancient foes are headed?"

Bale said nothing. Lorra squeezed close to him and grasped his hand.

"What is it you seek?" A'Sha asked.

Lorra spat into the fire. "Who are you to ask? Just because *she* trusts you, we should as well?"

Bale forced a polite smile. He waved a hand at Lorra but she brushed it away.

"You have no idea," Lorra continued, "no idea at all of what we've seen and what we've endured." She grabbed Bale's shoulder and held his eyes. "I say we'd be better off without the help of any more strangers."

A'Sha tangled a hand in his beard. "No doubt the two of you are anxious after all you've witnessed. I understand this land is strange to you, and you are wise to give your trust only sparingly. But I assure you, I am a friend."

"Bale," Alisa said, "you can speak freely here. Remember I told you of a disciple of the Sentinel Pastine, one who might help us?"

Bale's eyes widened. "Here? In this place?"

A'Sha swept his hands outward then bowed as deeply as his round belly would permit. "I am A'Sha, practitioner of ancient arts strange and wondrous, a Harkanian wizard, witch, what-have-you. And yes, my master was none other than Pastine, Sentinel of Rune."

"*Was?*" Bale craned forward. "Does she live? What can you tell me of her? Is she still dedicated to the safety of—" He stopped himself, realizing the words were tumbling too quickly from his tongue.

A'Sha laughed, the sound a joyful rumble. "You have many questions for me, Zandrachus Bale, and I have many for you. We'll answer them in time. For now, though, suffice to say I am a loyal servant of Rune. My purpose and yours are, at the end of things, the same."

Alisa looked to Bale. "During my last visit I told him of the murder of your Lector, of the displacement of Castor's spirit. You can tell him why you're here."

Bale tucked a wayward strand of hair behind his ear. Lorra gripped his hand almost painfully but he gave her a nod. He'd grown to trust Alisa and knew they needed all the help they could muster. "Castor intended to summon the Sentinels to Rune," he said, "and warned the Necrists were trying to recover Yrghul's power. I continue his errand, and have learned Kressan is somewhere in this city."

A'Sha looked to him intensely, his glare penetrating. "In Zyn? How is it you know this?"

"My order has means, methods taught to us by Castor. Kressan is here."

A'Sha shook his head. "I never... I came to Zyn a year ago upon learning troubling things of the Spider King's ascendance. What I found was a vile hive of Necrists, an unholy temple to Yrghul. I can't imagine a Sentinel would reside here. Unless... Unless she too learned of the Necrists' rise and their association with the Spider King, perhaps?"

Bale looked to the fire. "I don't know, though the possibilities are cause for concern."

A'Sha arose, drawing his fingers through his beard with eyes downcast. "But are you so sure?"

"I met with Lyan the Just in Cirak. She empowered me, and I have no doubt."

"He did these things, A'Sha," said Alisa.

A'Sha rounded the fire pit, robes rustling as he moved. "*Lyan!* You have been witness to a rare and spectacular thing, Zandrachus Bale!" He paused. "But in Cirak? I thought that place an abandoned ruin. Why there?"

"There is something beneath it," Bale said. "There is a

holy shrine to the Sentinels known as the 'Sacred Place.' Lyan waits for us there, where she intends to confer with the other Sentinels and decide whether to honor her old oath and defend Rune."

A'Sha let out a low whistle. "Then your task is indeed a profoundly vital one. But you must take great care in this city. Know that peril surrounds you at every turn."

Lorra stared at A'Sha sharply, yielding nothing. "Does it surround us now? Here?"

A'Sha froze, hand tangled in a loop of his black beard. "Yes," he said at last. "Even here, even now. But you do not face such peril from me." His dark eyes widened. "Aha! Our tea!"

The teapot puffed a steady steam from its spout. A'Sha strode to a cabinet and retrieved a few items, then returned. He handed them each a shallow ceramic bowl, wrapped a heavy cloth about his hand, then delicately removed the teapot from the tripod's hook. After removing its lid, he crumbled a handful of sprigs and spices into the pot.

"There," he said with satisfaction, falling back into his pillow. "The spices will steep for a moment and then you shall enjoy finest tea in all the world." He lifted the teapot and shifted forward, gesturing for their bowls. They passed them to him, watching as he gently filled them and then returned them full and steaming.

Bale sniffed at his bowl, a pleasant concoction that smelled of rare cinnamon from Khaldisia and even rarer clove from Rimgald. "Kressan is here, in this city," he said, sipping carefully from the bowl. "We must find her, or Rune may perish."

A'Sha lowered his bowl to the floor and looked to him with glittering eyes. "I will do anything my blood and bones will endure to defeat this so-called Spider King and save our dear kingdom. I will help you in any way I can."

15
THERE IS ONLY DEATH

ENCRESS GAZED OUT across the wet plain, a soaked, sweaty place thick with nagging mosquitoes. The Silverflow rumbled near, though the river's waters remained hidden beneath a mantle of fog. Somewhere—not far, she wagered—war seethed and a good number of poor, dumb souls were dying over some inane quarrel.

That's the thing with war, she thought. *Some bastard decides his greed, faith, or old grudge is so important it warrants a big fucking butchery.*

She wondered for a moment over the reason for this one, this war. She thought of her brief encounter with Arranan's Spider King, when that freakish, stitch-faced giant had inspected her like some whelp freshly plucked from the womb. She winced at the memory, of how he'd discarded her while mentioning she bore no mark of the gods.

Faith it is, then. The very worst reason of all, for that's the argument there's no solving no matter how many dead fill the graves.

She shook her head and pulled off her gloves. She flexed clammy hands in vain hope they'd dry in midday air that seemed barely more than stagnant. She then eased back her cowl and shook her ebony hair free. It was no use. Everything felt sticky and miserable.

"There," grunted Karnag from nearby.

Fencress looked to where the highlander gestured and saw naught but a heavy mist smothering the plain near the river. "Fog? Lovely. We're heading into even wetter, stickier air. Karnag, you really know how to entertain a lady."

"Follow me," the highlander said firmly. He whipped the reins of his horse, his flint-colored eyes fixed on some unseen point.

"*Fencress!*" hissed Paddyn from behind her. "Where's he taking us?"

She looked to her left—east along the river—where stood Riverweave perhaps a dozen leagues away. "Seems we're headed away from the front, boys," she whispered, her tone betraying a hint of relief. She still had no idea how she was going to sway Karnag, how she was going to help free him from the demon haunting him. But staying clear of the front seemed to offer damned better odds than rushing headlong toward it.

"Where?" pleaded Paddyn.

She nodded to him and turned to Karnag. "So we're not headed into the teeth of battle, eh? Perhaps a decent town with a few fat pockets and flea-riddled inns?"

Karnag stared blankly ahead. "I am the ruin not just

of the flesh of men, but of their hearts most of all. Today I take something."

"An excellent choice, Karnag!" she proclaimed with false cheer, shrugging aside her instinct to ask what this 'something' might be. She slapped a hand on her thigh and did her usual best to find some hope or humor— some promise of chance—in even the worst turn of the dice. "A good old-fashioned heist! A theft! A burglary!" She turned to the others. "Drenj? Any more poetic term for the task? You have the gift, as I recall."

The Khaldisian looked to her sadly, the kohl about his eyes smeared in black streaks across his olive cheeks. "Death," he sighed, hanging his head. "There is only death."

Karnag glanced back to Drenj. "There is wisdom in your words, Khaldisian, though your tongue intends it not. Death follows ever in my wake."

Drenj trembled beneath Karnag's gaze. "I should be home," he said with a quavering voice. "Home with my family…"

"I do not bind you," Karnag said. "You may choose your path."

Drenj shot up in his saddle. "I can leave? I'll not die if I do?"

Karnag looked to him for a moment then closed his eyes. "No. You will die."

"But I—"

"I tell you what is and what will be. Your sanctuary exists only at my side. Leave me and our pursuers will track you and exact punishment for your crimes."

"*My* crimes!" Drenj laughed woefully.

The young man's hopelessness troubled Fencress. She wished his heart weren't so burdened, but then she knew he had good cause to despair.

They all did.

They followed Karnag into the mist. The river's rush filled Fencress's ears though the steamy veil did not betray the water's location. Soon it seemed naught but oblivion surrounded them, a ghostly nothingness where anything just beyond her reach had vanished.

She slowed and at last halted her horse, lost in the cloud. "Karnag?" she called.

Several moments passed. A horse nickered somewhere. A cry, a grunt, then a splash.

"Come," came Karnag's voice from what seemed a great distance ahead. "This way."

Fencress could see nothing. She drew in a breath and eased her horse forward, the beast's hooves slurping and sucking the wet earth. After a dozen yards or so a silhouette darkened the haze. As she came closer the image resolved: Karnag standing beside his horse upon a platform propped against the riverbank.

"Come," Karnag said again. "Here we cross the river."

She studied the raft, a rectangular expanse of wood that no doubt served as a ferry for hire. The ferryman, though, was nowhere to be seen.

She slipped off her horse and tried leading it to the ferry. The beast stamped and then its legs stiffened, digging into the mud. Fencress cooed and clucked and snapped at the reins but the best the beast would do was crane its neck.

"Fencress," said Paddyn from beside her, his quiet

voice whistling through the space of his missing tooth. "My horse won't move either. They're scared, Fencress. Perhaps they sense—"

"Leave them," Karnag growled.

"We need mounts, Karnag," Fencress said. "This ground is a wet mess and—"

"Leave them. My horse can carry the supplies. You will all set loose your steeds. We will soon have others."

Fencress found her hand had moved to the shape of the totem she kept strung about her neck, the rough carving of a sun symbolizing the goddess Illienne. Any notion she had of faith was a wavering thing at best and she didn't fancy the idea of being bound by dead gods to a certain destiny. She'd always thought instead that life played out according to turns of chance, that those who made the smart bets could weather its troubles. Yet what she'd seen with Karnag—his talk of things yet to be and his inevitable march toward... *something*—left her unsettled.

"Karnag," she said, "you know I have no quibbles with killing when a job calls for it or a fellow is deserving, but gutting folk for nothing more than a few horses seems... unnecessary. We have good coin. Can't we just buy new horses?"

Karnag looked to her through a fraying curtain of black braids, his gaze empty. He closed his eyes and inhaled. He opened them—the eyes of the dead—and a sick smile twisted his mouth. "Those ahead have no need of their mounts."

"Karnag," Fencress pleaded. "We can't—"

"Their fate has been cast." The words rang like judgment.

Fencress swallowed back the bile rising in her throat and set about removing the satchels from her horse. "Very well," she whispered, shoulders slumping. She scratched her horse's withers then gave it a slap to send it away. "May good fortune find you," she said softly.

Paddyn and Drenj boarded the raft, stepping tentatively upon its swaying planks and moving as far from Karnag as the vessel would allow. Fencress followed, tugging her cowl and gloves back into place as she did.

"Now," Karnag grunted. He seized a long pole from the ferry's edge, pressed it into the water and pushed the ferry forward with a great thrust. The platform shuddered as it left the bank.

Fencress noticed a wet rope slithering across the ferry's center and realized the craft was guided by a line tethered to either side of the river. With the line the ferry held roughly to its intended course despite the river's swift flow. It held to a certain destination. The ferry was fated to reach the opposite side and could move nowhere else. The line directed it and permitted no deviation.

Fencress tucked the stray strands of her hair back within her black cowl and thought on that. She didn't like the notion, that certainty of fate.

But then a smirk found her lips.

The raft is fated to reach the other side, at least until chance snaps that line in two.

She studied Karnag through the fog, watching him work thick arms to dig the pole against the riverbed below. She wondered what sort of happenstance—what sort of chance—could shove him from his course.

She knew there had to be such a thing. There had to be a chance.

Karnag strode across ground that was barely more than a marsh, tugging along his sack-laden stallion. He paused and smelled the air. "We are not far now."

Fencress strained keen eyes against the endless murk and could discern nothing. She gave the air a sniff of her own. There was perhaps the odor of smoke, but mostly the scent of wet, boggy rot.

"Far from what?" she asked.

"Answers from the dead," Karnag said, then set off again through the muck.

She drew in a slow breath and followed him.

They moved along muddy earth that pulled at their boots. Ahead, a copse of trees emerged from the mist, trees with claw-like branches draped with vines. Fencress studied them and spied many birds fluttering about the boughs. The birds—crows—cawed and croaked, an incessant squabble of ill-tempered voices.

They slogged beneath the trees and the ground softened and grew more treacherous. The air thickened with steam that taxed the lungs. Karnag strode onward with powerful certainty though the others struggled to navigate the mire. Even Fencress's nimble feet found little purchase.

She paused and leaned against a slick tree trunk, then looked back to see her young companions trudging many yards behind. They looked utterly ridiculous in this mess, Paddyn in his foppish, stolen clothes and Drenj with cheeks painted like some circus performer meant to frighten children. "Hurry along, you swine-headed scape-graces!" she called over the squawking crows.

The boys could only nod tiredly in reply.

Fencress turned to find Karnag and just then caught an odor upon the mist, a smell quite familiar to one who'd done as much dark work as she. Sickly-sweet and pungent, she and Karnag had used lime to conceal it when they'd needed to stash a corpse for a day or two.

Nothing smelled quite like the decay of death.

She looked again to the crows and realized why they were so raucous: a great feast had been set for them not far away and the bastards on the boughs above were likely just giving their bellies a rest.

She pressed away from the tree and toiled on toward the source of the stink. Soon the ground firmed and the trees thinned and flies nagged at her from everywhere.

"Fencress," said Paddyn from nearby. "That smell…"

"It's death," Fencress said matter-of-factly, "and it strikes me you boys ought to be a little more used to it by now."

She moved onward and the thicket gave way to an open field. About it swarmed more cackling crows and buzzing flies than she'd ever beheld in a single place. Beneath that whirlwind of black birds and bugs bent hundreds of bodies, most dead and others almost so. Riderless warhorses wandered about, wet and wide eyes seeming to mourn the dead. Everywhere crows lorded over the bloated and broken corpses of men and their mounts, pecking gleefully away, and flies crowded upon the leftovers.

In the midst of it all moved Karnag Mak Ragg.

The highlander stalked the battlefield—the

graveyard—with apparent purpose. He'd pulled free his greatsword and swung it now in wide arcs before him. The crows flocked away from the sweeps of the blade, complaining and swirling about before returning to their meals once Karnag passed.

"Well, Drenj," Fencress said, "I suppose the good news is these folk are already dead or damned close to it. Your virgin hands should remain unstained by the dark work."

A retch and a splatter sounded behind her. She turned to see the Khaldisian swiping the back of his hand across a mouth dripping with spittle.

She sighed then straightened. "Well I suppose the stain of your puke is not quite as damning as that of blood."

"What is Karnag doing?" asked Paddyn.

Fencress drew her cowl tight and watched. Karnag took no spoils from the fallen and paid no heed to the cries of those few who yet lived. He moved about Arranese carcasses in their leathers and hides and amidst the dead soldiers of Rune cased in their gray mail. He seemed to watch only the flight of the carrion-eaters, watching as they wheeled away and settled once more.

"He seeks something," said Fencress. "Just as he said." Curiosity grabbed her and she strode out onto the field of the dead.

But what?

Karnag whipped his sword about, sending crows screaming and scattering. He crouched low, eyes trained upon the birds as they fluttered about the steamy air.

Fencress stepped around the tangled corpses, drawing nearer. *What do you seek, Karnag?*

Karnag stood straight, studying a black cloud of a

dozen or so crows. The birds croaked as they wound in a wide circle about the battlefield. Suddenly and as one they seemed to regroup, then sank as though to settle upon another carcass. But they fled their intended meal, squawking madly and breaking in all directions, then flapped their way clear of the field entirely.

Fencress looked to the spot the birds had abandoned though she could discern no details through the mass of dead bodies. She crept closer, steps careful upon ground still strewn with blood, gristle and entrails.

Karnag moved to the vacated place. His hard features sharpened to an intense glare, then he sank to a squat and set aside his sword. His mouth moved with words lost in the din of buzzing flies and complaining crows.

Fencress slowed, picking her way between severed limbs and crooked corpses. She came at last to Karnag's side. Her old friend knelt in a blood-soaked circle upon the field of the dead. Before him slumped a black-robed man—all but gone judging from his pallid color and arrhythmic, rattling breaths—waiting out his last moments with his guts in his hands. Flies clouded about, though seemed unwilling to spawn their maggots anywhere near the soon-to-be-corpse.

Fencress studied the fellow. He was covered in black from head to toe, aside from the red mess of bloody entrails. His face was masked in the shadows of his hood, but as she kept her eyes upon it she discerned a stitch that crept up the middle of his chin, through his lips, and toward his nose.

She thought—for the second time that day—of Arranan's Spider King. Of his stitched face. Of the monstrosity's companion bearing a face sewn in the same way. Faces of patchwork flesh writhing against stitches.

"No!" the man wailed. He shook, his body twitching with an odd quickness before abruptly falling still. His hood slipped aside to reveal a hairless head of sickly skin covered with even more barbed, black thread.

The same sort of witch as the one at the Spider King's side. The same sort we watched die in Shank's Hollow.

"Karnag…" Fencress said. "What is this thing?"

The highlander appeared to hear her not, or held no regard for her words. He spoke in a low mumble, a string of strange sounds Fencress could not understand. He beheld the witch with a terrifying glower.

"N-no…" the witch said through a cough, a dribble of dark blood falling from its lips and soaking into the thick stitch upon its chin.

"You are broken!" Karnag screamed, the sound of it jarring. He reached for the hilt of his sword *Gravemaker*.

The witch quivered. "Our secrets are our own," it hissed, spitting the words through bubbles of bloody spittle.

"Yield to me!" Karnag roared. His thick, muscled form seemed to grow, becoming all the more threatening. He held the blade against the witch's neck. "*Illienne abralide y alluma veras.*"

The stitched, hairless thing vomited forth a mess of blood and trembled before falling still. Its eyes remained open and a dark stain spread within to color them a deep black.

"Now," Karnag said, moving to stand, "you will surrender." He held the sword before him, his flint-colored eyes regarding it in an almost wistful manner. "You will tell me your secrets. Your secrets of death."

The witch seemed a corpse, and said nothing.

"Yield!" Karnag bellowed. "*Illienne abralide y alluma veras!*" Crows cawed and rose from all around, fleeing his presence.

Fencress watched with disgust as the stitches upon the head of the witch unravelled, its skin seeming to drip from its body. Wisps of what seemed shadows leaked from its pale fingers and spread upon the trampled earth like a spill of oil.

Karnag descended then upon the thing, throwing aside his sword to set hands against the creature's skull. "Yield!" he screamed, squeezing a skull set with two black orbs for eyeballs and covered only with gray sinews flecked with rot.

Fencress did her best not to sully the field with the remains of her meager lunch. She shied away, looking askance to Paddyn and Drenj still standing beneath the jagged trees at the field's edge. Their faces seemed hardly different from those of the dead.

"Yield," Karnag commanded, and a piercing shriek answered him. The highlander's hands flexed as they twisted the witch's skinless head. A crack sounded and Karnag pulled the skull and a fair bit of the spine free of the creature's body.

Fencress moved back, stepping between the corpses and even upon them. She felt a terrible sense of dread and wagered it best to allow plenty of space between herself and whatever the hell Karnag was doing.

"Yield!" Karnag roared again, holding the grotesque

skull level with his face. His hands worked against the rot-covered bone and he again spoke strange words. "*Illienne abralide y alluma veras...*"

The skull's jaw fell open to reveal a tongue, dark and discolored. At once the tongue twitched and fell still, then began rolling about. It swayed, slowly at first. Then Karnag drew the skull to within inches of his face and the tongue curled and twisted within the maw.

Karnag laughed, the sound of it awful.

Fencress realized then the rest of the field had fallen quiet, the crows and flies alike silent upon their feasts. She looked about, seeing the crows with wings folded and beady eyes upon Karnag. The flies formed muted crowds in the wounds of the dead and dying.

Only Karnag's laughter soared upon the fetid air.

"Now," he said, his chortle giving way to a grave tone. "You will tell me."

The tongue continued its dance and the jawbone began moving. It opened and shut with the click and clatter of bone against bone. As it chattered, tendrils of black formed an inky cloud before it.

Karnag drew back, stretching his sinewy arms to press the skull farther from him. The cloud grew, though, filling the distance. Soon it began to envelop him.

He pulled in a deep breath and shivered. His chest heaved and the cloud diminished. "I see..." he said. "Father?"

The witch's skull broke in Karnag's hands and its pieces tumbled through his fingers. The dark cloud vanished, its last wispy remnants seeping into Karnag's nostrils.

Karnag dropped to a knee, his head drooped and

hidden by his unraveling black braids. After a time he looked to the murky sky above. "Father..." he sighed.

Fencress kept still, her curiosity as bracing as her fear. *What sort of thing have you taken, Karnag? The spirit of another demon to torment you?*

Karnag did not move. He knelt there upon the bloody earth, quiet, with eyes tilted skyward. His expression seemed soft and contemplative, no longer the frightful mask of violence.

But Fencress knew that'd not last. She figured odds were whatever had just happened would make her friend even worse.

Something gave way beneath her and she nearly lost her balance. A pained groan sounded. Only then did she realize she'd placed a foot upon a poor fellow's ruined arm and her boot had just ripped away what was left of the flesh upon it.

"My deepest apologies," Fencress said.

The man, a soldier of Rune judging from the tatters of his red sash and his shredded chainmail, seemed nearly dead. His breaths came shallow and quick. He struggled to turn his head but at last regarded Fencress with eyes that seemed to wander in and out of focus. "Dead gods!" he wheezed. "We won..."

She looked to him, tugging the brim of her cowl. "Sorry, friend, but it doesn't seem you'll be enjoying the spoils of victory. I'd help you if I could, but you're well beyond helping." She tapped the hilts of her twin blades. "Unless you'd like a quicker death, that is? I can offer you that favor."

Tears twisted down the soldier's face and dripped

into the mud beneath him. "No," he croaked. "Just a few more breaths…"

Her eyes softened. "I suppose that's all you have," she said, drawing her hands away from her swords.

"The heavens… They are waiting for me…"

Fencress glanced back to Karnag, still kneeling in his bloody circle. He no longer looked to the heavy sky but to the ground below and that menacing glare once again darkened his face.

"Perhaps they are," Fencress said.

Or perhaps it's just as Drenj said. Perhaps there's only death.

Fencress sat in the campfire's glow, studying the pair of dice on the plate before her. They were the ones she'd stolen from *The Mewling Mutton* in Shank's Hollow. The wooden plate she'd taken from a wagonload of supplies no longer needed by Rune's fallen soldiers.

"A decent meal, at least," Paddyn whistled through a mouthful. He held a whole wheel of smelly cheese in his lap and a cheek-stuffed smile on his face. "Never knew soldiers ate so well."

"They're not eating anymore," Drenj said, taking a small bite of dried meat. He chewed slowly, his eyes finding the fire.

"All the more for us," answered Paddyn before sinking his teeth into the cheese.

Fencress stared out to the night, toward the battlefield a quarter mile downwind. Odds were Karnag remained there still, kneeling in that same morbid circle amongst the dead. She didn't know for certain, but knew she didn't want to head back to find out. Forces raged within her old friend, battling for his soul, and she had yet to figure out her best bet to change him.

She looked again to the dice. An excellent pair, fashioned from ivory and worn smooth along the edges. They seemed too fine for a place like Shank's Hollow, and Fencress wondered if the thane's dead brother had forgotten them at the tavern in some drunken stupor or perhaps lost them as part of a bad wager.

Regardless, they were hers now, as were the many turns of chance they held.

She snatched them up in her gloved hand and tumbled them across her wooden plate. Four pips and one. Honest dice, but lucky ones. It seemed most times she rolled them, one or the other or both would land with just one pip showing—the best face a die could show in deadman's dice.

Perhaps chance still favors me.

Drenj spat out whatever he'd been eating into the fire. He rubbed his eyes. "Where is he leading us? Why do we follow?"

Fencress grabbed the dice, tossed them upward then caught them. She again sent them across the wooden plate with a clatter. Two pips and one. Another fine roll.

"Fencress?" Drenj asked, running long fingers across his head. "Where does he take us?"

"Why he leads us to gold and glory, I'm sure!" she said, reaching for a bottle of whiskey she'd found amidst the supplies. "Considering what we've seen, I suppose Karnag could vanquish the whole of the Arranese army in mere days. Think of the loot! Before you know it the lot of us may be sitting atop a pile of coin as tall as the Southwalls!"

Drenj's eyes returned to the fire. "You know that's not going to happen."

She looked to him before taking a draw of the whiskey. It tasted like the harshest sort of rotgut. She swallowed and took another pull anyway.

"We don't belong in any war," Drenj said. "You know that, too."

Paddyn stifled a belch. He'd stopped eating his wheel of cheese in mid-chew and stared now at Fencress.

Fencress looked away. "Perhaps I do."

"I'm afraid, Fencress," said Drenj. "More afraid than I've ever been."

Fencress nodded. She felt the same but didn't want to say it. Given what they'd seen of Karnag in recent days she worried the words would weaken what resolve she still had.

"It's not just war he seeks," said Drenj. "I fear he seeks a destination much worse. I fear he seeks some kind of hell."

She tumbled the ivory dice across the plate once more. Six pips on one and five on the other—a bad roll at last. She seized them and tucked them inside a pocket sewn into her black cloak then stared again to the darkness. To that field of fatted crows and bloated corpses.

To Karnag and his demons.

She sucked in another mouthful of rotgut. "Who's to say? We may be in that very hell already."

Morning arrived heavy with dread. Fencress hadn't slept

well and wondered when she last had. She'd long ago grown accustomed to danger, but this endeavor was a thing entirely different.

"Breakfast?" asked Paddyn.

Fencress turned in her bedroll to see the skinny lad hunched over a heaping plateful of salted pork, cheese and crusty bread. "At least this foul task hasn't stolen your appetite."

Paddyn smiled, his lips curling to reveal the gap left by his missing tooth. "Never."

Fencress pulled herself upright to see a landscape still shrouded with mist. "Where's Karnag? Any sign of him?"

"None," he mumbled, struggling to bite off a chunk of the bread.

Drenj shifted nearby. "Perhaps he's left us? Perhaps we're free to go at last?" He darted upright, dark eyes lit by what seemed hope.

Fencress grabbed a few strips of salted pork. "I'd wager he's still crouched on that field of dead soldiers. He'll find us as soon as he's finished doing… whatever it is he's doing. As for leaving, you can do that any time you like. He's told you that."

Drenj sighed and fell silent, the only sound about them that of the occasional squawking crow and Paddyn's incessant chewing.

Fencress ripped into the pork. It was tough and stringy but tasty all the same.

At last Drenj spoke again. "I dreamt of my daughter last night," he said, mouth turning with a wistful smile. "Of little Ryaza. She was three years old when last I held her, though by now she's a few months past four. Her hair was long and black, perfectly straight like her mother's, and her brown eyes aglow with laughter. She was… She *is* beautiful."

"I very much want you to see her again," Fencress said. "I mean that."

Drenj held his dark eyes downcast. "I do too. I just fear that every day there is less hope of that. It seems the farther I go from home, the longer I stay with Karnag, the less hope I have of ever holding her again."

"He said you are free to go. You have that choice."

"Choice? He said I'd die if I left his side. What kind of choice is there when every choice leads to death?" He twisted his long fingers in his lap. "But I've begun to wonder, Fencress. I wonder if it'd be better to die away from *him*. That way at least I'd die away from this madness, this evil. And better yet, perhaps there's some chance he's wrong. You said something like that once, and you've talked about how you believe in chance. Perhaps there's some chance those hunters won't find me. Or perhaps some chance they'll not find me until after I've reached Raven's Roost and held my Ryaza once more. Some chance I'll see my Ryaza again. At Karnag's side there's no chance for that."

Fencress swallowed down the last of her salted pork. "I'd hate to see you go, Drenj, but I'd understand your reasons. You have family. I don't—none that I know of, anyways. If you follow the river west a few days and then break south for a couple more past the Drimrill you'll at least be close enough to find Raven's Roost by its stink."

Drenj sniffled and rubbed at his eyes, darkening the smear of kohl across his cheeks. "I would like that…"

"Go, then," Fencress said. "Take all you want from the supplies we found. Take the finest horse you can find from those milling still about that battlefield. I'll give you a good handful of coin, enough to make a nice start on a new life. Go and get clear of this. Go for yourself and your family."

Drenj held his gaze downcast for a time and his dark eyes welled with tears. He began to weep and cradled his head in his hands. "I w-would like that but… I'm so afraid. I'm a coward, Fencress!"

Fencress watched him as he sobbed, his form withered as a waif. She wasn't one to have much sympathy for those burdened by hardship—she'd shouldered plenty of her own. But she pitied Drenj. This dark venture had broken him.

"Drenj," she said, "not one of us has ever seen anything like what's happened to Karnag, what he's become. Only a fool would fail to fear him. You are no coward on account of that."

"I *am* a coward," Drenj said, wiping a mess of snot and tears and kohl from his face, "and the very worst kind of all. I stay at Karnag's side because I fear more for my own life than I do for my daughter's."

Fencress picked a chunk of salted pork from her teeth, finding its taste sour. Her eyes lingered upon the Khaldisian. "No one's as virtuous as they proclaim, especially those who give frequent voice to it. Every last one of us cares first and most of all for our own skin, for our own feelings. We just have a hard time admitting that until we're confronted with the hard choices."

Drenj shuddered and looked away.

Fencress adjusted her black gloves. She worried the short odds were the Khaldisian would find an untimely demise regardless of the path he chose.

A thud sounded. Then a rustle.

Fencress turned to see a man's head tumbling across the dew-tipped grass. It rolled to a stop just aside Paddyn's breakfast plate. A fat, pasty head that'd been severed just beneath its generous jowls.

"Behold." Karnag stood amidst them, towering and terrifying. He seemed even more fearsome than before, clad now in a mishmash of Arranese leathers, his burly frame and eerie eyes holding naught but the promise of death. Before him drooped his sword *Gravemaker*, fresh blood trickling down its length.

"Karnag?" asked Fencress, unable to bring her usual, practiced cheer to her words. She gestured to the severed head resting just beneath Paddyn's blanched face. "Who is—or was—this?"

"His name was Barly Stample," Karnag said. "He was an acolyte of the Ancient Sanctum of Illienne the Light Eternal. I…" His eyes wandered for a moment, as though confusion muddled his head. He breathed. "Castor presided over his induction into the order four years ago and regarded him a loyal though limited servant. And now he is dead."

Fencress studied Karnag's face. "You didn't find him dead on the battlefield, did you?"

Karnag looked to her, brow raised. "No. He was one of our pursuers, sent to scout our location. I sensed his presence then I took his head."

"Our pursuers?" moaned Drenj.

Karnag nodded. "The others will be upon us soon if we remain here. I intend to face them elsewhere, at another time. After I've mastered what I've taken. After I've… become."

"The rotted skull," Fencress said quietly.

"Arise," Karnag commanded. "We ride now."

Fencress stood. "What horses—" She stopped short. Over Karnag's shoulder she spied a line of a half-dozen warhorses ambling toward them from the battlefield.

Karnag smiled. "We ride upon the mounts of the dead. We ride them to war and to ruin."

16
TO WAR ONCE MORE

ANNICK SURVEYED THE many hundreds of soldiers about him, arms and armor reflecting the hard sun above. Some marched on foot, others rode horses, and others still guided wagons sagging with provisions.

All headed to war once more.

The air rose with an old but familiar song. Weapons clicked and clanked while wagons squealed and groaned. Horses nickered and men spoke in proud voices of deeds to come. Occasional orders or encouraging words were barked over it all.

"Two days to Riverweave!" shouted someone waving a red and black banner amidst the mass of men ahead. "Two and a half to victory!"

"Fuck General Fane!" howled another. Soldiers cheered in reply, smacking swords against shields and throwing fists into the air.

Lannick found himself smiling in wholehearted agreement.

Brugan would have loved this. He deserved to see it. If only...

He thought of the manner of his friend's death and his smile waned.

He knew at this moment Fane was heaping ever more lives upon the pyre of his ambition. More innocent lives lost to the man's madness.

Hatred filled his heart and he spat. He spurred his horse onward, wishing that doing so could bring him revenge just an instant sooner. He'd waited so long—too long—to make Fane pay for his deeds.

"You are mindful of your purpose, yes?" grumbled squint-eyed Ogrund from atop his drab horse.

Lannick looked sideways to the green-clad Variden. "Always."

Ogrund's head tilted upon his almost imperceptible neck. "Good," he grunted. "It is good to count you among the Variden once more. You should don your Coda."

Lannick ignored the words, his thoughts focused upon Fane. His ears still burned from the man's shrill voice and he could still see the scars striating the general's face. But most memorable were the eyes. Black eyes, ever intense and disquieting. Always calculating, always seeking an advantage. Always greedy with desire.

"Good," Ogrund grated in seeming annoyance. "I said it was good to have you with us, and that you should don your Coda. You should complete your rededication to the cause."

Lannick looked hard at the man. "You must

understand something, Ogrund," he said. "I have not returned to the Variden. Not yet. You and the others condemned me for seeking vengeance. Just because our purposes have become intertwined doesn't mean I'm ready to lash my Coda to my wrist and have you and Wil and all the rest poking around my head."

Ogrund shifted stiffly in his saddle and regarded Lannick with eyes almost closed. "There is far more at stake than exacting punishment for one man's past misdeeds. There is—"

"*Misdeeds?*" Lannick scoffed. "Dead gods! The man murdered my family and now my friend has been put in the ground as well!"

Ogrund raised a hand. "I mean not to diminish your losses. I mean only to illustrate what is at stake in this war."

"I'm well aware of the stakes and you'd not stand at my side now if I'd not learned Fane's place in all of this."

Ogrund stared to him with some sort of meaning, though the man's impassive features and eternal squint made that meaning impossible to identify.

At last Ogrund grunted. "One cannot simply wear a Coda whenever one pleases," he said. "It is no mere ornament, Lannick. You know that. Our Codas are sacred gifts from Valis. They bind us to his purpose and grant to us his power."

Lannick shook his head, weary of the lecture. "Yet my Coda hasn't left me, has it? Perhaps it *and* Valis understand my purpose more than you and Wil and Alisa and all those others who would question me."

"Our purpose is to defend Rune from its ancient and most dangerous enemy."

"And mine is to put my sword through Fane's heart!" Lannick growled. "I serve no other purpose until that one is fulfilled!"

"Well that's damned nice to hear." The voice belonged to Arleigh Lay. He'd come to ride alongside them and looked to Ogrund with his nasty sneer.

Ogrund turned to the man. "I am speaking with Lannick about things that do not concern you. He and I require a moment. Please ride along."

Arleigh pressed his remaining hand into the black jerkin he'd stretched over his chainmail, that part of the jerkin likely holding his dagger. "The fuck I will."

Ogrund pulled his horse to a halt. "I will not suffer such vulgar address."

Arleigh sneered. "Well you'd best ride the fuck elsewhere, then."

For just an instant Ogrund's eyes flared open before squeezing to a tight squint once more. He spurred his horse to a trot and wove between the soldiers ahead before becoming lost within the marching army.

"Thank you, Arleigh," Lannick said. He smiled crookedly, hardly believing those three words had just dropped from his mouth.

"Least I could do," Arleigh said.

"He's not a bad fellow," Lannick said. "He wants the same thing we all do. It's just that he and I have a… history."

"That I gathered."

Lannick looked ahead. "He's sworn to protect Rune from our oldest enemies. From those things that killed Brugan. He can help us in the war."

Arleigh grunted. "Always wondered why Fane accused you of being some kind of witch. After seeing what you did at Rellic, I suppose I know, and I daresay I'm glad you are whatever you are. I never would have believed the world held such… devils."

Lannick's hand fell to his Coda. "A war has been waged against them in the dark places of this world for centuries. A secret battle fought in the shadows. Ogrund's one of the soldiers fighting that war."

"And so are you."

"I was," Lannick said, glancing to Arleigh. The man's face twisted with its eternal scowl, though his eyes seemed to carry little of the hate they'd shown at Kevlin's farm. "I was," Lannick said again, "and I walked away. But now that other war is upon me—upon us all—once more."

"There's only one war now," said Arleigh. "Just our fight to stay out of the grave and put others in it." He chuckled. "I like to keep things simple."

"What say you, Captain?" said Black Jon, lounging on a barrel with his back against the tall spokes of a cart. He swiped crumbs from grubby hands into the campfire between them and gestured to the map aside it, the curled ends of the parchment set aglow by the fire's light. "Less than two days to the gates of Riverweave. We'd long thought to enter the city at its northern end, just as you had, but now that seems ill-advised. The latest additions to our number say the thanes finally prevailed in their demands to send more soldiers to the front. Now half a column—half the Fourth Column of Ironmoor—marches toward it. Mere days distant, they say. If we get pinched at the northern gates between Fane's men and the coming reinforcements then our little foray could be rather brief. The south? Then we're fighting Fane's men and the Arranese horde both at once. And the western edge of the city is wet, muck-covered sprawl, and no place to be fighting a battle."

Lannick tugged at the tasteless hardtack bread with his teeth. He ripped away a dry chunk and chewed it for a moment before deciding he needed a pull of ale to wash it down his gullet. He wiped the ale's foam from his face then looked to the map, shifting his crooked jaw. "We shouldn't try the northern gates. We—"

"Yes we should," interjected deMond. "We could double our pace and sweep around the city. Deception can be an elegant strategy…" he said, tracing a finger across the map. "It could be just like the renegade thanes' clash with High King Dermangorn three hundred years ago, when the High King used the brilliant strategy of disguising his men. Think of it: we still wear the red sash. Wash away the black mark we've placed upon it and we look no different from ordinary soldiers of Rune. The guards at the gate could be persuaded we're a vanguard of the Fourth Column."

Black Jon straightened atop the barrel. "But if the general learns of our approach and sends word to the new column? Then we're done for."

Lannick stared to the map. "The General Fane I know doesn't want us—or anyone else—coming to stand in the way of his mad ambitions. If he learns of our coming then my guess is he'll get word to the reinforcing column and order them to deal with us. Then Fane's taken care of both us and the Fourth. And if he doesn't learn of our coming? The northern gates still stay shut. He doesn't want the Fourth entering the city. He knows that's a column with a new set of officers certain to have heard the rumors and certain to be more inclined to question the general's decisions. Fane is a paranoid man, and he'll leave them encamped north of the city until he's finished slaughtering what remains of his present command."

Black Jon nodded. "It's a damned mess, whichever way we look at it."

Sergeant deMond stiffened and stared to Lannick. "Then what, Captain, is your *learned* recommendation?"

"Dead gods, deMond," sighed Sergeant Kaldare, staring to the night sky above the encampment. "We're here to find a way to *win* this war, not elbow our way toward some perceived position. The captain here is on the same side as us and knows Fane better than most."

Sergeant deMond fingered his patchy goatee. "No doubt the captain knows how to end on the losing side of the general. But does the captain know how to prevail against him, I wonder? Does he have any concept of a winning strategy?"

"Careful, bookish boy," growled Arleigh Lay from Lannick's side. "Captain Lannick here has already won a war. Did that fucking bastard Fane use his power to bring Lannick down afterward? Sure. But Lannick won that war." He took a draw from his tankard. "Where were you during Pryam's Bay? Judging from afar while doing nothing of consequence yourself?"

The sergeant's eyes bulged. "How dare—"

"Safe with your little books, were you?" Arleigh huffed. "You—"

"Arleigh," Lannick said, "enough." He uttered the words in a scolding fashion, though in his heart he was more grateful for the man's presence than he would ever have expected.

Black Jon shuffled atop his barrel. "We respect rank here, Corporal Lay."

Arleigh looked to Black Jon. "Then your sergeant here should remember he's addressing a captain."

Black Jon chuckled. "Fair enough," he said, eyes moving to Lannick. "My question remains, *Captain*. We have a quandary, as smart folk like deMond would call it." He winked and took a long pull from his mug, draining its contents. He looked about. "Harl?" he called. "More ale."

Lannick bent close to the fire between them. "We cannot afford to lose one more man than absolutely necessary, from Rune's army or your own."

"And hence our quandary." Black Jon hoisted his empty tankard and looked about again. "Harl! We've precious few moments left to enjoy a swallow of ale!" He shook his head and looked to Lannick. "Captain? What say you?"

There was a clatter near them and a hiss of steam from the fire.

"Sorry, sir," said Harl, standing at the fire's edge and clutching tankards against his chest. His dirty shirt was soaked.

"Ah, Harl," Black Jon said with a smile. "That's alright. So long as most of the ale is still inside those cups."

Harl peered into the mugs and nodded. "Aye, sir."

Black Jon held out a hand. "Then by the dead gods give me one. Either victory or death awaits us, and both are deserving of a drink."

Lannick watched as Black Jon snatched a tankard and drained it in a single swallow. Though his own thirst was still strong he waved away the mug Harl offered him. *Keep your edges sharp, lad*, he thought.

Harl looked to him with a narrow gaze then limped away into the night.

"So," said Black Jon, tilting his barrel forward to peer over the map, "you think the southern edge or the western. A choice among evils if you ask me."

Lannick stared to him. "Everything is now."

"Aye," Black Jon said. "That it is. Then how would you suggest we meet our glorious deaths?"

Lannick smirked. "I prefer that happen only after General Fane's." He studied again the map. "And I think the best way to ensure that is to march straight east. We spread out. We break into small units of a dozen or less and try to slip through the city's western edge. It's a mess, just as you say—the Arranese won't attack it for that very reason. It's also more difficult for Fane's men to patrol. Besides, Fane's attention will be fixed on the Arranese to the south and the Fourth Column to the north."

"Foolish," said deMond, waving a hand. "Utterly foolish. An army broken into that many pieces could never fight a battle."

Lannick looked to him. "We don't fight the battle in pieces. We regroup once we're in the city. Once we've—"

Sergeant deMond snorted. "We just march more than two thousand men through the city gates?"

"No," grated Lannick. "As I said, we move in small groups. We use the rivers, the canals, the channels and sewers. Folk are bound to be fleeing the city and the place will be awash with confusion."

"Ulder," grunted Arleigh. "Ulder Prane, one of our number, used to be a smuggler in these parts. Says his brother still is. If there's anyone who'd know the soft spots of the city and the best ways to enter..."

Black Jon rubbed his chin. "Sounds risky, Captain. If you'd not won one war already I'm not sure I'd consider it."

Lannick shifted his jaw and gestured to the map with his chunk of hardtack. "Once we've regrouped inside the city we make our purpose known. Fane may not want reinforcements but I reckon many of his soldiers feel differently. If those men have seen their brothers fall—if they've heard tell of defeat after defeat—and then see armed men arriving to help them? My guess is a good many will choose to march in our ranks instead of the general's. Soldiers value their lives more than their orders." He looked squarely to Black Jon. "You and your lot are proof of that."

"Fire! Fire!"

The shouting tore Lannick from his slumber. He struggled to sit, sucking in a sharp breath and looking about with bleary eyes. Dawn hadn't yet colored the sky but a harsh glow blazed but fifty feet distant.

A terrible clamor rose from the camp. Shouting. Men stumbling about and shaking away the fog of sleep. Others running, some away from the fire and some toward it. Others aflame.

Footfalls pounded close. Lannick just managed to avoid being trampled.

"What the fuck?" cursed Arleigh Lay from somewhere nearby.

There came the sound of shattering glass and fire engulfed a nearby tent. Men ran from it, screaming, their clothing afire. In an instant the tent became a tower of licking flames and billowing smoke.

Soldiers everywhere scrambled and the whole encampment seemed a frenzy of confusion. Men drew swords that shone in the blaze though none seemed to know where to thrust them.

A thickly-built fellow came near. "Lannick," the man grunted. It was Ogrund. "The camp has been breached. I will locate the raiders. Don your Coda so we can communicate. No doubt I will require your aid." He set off, slipping through the roiling crowd with unnatural grace.

Lannick tugged on his boots and stood. He fastened sword and purse to his belt, pulled on a padded shirt and coat of chainmail, then looked about.

Within moments wagonloads of supplies and more tents had erupted in flames. The strides and shouts of soldiers seemed to shake the ground beneath. The air seared the skin.

Then yet another blaze, this a tent mere yards from Lannick. The flames grew quickly, the heat singeing Lannick's face. Confused soldiers poured out as the flames consumed the tent's flimsy fabric. One man with clothes on fire ran close and nearly knocked Lannick from his feet.

More screaming.

More fire.

The camp felt like a furnace.

"Arleigh!" Lannick called.

"Here," came a groan, though from where Lannick couldn't guess.

Is he hurt?

Lannick spun about, searching. "Arleigh?"

"Right here," came a nasty voice.

Lannick turned. Something smashed against the side of his head. He staggered, eyes blurry. The warm drip of blood upon his cheek. "Ar—"

"Get him!"

Another crack upon his head.

He slumped to the ground.

Sinking, drowning.

And all turned black.

17
THE GRIP OF DARKNESS

PREFECT GAMGHAST STRAINED blurry eyes against the dying candlelight. The tome on the desk before him seemed covered by steamy glass, the stains of its text shifting and clouding over.

He squinted vainly, then sighed. A cataract had formed in his left eye and made an already difficult task all the more so. The Sanctum's healing arts could address many ills, though it seemed the withering of age wasn't one.

He eased back against the creaking spindles of his chair, his spine catching painfully as he did. Exhaustion weighed upon him, along with a growing sense of futility. The former he could manage but the latter troubled him deeply. He was a practical man by nature, and the task of saving the realm suddenly seemed an utterly impractical endeavor.

Defeat was all but a certainty.

Thoughts of the chamberlain and his foul Necrist companions haunted Gamghast's head. They had defiled the holiest of Rune's shrines, the Godswell. They'd bled the corpse of High King Deragol and seemed to commune with their dark, dead god by virtue of that hideous act. Rune's ancient enemy had taken hold like a cancer in the kingdom's very heart.

And all while we did nothing.

The cavernous library felt still as a crypt, a stale thing that seemed to Gamghast a fine symbol of the Sanctum's stagnation. He smacked a hand against the desk, knowing the Sanctum's inaction to be the very worst of things. His ignorance—indeed the ignorance of the whole of his order—confounded him. He thought of those countless years the Sanctum had devoted to prayer and study and healing yet none to preparation. None devoted to mounting a defense against an old foe they'd permitted themselves to all but forget.

He'd spent much of the last week here, secreted away within the musty expanse of the Abbey's library. He'd tried to recover what the Sanctum once knew of the enemy and the weapons to fight them, scouring the library's deepest recesses and the Lector's collection of banned books. He'd forced failing eyes upon forgotten tomes and dry, crackling scrolls that nearly crumbled when unfurled.

And he'd found precious little. For all the wisdom the Sanctum hoarded it seemed only meager scraps had been saved of the knowledge he needed most.

He wondered at the wisdom of their Lector, of the Sentinel Castor. He wondered why Castor would have failed to prepare his pupils, why he would have disregarded the threat the Necrists posed.

Could he, too, have been blind to their coming?

Gamghast shook his head. *No. His journey and the note the chamberlain claims to have intercepted indicate otherwise. But if Castor knew, why did he not tell us?*

He smoothed the wild wisps of his beard. Doubt nagged at him. *Did he not trust us? Did he not trust us because Rune banished him and his kin so long ago?*

Or worse, could he have meant to betray us?

His mind reeled with these thoughts, these troubling possibilities. He contemplated them for a moment, staring out upon the darkness.

But then he shook his head once more. None of it mattered. He needed to be practical, to find solutions. What the Lector *could* have known, or *could* have done, did nothing to help Rune now. What mattered was finding a means to save the kingdom, a means to keep all from surrendering to the dark and to the Lord of Nightmares.

He leaned forward to again pore over his book. It was one of the very few things he'd uncovered that seemed of use, an ancient text he'd found buried beneath a mountain of rolled scrolls and maps. The brittle book appeared to have been written when the War of Fates and its aftermath were still wet upon the tongue of history. It whispered of days when the Sanctum and the Variden worked in concert to hunt down and finish what was left of Yrghul's disciples, of old magic and old foes.

The tome spoke of the Necrists as a very real and present danger and with an urgency Gamghast hadn't read in any book penned in more recent centuries. Gamghast read of a hidden stronghold where the Necrists plied their darkest secrets, and of a desperate venture to destroy them forever.

He strained his eyes now to read of that effort, of that mission to annihilate the enemy. He focused his rheumy vision and read of members of the Sanctum and their Variden brothers discovering a shadowpath, an invisible passage used by the Necrists to travel beneath the shadows of the world. And he read of two scores of Necrists and their abominations discovering the intruders and the battle that ensued.

He read of the Variden using their sacred instruments—their *Codas*—to muster their powers. He read of their inhuman agility, their gift of concealing themselves from eyes unwanted, and of swords dripping with flames that cleaved the darkness. He read, too, of long-dead prefects proclaiming forgotten words of spellcraft, incantations that pulled lightning from the heavens. Spells that stole the life from the Necrists and turned to ash the dead flesh they wore.

The prefects and the Variden had prevailed. They'd prevailed despite losing half their number and facing many foes.

Prefects, Gamghast thought. *Prefects worked these powers. Not just Castor. We once possessed the tools to defeat the enemy.*

He resumed the tale, reading of how after the battle the victorious prefects and Variden had found the shadowpath altered and misdirected. They wandered lost for days. When at last they found the Necrists' stronghold they found it abandoned and its contents burned.

Gamghast closed the book. In spite of its ending the story imparted hope. It seemed, he thought, there had to be some way to beat back the grip of darkness.

He took a ragged breath and withdrew from the tome, eyes drifting about the library's expanse. Shadows crowded all about, oppressive and impenetrable. The ceiling above, where stretched great arches of stone, was lost behind a blanket of black.

Gamghast shifted in his chair and held a hand upward. He drew in a long breath and brought certitude to his voice. "*Illienne abralide y ganode allum!*" he commanded. *Illienne awaken and give me light!*

Light, white and pure and brilliant, erupted from his hand. The shadows—all of them—cowered and vanished, and the whole of the library seemed lit with a radiance as blinding as the midday sun. Gamghast smiled even as the fleeting light dimmed and gave way once more to the heavy dark.

If we can but find the tools, we can find a chance of victory.

A door creaked open somewhere behind him followed by shuffling steps upon the tiled floor. Gamghast turned as far as his achy spine would allow and spied the glow of a candle moving between rows of sagging shelves. A rotund figure emerged, round features muddled by apparent concern.

"Good evening, Borel," Gamghast said.

"Evening?" Borel said, jowls swaying. "Gamghast, it's well past midnight. You need sleep."

"Sleep?" grumbled Gamghast. "Sleep?" He smacked a hand upon the old tome, sending a shower of dust from its cover. "Sleep is the last thing we should worry over! We've been sleeping for centuries, Borel. We've slept while our enemy has awakened and thrived in the shadows. We've slept and have allowed ourselves to forget the very things we need most."

Borel thumbed his chin. "You're certain? You're certain those old spells exist?"

Gamghast lifted the book before him with a grunt. "This account speaks of such things. There must be secrets we've forgotten, secrets buried somewhere within this place."

"You and I have only four eyes between us, Gam. It could take us years—decades—to find such things."

"That is why you will summon every able body in the Abbey. Summon them and tell them the stakes of this war. Tell them the truth, the truth of Castor and our charge. All—"

"But the Crown! Such would be deemed treason by the Crown!"

"Damn the Crown!" Gamghast spat. "You will tell the acolytes the truth! All of it. And tell them to empty these shelves—every one of them—and read every word written in every book and every scroll of this library. Tell them to turn over every stone in this tomb we call our home. Tell them the whole of the world depends upon them finding the precious secrets we have lost. Tell them to find our old weapons against the enemy."

Prefect Gamghast leaned upon his staff near the library's entrance, watching as more than a hundred acolytes scoured the massive chamber. The place, generally one of quiet contemplation, had become a chaotic mess the moment dawn streamed in colored ribbons though windows of stained glass. Brown-robed acolytes tore down shelves and flipped through pages of countless books, discarding irrelevant tomes in great, heaping piles. The rare books holding a hint of promise stood in stacks upon a table manned by Prefect Borel and a few of the Sanctum's more senior acolytes.

Gamghast strode inside with a click-clack of his staff. "Do not ignore the scrolls!" he demanded, gesturing toward the library's northern end. "Scour every word in this musty cave!"

Several acolytes darted toward those shelves and in their eagerness managed to send a dozen or so scrolls rolling haphazardly across the library's floor.

Gamghast shook his head. *Ah, Acolyte Bale*, he thought, smoothing the wisps of his beard. *You would have reveled in this work and no doubt would have had a better idea where to search than this sad lot. I pray that by the grace of Illienne you're still alive.*

He thrust his staff ahead then dragged himself forward, shuffling his way deeper into the chamber. The shelves were in shambles, now, their old order overturned. Gamghast grunted, finding the sight well suited to the times.

"Tear this place apart!" he shouted, guiding his way about a jumble of books. "You know now the Lector's true identity and you know that he was slain! A Sentinel among us—a Sentinel slain! If that doesn't impart to you the urgency of this task then you should be sifting through sewers rather than shelves."

The acolytes hastened their work, some even trying to rifle through two books at once. Prefect Borel, too, hunkered closer to his tome, dragging a pudgy finger across lines of text.

Gamghast drew near his fellow prefect and braced himself against the table. "Anything?" he asked.

"Only prayers and incantations we already possess," Borel said, his heavy head still lowered over the book. "But there are histories... histories with unusual accounts. Accounts of the Necrists and of members of our order using prayers of great power against them."

"But no recitations of those prayers themselves? No descriptions of the gestures and reagents employed? Such texts *must* exist. Lector Erlorn was always digging around in here, always digging through so-called 'banned texts.' Certainly he wasn't just reveling in tired nostalgia."

Borel raised his eyes to Gamghast. "He did have an odd fascination with our lesser-known volumes. A blasphemous fascination, if you believe Dictorian Theal."

"Do you?" Gamghast said, striking his staff upon the stone tiles. "Do you believe Dictorian Theal? That most pious and pompous soul who is no doubt lounging in the Elder God's heavens as we speak?"

"Gam, you know how I feel about that. I would have left with Prefect Kreer if I felt otherwise. I'm merely recalling what many thought of the Lector's interest in old books."

"Perhaps he, too, was trying to remember how to defeat the enemy. Perhaps not, and perhaps we will never know. Regardless, we must keep searching. The Crown can't have burned every book of value, and Castor or

Erlorn or whoever *must* have known something to have spent such time here. Acolyte!" he said, leveling a finger at one of the men seated beside Prefect Borel. "Fetch me a chair and a stack of books not already deemed worthless."

Gamghast rapped his knuckles on the table, the sound jarring now that night had dulled the day's commotion. "Still nothing?"

Borel looked up from his candlelit book, eyes baggy and bloodshot. "Just more histories," he said weakly. "Little different from what you discovered earlier. There are more detailed descriptions of the Necrists than I've ever encountered—they're quite frightening. And there are stories of battles against them. There are accounts of pilgrimages to ancient shrines and of the use of forgotten prayers and powers. But not a detail on the means and methods of more potent spellcraft. Not things we don't already know." He rubbed at his eyes with thick thumbs. "I'm sorry, Gamghast."

"There are poems, too," muttered an acolyte seated beside Borel. "Poems and—"

"And not a word of sacred spellcraft," interjected Gamghast.

The acolyte shook his head. "No, Prefect. Not a word."

Gamghast gripped his staff and arose, frustration stifling all other thought. "Then perhaps the gods, and Castor, have forsaken us indeed." He turned from the table and trudged away.

"Gamghast?" Borel called after him.

Gamghast made a shooing motion and walked, leaning heavily upon his staff as he exited the library.

Gamghast found the Abbey's corridors had surrendered to darkness at this late hour, the stonework lit only by occasional, sputtering torches. Most of the acolytes had abandoned their efforts, the doors of their quarters shut and showing no hint of candlelight beyond. He moved along, wondering if they, too, felt bound by the shackles of futility.

He walked aimlessly through the shadows, listening to the thud and clack of his uneven stride. His journey lacked purpose, aside from what he guessed was some effort to either hide from others or become lost himself. He wandered and as he did his thoughts drifted back to his conversation with Tolem. *"How can I have faith in the absence of hope?"* he recalled asking.

He worried over that question again, that question of faith. He'd devoted decades—every good year of his life—to the Sanctum, and now it seemed that time was coming to an end. An end with an ancient enemy's hands at his throat and his kingdom in ruins.

He came to a stop and closed his eyes. *Will this be how we're remembered? Old bones in an old grave, powerless against our foe?*

He straightened his spine as much as his aches would allow. *No. I will meet my end with dignity, and fight until the end.*

He looked about his surroundings, an intersection of cramped corridors hazy with the smoke of torches. Though nearly identical to many other crossings in the Abbey, Gamghast knew this one. He'd visited it many weeks before, just hours after receiving word of the Lector's murder.

He found the door to the Lector's quarters and approached. Curiosity seized him. He grasped the knob and turned it, pressing open a creaking door to reveal the dark room beyond. He squinted and spotted a candle on a desk inside. He snatched it and fired the wick on a coughing torch, tugged in a breath and entered.

The Lector's quarters were as he remembered, small and simple. Erlorn's few personal effects had been sent to his family—a sister and two nephews near the Waters of World's End—shortly after his death. What remained were neat piles of ceremonial garb and ornamentation, a shelf bearing a careful arrangement of statuettes, and a haphazard assemblage of books.

Gamghast bent close to the jagged stacks, bringing the candle's flame as near to the wild wisps of his beard as caution would allow. He supposed these were the last dozen or so tomes the Lector had taken from the library, the last things he'd thought to read before his trek southward. The last he'd thought to read before his death.

Gamghast had given the books only a cursory inspection when he'd last visited this room, glancing at the spines and the titles written upon them. This seemed the same collection. Books on the divinity of the High King and his line, volumes on the healing of the sick, old hymns to Illienne and the Elder God.

Before, in those hours after learning of the Lector's death, Gamghast had searched for journals, for personal letters and notes. He'd not given much consideration to these books. Now the texts puzzled him, for they hinted at nothing of the Lector's so-called 'blasphemous' interests.

Each of these volumes adhered to the Sanctum's modern—or at least publicly proclaimed—doctrine on the Old Faith. Each had been scribed after the Crown banished the Sentinels and banned their veneration. These were elementary teachings, the sorts of books read by new acolytes upon admission to the order.

He furrowed his brow, wondering if the works had provided an innocuous distraction for the Lector, a simple diversion for a soul who'd certainly read every work in the library already.

He stretched his crackling spine upward to stand. *Nonsense. A Sentinel wouldn't dwell upon such trifles.*

He tapped the butt of his staff against the floor. He recalled when he'd received that terrible news, that news of murder. It'd been the wee hours of morning, the day's first hour, perhaps…

Gamghast himself had been first to hear it, to hear the green-cloaked Variden—Ogrund, he was called—speak of the death of Erlorn's body and the displacement of Castor's spirit. Gamghast had summoned Dictorian Theal and Prefects Borel and Kreer, and the four of them had listened to the Variden with rapt attention. Borel had nearly fainted, Gamghast remembered. Kreer had quoted old platitudes and hollow scriptures. Theal had fled the room to focus all his soul on prayers to guide the spirit.

Or had he?

Gamghast thought of the Dictorian, particularly his mad desire to pry Castor's spirit from the highlander and possess it himself. It had seemed an act of hubris then, and seemed even more so now. Gamghast worried what motivations would have moved Theal in those moments after learning of Erlorn's murder.

He looked again to the stacks of books, the precarious pillars a contrast to the arrangement of the rest of the Lector's belongings.

He squeezed his hand about the staff, knuckles cracking as he did.

With a curse he spun away from the books and stormed from the room. He trampled through the Abbey's corridors with his crippled, crab-like stride. A couple of bleary-eyed acolytes walked the same passageway and he swatted them aside with his staff.

Down another corridor he turned and nearly collided with a candle-toting acolyte. "Prefect," the fellow yelped. "Prefect! There you are! Someone is asking—"

"Not now!" Gamghast barked, shrugging aside the man and hobbling along.

"But Prefect Gamghast!"

Gamghast ignored the words and worked his way through the stony catacombs, through hallways bearing only rumors of torchlight. At last he came upon the doors to Theal's chambers. The knobs of the double doors were gilded—a rare opulence amid the Abbey's gray masonry. The room hadn't been disturbed since the Dictorian's death, there being no new Dictorian named. Kreer had demanded no decree be made until he'd returned from his journey and lent his voice to the process. Gamghast knew the man's motives were less than noble in this regard, certain Kreer thought he'd command Castor's spirit by then.

He scowled. *Can good intention ever triumph over greed when both stir within the same soul?*

He huffed and approached the door, twisted a knob and found it locked. He grunted and dug into his robes, at last producing a ring jangling with keys. He and the other prefects now possessed keys to every door of the Sanctum, including those to areas formerly accessible only to the Dictorian and Lector. He fumbled with them, candle in one hand, keys in the other, and staff squeezed in the crook of his elbow. At last he found a key scratched with Theal's name and guided his shaking hand to the keyhole. The tumbler turned with only minor protest and Gamghast threw open the door.

The dark room smelled musty, little different from the crypt beneath the Abbey. Gamghast moved within, his candle's wax dripping from its narrow holder onto his hand. It seared his age-thinned skin for an instant though he cared not. With bleary eyes he scrutinized Theal's every possession.

The room off the main doorway was all bejeweled boxes, imported silks and valued artifacts. A tight grouping of ornate chairs for quaint discussion. A tall mirror no doubt used for the Dictorian's daily ritual of self-admiration.

Gamghast turned to the next room, the Dictorian's study. Its shadows gave reluctant way to the candlelight, retreating to reveal a decorative desk and a wooden case displaying an array of baubles and books. A sheaf of scrolls tied with ribbons lay heaped upon the desk and bound volumes lined the bookcase. All seemed fat with promise.

Gamghast shambled to the desk, rested his candle

atop it and sank to a seat in its plush, red-pillowed chair. As much as he rejected opulence and its comforts, his aching back was thankful for the chair's design. He eased in a breath and set about inspecting the scrolls.

A commendation from Thane Vandyl for healing soldiers who'd been gravely wounded in a skirmish near Rellic. Correspondence from an acolyte in Raven's Roost seeking counsel over worrisome practices in the city, theft and gambling and prostitution and such. Three letters from some confidant in Pyrene inquiring after the troubles in Rune and the devastation of its war.

All utterly worthless.

Gamghast forced himself upward and turned to the bookcase with a grimace. He brought his candle near, reading words upon weathered spines, some etched with artful script and others with simple scribbles. These volumes were well-known, innocuous titles holding psalms and hymns and similar dross. Gamghast flipped through their pages in hopes of finding some secreted note but, of course, there was none.

His shoulders slumped. The weight of defeat—of futility—pressed upon him. He gathered his staff and trudged to the remaining room.

The door to the Dictorian's bedchamber rested slightly ajar. Gamghast whacked his staff against it, sending it squealing upon its hinges. *Out with you demons*, he thought half-heartedly before shuffling inside, candle in hand.

A four-poster bed with a fluffed mattress dominated one wall and a tall wardrobe another. He tugged open the doors of the wardrobe and was struck by a waft of potent fragrances. Clothing—fine clothing by any standard—hung within, and shelves held ivory combs and hand mirrors and vials of scented oils. Gamghast swept the clothing aside but, alas, the wardrobe revealed no secrets.

He sighed and turned to the bed. Nothing rested atop it. He sighed again, braced himself upon his staff and sank to a knee. Pain shot through his back and he winced, almost dropping his candle. He grimaced and pressed low and lower still and at last came near enough the floor to spy beneath the bed. He eased the candle outward and opened wide his eyes.

He gasped. There, hidden below the bedframe, rested a sack or satchel of some sort.

Gamghast moved the candlestick to his opposite hand, flattened himself against the stone tiles and threw an arm outward. He strained to straighten fingers that'd been bent for years. Still nothing. He shifted closer to the bedframe, wedging his shoulder between its wood and the floor. Finally, his hand found the sack's cloth.

He dragged the sack—a heavy thing—across the floor and then pulled it and himself upward with a groan. He drew in a deep breath and dumped the bag's contents onto the bed's feather mattress.

Books. A dozen of them, all worn and weathered and ancient. Even in the dim light of the candle his weak eyes could make out covers telling of spellcraft within their pages. There was another book, too, a seemingly newer volume with an unadorned binding. He opened it and spotted a simple letter, "*E*," atop the first page, and handwritten entries beginning beneath it.

Erlorn's journal.

He chuckled and shook his head. *How utterly childish of you, Theal. How utterly childish, and how dangerously selfish.*

His heart soared. He grabbed one of the older volumes and thumbed through it, soon finding instructive passages reciting forgotten prayers, their powers, and how to employ them. He held the candle close, reading the passages quickly but with care. His mouth moved with the sacred words— committing them to memory—though he dared not give them voice. These were real powers and his spirit lifted with the confirmation of their existence.

"At last," he said, sweeping up the books into the satchel. "At last."

He snuffed the candle and shouldered the sack. In the dark he made his way back to the door, leaning as much as ever against his staff. He breathed deeply, relieved, as he turned the knob and exited to the torchlit hallway.

A few steps away stood Prefect Borel.

Gamghast smiled. "We have them," he said. "We have our weapons."

"Gamghast?" said Borel, his voice unsteady.

Gamghast gestured to the sack sagging over his shoulder. "Not to worry. I've found what we need."

Borel's entire form trembled. "Gamghast… it doesn't matter now. There's a herald at the door. A herald bearing a warrant from the Magistrate Examiner. We are to be tried for treason."

"Treason?" Gamghast croaked. His mind whirled and he seized Borel's collar and pulled him close. "Is it the queen?" he whispered. "Has Alamis discovered her whereabouts?"

"N-no," Borel stammered. "But he's discovered we harbored Castor in violation of the banishment. Someone—one of the acolytes, likely—must have revealed the secrets we disclosed. Now every one of us stands accused."

18
THE HOME OF THE SPIDER KING

ANDRACHUS BALE SQUINTED skyward, the sun's blaze burning his eyes. The noon hour set fire to Zyn with a withering heat and blinding brightness. Everything—every sandstone structure, every dusty cobble, every stretch of dirt—seemed colored a fierce yellow hue as though mirroring the sun itself.

"This will prove our finest chance," A'Sha said from behind him in his deep, ponderous tone. "Now their magic is at its weakest. What is more," he said, gesturing toward an edge of the sky painted the color of wheat, "a sandstorm is coming. It will grant us cover during the day's late hours."

Bale crept ahead, clumsy boots scraping on the ground. He felt stifled beneath his brown robes and fearful of the shadows they'd seen during their last foray onto the city's streets.

Alisa came alongside him, her green cloak draped across her shoulders. "Well?"

Bale nodded and concentrated upon the seeking stone held in his hand. "West. And south, but mostly west."

Alisa shaded her wide brown eyes and gazed in that direction. "Toward the city center. Toward the tower. Let's go. We must discover all we can while the sun is strong. Every day we linger in this accursed city is another day Rune bleeds."

"A moment," said A'Sha. He retreated inside his tent but soon returned with several wicker cages filled with chirping, fluttering birds. He set them gently upon the ground, untied their tiny doors and watched in seeming satisfaction as the birds fled their confines. "There," he said, folding his arms across his chest. "They will find Pastine's other disciples, and let them know of Cirak."

Bale watched the birds scatter to the sky and then nodded. He grasped Lorra's hand then began walking down a narrow street crowded by shanties. His eyes darted about, studying every stubborn shadow that refused to yield to the sun's brilliance. He watched but they did not deepen and they did not move. He sighed with timid relief.

"Make haste," A'Sha said, jogging to take the lead. His many-colored robes snapped like pennants behind him. "The daylight is most precious and sandstorms most treacherous! We've not much time!"

Alisa strode at the man's heels, her stride graceful. "Quickly!"

"Move, Bale," came Lorra's annoyed voice. She yanked his hand and tugged him forward with surprising force. "Move."

Bale lurched ahead on creaky knees, trying to manage his way along a street littered with sacks, refuse and the residents of this place. He stumbled more than once, though Lorra was always there to catch him. She loped at his side, hand firm in his own.

He clutched his seeking stone, feeling it shift and pull against his palm as they travelled. Its movements were powerful, now, more powerful than they'd been their entire journey. He sensed—no, *knew*—that the Sentinel Kressan was near.

Their path zigzagged through the slums but they managed to keep sight of the green stretch of Lorra's cloak and the rainbow swirl of A'Sha. Bale glanced upward, through the stretched fabrics shading the path, and spied the black peak of Zyn's great tower, home of the Spider King.

After a time he realized the stone remained fixed in the direction of the obsidian spire. Even at this distance he could see its dull black surface scratched with jagged glyphs. The sight of it nauseated him; it seemed a blasphemous evil given form.

After a weave of tiny streets they came upon a tight passageway. Beyond stood a grand bazaar, an immeasurable tangle of people, tents and wagons. The smell of exotic spices and musky livestock mingled upon the hot air, as did the din of accented voices. It seemed to Bale the whole of some strange world had gathered at this place, here at this dark jewel in the heart of a desolate land.

"Where?" asked Alisa. "Can you tell where the stone points?"

Bale pulled his eyes from the market and drew his fist near his face. He unfurled his fingers and allowed the stone to twitch upon his palm. The stone, an oblong and well-polished thing, pointed due west. Bale traced his eyes across its length, through the bustling market and to the row of tall sandstone buildings beyond. And beyond them, the obsidian home of the Spider King.

"There," Bale said with a nod. "The tower. It's held to that direction no matter how many turns we've taken."

Alisa came near and stared at the stone. "Perhaps. Perhaps a Sentinel is there, in or near the tower... But we've only made our way through a small corner of the city. It may be the stone points somewhere on its opposite side." She looked toward the tower. "Either way, the sun stands high, and while it does we are safe from the shadows. Let's go."

They squeezed their way through the vast market, through great throngs of people of every shape and shade and past carts and tents displaying goods from across the world. Bale searched for suspicious eyes, though it seemed the many merchants and haggling customers paid mind only to their business.

"Five hundred *sheleks*!" shouted a sweat-soaked man, shaking a bulging purse of coins near Bale's ear. "I bid five hundred sheleks!"

"Bah!" spat another. "A sad pittance for this specimen... This is a rare *raggaan* from Rimgald, one of the last of its breed! Think of the fortune this prize will win you in the fighting pits!"

Bale turned to see a gold-caped Khaldisian standing before a scaled thing tall as a man but almost twice as wide, a thickly-built beast all claws, teeth and muscle.

It snarled and snapped its heavy jaw, struggling against many chains and darting gem-like eyes about the crowd.

"A monster," said Lorra.

A'Sha chuckled grimly. "Alas, Lorra, I fear you are doomed to find Zyn is home to many monsters."

Bale shuddered and hastened his pace, moving behind Lorra to wedge through a train of sack-laden donkeys. A dung-scented tail smacked him square across the face and showered him with dust and debris. He blinked away painful grit and rubbed at his eyes, his vision blurring. "Wait…" he coughed, slowing.

"No time for that," grumbled Lorra as she tugged him along.

He staggered along, half-blind. The crowd jostled him and some cursed as he blundered his way amid and against them. He winced at sharp elbows and hard shoulders and apologized to those offended in his wake, yielding to Lorra's tow and stumbling ahead.

At last the crowd dwindled and Lorra drew them to a stop. Bale rubbed away grime-filled tears and looked about, seeing two-storied buildings of sun-bleached stone—shops and storehouses—that formed the market's western edge. Beyond them, another half-mile perhaps, loomed the tower, its black surface yielding nothing to the sun above.

Alisa shaded her eyes and looked to the obelisk. "Let's waste no time. We must do all we can to find Kressan this day."

A'Sha moved beside her, folding his arms across his chest. "So long as we are off these streets by twilight.

We risk capture, or worse, otherwise. What say you, Zandrachus Bale?"

Bale stared at the tower. He had no idea what horrors awaited him within it, though was quite certain they'd prove quite terrifying. He worried this could mean his ending, an awful ending in a fearsome place far from anything that seemed like home. Heat and despair pressed upon him.

I am too weak an instrument…

Lorra gave his shoulder a rough rub. "Bale?"

He looked to her. Her face was dirty, her sharp features caked with crud. Her fierce eyes burned from the slits of their lids and she swept aside clumps of hair matted with sweat. She had seemed coarse and surly to him weeks before, but now…

Now, in this place and in this moment, she inspired him more than ever. She held his shoulder and his heart lifted at her touch. He nodded again, holding his eyes only to hers. "We *will* see this task through, you and I. The whole world depends upon us, and we will not fail."

The tower of the Spider King dominated the sky before them. The harsh sun tilted westward as the day wore on, leaving them within the tower's chilling umbra.

"Still the tower?" asked Alisa, crouched behind a sack of grain at the alley's mouth.

Bale's hand shook from trying to contain the seeking stone's pull. "I've never had a seeking stone behave in such a fashion—it's as though it wants to fly from my hand and it's taking much of my strength to contain it. It acted nothing like this when I sought the Lector's remains."

He peered across the crowded promenade, over the dusty passersby and the buildings on its opposite side, to study the tower once more. "The Sentinel is inside. I wish it weren't so, but the dead gods seem to have no care for the wishes of their creation."

Alisa stared at him for a moment. "Our task takes us where it does. We serve Illienne, Bale, and only by her grace will we survive."

"The Spider King still has eyes within it," A'Sha said from over Alisa's shoulder. "Though most of his army and foul allies have marched north, some still tend the tower."

"We are not without some advantages," Alisa said, rubbing at the black metal of her Coda. She closed her eyes and muttered something.

"Your magic?" A'Sha asked. "Can it protect us *there*?"

Alisa stood and as she did she *changed*, assuming once again the appearance of a simple, road-worn pilgrim wearing little more than rags. She looked upward, to the blazing glow of the sun. "I hope for now it will. If it fails, we may need to call upon yours."

A'Sha grimaced and smoothed his colored robes with ringed hands. "Let us hope it does not come to that."

Alisa left the alleyway and slinked onto the avenue beyond. They stayed near, shambling about her as she guided them past beggars stretching cupped hands, wild tribesmen with taciturn faces, and zealots chanting in praise of the Spider King. None paid them any regard.

Bale felt a touch of relief though that vanished the moment his gaze returned to the massive obsidian column. He stood far closer to it now than he'd ever been and his heart quaked before it. The structure seemed a malignant evil, a great horn impaling the heavens. Its black stone bled the sun and its unreadable glyphs howled profane curses against all the world.

They crossed the promenade and moved down another street, the tower directly before them. It stood within a circle of bleached tiles, and in that circle bent figures cloaked in white kneeling and murmuring toward the tower in reverence. A smattering of other worshippers gathered, too, bowing while staring wide-eyed upon the edifice.

Alisa slowed as they came to the plaza's edge. "Do not wander, and do not make a sound." She entered the ring of stone, shuffling along its outmost edge and bowing occasionally toward the tower in the manner of the worshippers.

He sucked in a breath and looked to the structure's dark exterior. It seemed a great, swallowing shadow, only the glyphs discernible. All the rest of it remained cloaked in the blackness of night.

At last they came round to the tower's southern edge—out from beneath its heavy shadow—and walked in sunlight once more. Beneath the sun's glare the tower's features became visible. Its exterior—a massive spire of near-seamless blocks resembling basalt—was punctuated by tiny, pinprick windows, all far above the plaza's bleached stone.

"The main gate is ahead," whispered Alisa.

They tiptoed around the plaza's edge and found the tower's western side, the whole of it bathed in the light of the tilting sun. There, at the center of its base, stood a gate, a decorated archway bearing great thorns of stone.

The gate's giant obsidian doors were thrown open to reveal a darkened passageway. Ragged worshippers neared and walked into that maw, backs bent in what seemed either reverence or terror.

Alisa halted, eyes trained to the gate. "A'Sha? Is it the wisest way?"

A'Sha leaned close. "With the Spider King gone, the tower is more monument than palace, and during the day the gate opens to his faithful. There is no easier path."

Bale looked to Lorra. She pressed a hand upon his shoulder. "We can do this, Bale."

Alisa nodded. "Stay close, all of you. My Coda can obscure our presence, but the Necrists' power will wax as the day wanes. We must hurry."

The pathway to the gate angled upward to rise above the plaza. They ascended, shuffling upon the sun-drenched tiles toward the impenetrable shadows of the tower's interior. Rows of guards—tall and sinewy Arranese—stood along the pathway's sides near the gate, stoically observing the worshippers as they entered.

"You're certain they'll not see us?" whispered Bale.

Alisa slowed. "They will see us, but to their eyes we'll be but a huddle of pilgrims in tatters. Their ears, however, will not be deceived. Speak no more until we're clear of them."

She led them onward, up the ramp toward the tower. Bale kept close, bending low like the scattered zealots walking ahead of them. He studied the ragged procession beside and behind him, a sparse parade of beggars with hands upraised and grubby faces lined with tears. They seemed a most desperate lot, causing Bale to wonder what horrors had been wreaked by the Spider King to compel his faithful to regard him so.

He rubbed away a dribble from his large nose and tried to gather what wits he had. Then he looked ahead to the gate and his guts roiled.

Macabre carvings decorated the massive archway of grainy basalt, bodies of black rock with screaming mouths and clawing hands, frozen as though in the midst of trying to escape the tower's confines. Some clutched the great thorns while others seemed impaled upon them. As Bale watched he was sure the stone shifted and churned, slowly easing bodies aside to allow others to rise from the stone. Some were barely more than infants.

He recalled Alisa's account of seeing a cartload of children wheeled into the tower and a cartload of small bones wheeled out of it. He wondered if these were whatever else was left of them.

Could we be the tower's next carvings?

His knees nearly buckled but Lorra held him fast. He felt strength in her embrace and did all he could to summon some semblance of the same.

They moved closer to the tower, between guardsmen clad in oiled leather and hefting long spears and curved swords. Their weapons carried little menace, though, here beneath the tower. Bodies could be poked and cut and bled, but Bale worried the tower held fates far more frightening.

At last they entered, swallowed by the tower's heavy shadows.

Sweet Illienne please spare your loyal servant…

The gate gave way to terrifying darkness. A cold wind whipped from ahead and carried a foul stench upon it. On either side of them candles flailed against the shadows but appeared no more than rumors of stars on a cloudy night. Wayward pilgrims stumbled ahead, uttering prayers and praises in a muted drone.

They followed the trail of zealots down the wide passageway. Between the sounds of their prayers slithered strange voices, a hissing chitter that made Bale's ears itch and his stomach churn. The seeking stone twitched madly in his hand, causing his fist to jerk about. He steeled himself as best he could, creeping forward and concentrating on Lorra's hand upon his shoulder.

There seemed a doorway ahead, a rectangle of light pushing aside the passage's heavy dark. The zealots drifted inside, into a heavy haze of orange. They seemed ghost-like as they moved into that glow, shifting silhouettes that withered and vanished like parchment put to flame.

They came to the door's edge and paused, beholding a smoked-filled chamber so vast its boundaries were lost to the eyes. Within stood a ring of iron braziers blazing with fire. Behind those another ring, this of smallish, crucified corpses in varying states of decay. And within that circle a massive column of rounded, ebony stairs ascending to a platform twenty feet from the chamber floor and cresting just above the smoky haze. Atop it stood a hulking, ivory throne hewn for a giant.

"The throne of the Spider King," A'Sha whispered. "Built from the bones of all who opposed him."

"And who are, or were, they?" Bale asked, gesturing to the dangling, crucified remains.

A'Sha's mouth tightened as he looked upon the dead. "Their children. Some the Spider King had hunted down more recently than others."

Bale grimaced. The foul scent upon the air was indeed that of death.

Alisa drew near. "Careful now. The eyes of the enemy are upon us all."

He studied the other figures shuffling about the chamber. Most were pilgrims and zealots, beholding the throne as though it were the very countenance of the Elder God. They shook and stammered and wept, many falling to their knees as they did.

There were others, though. Others at the chamber's fringes, barely visible figures cloaked in black robes and stalking the deep shadows. Bale did not need to survey their stitched faces to know what they were.

"Here?" he whispered, using both hands to contain the seeking stone. "They are here even during the day?"

Alisa nodded. "Their powers are muted at this hour, though here in their sanctuary they are formidable still. I should be able to conceal us, but we'd be wise to stay clear of them."

They crept onward. The stone's draw grew stronger, almost irresistibly so. Bale struggled to hold it and his arms stretched outward. Sweat dripped from his brow. "We must be close," he wheezed. "I can hardly—"

The pull proved too powerful. The stone slipped from his twitching grasp and flew into the hazy air of the chamber, through the licking flames of a wide brazier before cracking against the second ring of stairs rising toward the

Spider King's throne. It skittered about from there, beginning to round the stair's ring with a scrape.

Alisa stiffened. "Quiet."

Bale followed her gaze and spotted three Necrists crowding together in the shadows of the nearest wall. The hooded figures pressed close then one raised a hand, pointing a pale finger toward Bale and his companions.

Alisa turned to Bale, brown eyes ablaze with the light of the chamber's flames. "Follow the stone. A'Sha, can you deal with them?"

The Harkanian combed a hand through his beard. "I can," he said, his baritone sounding tinged with melancholy.

Bale stood slack-jawed for a moment, counting the many Necrists gathered near the edges of the chamber. A dozen at least.

"Move now!" Alisa snapped, grabbing hold of Bale's other arm. She and Lorra pushed him ahead in their rough grasps.

Bale glanced back to see A'Sha standing in his rainbow-colored robes while the clutch of black-clad Necrists moved toward him from the shadows.

Sweet Illienne…

Alisa squeezed Bale's elbow. "The stone? You've not lost sight of it, have you?"

Bale shook his head and pointed. "It moved along the stair, away from those Necrists…" He listened as much as his rattled nerves would permit and after a moment heard it still, the rasp of stone upon stone. "There. That way."

Lorra strode ahead and dragged Bale along, her stare fixed on the stone's trace. Bale followed in her tow.

Alisa trotted behind them. "You see it?"

Lorra nodded and led them round the column of stairs, all the way to the end opposite the entrance. It was a bleak, blackened area where no fires burned. Bale searched the shadows and found nothing.

Lorra stopped, tugging Bale to a halt beside her.

"What is it?" said Alisa.

"The stone," Lorra whispered. "I've lost it."

Alisa crept ahead. She rubbed her Coda and the illusion of her pilgrim garb melted away. "Do you sense it, Bale?"

Bale rubbed his nose. "I…" he faltered. "I can try…" He stared into the darkness and slowed the stutter of his heart. For a moment he pulled *within* himself, inside that place of solitude he'd always treasured. He'd spent much time in the sheltered secrecy of the Abbey's library, where any manner of sound niggled at his concentration. He thought of himself there now, reading. Reading and at ease and tucked away from the troubles of the wider world. Enveloped in comfort and silence and safety.

He thought also of Castor, of Lyan the Just, of Kressan. He thought of the words of the Spell of Divination—quietly reciting them over and again—and of the stone upon his palm, twitching and poking…

All fell quiet in his ears.

And then he sensed it. No more than a tiny, mouse-like scratching.

He knew not whether his ears or his mind perceived the sound but he was certain he heard it, ahead and against the chamber's wall. His eyes widened and he eased toward the noise, uncertain at first but his stride gaining confidence. He pressed a crooked finger outward. "There."

He looked to the blank wall, searching the rock for some sign of the Sentinel though he knew not what to search for. *Some golden titan? Some bloodied husk?*

Lorra and Alisa drew to his sides and together they found the wall's rough surface. Bale bent low to recover his wayward stone and felt it twitch about, seeking the wall and whatever stood beyond.

"Another chamber," said Alisa. She examined the wall with deft hands. Her Coda seemed to wake, thin lines of text upon it glowing with a faint, greenish hue.

Just then a hideous roar shook the chamber, a feral scream that ripped through the heavy dark.

Bale jumped and hunched close to Lorra, his empty hand seeking hers. "What *was* that?"

"A'Sha," Alisa said. "He's buying us time."

"Will he be safe?"

Alisa spun from the wall and squared to him. "You must worry only about our task, Bale. The greater good always demands sacrifice. A'Sha knows that. You should as well."

Bale sucked in a slow breath of the foul air and held fast his seeking stone. The stone and air both had a chill to them now.

Another roar echoed through the chamber, as did a clamor of voices and weaponry.

"I find no seam or latch," Alisa said, again inspecting the wall. "Nothing."

"There must be something." Bale's eyes strayed, looking farther down the wall. All was cloaked in darkness. He rubbed his nose, wondering how many Necrists lurked nearby.

Dare I?

Is there any choice?

"*Illienne…*" he whispered, stretching his hand toward the dark and focusing with reverence upon the words. "*Illienne abralide y ganode allum.*"

Light exploded from his hand, burning away the shadows with brilliant radiance. It was as though the chamber's ceiling had been torn away and the searing sun now burned within. Bale shielded his eyes, blinking and nearly blinded.

Alisa gasped. "What—"

"Look!" said Lorra.

Bale stood with mouth agape. About the chamber stood many doors and passages and above, far above the giant throne, stretched countless bridges all the way up the great tower's height.

Nearest them, just a dozen feet away, stood a squat door carved into the tower's basalt rock. No Necrists or guards stood beside it, though Bale spotted two figures robed in black retreating toward the chamber's far side.

The stone sought it, jerking in Bale's hand. "That must be it."

Alisa leaped ahead and Lorra moved after her, tugging Bale along the wall. Together they came to the door.

A roar sounded again, fiercer and louder this time.

Bale's concentration wavered, and as it did the light vanished. The opening before them disappeared.

Bale furrowed his brow. "How—"

"Necric charms," Alisa spat, swiping her hands swiftly about. Her Coda glowed. "Their vile sorcery closes the passage though it seems your powers may reveal it. Cast your light again!"

Bale threw his hand upward. "*Illienne abralide y ganode allum!*"

Once more the light erupted, pure as it blazed against the dark.

Before them stood the door, a square of stone resting on iron hinges. Upon it were carved the same glyphs that decorated the tower's exterior, the same blasphemous, nauseating symbols that poisoned Bale's mind. He felt a terrible unease as he looked upon them, a gut-wrenching sensation that made him want to flee this place and never, ever return. He turned to Alisa. "No guards?"

Alisa found a latch. "Such a door requires no swords to protect it." She eyed him. "You feel it, don't you?"

"Bale…" Lorra said beside him, a rare fear upon her voice. "What is this?"

There came the ring of steel and then another roar. Harsh voices and things clattering upon the stone floor. Then, silence.

"Hurry A'Sha," whispered Alisa, staring out to the throne room.

Bale looked nervously about the room. He spied only the two Necrists huddling against the far wall more than fifty feet away.

Just then A'Sha rounded the ring of stairs with a lumbering stride, his rainbow robes reduced to ribbons. His black skin shone with blood and his linen undergarments were stained red.

"A'Sha," Alisa said, her tone one of relief. "Can you continue?"

The large Harkanian trudged near. Bale noticed more splatters of blood coloring his shaking hands and sweaty face though he saw no wounds on the man. His breathing was labored and his expression grave. At last, he nodded.

Alisa turned the latch and the square door groaned upon its hinges. The chamber's cold air rushed to fill whatever lay beyond, whipping through the long strands of Bale's graying hair and fluttering across his robes. The door swung wide and the light of Bale's spellcraft failed like a candle snuffed.

"Go," Alisa whispered. "We've not much time before the Necrists recover and learn where we've gone."

Dead gods.

The descending passage—dimly lit by no apparent source—struck Bale as something carved through the old hells themselves. It was a twisting, cramped tunnel, a wet space choked with creeping, thorny growths and reeking of death. The floor was moist and it *moved*, rising and falling like the slow pulse of a living thing. The chittering seemed louder here, echoing through the corridor as though given voice by every wall.

Lorra pressed close. "Bale, this is a bad place."

Bale glanced back, wondering when a horde of Necrists would come chasing them. "Perhaps the worst of all."

"I'm with you," she said, "wherever you go. But this feels wrong. Like a nightmare, only real. Your Sentinel cannot be here. If she is, then she's not someone we should be trying to find."

Bale held his stone and felt its dreadful pull. "I

must…" he said, eyes drifting down the strangled passage. "I must," he said again, quelling the tremble in his voice.

Alisa tiptoed down the tunnel, one hand upon her glowing Coda and the other pulling her green cloak tightly about her. She turned her head. "The stone?"

The small rock held firm upon Bale's palm, seeking some unseen place. "It shows the way."

"To their sanctuary?" said A'Sha, frowning. "You are certain of this path?"

Bale nodded. "Kressan must have been taken prisoner, somehow. Alisa? The Variden know nothing?"

She clasped her Coda and stared ahead. "We know precious little of Kressan the Kind. Rumors only, and all those ancient. Like many of the banished Sentinels, she's not made her whereabouts well known."

"You've not heard of her taken prisoner?" Bale asked. "Or… being in league with the enemy? Nothing?"

Alisa shook her head. "Your stone has been our only hint in ages."

Down and round they went, through other doorways and down many winding paths. All the while Bale's stone guided them, leading them deeper beneath the tower. The slope sharpened and the wet floor sucked at their feet and the thorny growths clawed their clothes and skin. The harsh chatter upon the fetid air grew steadily louder, sounding like the song of many locusts.

Bale's heart thumped and his breathing grew shallow. Cold sweat dripped through his hair and across his brow. He pressed ahead, trying to dull his senses and focus only on Lyan's charge to find Kressan. He felt as though he moved according to forces both powerful and divine, an unwitting pawn of the dead gods.

His hands tightened upon the stone, its draw like shackles dragging him onward. *I am too weak an instrument!*

They trudged down the pulsing, curving burrow, deeper and deeper beneath the Spider King's throne. The odd, faint light assumed a reddish shade and the air thickened to a steamy, coppery stink.

Soon the passage forked, one way a twisted and looping drop and the other a rising slope bending toward places unseen.

"Bale?" Alisa asked, slowing to a halt.

Bale gripped the stone. It shook in his hands, its pull undeniable. *She must be close.* He leaned his head to the left. "Upward," he breathed. Lorra placed a hand upon his shoulder, though even that granted no comfort.

Alisa paused, silent, her wide eyes upon him. Then she nodded and turned, slinking up the passage with A'Sha just beside her.

Bale rubbed snot from his nose and drew his robes close. He felt cold—terribly so—and it seemed all the stones of the massive tower above weighed upon his skinny shoulders. "We're not far," he whispered with far more apprehension than relief.

"Let's go," came Lorra's soft voice in his ear. "As bad as this is, it'd be even worse to turn back. Either we face this fear or we fail."

He sighed then yielded to her hand. She eased him forward and together they plodded up the twisting pathway.

After only a few steps up the winding passage they came upon Alisa and A'Sha, both standing motionless.

Bale peeked between them and beheld a chamber roofed by a low dome of black rock just taller than a man. In the room's center yawned a wide, circular maw from which drifted scarlet smoke.

"What is it?" Bale said, struggling to take in details between A'Sha's thick form and Alisa's long cloak.

Alisa turned sideways, allowing Bale to move within the space. "I fear we may have found Kressan."

Bale stumbled through and onto a flat ring of black stone that surrounded the opening. His eyes darted about. "Where—"

"There," Alisa said, standing aside him.

Bale looked downward into the opening and saw, far below, a great pool of blood-colored liquid. About that pool knelt hundreds—*hundreds!*—of Necrists draped in their black robes. Their insectile drone swelled from the depths and seemed to tremor though the rock. Great creatures stood amongst them, massive, misshapen beings that seemed cobbled together from lesser things. Someone screamed, a pained, terrified shriek. Bale tilted his head to see a dozen or so naked prisoners cowering in a corner as one of their number had its arms ripped away by some bestial thing. Other abominations held the man in place while three black-robed Necrists worked knives upon the body. The man's screams soon fell silent and his skinless, armless body was cast into the well, the blood-red liquid swirling and rippling unnaturally as it swallowed the corpse.

Bale shuddered and withdrew.

"She's not in that damnable pit," said Alisa, her tone grave, "but just there."

Bale felt the stone's pull and his gaze followed it to the opening's opposite edge, just across the domed room. His jaw dropped. "Dead gods…"

He beheld two wretched figures dangling limply from the lip of the circular maw. Their skin held a pale hue like the bellies of dead fish washed ashore. Their bald, ashen heads stretched unnaturally, mouths agape with gruesome spikes jutting from them. Grotesque hooks protruded from their elbows and hands, too, fastening them against the opening's rim. Blood drained from their wounds, dripping down their drenched, ragged forms to fall into the well far below.

Bale sank to his knees. He felt like vomiting, his stomach filling with the sickness of abject failure. His hands went slack. As they did, the stone slipped from them and fled toward the figures, landing against one with a wet, ugly squelch.

"No…" he whimpered. He looked upon the desecrated bodies and thought of the many, many miles he'd come, the many horrors and hardships he'd endured. He thought, too, that someone younger or stronger or braver could have made the journey in less time, and perhaps could have found Kressan before *this* had happened to her.

Someone other than Zandrachus Bale could have saved her.

Tears welled in his eyes.

I am too weak an instrument.

Alisa jabbed an arm under his and began pulling him to his feet. "Get up, Bale," she said gruffly. "We cannot countenance a Sentinel being left this way. A'Sha? Lorra? Help us."

Bale resisted at first, fighting away a sob, but Alisa seemed unwilling to allow him a moment. He sniffled and straightened upon creaking knees and followed Alisa round the ring of black stone. Lorra came to walk beside him though she said nothing, eyes fixed on the grim gathering of Necrists beneath them.

Bale came to the dangling figures, heads and arms nailed just level with the stone floor. They were nearly identical in appearance, both smallish and seeming hardly more than children.

He drew low, stretching shaking hands outward though he was not quite sure what to do. He noticed then his seeking stone. It moved slowly between the two beings, touching the palm of one and then sliding across the stone rim to that of the other. "Have we found *two* Sentinels? Two Sentinels slain? And… if one is Kressan who is the other?"

Alisa stood above him with eyes distant, her hand gripping her glowing Coda. "Retrieve them both. Then we must leave this place."

A'Sha knelt beside Bale. He grabbed one of the figures by a wrist then worked it away from the hook piercing its hand. "Can you get the other?"

Bale nodded and scooted over. He seized the creature's wrist—slick with blood—and moved it about the twist of rusted metal affixing it to the stone. He squeezed and pulled and at last it came free. He did the same with the elbow but the weight of the arm caused it to droop and Bale was pulled with it. "Ah!" he yelped, heart in his throat as he stared wide-eyed upon the vast drop into the pit below.

Lorra grabbed his shoulder and withdrew him from

the edge. "I have it," she said softly, easing him back and taking hold of the figure. Together she and A'Sha removed the thing from the nasty spike impaling its mouth—its skull scraping against the rough metal—and dragged it to the floor beside Bale. They then moved to the other.

Bale sat with eyes upon the sad creature laid beside him. Its limbs were thin and its pallid skin almost translucent. Its eyelids tilted open, revealing orbs entirely white and lifeless. It seemed so weak, so frail, and so very unlike a being of eternal power. Blood pooled beneath it.

Gravely wounded? Dead, maybe?

Could this have been Kressan?

Soon its twin was stretched aside it. It looked no different, no less pathetic.

Or this one?

He spied his seeking stone caught in a sunken groove between its protruding ribs and moved delicate fingers to retrieve it. As he pinched, he realized the stone's pull had faded. It was a simple rock now, no more than an ordinary object in his hand. He wondered if its stillness meant the Sentinels had died.

Just then a terrible cry arose from the pit, a pained shriek voiced from what sounded a hundred throats. A horn sounded, too, a shrill wail that came from every direction.

"Carry them!" Alisa cried, her voice cracking. She stared wide-eyed through the opening. "We must leave!"

Bale listed about, swooning. He pressed his hands against his head and heaved a ragged breath. Everything about him seemed a hopeless, horrid madness. The futility, the smell, their awful surroundings. It burdened his every thought.

"Bale!" said Lorra, bent at his side. "We've come too far. Get up!"

"I…"

She snatched his chin in her hand. "You'll stand and you'll move! *You* said we'd see this through and *you* said we'd not fail. I'm not dying in this hole because *you've* decided to give up!"

He blinked. He blinked and he staggered upward, leaning against her. Her glare was a command and he followed it.

A'Sha gathered both bodies and slung them over his broad shoulders. Both swayed with sickly noises against the Harkanian's back. "From whence we came, Alisa?"

Alisa stood at the room's entrance, peering down the winding corridor. "I fear there's no other way. Bale, be prepared to summon your light. And A'Sha, be ready also. Be ready for the worst."

The horn's blare chased them down the strangled passage and the maddened screams followed just after. The tight corridor echoed it all.

Bale stumbled ahead, gripping Lorra's arm and warding away the sharp thorns with an upraised sleeve. Behind them A'Sha hefted the Sentinels' bodies, moving his big form with agile steps.

Alisa's Coda pulsed with a strange luminescence. She unsheathed her sword and brandished it before her. "They're coming," she hissed.

Bale felt *something*, an icy chill and a change in the air. The passage's movement—the pulse of its floor—seemed stronger now, pressing them onward like waves of a rising tide. The wind moved differently, too, rushing toward whatever lay ahead.

He cringed and held close to Lorra, wanting to stop this fool's crusade and find some secret refuge. He knew, though, the only safety he'd find was away from this tower, far away. Fear stoked his stride.

"We'll make it, Bale," Lorra said over the shrieking din.

Bale nodded and plummeted on, clutching her. She held him, supporting him and guiding his steps through the twisting corridor.

A sharp groan came from behind. Bale jerked his head to see A'Sha hoisting the two bodies upon his shoulders, his dark brow pinched in apparent puzzlement.

"They move," the Harkanian said, turning to look upon the things.

"They move..." Bale said, hope finding his heart. "Alisa! They move! They may yet live!" He grabbed her cloak but she shrugged him aside and charged ahead.

"We've no time for that now," she commanded, urging them onward through several more turns of the passageway.

Suddenly the horn and the screams fell silent. In their place a dreadful quiet filled the air. Bale felt even the rustle of his robes seemed an offense to it.

Alisa brought them to a stop. "The doorway..."

Bale craned his neck to gaze over her shoulder and upon the steamy stretch before them. Ahead, not more than twenty feet, the door stood open to the dark expanse of the throne room. In the midst of the chamber rose the great dais of ringed stairs. Near the base of the dais, not far from the door…

I am too weak an instrument.

A black rent appeared to be rising from the chamber's floor. It shifted and shook, a tear in the drifting haze. Something deeper than shadow, a black chasm opening upon the world.

"Bale," whispered Lorra, "what is that?"

"Necrists…" he breathed.

Bale peered into the vast room and squinted toward the growing rift in the dark. He tried to deepen his shallow breaths and ignore the harsh words he heard shouted from some far corner of the expanse.

Alisa stood by him, rubbing her Coda with eyes fixed on the void. "A shadowpath," she said. "Who knows how many travel within it…"

Bale darted blind eyes about, finding the whole of the chamber draped in darkness. "Can it be the gate still stands open?"

"What is that?" said Lorra beside him, grabbing his shoulder to turn him about.

He looked to see A'Sha behind him, slack-jawed with fingers knotted in his beard. Before the Harkanian, looking little more than children, stood what Bale guessed to be Kressan and the other being they'd rescued. Their small, naked bodies still ran with blood though their grievous wounds seemed to be healing.

"Kressan?" Bale exclaimed, his fear momentarily forgotten. "You live!"

"I live, Zandrachus Bale," said Kressan, her voice barely a whisper. Her hairless body had turned a deep gold stained red in many places. She gestured in seeming pain toward the other small being. "As does my twin Sienne."

Sienne, identical but for her silvery hue, tilted with a slight bow. "You have our gratitude," she said.

"Bale!" urged Alisa.

Bale remained transfixed by the twin Sentinels, his head lost in old tales. "I-I…"

"Now!" Alisa barked again, seizing a handful of his robes. "We must run *now*!"

Bale shook himself from his trance and turned to see the rift had grown to several yards across. It convulsed and squirmed, its shape shifting as it opened wide. At its edges he could see gnarled hands gripping and tugging, tearing a larger hole into the space of the chamber.

The hideous shrieking began anew, the sound of it cascading from the void. A bell tolled, loud and terrible. Many shouts came from across the chamber and its heights.

Bale's heart quailed. "I-I…"

"Run!" screamed Alisa. She bounded wide of the void, her cloak whipping behind her. A'Sha moved just behind, helping along the limping Sentinels. Their metallic faces were impassive, statuesque, and they seemed to pay no heed to their hunters.

Bale leaned upon Lorra as they scurried after. He looked to the opening shadowpath and saw figures— *things*—emerging from it. Black-robed Necrists poured from its depths, swarming into the great chamber with shadows coiling about them like snakes.

Others came, too. Hobbling, hump-backed dwarfs

and lumbering, misshapen giants groaning as though every step were a dagger in the back.

"Dead gods!" Bale drew a breath of the cold air and blinked away tears. He sagged against Lorra, almost collapsing.

"Run, spooker!" she scolded. "You run or we die!"

Bale whimpered and surged onward. He glanced back again. The Necrists and their malformed progeny pursued, not more than twenty yards away. The Necrists jerked and spasmed but ran frighteningly fast and were gaining. Others materialized from the mouth of the shadowpath and they too gave chase.

Fear choked him and he looked to the chamber ahead. They'd begun to round the great ring of stairs and he could now see the crucified bones of children and the fires of the blazing braziers. Beyond the fires he spied flashes of steel. Spears, swords, axes. All wielded by Arranese warriors.

Alisa drew to a stop, boots skidding on the black stone beneath. Bale and Lorra nearly slammed into her but managed to come to a halt at her side.

"We can't stop!" pleaded Bale over the piercing wails. He glanced back to the Necrists dashing toward them from the dark. "We mustn't stop!"

"You'd have us run headlong into Arranese blades?" Alisa snapped. "A'Sha! Can you handle the warriors? We'll deal with the Necrists."

A'Sha stepped ahead, shaking his hands. "It seems I must."

The Harkanian threw his arms outward, upward, and as he did he transformed. New sinews seemed to ripple and surge from within his hefty form. His neck cracked and his head cocked at a sharp angle. A second set of arms sprang from his ribs. He roared, the sound of it harsh and feral. His many fingers twisted and sprouted long claws and his body contorted and grew to nearly triple its size.

Dead gods!

A'Sha roared again, spittle spraying from a jutting maw. He'd become a fearsome beast, like some massive, hairless bear, and the Arranese warriors retreated.

"Bale!" Alisa said with a stern gaze. "Light this tower!"

Bale, bewildered, turned to behold more than two dozen Necrists and their twisted creations charging toward them. They seemed a gallery of horrors wearing masks of the dead. Black eyes glared from black sockets. Shadows spun from their hands and seemed to swell with every stride.

"*Illienne…*" Bale said, stretching a timid arm toward the coming dark.

"Bale!" snarled Lorra. "Make your light!"

He threw out his hand, firmly this time, and his mind focused on every syllable of the sacred words. "*Illienne!*" he shouted. "*Illienne abralide y ganode allum!*"

Pure, brilliant light flooded the great chamber. The Necrists and their creatures staggered as though blinded and their shrieks fell silent. They faltered to a stop, many clawing at the light as though it were a physical thing. The flesh of those at the fore smoldered. The shadows they held withered, diminishing to almost nothing.

The trembling hint of a smile lifted Bale's face. It's working!

But some of the Necrists seemed to gather themselves. They bent behind nearby comrades and worked pale, sickly hands as though kindling the wisps of shadow within them.

A Necrist at the rear began barking at the malformed creations and the cow-eyed giants lumbered ahead. They limped through the cringing crowd then lurched forward upon legs that looked to be braided from those of many corpses. Fists like anvils swayed at their sides and the ground shook beneath their march. Behind them, Necrists crept in the shade they cast and the shadows they held grew and darkened.

Alisa shouted something, some arcane command, and her sword erupted with green fire. She sprang upon the enemy. She slashed her weapon at the first monstrosity, cleaving away a chunk of its thigh. The giant moaned but then threw down a massive fist. Alisa just managed to avoid the blow.

The Necrists behind the beast muttered madly, speaking a harsh language of insectile chitters and guttural noises. Shadows spread from their hands like smoke from fire.

Alisa swept her blade at the dark and dodged another strike from the giant before cleaving its belly. Its innards spilled upon the stone, a bloody stew of what appeared to be small fingers, eyeballs and brains.

The wounded giant teetered and fell. The Necrists shrieked.

Bale sucked in a horrified breath and turned his head about. Lorra stood beside him with a hand on his arm and mouth agape. Behind them, A'Sha—or whatever he'd become—growled and lashed his claws at a clutch of Arranese warriors.

But the Sentinels were not to be found.

"Where…" Bale breathed, his focus wavering.

His light flickered.

Alisa cursed.

Bale looked to her. She danced about, slashing her shining blade at the legs of the two remaining giants. The Necrists' shadows groped at her like the tentacles of some undersea monster. One coiled about her waist. She cut it away but another quickly wound about in its place.

Bale took a stride forward though his heart stammered. He pressed his hand farther ahead and concentrated, willing himself courage. He drew a deep breath, hoping—praying—the divine illumination would prevail against the night.

The light shone, but it didn't seem to be enough. Not in this shrine of evil nor against so many foes. The light was failing and the Necrists seemed to be recovering, their shadows deepening and darkening.

And at last the light died.

The air filled with the Necrists' loud chitter, the scuffle of Alisa's movements and the violence of A'Sha and the Arranese behind. Bale's eyes darted about, desperate, adjusting to the renewed dark. Thick shadows obscured the whirling flame of Alisa's sword, and the dull illumination of the chamber's braziers seemed but a rumor. There came no hint of sunlight and he was certain the tower's gate had shut.

All of it, all the darkness and the madness within it, surrounded him now and appeared to be closing.

His heart sank. Enemies were everywhere, and he could find no sign of the Sentinels.

Have they abandoned me? And after so great a journey to find them?

He cast his eyes downward and drew his hands into fists. He pounded them against his hips and shook with a sob. *Are we to die here?*

"Bale," hissed Lorra. "Look."

He sniffled then lifted his head to search the dark. The Arranese warriors lay in shattered heaps among pools of red reflecting the tower's fires. A'Sha, still in his monstrous form, stood doubled over, the wide breadth of his back heaving. After a moment he straightened and roared, the sound more tragic than ferocious.

"A'Sha!" Bale said.

A'Sha turned to reveal a massive body torn by many grievous wounds. He flexed and shook the great claws of his many hands, splattering gore upon the stone tiles. He pressed himself ahead with a snarl.

Lorra held Bale's arm as the great beast approached.

"A'Sha?" Bale said, shrinking.

A'Sha paused and looked down to him, his bestial, bear-like face softening with seeming sadness. "Bale," he said, his sonorous voice unaffected by his transformation. "We will delay the enemy. Go now. They await you." His expression hardened once more and he trudged away.

"But…" Bale said, his head tangled with fear and confusion. "Who waits?"

No answer came.

Bale's eyes followed A'Sha and he saw beyond him Alisa still battling the Necrists and their giants. She swept her fiery sword about but the darkness seemed to be engulfing her. A'Sha came beside her, flailing at the enemy, and soon shadows entwined him as well.

"*Zandrachus Bale*," came a voice.

The voice, Bale knew, sounded only in his head, just as when Lyan the Just had first communicated with him beneath Cirak.

Bale's looked about. "Kressan?"

Lorra squeezed his shoulder. "Bale! We can't just stand here!"

"*You must come to the gate,*" said the voice.

He stared again to Alisa and A'Sha. The shadows around them had grown and more foes had joined the fray. Alisa cleaved her sword into a Necrist's skull then reeled as a giant smashed her side with a mighty fist. A'Sha howled as black tendrils coiled around him.

"I can't..." Bale breathed. "I can't leave them."

"We must run!" pleaded Lorra, her hand knotted in his robes. "We can't fight these things and you must save your Sentinels!"

"*Come now, Zandrachus Bale,*" said the disembodied voice. "*The gate will not open for long.*"

He glanced over to where he remembered the gate to be. Something shimmered there, a figure distant and small and gold. The Sentinels were his charge, he knew, though leaving his new allies—*new friends?*—to fight the enemy alone tasted of cowardice. He tried to think of what he could do to help them, rummaging through cobwebbed memories of old books he'd read. He wondered about an exorcism, but knew such things required much time and preparation. He thought also of powerful blessings and curses he'd learned, but those too demanded profound concentration.

He wrung his hands, helplessness and fear consuming him. *Is there nothing I can do?*

"Bale!" shouted Lorra. "We'll not die here!"

He looked to her, her face mere inches from his own. Her sharp features pinched with what seemed panic and desperation. She braced his arm with hers and tried towing him toward the gate.

"Now. You must come now, or you will perish."

Bale dug in his feet. He felt his lower lip shaking and his limbs ran cold. He looked ahead and saw only the failing light of Alisa's blade. He listened to the harsh drone of the Necrists and heard within it a muted roar from A'Sha.

I am too weak an instrument...

He whimpered and succumbed to Lorra's pull. She dragged him backward along the slick stone tiles, between broken, bloody bodies of Arranese warriors ripped nearly to shreds. "Move your damned legs!" she said.

He turned toward her and spotted Kressan at the chamber's far end, still and golden and regal as a statue. Her twin, Sienne, moved to stand near, her silver hue catching the fires' glimmer.

"Alright," he said with a quavering voice. He clung to her and together they ran, his stride ragged and clumsy but determined. The came nearer the Sentinels and he could see beyond them the gate cracking open to a blaze of sunlight and a rush of hot wind and sand.

The Sentinels drew to his side and they hastened onward. Onward to the light, and to hope. He drew a sharp, elated breath.

But his eyes fell one last time to Alisa and to A'Sha, far behind him. He could just see A'Sha tearing clawed hands into the growing darkness. Shadows surrounded him. Alisa, too, was fading, the gleam of her sword now hardly discernable. More shadows, more Necrists...

A distant roar sounded though it spoke only of pain. A thud and a pitiable groan followed.

Bale heard Alisa's scream—a terrified scream that penetrated the dark—then the clang of metal against stone.

The sword's flame vanished. Bale could see nothing more of his friends.

Only darkness.

He reached out an arm though knew he could do nothing to save them.

They were dead.

And there was only darkness.

He clutched Lorra and together they fled the tower.

19
OLD ACQUAINTANCES

YANNICK WOKE TO a thunderous pain in his head, a thick tongue and a burning throat. He drew in a breath of hot, stinking air and moaned. He rolled to his side but his shoulder caught hard wood and splinters just above him. He leaned back and eased a hand to a head topped with hair crusty in places and sticky in others, as well as with two massive, throbbing lumps swollen and smarting.

His bed lurched. It jolted about and swayed and groaned.

Am I moving?

He eased open his eyes, finding his surroundings a darkened box. Threads of light striated the tight enclosure, and the whole of the thing seemed fashioned of wooden planks.

A coffin?

Dead gods!

He jerked his head about as fear seized him. Whatever

he was in creaked and listed. A horse nickered somewhere outside. He guessed his box was borne upon a wagon of some sort, and worried he was about to be dropped in a newly-dug grave.

"I…" he croaked. "I'm not dead yet!"

Laughter. From without the box came hard, hateful laughter. "Hear that, boys? The captain's not dead!"

The wagon crawled to a halt. Shapes moved outside, darkening the thin light within Lannick's enclosure.

Lannick frantically felt about. He still wore his chainmail and cloak though his sword and the purse containing his Coda were gone. *I'm defenseless!*

There came the sound of jingling metal. The box shifted like someone pushed against it. A click. The squeak of a turning key then a clack. "Here you go," grumbled someone. "Unlocked and all."

Lannick lay still, terrified. He held his eyes to the box's lid. With a searing head he recalled the last night at the camp. The fires, the chaos. He'd called out for Arleigh and heard Arleigh answer. Then a crack on the head and nothing after.

Was I betrayed?

The lid above swung open with a squeal, bathing Lannick in a harsh, blinding light. A figure loomed above, a black silhouette framed by the sun. Whoever it was seemed an imposing sort squeezing a knife in a fist.

"Remember me?" The man grunted the words with distinct disgust.

Arleigh?

Lannick raised a trembling hand, shielding his eyes from the light and trying to make sense of the scene before him. He could discern no details, but whoever it was seemed ready to plunge the knife downward into one of his soft places.

"Course you don't," the man continued, shaking a head of long hair. The voice wasn't Arleigh's, though if anything it sounded angrier. "You don't remember because you were dead drunk. Well I'm guessing your little ride in that little box has sobered you up some. Good. I want you to be as afraid as you can be, you fucking bastard."

"Who are you?" Lannick whispered, struggling to make out the man's features.

"One of your old acquaintances."

The man slammed shut the box's lid with a fearsome crack. Lannick cringed as the latch and lock snapped back into place.

The man laughed. "You'll get yours soon, Captain. Real soon."

Dead gods.

"Water," Lannick wheezed. The box seemed a cauldron. The searing, steamy air choked him as he breathed it. His chainmail coat weighed upon his chest and made the heat all the worse. "Water," he pleaded.

A spiteful grunt. "Anyone want to give the good captain a drink?"

Laughter followed.

"Alright, then," grated the voice. "Leave it to me, boys."

Footfalls shuffled outside and the cart shifted and creaked like someone clambered atop it. The ribbons of light above Lannick darkened with shadow. After a moment there came a trickling noise and droplets tumbled through the box's cracks.

"Drink up!"

Lannick craned his neck, mouth agape as he contorted to catch the drops. At last he managed to wet his tongue. He winced, finding the taste bitter and briny. He swallowed, though, for his throat felt as though it'd been flayed.

The trickle slowed and ended. Lannick twisted his head and tried to seize more of the water but could only catch a tiny mouthful. He swallowed again.

More chuckling.

"So how's my piss taste, Captain?"

Lannick retched. His stomach turned and he spat, head smacking against the box's splinters as he did. He heaved up the sour remnants of whatever he'd last eaten and whatever he'd just swallowed. He fell back with a whimper.

"I'll take that as a compliment!"

Nasty, vile laughter.

Lannick gritted his teeth and hate filled his heart. "You bastards... As soon as I get out of here I'll—"

"You'll what?" A boot pounded against the box. "Open this damned thing! It's high time we got reacquainted."

The lock clicked open and the lid was yanked aside. Again a black silhouette framed by blinding sunlight. Lannick tried to rise but a rough hand held him and a knife pressed against his throat.

"Easy there, Captain," said the man, bringing the blade to Lannick's jugular. "You can't be dying just yet."

Lannick drew in a breath and tried to settle his nerves.

He squinted and made out a big head draped with long hair. "Who are you?"

"You really don't remember, do you? You destroy my fucking life and can't even recall my face."

At last the features resolved in Lannick's eyes. An angry face scarred in places. Scruffy, matted hair. *Black Jon's attendant?* Confusion clouded his head. "H-Harl? Black Jon's man?"

"I figured that's all you'd know me as. A fucking serving boy! Fetching your fucking ale and emptying turds from chamber pots." Harl's face twisted to a vicious glower and his knife hand trembled. "You're *why* I was reduced to that."

Lannick's head still rang from the blows, from retching piss and from the blazing sun above. He had no idea who accused him now.

"I was a fucking Scarlet Sword!" Harl roared. "For five years I answered only to General Fane! Then you cut my hamstring outside your shit-stained quarters in Ironmoor and I lost *everything*! General Fane discharged me from the ranks because of you! I found my way back into the army, but the only work for a man with a leg like mine was doing the shit no one else wanted to do. The shameful jobs. The work of the wretched and the wounded. Well, you're my way back, Captain. You're my way back to the general's side."

"I-I…" Lannick stammered, struggling to recall foggy details of that morning after his night with Fane's daughter.

Harl shoved himself away from Lannick. "Lock it," Harl growled. "Let this fucker soak in piss for a while."

Lannick awoke in the dark, head stinging and body aching in every joint. He shifted but could find no comfort in the box's confines. His throat burned though he dared not ask for drink.

He turned his head and spotted the glow of a fire not far from the cart. He heard the snap of flames and foul, guttural voices upon the night's still air.

He drew in a shuddering breath. He wondered how many of his comrades lay dead, how many of the old soldiers of Pryam's Bay had perished that night at the camp.

All of them?

He felt a sick, cold pit in his guts and his lips trembled.

Has this all been for naught?

He fought away tears. He thought of his family, of Brugan, and of his many old comrades.

And he thought too of General Fane, the man responsible for every last one of their deaths.

He cursed and bunched up his fists then heard shuffling steps approach. He heard the click of a lock and felt the box lurch sideways. "What?" was all he could say before tumbling out into the night and onto the wet ground.

"Pick him up!" Harl growled.

Hands heaved Lannick upward then slammed him against the side of a cart. Three burly soldiers wearing the red and black sashes of Black Jon's deserters faced him with hateful eyes. Behind them, on the other side of their campfire, moved Harl. He limped through tall grass and drifts of mist, dragging his bad leg behind him. He was a big fellow, clumsy but undoubtedly strong.

Harl made his way toward Lannick. "Keep him standing," he said and the soldiers held Lannick firm against the cart. "Good. General Fane wants him alive, but he probably won't mind if he's missing a piece or two."

Lannick saw then the gleam of a sword—his own prized sword—in Harl's hand and the former Scarlet Sword gripped it with certain intent. Lannick struggled against the soldiers' grasp but it was no use. His eyes darted madly about. "Help!" he screamed.

His words died in the steamy air.

Harl moved closer. "Turn him round, boys."

"Help!"

The soldiers did as ordered, spinning Lannick about and forcing his head down to the rough wood. He squirmed, turning his head aside. In the darkness he spotted a purse, his purse, just a few feet away atop the cart. *My Coda! If I can but grab it...*

He twisted and jabbed his elbows backward, flailing against the men holding him. They loosened their grips for an instant and Lannick lunged toward the satchel. He managed to tug it close, near his box, but the soldiers grabbed him and held him fast once more.

There was a hot breath in his ear. "It's only fair, you know," said Harl. "Folk where I come from say dark work brings dark rewards. Well, *Captain*, you're about to get yours."

"No!" he wailed. "No!"

"A fine blade," said Harl. He chuckled. "You probably never guessed it'd be used this way. Well, fate's a funny thing, Captain."

"This one?" asked one of the soldiers.

"Why not," Harl said with a laugh. "We can start small. We have plenty of time."

Lannick gasped as he felt the small finger of his left hand yanked upward. The soldier gripped it in a fist at a painful angle, pulling it against the joint's bounds. Then, with the soldier's sudden twist, the finger snapped.

Lannick stared slack-jawed at the digit, its tip now pointing sideways from the middle knuckle. The pain was awful.

"It hurts?" sneered Harl. "You fuck!" he screamed against Lannick's ear. "You turned me into a cripple!"

A fist or knee smashed into his crotch and crushed his jingles. He heaved out what air remained in his lungs and sucked in a shallow, stunned breath. He wheezed and wilted against the wood.

"Up, now!" spat Harl. "Keep him up! We've more work to do!"

Lannick felt hard hands seize him and slam him against the cart. They yanked his left arm outward and splayed it upon the rough wood. One of the soldiers tugged at his broken finger and he wailed.

"That one hurts, does it?" said Harl. He leaned forward, his angry face coming even with Lannick's. "Don't worry. I'll not let you suffer that pain for long. After all, you're a decorated hero!"

He pressed back and shoved Lannick against the cart as he did. He kicked Lannick again in the crotch. Harder this time.

Lannick slumped against the cart's side. His head spun with pain and he let out a cry.

Harl laughed his ugly laugh. Then he braced Lannick's hand and chopped away his broken finger.

Lannick looked in horror at his bloodied hand and groaned.

"You see, Captain!" crowed Harl. "I'm a man of my word! I told you I'd not let you suffer the pain of that broken finger!"

His men chuckled. "Another?" said one.

"No…" Lannick whimpered, sinking against the wood. "No…"

Harl snorted. "Sure. Try the one beside it."

A hand around his finger. A twist.

Crack.

The pain made him swoon. His vision blurred red and black and then, just barely, focused on the image of the ruined hand.

"There, Captain!" Harl said, a sick satisfaction in his tone. "Boys, after he's admired his new hand you can bandage him up."

"*Bandages?*" asked a soldier.

"I'm a charitable man!" laughed Harl. "General Fane wants him alive. No doubt he'll want to finish this bastard himself. We should let the general have his due."

The soldiers laughed and dropped Lannick to the dirt.

"Perhaps we'll take a few more parts before Riverweave," growled Harl. "When you bandage him, find our filthiest rag and wrap it good and tight around that wound. Then bind his hands together and throw the bastard back in the box."

Lannick winced, a terrible pain searing through his left

hand and up his arm. He'd tried shifting the wet rag about his hand but it proved no use—his mess of a hand remained trapped in an agonizing contortion. His eyes welled with tears and he drew in a slow breath. He reckoned he had precious few of those remaining.

He had no means of escape, he knew, not unarmed and trapped in what might as well have been a coffin. But at least it seemed he'd have one last audience with General Fane—at least these foul bastards were taking him exactly where he wanted to go.

And maybe, just maybe, I'll have one last chance to stick a knife in Fane's black fucking heart.

He blinked away tears and squinted through the cracks of his box. Dawn had broken upon a steamy landscape. Frogs croaked and cranes chattered. He caught the scent of bacon on the air and realized he'd not consumed anything in days.

Unless you count Harl's smelly piss, that is.

He convulsed, not sure whether it due to an aborted laugh or a near retch. The pain seared up his arm anew.

Someone belched. "Two more days, you think?"

"Likely," came Harl's gruff tone. "This ground between the rivers is a shitty mess. But give us two days more and we'll reach Riverweave."

"You sure the general will take us back? You sure we'll be pardoned?"

"Of fucking course. He'll not have forgotten me. Named me a Scarlet Sword, he did, and for good reason. And with the gift we're bringing him? Ha! We'll be real soldiers, promotions and all!"

Low laughter. Another belch. "*Captain* Harl. Has a fine ring to it."

"Damned right it does. Toss me another rasher of that bacon. I'm soon to be a captain, after all."

They laughed all the more.

Lannick smelled again the pork and his stomach roiled and rumbled. "Food?" he chanced.

Silence.

Then a chuckle. "Why not. General Fane won't want him too close to dead. He'll want to do most of the killing himself. Open the box."

A shuffle sounded, then the click and squeak of the lock. An arm tossed open the lid and another two plunged into the cart to yank Lannick to a seat by his bandages. Lannick gnashed his teeth but managed to keep quiet. The rough-faced soldier dropped Lannick's hand with a snicker.

Lannick blinked, eyes adjusting to the light of morning, and turned to see Harl pressing himself upward with a grunt. He limped the few strides between the campfire and the cart, mouth curled to a sneer. Then he dropped a bowl of fatty bacon and crusty bread in Lannick's lap.

Harl regarded him with a nasty look. "As I said, I'm a charitable man. But you'll eat with *that* hand. Boys, unwrap that and bind his good one behind him."

Harl's men did as instructed, the bandages ripping away scabs and jerking about Lannick's broken finger as they unfurled from his left hand. Lannick winced, yielding defeatedly as his right arm was tugged, twisted and tied.

"Enjoy your breakfast," said Harl with a snort. "You

try and run and we'll add a few limbs to your list of missing parts." He returned to the campfire and plopped to the ground with a thump.

Lannick studied his hand beside the bowl, fresh blood trickling from the hole left by his severed finger and the one next to it turned in ways fingers weren't meant to turn. He pinched just his forefinger to his thumb but even that shifted the wounds and sent a pang through his hand. He tested it a few more times before gingerly drawing the bacon to his mouth. He chewed and it tasted delicious, though he reckoned just about anything would now.

"Two damned days," said Harl to the soldiers seated again beside him. "Two damned days and we'll have our lives back."

"How you figure we'll find the general?"

"With our prize? We just need to get to Riverweave—he's known to be holed up there. Once in the city we'll have no trouble finding him. We'll have the attention of a Scarlet Sword soon enough, and those fellows are certain to remember me. We'll get our introduction."

Lannick's hunger prevailed against his pain and he swallowed the last of his bacon. His eyes drifted. All the land about seemed a flat, steamy mess, broken by rare, gangly trees and tall reeds and nettles. There seemed no one—no help—anywhere near.

His wounds brushed against his bread's crusted edges. He hissed and looked to his bowl. The crust seemed to have been salted and he felt the sting of it. He tilted his elbow outward and pulled the bread from the bowl with the few whole digits left on his hand.

He gnawed at the chunk, wanting water but knowing

better than to ask. He looked around the cart and there—just there aside his box—slouched his satchel. He remembered it used to hold a flask, but then recalled it held something far more important.

My Coda.

He glanced to Harl and his men. They hunched over their bowls near the fire, seemingly content to spend their morning feasting over glories yet to come. They paid him no mind.

He set his bread back in his bowl and flexed his wounded hand again. It hurt, terribly so, though he could still use it. He twisted and pressed it outward, fumbling briefly with the flap of the satchel before easing it open. He slipped his ruined hand within—eyes shifting back to Harl and his henchmen and seeing them occupied—and at last found the box holding his Coda.

He felt about and used thumb and forefinger to draw the metal from its container. He pressed it open and slid his hand between. With a twist of his wrist the metal closed upon his forearm with a dull click. He withdrew his arm from the satchel and watched as the iron began to glow a cool green.

"*Find me, Ogrund!*" he willed through the torrent of visions. "*Find me, Wil and Alisa!*" He looked wide about his surroundings, hoping someone would recognize the landscape, the location. He threw his thoughts outward, where he'd been and where he knew his captors were taking him.

"What the fuck is he doing!" snapped Harl. "Get that fucking thing off his wrist! I'd heard he was a witch of some sort. The general will want that! If our prisoner here puts it back on his wrist then cut his whole fucking arm off at the shoulder."

The soldiers pried away the Coda and tossed it somewhere atop the cart. They shoved Lannick back in his coffin and turned the lock. The air was steamy and the confines tight, though Lannick knew the message had been sent.

He just hoped his former brethren had heard it, and that they'd prove more loyal to him than he'd been to them.

He shook his head, vowing to one day make amends for his many mistakes.

"*Find me*," he hoped.

"*Find me*," he prayed.

20
DESPERATION AND DEPRAVITY

"WAR," SAID FENCRESS, the word a curse upon her tongue. She tugged at her cowl and stared though the swaying sedge of the hillock to the darkening landscape beyond. It was a flat expanse of trampled weeds and grasses leading to the sea a league or so distant. Countless pools of water reflected the setting sun, shining like a fortune of gold spilled across the plain.

And upon it all seethed the battle. Several thousand poor fools clashed in the waning light, Rune's soldiers in their rectangular bunches with shields raised and mounted Arranese swirling about them like tongues of fire.

"War," she said again. "As profound a tragedy as anyone could witness."

Drenj crouched low beside her. "Odd words from an assassin," he said, his voice wielding an edge.

Fencress shifted on her elbows. She looked to the

Khaldisian and Paddyn nearby. "Ever the pious one, the one who claims his hands have never been sullied by the dark work?"

Drenj seemed not to hear, his dark gaze trained upon the combat. Men screamed and orders were shouted in the distance. Steel hissed and rang. "An assassin calls war a tragedy?" he said after a moment. He rubbed eyes moist with sweat and perhaps a few fallen tears, smearing a black mess across his sunken cheeks. "You permit yourself to judge the righteousness of the means of men's deaths?"

"Women die too, you know," Fencress said, mouth curling to a smirk. Drenj was troubled, she knew—his haggard, stained face told of despair and little else. If this were deadman's dice, he'd be the dead man. "The tragedy of war, though," she said, "is in its absolute stupidity, the fact that so much death happens at the same time and in the same place and for reasons not shared by those doing the killing. You think any of those poor sods out there are throwing around their steel for the *glory* of Rune? For the glory of Rune's dead king? Nonsense. They're doing it because they're *told* to and nothing more than that. Sounds like no reason at all, if you ask me."

Drenj sniffled. "When do we ever get to choose our *reasons* for dying, Fencress? A knife in the back or a spill from a horse is no choice. Death by red fever is no choice, nor is death by..." he said, his voice cracking, "some kind of plague."

Fencress tucked a stray strand of black hair back within her leather cowl, knowing the Khaldisian remained troubled by Karnag's words. "Death finds us all and we have little or no choice as to when or how," she said, meaning the words as some sort of comfort. "But I wasn't talking about dying. I was talking about killing."

"And you believe there's a choice in that?" asked Drenj, eyelids drooping with sadness. "That people can choose why and when they are driven to such acts, and that some choices are better than others?"

"I do," she said, with conviction. "Coin is always a better cause for me than country. My cause is ever *my own*. Show me a man whose cause is anything other than a selfish thing and I'll show you a damned fool. When I kill, it's for my own reasons, for my own cause."

"I'd say there's no choice at all. Killing is the very worst of things. Why would anyone *choose* to do that? I'd say there are only two reasons that'd compel a person to take the life of another: desperation and depravity."

Fencress looked to the Khaldisian, her eyes narrowing to a squint. "Now who's the one standing in judgment of others, Drenj? I for one will never be judged by the likes of you or any other man for that matter. My conscience is clear."

Drenj held her gaze but said nothing.

Fencress stared again to the battlefield. "Fools," she said, meaning the word as much for Drenj as the soldiers below. "Bloody fools."

"You're not unlike *him*, you know."

Him.

Karnag.

Fencress peeked back above her shoulder, back to where Karnag… rested or meditated or did whatever it was he did.

Paddyn shifted closer. "What's he doing, Fencress?"

he said, the words whistling through the space left by his missing tooth.

Fencress scowled. "Probably making ready to kill someone."

Evening had long ago given way to night. Fencress shook her thin blanket and shifted upon the lumpy ground. After a moment she lay still, sucking in steamy breaths while listening to the clash of distant combat broken only by Paddyn's clumsy snore.

She turned to where Karnag had bedded down and saw only a bundle of rags. He—and *Gravemaker*—were not to be found.

She tugged gloves upon her hands and flexed her fingers. She drew her twin swords closer, even though they'd already been within a comfortable arm's reach. It was too dark, too quiet, too unsafe. Even here at their hilltop encampment far enough from the fighting things seemed… dangerous.

She cursed and pressed herself to a seat. She'd not slept much this night, nor did she reckon she would in the few remaining hours before dawn. Too many unknown perils lurked about and she didn't fancy the notion of being caught unawares.

She needed to case her surroundings and get a clearer idea of what and where those dangers were.

And of those, perhaps Karnag most of all.

She withdrew from her makeshift bed and pulled on boots, cloak and cowl. She cinched the belt holding her scabbards, slipped the blades into place, and widened her eyes to the night.

She tiptoed through their small camp, about the

doused fire pit and between the dozing forms of Drenj and Paddyn. She paused for a moment, eyes upon them. She'd heard the Khaldisian weeping earlier and knew the young man had broken. It troubled her, but not enough to sway her intentions. She'd pushed too large a wager to the table's center to quit the game now. She'd tied her chances to Karnag and needed to see things through.

She came to the hilltop's crest. Karnag had chosen this spot—indeed, he'd insisted upon it. "*This is the place,*" he'd said. "*An old and sacred place, and one perfect for my purpose.*"

She'd shrugged off the words at the time, but now reckoned it offered a fine view of the battlefront, the Sullen Sea just east of it, and—when she squinted—the faint glow of Riverweave a few leagues to the north.

A fine view of all the killing.

The size of the gathered forces was staggering. Many thousands occupied the broad swath of land below, Rune's soldiers behind trenches and wooden fortifications and the bulk of the Arranese encamped a mile or so to the south. Moonlight played upon the field between, across ruined armor and rivers of blood and the wreckage of men and beasts, and caused it all to twinkle like some deranged fairytale sky.

Fencress grimaced and found a flask she'd salvaged from an abandoned supply cart. She twisted off the cap and sucked down a swallow. It wasn't good whiskey— she'd not had that since Ironmoor—but it'd dull the edges and shove some courage in her heart.

She thought about that for an instant. She wasn't

normally the sort to need drink for bravery. But then things were anything but normal now.

She took another sour pull and examined the downward slope and the land beyond. Tangles of bodies, warriors of both Rune and Arranan, piled about. There was movement, too. Occasional Arranese war parties ranged across the field, as did a handful of scouts from Rune. In the midst of it all struggled groaning bastards with missing limbs or broken parts, toiling as though their sad efforts would buy them another meaningful day in this hell.

"Bloody fools," she whispered.

But as awful as it all was, as wretched and as wound-filled, there was something worse. Fencress felt it like the gnaw of sickness in her belly.

Somewhere Karnag stood. Somewhere he raged. Somewhere he *killed*.

But where?

She looked to the sea and then southward, to the Arranese army and the darkened land beyond. She wagered they weren't terribly far—thirty leagues at most—from where they'd found Karnag weeks before. That place where he'd killed countless Arranese and made some sort of monument from their bloody bits.

Could he be doing that again?

She shuddered and took another sip of whiskey. She wondered where all this was headed, to what fortune, or misfortune, chance would take them. She knew what she hoped for but worried the odds of changing or saving Karnag became slimmer by the moment.

She took a few skulking steps down the hillside, keen eyes trying to take in those things she'd not seen already.

She scanned the Arranese war parties, all groups of seven riding in wedged bunches. One, though, had scattered and rode about haphazardly. It had now but six riders, all those hoisting weapons and torches.

She knew what troubled them.

Karnag.

She watched the scene play out, the Arranese horsemen wheeling, searching. She heard their distant, accented words. Words of confusion. Words of fear.

And she saw them fall.

One by one they fell.

More shouting on the air, this in a gravelly voice familiar to her. Karnag's voice.

All but one fell. That last rider fled to the Arranese encampment and Fencress swore she could hear the echo of Karnag's laughter chasing him down.

She sank to the scratchy weeds of the hillside and drew her twin swords. These were dangers she could not understand. Chaos swirled about her and chance seemed more random than ever.

There seemed no safe bet.

She tightened her cowl and tried to follow Karnag's dark shadow across the plain. She thought she saw him come near a scout from Rune and heard the soldier shout. Then a squelch, a pained moan, and silence.

She sheathed one of her swords and grabbed the flask once more. Karnag seemed to desire more than wanton murder. He had a plan, she knew.

She took a long pull of the rotgut and wondered about the killer's motives.

Her friend's motives, she reminded herself.

His strange talk had troubled her and thus she'd tried closing her ears to it. But sorting over it now she knew he'd been speaking of things both long ago and yet to come. Histories and prophecies mingled in his mouth. Threats against this 'Thaydorne' and Arranan's Spider King, names spoken together as though one and the same.

Another awful laugh sounded. This one not far away.

She stared into the night, down the slope of the hill and toward the battlefield. She spied him at the hill's base, an imposing, fearsome figure clutching a bulging sack. He strode up the incline, shouldering the sack and shaking a wet mess from the massive sword gripped in his hand.

Closer he came, nearer to Fencress. The moonlight caught his face, his countenance pale and cut by a grin. It struck her as little different than a bleached skull, all bare bones and hollow eyes and toothy smile.

She gripped the flask and took another swallow. She gave half a thought to slinking back into her bedroll but knew Karnag had spotted her by now. She didn't want to show more fear than she knew he already perceived.

He came near and tossed the large sack to the earth. It landed with a thump, shifted then settled. Karnag paused and seemed to admire it, his sick smile widening all the more.

Fencress looked to him, whiskey warming her head and stoking an ill-tempered feeling within. "You've brought me a birthday present? How kind. It was only a day or two ago, I think." Her words fell without humor, though she suspected that mattered not with Karnag. The only laughter he knew now was born of cruelty.

He dropped to a seat beside the sack. "Birthday?"

he asked with what sounded utter confusion. His head seemed to wrestle with the notion but then he shook his mess of fraying black braids. "I've brought no gifts. I've brought invitations."

"Ah," Fencress said. "You're throwing me a party, then?" It was the sort of line that, months before, might have drawn a slight smirk to Karnag's lips. Fencress worried, though, the Karnag she'd known then was all but gone.

Karnag looked to the bloodied plain below, to that great mass of dead and dying, and the discomforting smile returned to his face. "Invitations…"

Fencress stared blankly.

"Yes," Karnag said, "indeed these are invitations. They are invitations for my brother. With each I send him a new request to parley, and the tongue of our talk shall be violence. Behold…" He pulled apart the strings binding his sack and rummaged within. His hands returned with a severed head, a face of angled features with olive skin slack upon it. Blood dripped and slopped into Karnag's lap.

Fencress grimaced. "An Arranese warrior," she said flatly. "Or at least the topmost part of him. Forgive me, Karnag, but if severed heads are serving as your invitations I don't wager many will want to attend this party."

Karnag turned the head's face toward his own and seemed to study its eyes. "I've learned the dead hold secrets, secrets they reveal only to those who've discovered how to ask for them."

Fencress sucked down the last mouthful of whiskey, the burn bothering her not at all. "What secrets are those, Karnag?"

Karnag's eyes fluttered for a moment. Fencress couldn't be sure but she thought she saw a string of dark shadows—an inky black darker than the night about them—stretch from the disembodied head toward Karnag and he appeared to inhale the eddies from the air. It seemed no different from what she'd seen in that field of dead men and silent crows just days before.

Karnag grinned again. "The secrets are many."

She looked to him, silent, and fear filled her heart.

"This man," said Karnag, staring at the severed head, "was Hashaan. He was a warrior and breaker of horses of some renown among his people. He served as one of the Spider King's most trusted commanders. His death will trouble Thaydorne and Thaydorne will send soldiers to seek out his killer and the killer of the other corpses I've left upon the field this night. And when those who seek out the killer suffer death themselves, my brother will seek the killer himself. Thus, the headless corpses, and the heads themselves, serve as my invitations. He will come to me."

Fencress swallowed, wishing she had a few more sips of whiskey in her flask. "And so that's why you've come here."

Karnag lowered the head and looked to her. "I've come for Thaydorne."

"Thaydorne," Fencress said. "Arranan's Spider King."

"The same. I come to destroy him. He seeks to steal something from me. He thinks he commands the ending of things but has yet to understand death is mine alone to wield." He glanced northward. "Father need choose but one son."

"Father?"

Karnag seemed not to hear and dug again into his sack of human parts. His hands emerged with another severed head. This, it seemed, was that of a soldier of Rune, the pale countenance still stuffed within the steel casing of its battered helmet. "And this was Elmin Pine, son of a fisherman from a village near the Waters of World's End. He..." Karnag looked upward toward the night. "He will be a beginning."

Fencress tugged tight the gloves upon her hands. Her hopes for answers were bleeding away though still the question found her mouth. "Karnag, what is happening? Where does this path lead you?"

Karnag looked to her, empty eyes reflecting the moonlight like a pair of distant ghosts. "To the end."

She sat for a time longer, waiting for more words to come, but they did not. Instead Karnag's gaze returned to the severed head in his hands. He mumbled words Fencress neither understood nor cared to. He tossed aside the head then arose, looking back toward the battlefield.

Fencress stood also, stared to Karnag, then turned her back to her friend. She heard him walk away, stomping back down the hill's slope with a low, disconcerting laugh. After a moment she strode back to her bedroll.

Sleep did not come easy.

"Thaydorne," Karnag said with a strange chuckle from across the morning campfire. He tore dirty teeth through salted pork then laughed again. "Thaydorne was nothing before that battle..." He twisted about to regard the war raging on the plain behind him, the many soldiers of

Arranan and Rune clashing almost a mile away. "Nothing. A mercenary, a strongman. But he was no slayer."

Fencress gnawed at her chunk of pork, the meat sour in her mouth. Breakfast with Karnag was no longer a pleasant thing—his company well worse than the sour pork—and she wagered it'd only grow more horrible.

"He was never worthy of the gifts Illienne imparted," Karnag continued. "Had he not curried her favor with deeds at Cirak—simple deeds any soldier could have performed—he'd never have been among the chosen. His brother Vellinor was twice his measure!" He shook his frayed braids. "I gave Illienne my counsel, but she did not listen. Perhaps… Perhaps that is why she granted wisdom to me. Perhaps she thought I'd not seen the truth of things. But I did, and now I know that truth more clearly than ever…"

Fencress stopped chewing and looked to Drenj and Paddyn. The young men huddled far from the fire, wide eyes upon Karnag.

"Thaydorne!" Karnag said with another odd laugh. "Illienne instructed that his role in the last battle had been foretold, that it would be Thaydorne who'd deliver the decisive blow against Yrghul. Thaydorne's strike proved to be the last though it could have come from anyone, from any blade. Yrghul was weak, broken. He was all but defeated when Thaydorne came upon him. Thaydorne was no slayer. His was no more than the fall of an executioner's axe. He is nothing like…" He turned to stare upon the battlefield, to the soldiers of both armies clashing upon it.

Fencress began chewing again then swallowed dry meat into her dry throat. "Nothing like what?"

Karnag looked to her, dead eyes displaying what seemed a hint of surprise. "Nothing like me. I have become the greatest slayer the heavens have ever witnessed. I have become death, and the days to come will chronicle my triumph. Thaydorne will fall, and he will fall by my hand."

21
THE WORST OF TREASON

"PREFECT GAMGHAST GRAYSTONE!" announced the armored bailiff, voice booming through the dusty, column-lined chamber. He thrust his halberd upward, its steel reflecting the gleam of many torches illuminating the courtroom. "Proceed to the chair!"

"If I must," Gamghast spat, shifting painfully upon his seat at the chamber's rear. He grabbed his staff and looked to Prefect Borel and the dozens of acolytes about him. He patted his robes and felt both the folded note he'd kept and the vial of quicksilver he'd secured from the Sanctum's apothecary. "This will not be our ending, my friends," he whispered, then pressed against his staff to stand.

"I pray you're right," said Borel, jowls quivering.

"This way, Prefect," barked the bailiff. He gestured

down the length of faded carpet laid between rows of scattered dignitaries and stretching toward the bench of the Magistrate Examiners.

Gamghast grunted and trudged along in the bailiff's tow, the clack of his staff resounding though the ancient chamber. He turned his head about, watching the tired, disdainful eyes of the seated onlookers follow his march. He wondered if these so-called dignitaries did anything other than attend coronations, condemnations, and funerals.

He sniffed, thinking how a level of supposed 'importance' could doom a person to irrelevance in the greater picture. Life, he thought, must have become to them all ballrooms and burials, a strange sense of majesty in the mundane memorials of society.

He heaved a sigh and stared ahead, the image of the courtroom's bench slowly resolving in his rheumy eyes. It was a heap of dark, decaying wood and upon it perched three Magistrate Examiners, their bald or balding heads and bunched, black robes making them seem a wake of vultures atop a corpse.

"Kneel before approaching!" croaked one.

"My apologies," Gamghast grumbled, bracing against his staff and sinking to a complaining knee. As he did he glanced to his sides and noticed the first two pews of the chamber were stuffed with armed guards. He shook his head and arose, doing all he could to maintain a scornful expression. This whole proceeding felt a profound insult.

The bailiff thrust his shiny halberd to a single chair positioned before and beneath the massive bench. "The accused will sit here," he commanded.

"Accused?" he hissed. The word, the notion, angered him.

The bailiff, a ruddy-cheeked man with a flattened nose, looked to Gamghast impassively. "To the chair, Prefect," he whispered. "I assure you the jails are most unpleasant, and I'd rather not be ordered to escort a man of the faith to such places."

Gamghast huffed and made his way to the chair, the bailiff walking to stand beside him. Gamghast dropped to an uncomfortable seat then looked to the three men waiting to determine his fate.

"Prefect Gamghast Graystone," said the one in the center, a man whose bald head was crowded by liver spots. He pored for a moment over a ledger then turned a page with angled fingers. "Your order stands accused not only of harboring a banished traitor of the realm, but also of complicity in summoning other such traitors to our kingdom. These traitors were banished a *thousand years ago* by decree of High King Derganfel, a decree honored by every High King to follow him. How do you answer these charges? How can you excuse such a thing, a thing that strikes me as the worst of treason?"

Gamghast pressed a hand against his back and stiffened in his chair. He was certain the examiners had some measure of evidence—the summons had come too soon after Gamghast ordered that the acolytes be informed of Castor's presence.

Someone had betrayed them.

"Prefect?" the examiner asked, his voice pitched with obvious irritation.

Gamghast looked to his inquisitors, defiance in his

eyes. "As prefect I came to learn the Sentinel Castor honored the oath he swore to Illienne the Light Eternal. He *rightfully* regarded that oath more binding than any kingly edict. Thus, as my order's Lector, he continued to tend to the High King's faith and wellbeing for centuries. He kept track of threats to the kingdom for centuries. He helped ward away our oldest enemies for centuries. He helped to keep us, *all* of us, safe from ancient evils *for centuries*. Considering the foes facing us, are we the sorts of 'criminals' Rune's Magistrate Examiners choose to prosecute?"

The codger in the center settled back in his tall chair, slinking into his black robes. "An honorable judge does not choose to whom the rule of law applies, for law applied unequally is injustice. Further, an honorable judge knows all citizens must stand alike before the law, with the law blind to their stations. Finally, an honorable judge knows high-minded intentions cannot be weighed against illicit acts. Your order, Prefect," he said, craning his speckled head, "stands accused of conspiring with traitors. Such would make your order traitorous as well. I ask again, how do you answer these accusations?"

Gamghast felt a fire rising within him. He swatted the wisps of his white beard. "And I ask, Examiner, who is my accuser? Who is my accuser and what is the proof?"

The Magistrate Examiner leaned forward, the bench's wood creaking beneath his elbows. "The proof? You've just admitted that, as prefect, you learned your so-called Lector was the Sentinel Castor. When did you learn this? I suspect it wasn't only upon the day you received your summons. Why did you not approach this body and report the crime of a Sentinel defying banishment? How long did you continue to commit treason against the realm?"

An examiner to his side raised a thin and trembling hand. "As the most senior member of this body," he said in a voice as thin as his wreath of white hair, "I would remind you, Examiner Lagdall, the prefect is a respected member of the Sanctum, a man pledged to serve the Crown who—"

"Duly noted," the bald man—Examiner Lagdall—said, glaring at the other examiner. "However, I have been designated Lead Examiner for this inquiry, and, as such, my questions *will* be answered. How long have you conspired with a traitor, Prefect?"

Gamghast gritted his teeth. "I will concede there are some who conspire with our oldest enemies. However, I assure you they have no home in the Abbey. Indeed, there are some who work in the shadows against the Crown and the whole of the kingdom." He looked about the chamber's sparse crowd, his glare a challenge. "I daresay Chamberlain Alamis has arranged this farce, and it is he who betrays Rune. And I ask once more, who accuses the Sanctum?"

He heard scattered, fleeting gasps in the chamber. Then the sharp, intoned whispers of gossip.

And then laughter. Laughter light as a spring rain. From behind the wooden bulwark of the Magistrate Examiners slipped Chamberlain Alamis, impeccably groomed and draped in blue silk. A thin, golden band rested upon the trimmed bowl of his blond hair, just above his pale eyes.

"My dear Prefect Gamghast," said Alamis, his tone

patronizing. "How utterly unfortunate to meet under such circumstances."

Gamghast scowled at the chamberlain. With a gnarled hand he found again the shape of the vial of quicksilver secreted within his robes. "You are the traitor, Alamis!"

Examiner Lagdall banged a mallet upon the ledger before him. "We will have order in this chamber, Prefect."

Gamghast gripped the arms of his chair and pushed himself upward. "Alamis should be the one confined to this damned seat!"

"I said order!" demanded Lagdall. "Bailiff!"

The armored man jabbed his halberd before Gamghast, the blade pressing against his belly. "Please, Prefect," he said quietly. "Return to the chair."

Gamghast huffed but slumped backward. "Very well."

"Once again," said Examiner Lagdall, "I pose my queries. When did you learn your Lector's true identity, and why did you fail to report such treason to the Crown?"

"Treason!" Gamghast exclaimed. "My order serves to *protect* the Crown, to protect the whole of Rune. I urge you, it is my accuser who should stand accused."

Examiner Lagdall pounded the mallet against his ledger once more. "You fail to answer my questions, Prefect. I would suggest you not take our inquiry lightly nor attempt to distract or obstruct it. This body can be quite understanding, but severe in equal measure."

Gamghast eyeballed the lead examiner. "If it is the Bastion's *chamberlain* who accuses my order, then my truthful and resolute answer to your inquiry is that any and all charges represent a desperate attempt to distract the kingdom from far more vile betrayals. I witnessed with my own eyes the chamberlain sharing the company of necromancers in the Godswell as they summoned Yrghul's spirit from the depths of oblivion. I say again it is the chamberlain who betrays all of Rune!"

Alamis smiled and leaned against the bench, elbow rested upon its lip. "Our king is dead, Prefect, and, in the wake of his tragic passing, the nobles and dignitaries of Rune have named me Sovereign of the Realm until a worthy successor can be named. I'd suggest you reconsider your words. They are, in my estimation, even more treasonous than those crimes of which you already stand accused. I am Sovereign of Rune, our kingdom's ultimate authority during this delicate time, and, as such, I stand in place of its High King."

Gamghast knotted his hands into fists. "How dare you, Alamis. I know it was you who murdered the High King!" He pulled from his robes the note of the now-dead scullery maid. "Behold!" He unfolded the brittle parchment and brandished it. "A scullery maid from the Bastion, months ago, knew the chamberlain was poisoning the king to prevent him from siring an heir! She summoned us under the auspices of an exorcism so that she could deliver the news, then died under quite suspicious circumstances shortly afterward. I say she told the truth, and the chamberlain had her murdered on account of it!"

"A scullery maid?" Alamis laughed. "A note from a *scullery maid?*" His smile fell to a glower and his pale eyes burned. "And just who is the one offering desperate attempts at distraction, Prefect? Who is the one lacking proof, lacking evidence, lacking witnesses?" He spun toward the examiners upon the bench. "I say this man should be led in chains to the jails, lest his treason spread even further during wartime! As the sovereign I demand it!"

Examiner Lagdall looked to Alamis for a moment then tilted his splotchy head to regard the whole of the chamber. "Treason," he proclaimed, "like any infection, cannot be allowed to spread or fester!"

The elder examiner to his left again raised a tremoring hand. "This is not justice, nor has this been a trial," he said, his withering voice nearly lost amidst the growing commotion within the hall. "No matter the accuser, be that a commoner or the kingdom's sovereign, justice must be served. This body does not convict those merely accused. A proper hearing must be held and evidence presented."

Alamis thrust a pointed finger at the man. "I assure you, Examiner, there is evidence. There is a witness. And, most importantly, there is my *mandate*. I decree the banishment of the Sentinels will and must stand, and thus the law has been immutable for a millennium. For his admission of conspiring with the Sentinel Castor, the prefect has confessed his crime, and a serious one at that. If he wants a witness I will gladly provide that."

Lagdall looked to Alamis with a cocked brow. "Sovereign, would you like to summon your witness for inquiry?"

Alamis sighed and smoothed his silken tunic. "If this honorable body deems it necessary."

"I," said the old examiner in his weak voice, "most certainly do."

"Then by all means," Alamis said with a flourish of his hand, "summon my witness."

Examiner Lagdall nodded his liver-spotted head toward the bailiff. The bailiff bowed stiffly then marched about the bench to its rear.

Gamghast twisted to peer to the back of the chamber. He saw only a blur of brown robes—all acolytes were accounted for. He turned again to the bench and grunted. *What lies will Alamis weave next, and through what puppet?*

After a moment the clink and clank of metal sounded. The bailiff returned, followed by two red-sashed, armored guards bullying ahead a limping, lanky fellow in chains. His long face, stretched beneath a messy thatch of hair, wore a pained expression.

"Wit!" Gamghast screamed. "Wit, what have they done?"

The simpleton stared to Gamghast with tearful eyes and he shook the shackles upon his wrists. "I had to answer their questions, Prefect," he said with a whimper. "They said I had to. I had to on account of the High King and such. Every week they'd catch me outside and ask them. I only told them what you told everybody... I didn't tell no lies but they broke my toes for what you said! Broke my toes and tossed me in the jail!"

Gamghast steadied himself against his staff and stood. He brandished a fist toward the bench. "This is justice? This so-called 'honorable' body permits the coercion of innocent witnesses? It permits the *torture* of innocent witnesses? Again, I say it is Alamis who should be tried for treason! The whole of Rune cannot be made to suffer because its examiners turn blind eyes to the kingdom's most dangerous traitor!"

"Ah, Prefect," sighed Alamis, still lounging against the

bench. "You are charged with—and have confessed to—the most serious of crimes. Your man, this 'Wit,' has confessed his knowledge of your order's treason. In doing so he's also confessed his complicity with that treason. There comes a time when a guilty man must admit—"

"There will be silence in the chamber!" shouted the old examiner with surprising force. He turned to his brethren, bracing himself upon his thin arm. "Did this treatment occur while the witness was in our custody? Who permitted this?"

Alamis spun toward the bench. "*I* commanded the detention of this man, Examiner. *I* commanded it upon learning of the Sanctum's treachery, as he is as much a traitor as the prefect himself. Let us not forget the order of things, Examiner. My command carries the weight of law." He looked back and swept a hand toward the gathered acolytes. "The whole of the Sanctum stands guilty. Do you deny the confession the prefect has already delivered?"

The old examiner looked to Alamis. He seemed to suck at his teeth and swallow, the large lump of his throat dipping downward then slowly rising. "The law, even *your* law, Sovereign, demands the application of justice. I will not—"

The examiner stopped short and rose from his seat, peering with fluttering eyes past Gamghast and down the chamber's length.

A clamor arose. Many murmurs mingling to a din. Startled exclamations. Sounds of bodies shuffling upon the pews and rising to stand.

Gamghast struggled upward and turned. He saw light—daylight—pouring into the chamber, blinding in the stuffy darkness. It appeared the doors had been cast open and a clutch of figures stood silhouetted there. The acolytes seemed to be bending to kneel, as were a number of the gathered dignitaries.

"You will stop this charade *now!*" cried a clear, strong voice. A woman's voice.

Gamghast stumbled around his chair, mouth agape.

The queen?

He squinted, trying to make out the figures now marching down the length of carpet toward the bench.

"Alamis!" Queen Reyis shouted again. She wore a heavy cloak over purple robes and a gold crown atop her head. At her side strode ten or so soldiers, one-eyed Tannin among them. "You will stop this!"

Gamghast grabbed his staff and braced against it as he lowered to a knee. He watched the queen approach for an instant longer before twisting his gaze to Alamis. The chamberlain—or sovereign, as he'd proclaimed—stood immobile, fists and jaw clenched.

After an instant Alamis swept hands across his blue tunic. "You?" he said, voice seeming to seethe with anger as he looked to Reyis and her entourage. "You have no authority, Reyis. Your authority died with Deragol."

"I am your *queen*," she said, her tone an edict.

Alamis snarled. "You are naught but a widow, and you will leave this place now. Guards!"

The front pews groaned with the sound of soldiers rising to attention, armor and weapons clinking and clattering. Two dozen or more armed men pressed into the chamber's center aisle. Many looked to Alamis, seemingly seeking his command.

Gamghast drew a sharp breath and slipped his hand within his robes to find the vial of quicksilver. *Sweet Illienne, dare I even try this?*

"Guards!" Alamis demanded again, thrusting a finger toward Queen Reyis. "Dispose of this rabble!"

Alamis's men drew their weapons with a collective, steely hiss.

"Sovereign Alamis!" said Examiner Lagdall, voice uneasy. He'd risen from his seat and stood with a hand splayed over his liver-spotted head. His eyelids twitched. "I assure you we will hear all your evidence and what you've submitted already I've found quite compelling. However, this is a hall of justice and we deliver verdicts, not executions. There will be no bloodshed here!"

Alamis shooed a hand at the examiner. "The whole of this kingdom yields to my command. That includes this chamber, my soldiers, and this so-called 'queen.'"

"I *am* your queen!" Reyis declared. She and her men had stopped and now stood midway down the long aisle. "I am your queen, and I carry within me the next High King of Rune!" She threw aside her cloak to reveal the swell of her pregnancy. "You, Alamis, have no right to assume the throne when High King Deragol's true and only heir has been sired!"

A hush fell over the whole of the chamber.

Alamis seemed to stagger. "What..." he said in a low, level voice as he appeared to gather himself. "Whatever grows in your belly cannot be the High King's heir... How—" He tugged in a breath, smoothed his tunic and took a hard step ahead. "How can we even know this child is Deragol's? How many miscarriages did you have, Reyis?

How many times did he fail you? Indeed, can you prove this is Deragol's child and not the product of some lurid affair? I doubt it."

Gamghast withdrew the vial and clutched it close to his chest. He bent low, his head struggling with the words, but soon he saw them clear as though they'd been scrawled on the stone tiles beneath him.

"How dare you, Alamis," Reyis said, her tone stern and commanding. "I took *your* ministrations in hopes of having a child, and those resulted only in tragedy. As soon as I ceased taking them—as soon as I sought the help of Prefect Gamghast—my child survived." She shook her head. "I had no affair, and may the dead gods curse you for suggesting such. And may the dead gods curse you most of all for murdering my husband."

Alamis strode forward. "Lies." His face shook. "Lies! I sit on Rune's throne by right!"

"You are a usurper, Alamis," said Reyis. "You are a usurper, a liar, and a murderer. The law decrees I am the rightful ruler of Rune so long as I carry the High King's heir. As such, I pardon Prefect Gamghast and the whole of the Sanctum, and order your arrest for threatening me with violence."

Alamis's men slowed and several looked back to him, uncertainty clear in their eyes.

"Whore!" Alamis screamed. "This is not the High King's child—I was Deragol's closest confidant. He knew of your licentiousness and he despised you for it. Guards! Throw this rabble in chains and kill them if they resist!"

Alamis's men moved forward and the queen's entourage drew their blades. Tannin moved to the fore, longsword brandished. "You'll stop there or blood will be spilled," Tannin warned. "Many of you know me, and know full well I don't trifle with false talk."

Silence.

"Throw down your arms, brothers," Tannin said. "Throw them down so you might take them up again."

"Take them, I said!" howled Alamis.

"Onward!" commanded one of Alamis's guardsmen. "You've heard the sovereign! At them now!"

Weapons rattled and Alamis's men rushed forward, swords and halberds at the ready. Shouts and the clash of steel. A cacophony of violence filled the hall.

Gamghast gripped the vial of quicksilver in a fist. "Do I have no choice?" he muttered to himself. He squeezed shut his eyes for a moment and prayed for guidance, but there came no answer.

He focused upon the silvery substance, the words and the Old Faith. Then he drew his arm back and hurled the vial toward the floor near Alamis. The glass shattered and the fluid shimmered upon the tiles like a misshapen mirror. "*Illienne abralide y ganode ferum!*" he growled. "*Kallude axuma sacridum!*"

Illienne awaken and grant me fury! Destroy our enemies with your sacred power!

Thunder rolled. The chamber's vaulted ceiling trembled and debris drifted downward in a slow, wayward shower.

A pause, a breathless pause in which the fighting stopped.

And then came the heavens.

Bright, brilliant light crashed though the hall, forks of lightning searing the eyes. Concussions shook the chamber's stonework. Chunks of rock fell from the roof, smashing through wooden pews and thudding against the tiles. Soldiers lowered blades and fled about, their fight forgotten.

Lightning struck again and again. Blinding spears rained from the sky, stabbing across the chamber. Soldiers fell in twitching heaps, armor and weapons sparking with the light's glow.

Only after a long moment did it stop, the chamber left deadly quiet.

Gamghast turned to Alamis.

The so-called sovereign lay there, motionless. His perfect, blue tunic was spoiled by a smoldering hole in the center of his chest. His pale eyes and thin mouth were agape.

I did it, Gamghast thought. *I did it.* His shoulders drooped with a relieved sigh.

A groan came from the bench. The three examiners slumped upon it amidst scattered stones, each listing about and clutching apparent wounds. Below them, against the bench's wooden front, slouched the bailiff and Wit. They, too, seemed wounded but alive, Wit fumbling with his chains.

Then someone screamed.

"See to the queen!" came Tannin's voice. "Queen Reyis!"

Gamghast turned to the sound and stumbled ahead, trying to peer through the haze of dust and smoke. He could see Alamis and most of his men were dead, torn through and burned by lightning, but he could see nothing of the queen. He snatched his staff and picked his way through the mess of smoldering bodies.

"Careful, my queen!" came another, desperate voice.

Dread weighed upon Gamghast and he quickened his pace, stumbling and nearly falling. Debris still rained from the ceiling, falling to the tiles with a hiss and obscuring his already blurred vision. "Queen Reyis?" he asked, his voice drained of strength.

He pressed onward, dragging himself along with his staff as though it were an oar. The heaps of bodies made for slow going but soon he neared the tight circle of soldiers kneeling around Queen Reyis. She lay upon the floor, face clenched in obvious pain. Much blood spread from a wound on her forehead and another on her thigh.

"My queen," Gamghast heaved, clutching his staff. "How—"

"The roof's stones rained upon us," said Tannin, pressing a bloodied cloth against the queen's brow. He turned to Gamghast. "She should make it, though. These wounds look worse than they are."

"And the child?"

Queen Reyis's eyes fluttered and she looked to him. "I hope... It seems my child is unharmed, Prefect. I... I saw Alamis fall."

Gamghast nodded. "He's dead. He and his men."

She struggled upward to sit, Tannin aiding her. Her bloodied face was solemn. "Death is never a desired outcome, even with the worst of men." She inhaled deeply. "Yet, Prefect, whatever you did saved us, and perhaps the entire kingdom."

Gamghast bent his head low, uncertain how to respond to any appraisal of the carnage.

"My queen," said Tannin. "We should leave this place if you are able. Who knows how long this roof will hold. And Alamis has many allies."

Gamghast rapped the butt of his staff against the tiles. "Acolytes! Prefect Borel! Help us bring this rightful queen and this rightful heir to the Abbey!"

"Wait," Queen Reyis said, moving to stand on unsteady feet. Tannin and the other soldiers braced her. "Wait," she said again. "We'll go to your Abbey for a time, Prefect, but we'll not tarry there for long. We must soon return to the Bastion. The people of Rune deserve to know the usurper is dead. They deserve to know the High King's line survives."

22
THE SANDS OF FOREVER

ZANDRACHUS BALE SAT at the fire's edge, still dumbfounded at the sight before him. Not one but two Sentinels sat before him, sharing Lorra's stew of smelly roots and turnips. It seemed surreal, beyond understanding. Here he was, a misanthropic acolyte who'd always preferred the company of books. Now he dined with demigods.

Kressan, her golden, hairless body healed and grown to the size of an adult human, studied her wooden bowl impassively in the dying light of day. She tasted the concoction then stirred it with her spoon. Her twin Sienne—also fully grown but silvery-skinned—disregarded the stew and stared north with white eyes devoid of pupils, gaze seemingly fixed to the faraway Southwalls.

"Lyan awaits us," Kressan said, her narrow face showing

little emotion. "Never would I have expected to be asked to return to Rune, though Thaydorne's actions demand it."

Bale swallowed his mouthful of stew. "*Thaydorne?*"

Kressan looked to him, her gaze penetrating. "Our brother. Thaydorne the Sentinel. The strongest among us. He is Arranan's so-called 'Spider King,' and the force driving the invasion of Rune."

Bale's hands slackened and he just managed to catch his bowl before spilling it into the fire. "He *betrays* Rune? He betrays the Old Faith and the whole of the kingdom? A Sentinel turned against us," he said, voice little more than a whisper. His thoughts turned to the Spell of Recounting, when he learned of Lector Erlorn's summons and his warning. "So it is Thaydorne who aids the Necrists? It is he who endeavors to pull Yrghul's power from the Godswell?"

"It is," said Kressan, rubbing a slim hand against the nape of her neck. "I discovered his treason. I sensed Thaydorne's thoughts, his intentions. Just as I do those of others, for it is my divine gift. I… I *knew*, and I told my sister Sienne of his betrayal. We entered his tower together and we confronted him. But he was too strong when partnered with the sorcerous works of his Necrist allies. We were tortured and nailed to those spikes to provide endless blood for his hideous associations. We were impaled upon those things for months." She shuddered and looked away toward the waning sun.

Bale pulled a hand from his bowl and rubbed away a dribble of snot. "But you could not die? You are immortal, and could not die?"

"Imagine an hourglass," said Kressan, her thin hands mimicking the shape. "The top of yours—of any mortal's—is filled with but a limited amount of sand. Ours, though, are filled and refilled again endlessly, with the sands of for-ever. It… It makes the flow of grains meaningless, and there are times I struggle to recall when people I knew—people I loved long ago—died. When those I cared about evidenced their mortality with their *endings*. The endless flow of new sand replaces that which falls away." She looked downward. "There is a sadness to that, though it has become a sadness I can no longer attach to others. Everyone dies. Everyone but us."

"You bled for months…"

She nodded. "Months of agony. We—we Sentinels—feel pain, just as we did before our choosing. I could feel the life draining from me every moment of every awful day, though my vitality would never diminish completely. It is said only the complete destruction and desecration of our bodies could accomplish such a thing, and nothing like that has ever happened to one of our number. But now it seems we must consider taking such measures with Thaydorne."

Bale scooted closer to the fire. "So you will come to Rune's aid?"

Both Sentinels held quiet.

"You *will* help Rune, won't you?" Bale pleaded.

Kressan's eyes, and those of Sienne, flashed to Bale. "We feel emotions we've not had in many years. Centuries, even. We feel anger, and we feel wronged by the worst of betray-als. We will speak with Lyan and decide upon a just course. I would hope that course entails revenge upon Thaydorne for his actions. I regard those actions as treasonous, but those Sentinels who remain must act as one in such matters."

"You've not decided, then?" Bale asked.

"We are indebted to you, Zandrachus Bale, and we do

not regard debts lightly. But the decision to defy the banishment and take up arms against one of our own is not something we regard lightly, either. We must seek Lyan's counsel for this."

"You just said Thaydorne's actions were treasonous but you will not stop him?"

Kressan's eyes locked his, her gaze piercing and discomforting. "You have known of your own Sentinel's—Castor's—presence for mere months, and of Thaydorne's for mere moments. Yet you presume to counsel us? We, who have known these things for a millennium? We, who have contemplated our banishment for a millennium? When the High King cast us from the kingdom our bond with Rune—and with each other—was broken and each of us charted our own course. Those bonds will not be reforged simply because war is waged upon Rune, even if that war is brought by the hands of one of our own."

Bale's eyes widened, watching the dirt and scrub of the Arranese steppe blur beneath his stride. He felt as though he walked upon the same creaky knees and clumsy feet but the ground moved so swiftly as to defy comprehension. He turned his head about—Lorra beside him and grasping his hand—and marveled at how the landscape swept by. It seemed he rode upon a galloping steed, faster even, though only his legs propelled him.

His legs, and the presence of the Sentinel Sienne.

The silvery-skinned Sienne moved at the front of the group, her power appearing to shimmer from her skin like the sun's heat from the dusty waste about them. In the wake of that power it seemed they were all able to travel at both a tremendous and tireless speed.

He looked to Lorra again. She walked onward though her eyes were squeezed shut. Bale spotted the drip of a tear beside her nose.

"We're safe, Lorra," he said, the sound of his voice unaffected by their rapid travel. He held her hand more tightly. "We're safe."

She glanced to him, opening her eyes but briefly. "Of all the mad things I've seen at your side, Bale, this is the maddest. It's *unnatural*."

"It is unnerving," he said, though it'd been in the heart of the Spider King's tower and when they'd been chased by hobblers in Cirak that his heart had quaked most. He looked to her and it seemed fear tightened her features. "We're safe," he said again.

"I believe you, Bale," she said, tightening her grasp.

Comforting her gave him courage. He found it filled what he knew to be his own shallow reserve of the stuff. He smiled at her, though she'd closed her eyes again.

His thoughts turned to what awaited them, to the forthcoming meeting with Lyan the Just and, now, other Sentinels. He wondered what counsel these immortals would share, what eternal truths would inform their conclusions. He wondered also how these eternal beings would regard the likes of him and Lorra. How would they countenance mortals from the very kingdom that had banished them?

He drew in a deep breath. *I must not cower*, he thought, scolding himself. *Not this time. The stakes are too great.*

Kressan's gaze darted back to him then she slowed to stride beside him, her gold skin reflecting the shifting, sunlit panorama. "Zandrachus Bale," she said. "Sienne and I have conferred and have arrived upon a decision. When we reach the Sacred Place in Cirak we will demand all Sentinels allow you to speak on Castor's behalf. You will give voice to his judgment among those chosen. I sense your thoughts on this matter, and they will be heard."

Bale gulped. "Th-thank you."

She cocked her head and stared to him. "You are the one owed gratitude, Zandrachus Bale. You will speak for your Sentinel, and your word shall be as binding as that of any other. You needn't fear how the Sentinels will regard you. I promise you that."

Bale lay upon the rocky ground and stared northward as dawn painted the sky. The Southwalls loomed like a wall of shadows in the distance. He guessed at a normal pace they'd be a week from Cirak—and the Sacred Place beneath it—though with Sienne's power he knew it'd be much less.

He knew not whether to be eager about the coming meeting or regard it with dread. It was such a gravely important thing, the fate of the very world seeming to rest upon the decision to be made. He hoped he had the strength within him to persuade immortal beings to put aside grudges held for centuries.

He sighed and turned his gaze to Lorra, now setting about making breakfast. She'd slept beside him, or at least *near* him, and the thought of it warmed him.

She shot sparks across kindling with a strike of her flint and steel. "Where do you think they are?"

"I don't know. I awoke before dawn and found no sign of them. I'm not sure they sleep, though." He shifted up to his elbows. "After we bedded down they seemed to enter some sort of trance, eyes open but bodies still. I suspect now they may be off speaking with each other or perhaps with the other Sentinels, somehow. Regardless, I'm sure they've not deserted us."

Lorra poured water into a pot she'd placed atop her small fire. "I'd not complain if they had. I worry about them, Bale. With the way they've spoken to us, there's no telling whether they're on our side."

"Perhaps. Perhaps that's true of Lyan, though I'd hope what happened to Kressan and Sienne in Zyn will ultimately sway their feelings. They've seen one of their own turn. They saw Thaydorne turn not only against Rune but against them as well."

"Thaydorne. Another one of these Sentinels."

"Said to be the strongest among them, blessed with the might of the goddess Illienne." Bale pulled himself upward to sit then tucked a stray strand of hair behind an ear. "It was Thaydorne who dealt the final blow to Yrghul the Lord of Nightmares, thus allowing Illienne to drag the dark god into oblivion where he remains confined to this day. And now Thaydorne moves to…" He fell quiet, head awash in worry as he troubled over the implications of Thaydorne's intent.

Silence fell upon them. After a few moments Lorra produced a handful of eggs and began placing them into the pot of now-steaming water.

Bale looked to the eggs, their shells a greenish hue, and thought of Alisa. When they'd met she'd brought eggs much like these, and now, somewhere in the depths of Thaydorne's tower, her corpse decayed. Bale grimaced, knowing the Necrists were certain to have set about defiling the body, likely peeling away the skin and chopping up bones and sinews to use in making their gnarled dwarfs and lumbering giants.

The thought sickened him.

He drew away from the fire and fell back to his bedroll, pulling his blanket overhead.

"Bale? I'll prepare a bowl for you."

"Sorry," he said. "I can't eat just now."

Sienne and Kressan returned just before midday, metallic bodies agleam in the sun's splendor. They appeared weary but unharmed, and between them they dragged something, a sack holding what seemed a heavy load.

Bale shoved himself upward to sit, tossing aside the blanket he'd wrapped himself in despite the growing heat. "You've... You've returned?"

Lorra shifted nearby, tossing water upon her small fire with a hiss. She grumbled something and held a suspicious glare in her eyes.

"We ventured ahead in the night," Sienne said. She gestured toward the load. "Kressan sensed a presence."

Bale looked to the thing they pulled, a burden wrapped in a swath of brown cloth with a billow of yellow dust slowly settling behind it. "A presence?"

"Necrists," said Kressan, nodding toward the heap.

Bale drew back. "And you've brought them *here*?"

Sienne set about untying the knot holding shut the sack. "Any life they had has left them. Any evil Yrghul could work though their forms has been extinguished."

Kressan nodded. "Three Necrists and a number of their creations. They were searching for us several leagues north.

We found them before they could descend into their shadowpaths, though they and their minions proved powerful in the darkness. Your gifts would have been useful, Acolyte."

The sack fell open and three bodies fell limply to the dirt. Black stitching crisscrossed their bald, pallid heads, and their robes were ripped and wet with wounds in many places. Steam or smoke seemed to rise from the dead flesh as the sunlight blazed upon it.

"Yrghul's power survives in them, somehow," Kressan whispered, coming close. "Necrists served always as his disciples. However, they've gained new potency in recent years, assisted certainly by Thaydorne's betrayal. Sienne worries he's helped them worm through the dark to extend their shadowpaths near oblivion, near the very place in which Yrghul is confined. If they've found such a path, Yrghul could escape even with the Godswell sealed. If that happens he'll be the doom of the kingdom."

Bale looked to Kressan, his large nose catching the sickly scent of the Necrists' burning flesh. "So you'll come to Rune's aid, then?"

Kressan held her eyes to his. "The Sentinels will hold their council and we shall abide its decision, whatever that may be."

"But you'd abandon the whole of this world by ignoring Rune's plight. You'd leave us all to darkness."

"Be grateful, Zandrachus Bale, that you have an equal seat at that table. Understand, though, that eternity recounts but precious few events. I wonder if the ruin of Rune would be such a thing."

23
RIVERWEAVE AT LAST

"RIVERWEAVE AT LAST!"

Lannick would have otherwise been overjoyed at those words. Barked from Harl's rotten mouth, though, they seemed ominous, threatening.

He shifted against the splintered backing of his box and caught what sights he could through the thin slits between the wood. Judging from the misty, barren land about they seemed still a distance from the city, though they were certainly coming closer. Lannick wasn't encountering General Fane in the manner he'd hoped, and hope was becoming a vanishing thing.

"Let's rest the horses, boys," said Harl. "Rest the horses and have a decent lunch. Who knows how things are nearer the front."

"The onions and leeks?" came a voice.

"Fuck no," grumbled Harl. "Cook up the rest of that bacon. The lot of it. It's high time for a victory feast. A fine feast before the general serves me an even finer one."

"As you command, *Captain* Harl," said a man. Hard laughs followed.

"You lads laugh at that," Harl said, no humor in his tone. "Well just remember I was the Scarlet Sword. *I'm* the one the general will recognize, the one he'll respect. You keep up your laughing and maybe I forget to tell the general of your loyalty to his cause."

The laughter fell silent.

"Like I said," Harl grumbled, "cook the fucking bacon. Gather up some kindling and make my damned lunch."

Lannick could spy Harl's soldiers trudging out into the mist, bending occasionally to yank brush from the soil. They mumbled among each other, though the words were lost upon the air. Soon they vanished in the gloom. Harl, meanwhile, had hefted a sack from the cart and reclined against it, seemingly waiting for his meal to be served.

Harl chuckled and knotted fingers behind his greasy head. "Hope you're still alive in there, Captain Lannick," he said, his voice almost wistful. "You'd better be, because you're my best chance at getting my life back."

Lannick said nothing, though he sensed a perverse kinship with the man. At this moment he hoped Harl could provide him redemption as well, that Harl could get him close enough to Fane that Lannick could drive a blade through the general's chest.

Harl grunted and sat straight, fussing with what meager kindling he had. "Hurry, lads," he said. "My belly ain't getting no fatter with the three of you traipsing around the wild like fairies."

A shout sounded.

"The fuck?" said Harl, shifting upward.

Then the thump of hooves and the creak and jingle of tack.

Harl's men dashed back to the camp, desperate looks on their faces and their kindling either dropped or forgotten. They scrambled for weapons.

"The fuck!" Harl barked.

"Ho there!" hailed a high, raspy voice. "Illienne's light upon you!"

"Who the fuck comes?" demanded Harl. Lannick squinted through a gap in the box's boards to see the nasty fellow staggering upward to stand. From the heavy mist beyond emerged a rider upon a white steed.

The rider, a bald man in brown robes hefting a staff, cleared his throat. "I am Prefect Lavris Kreer of the Ancient Sanctum of Illienne the Light Eternal."

Harl chuckled. "You're in the midst of a war, old man. War's no place for spookers."

"I'm acutely aware of the peril. Indeed," said the prefect, rising tall in his saddle, "I pursue it."

Harl shuffled his feet and placed a hand on the hilt of a sword—Lannick's own prized weapon—resting in a belted scabbard. "We've no spare food or supplies, if that's what you're after. Boys!"

"Not at all," the prefect said, drawing closer. "We've no need of supplies, as Illienne has blessed us with her bounty. We merely seek information."

"*We?*"

"Forgive me," the robed prefect said, raising a hand. "My associates tend to shy from strange eyes. Come, my friends."

Three more riders appeared like apparitions becoming

415

flesh as their horses sauntered through the mist. One wore heavy brown robes, two others cloaks of forest green.

Variden?

Lannick turned about, struggling to catch a better view through his splintered coffin. Harl paced between the cart and the newcomers, and Lannick's thin view and the thick haze made details difficult to discern.

"Help!" Lannick chanced, his throat ruined by dehydration and a night spent groaning in pain. The word sounded barely more than a rasp.

None seemed to hear.

"As I said," continued the prefect, "we merely seek information. We're on the trail of a killer, the most awful sort of man. A highlander from the north, a filthy barbarian who's taken something from my order. We've tracked him and his band and they've passed near this place, murdering one of my acolytes just two days ago. Have you seen this man? A large fellow with long braids and a fierce countenance? He's undoubtedly committed unthinkable atrocities. Have you seen him?"

Harl stood still for a moment. "There are plenty of killers in this war, and plenty more heading toward it. Hard to single out a man."

The prefect patted his purse and a purple smile curled beneath his long nose. "I know that information—*valuable* information—is not always freely given."

Harl ran a hand through his matted mess of hair. "Well, now that I think about it… A big man, you say? Mean-looking bastard?"

"Help…" Lannick whimpered.

"He would have had companions with him," said the prefect.

"Hmm," Harl rumbled, rubbing his chin in what seemed an attempt to appear thoughtful. "Boys? Do you remember those marauders we saw yesterday?"

"Uh," answered one of Harl's companions. "Ah, yes! The marauders!"

One of the green-cloaked men urged his horse forward a few strides. He had a round, boyish face beneath a bowl of brown hair.

Wil?

"Of course!" boasted Harl. "It *was* yesterday. They were headed off south," he said, jerking a fat thumb over his shoulder. "Due south, right toward the front. A vicious-looking lot—worse than any others we've seen."

"Indeed," murmured the prefect, rubbing his narrow chin as though the information were particularly profound. "The highlander travels to embrace the Spider King. The stone does not deceive, and reveals just what I've feared all along. We should ride."

"Wait now!" barked Harl. "My coin! You promised me coin, spooker."

"We should wait, indeed," said the green-cloaked man with the youthful face.

The prefect clucked his tongue and fiddled with the strings of his purse. "Coin, ever the sad pursuit of lives resigned to mortal needs." He tossed the coins toward Harl. "Our business is done, then. May Illienne light your path during these troubled times. Friends? Let us be on our way."

"Not just yet," said the green-cloaked, brown-haired man.

"You sense something else here?" asked the prefect. "Your missing comrade, Wil?"

Wil!

"Wil?" Lannick croaked. "Wil!" he said, his voice like the scrape of a whetstone.

"I do," said Wil. "Your prisoner. Whoever you're holding in that box. Who is he?"

Lannick sucked at his teeth and drew up all the bile and spit he could manage then tugged it down his throat. "Wil!" he screamed, voice finally forceful. "Help me!"

Wil drew his horse closer and cocked his head to a side.

Harl wheeled toward the cart. "Shut up."

"Wil!" yelled Lannick, desperation fueling his words. "Help!"

Wil placed a hand on the hilt of his sword. "Identify your prisoner, soldier."

Harl drew his weapon—Lannick's own sword. "A prisoner for General Fane. None of your concern."

"It appears it *is* my concern," said Wil, his tone level and meaningful. "Your prisoner asks for me by name."

Harl laughed but sounded uneasy. "Nonsense. He's a deceitful bastard. Probably just heard your spooker say it and now he's playing games. We'll deal with him. Boys!"

Again, no answer from Harl's men.

Lannick sucked in a sharp breath. "Wil! It's Lannick!"

Wil glared at Harl. "What's more, you're holding his sword."

"This thing?" Harl asked, looking at the blade as though the weapon had grown eyeballs. "Just a weapon I found after a scrape with Arranese scouts a few leagues back—"

"Wil!" Lannick shouted again.

Wil rubbed his Coda and looked to the other Variden. They exchanged a nod.

"I said we'll deal with him!" spat Harl.

Boots thudded toward Lannick and a sword slipped through a slit in the box, jabbing against Lannick's shoulder. "Shut your mouth," growled Harl's man.

"You'll hand over your prisoner," Wil said, his voice grave. "Then you can be on your way with no quarrel from us."

"The prisoner is mine," Harl said, his harsh voice rising. "You fellows should ride along."

"Release him. Release him now."

Lannick heard the hiss of drawing steel. He tried to see something, anything, but the pressing blade kept him against the far side of the box.

"I said the prisoner is mine. Ride along before there's trouble."

"Trouble it is, then," said Wil.

Shouting.

The clash and clang of weapons.

More shouting and the thuds of forms falling to the ground.

The sword withdrew from Lannick's shoulder and the scuffling sounds came close and then fell quiet.

He shifted to the box's wall and saw what appeared to be the end of a short encounter. Harl and his men lay face down the mud, pools of blood forming beneath them. Wil and his lanky companion sheathed their swords, the green glow of the blades waning.

"Wil…" Lannick wheezed, eyes welling with tears. "It's me. It's Lannick. Help me…"

"The broken finger will mend in its splint," said the old, droop-nosed prefect seated across from Lannick atop the cart. He inspected Lannick's hand with jaundiced eyes. "I can't replace your severed finger, but the poultice will ease the pain and ward off any infection. Your hand won't be the same, though still far more usable than it would've been had Illienne not intended our meeting, Lannick deVeers."

Lannick pressed himself from the cart and stretched out his hand. He winced at the pain in his shoulder, but that too had eased with the prefect's ministrations. "Thank you, Prefect," he said. "I reckon I'd be headed to my death if you and your companions hadn't arrived."

"Who knows?" said Wil, standing nearby. The still-rising sun of late morning gave a glow to his round, youthful face. "You may be headed there still, Lannick."

Lannick looked eastward, across a plain of muck and mist toward Riverweave. The sun had burned away much of the mist, though at this distance the only hint of the city was a smear of dark smoke. "I *have* to, Wil. I've come too far and suffered too much to choose a different path now."

Wil held quiet for a moment. "I'll not try to sway you. Not anymore. Your purpose, regardless of the motive driving it, serves ours and thus it serves Rune. Indeed, Ogrund marches with your ragtag army even now. He tried to find you, but too many fled in confusion that night for him to track you."

"And where's the army? Have they engaged Fane?"

"Not yet. Ogrund tells me they're near the city but must slip inside in smaller groups with the aid of smugglers. Smugglers," he huffed. "An unseemly process, though I suppose it's necessary."

Lannick felt a smirk tilting his face. "They're doing just as I suggested," he said mostly to himself. *And perhaps there's time yet for me to join them...*

"When you're done with this, we could use you, Lannick," Wil said. "We've lost another of our number. Alisa. I trust you remember her."

Lannick's smile fell. "I do."

"She died just days ago," Wil said, hand caressing his Coda.

Lannick swallowed hard. "How?" he asked.

"She died at the hands of Necrists while trying to rescue two Sentinels from the tower of the Spider King in Zyn. A most courageous endeavor in a most fearsome place."

Lannick grimaced and looked to Wil. "I only met her on a handful of occasions though all were important. All changed me for the better. When I'm through with the general I'll do my best to help you."

"We *need* you, Lannick. We believe the Sentinels escaped the tower, though we've no way of knowing for sure. I pray they did, for I fear we're in a fight as dire as the War of Fates. The Sentinel Castor—who'd tried summoning the Sentinels back to Rune—was murdered and his spirit is now held by his killer. We track the assassin now, and I'd demand your help in doing so if I didn't know your task may prove just as important."

"I promise you, Wil. I'll be back. I owe you—and Alisa—as much."

A slight smile dimpled Wil's face. "I'm glad to hear it. Take one of these horses and head to the western side of Riverweave. Ogrund and your men are but a mile or two from the city, right along the Silverflow, and I'll let Ogrund know you're coming." He rummaged through the cart's various sacks and crates then hefted the purse containing Lannick's Coda. Wil tossed that and Lannick's prized sword to him.

"Thank you, Wil," Lannick said.

"Don't lose these again."

Lannick wove his new drab mare through muck and a mass of people beside the Silverflow, tugging the reins with one good hand and another ruined. Countless folk moved along the northern riverbank, fleeing the war clawing at the city's southern edge. They passed Lannick, carrying meager belongings, faces muddied and desperate.

He could see it now—Riverweave—perhaps two leagues distant. From this vantage the city seemed a smear of cheery colors beneath the clearing sky, though he knew better than to expect any cheer within the walls. Just to its south rose heavy columns of black smoke.

He swallowed hard, knowing many good soldiers were dying on orders from a man unhinged. Much blood had been spilled, and many wounds inflicted.

He searched about for signs of Black Jon and his men, for red flags or sashes crossed with a black stripe. Amidst the swollen throng, though, he could find nothing.

At last he looked to one of the grimy travelers and bent low. "Have you seen soldiers along the river? Any folk west of the city who aren't fleeing it?"

The traveler, a man with hollow cheeks and a back bent beneath the load slung upon it, stopped and stared to him wide-eyed. "Who'd *not* flee?" he asked, voice hoarse. "There's naught but starvation, disease and death there, and the Arranese are certain to overrun the city within days."

Lannick sighed. "I wish you better fortune than you've found."

"By the looks of you," the man said, nodding to Lannick's bandaged hand, "I should be wishing you the same."

"Better fortune is precisely what I'm hoping to find." *Especially after the hell of these last many years.*

"Well, you seem to be going in the wrong direction then."

Lannick grinned crookedly. "I've an overdue debt to pay, and the man I owe it to is somewhere within the city walls."

He flicked the reins and moved onward, deeper into the horde of refugees. They shuffled aside to let him pass but the sheer numbers made for slow going. It seemed every resident of Riverweave had poured from its gates. They were clad in rags of every color, so finding however many of Black Jon's men were still outside the city seemed impossible.

He thought of donning his Coda and reaching out to Ogrund but decided against it. He didn't feel quite ready to open his head to his old order—he needed Fane dead first. That, and the next time he wore the Coda he knew he'd not be able to remove it. He'd betrayed the Variden many times and, despite that, they'd saved his skin not once but twice.

That, too, was a debt that needed repaying.

He'd kill Fane as a soldier, not as a Variden. Then he'd rejoin the order and do his best to save Rune from the ravages of the Necrists and the Spider King.

He studied the moving multitude, determined to find his companions. The occasional glint of steel drew his eyes, though it seemed a good number of those fleeing the city had armed themselves with spears or swords or the like. He looked also for the gleam of armor, but after seeing none he reckoned the old soldiers knew better than to reveal themselves so close to Riverweave and the general's men.

The river, too, appeared a cluttered mess. Boats well-built and others cobbled from scraps bore sad-eyed passengers. Some desperate folk even clung to chunks of driftwood, kicking legs and churning arms to propel themselves against the river's flow. Few managed to move forward, and Lannick reckoned fewer still would survive.

He flicked the reins again and moved on, steering his horse close to the river's edge. He kept eyes trained upon the boats riding the Silverflow and at last spotted something out of place. There, fifty yards or so away, floated a skiff bearing a handful of ragged passengers, riding the river's run against the drifting flotsam of refugees.

Lannick rode closer and closer still. As he came near he spied a green-cloaked man at the riverbank near the skiff. The man had a shaved head set low upon his shoulders and eyes squeezed to a squint.

Ogrund.

Lannick dug his heels into his horse, the beast lurching to a trot through the mire along the riverside. The horse tottered and Lannick clung to it, and only after a few wobbly strides did it find its footing.

He tugged in a breath and looked ahead again. Ogrund stood straight and stoic as he eyed the skiff floating toward Riverweave. Several men alongside him—hearty lads draped in paupers' blankets—pushed another skiff into the water, eased themselves upon the thing and used a long pole to shove off.

Lannick slowed his horse and raised in his saddle. "Ho there!" he called. "Is there room for another on that boat?"

Ogrund spun toward him, hand upon the hilt of his blade. His eyes popped open. "Lannick!" he said in a high-pitched cry. "You made it!"

Lannick nodded, stretching his damaged hand. "Not without a bit of trouble."

The man's gaze retreated behind a tight squint once more though a grin rose at the edges of his mouth. "Lannick," he said, his voice again the gravelly monotone Lannick had grown used to hearing. "It pleases me to see you again."

"Well fuck my eyes!" came another familiar voice. From out of the crowd slipped one-handed Arleigh Lay. Dirty rags concealed his armor and a bloodied bandage wound about his head. His sneer, though, remained fully intact. "Your friend Ogrund here said you'd survived but I didn't dare believe it."

Ogrund turned his squint to Arleigh and folded arms across a thick chest. "I speak no lies." He looked again to Lannick. "We searched for you, but many scattered from the camp the night you were captured. There was no way to track one person. If you'd but worn your Coda..." He shook his head in what seemed a scold.

"Soon, Ogrund," said Lannick, eyes turning to the bandage about Arleigh's head. "And what of that night? How many men did we lose?"

Arleigh pressed his hand against the wound and spat. "Too many. A hundred at least, and perhaps twice that many wounded."

Ogrund nodded. "Your captors did not work alone. It seems a number of men still loyal to the general had infiltrated our number."

"There was a good deal of confusion and screaming and

fire," said Arleigh. "A mad night. Who was it that took you from the camp?"

Lannick grimaced and looked along the water toward Riverweave. "One of Black Jon's men was a Scarlet Sword once, one I'd wounded. He and his companions meant to take me back to the general as their prize." He lifted his bandaged hand. "Before I was rescued, they took a finger and broke another."

Arleigh shrugged. "Well, you still have more of a hand than I, and you'll have your revenge soon enough. Stay with us," he said, swaying a pointed thumb between himself and Ogrund. "This fellow's more useful than I'd guessed." He ignored a grunt from Ogrund and continued. "Plan is to take separate routes through the city then mass near a ruined storehouse not far from the old governor's palace. Black Jon received word Fane's made that palace his home. He's there, or at least near it. Least till he loses Riverweave, anyway."

Ogrund looked to him. "What Arleigh says is correct. We'll have another skiff soon. We waited for you, and thus we'll be among the very last to enter the city."

Lannick dropped from his mount. "Thank you, Ogrund."

"Now give your horse to one of these poor folk fleeing the fight and make yourself ready."

Lannick grabbed the small pack of provisions he'd taken from Harl's cart then adjusted his purse and his sheathed sword. "I'm ready, Ogrund."

Ogrund dipped his head with the slightest of nods. "I know, Lannick, and that is a fine thing to hear."

24

THE HEADS FROM
THEIR BODIES

KARNAG MAK RAGG sat upon the hilltop, eyes trained on the nighttime battle below. Fencress Fallcrow sat at his side, though not close. She remained far too wary of whatever thoughts tumbled through the man's head.

The battlefield before them churned, forces clashing in the dark. Rune's soldiers continued to suffer, their fortifications set aflame by fiery arrows that streaked across the field like shooting stars across the night sky.

"How long will you watch this?" she asked.

"I do not watch," Karnag said, shifting beneath his coat of Arranese hides and leathers. "I wait."

Fencress fell silent and knotted her hands.

"I wait," Karnag continued after a moment. "I wait for Thaydorne's champions. They will come. They will come before morning, and I will take the heads from their bodies."

"You've foreseen this?"

"I see many things. Things yet to come. A vast number of those things shift upon the atlas of fate by the hands of both mortals and immortals. Some, however, are a certainty. The encounter I foresee is one."

"So I'm to stay awake this night while awaiting an ambush? Lovely. Karnag, I do tend to enjoy a decent night's sleep from time to time." She tugged at her gloves and shook her head with a smirk. "That, and the occasional dream of a pampered life full of perfumes and princesses. I don't suppose our endeavor will make such dreams come true."

Karnag remained impervious to any attempt at humor. "Dreams are the refuge of the desperate and the dying. I behold eternity. I behold what will *be*. Remain awake if you wish. Otherwise sleep until I call upon your help."

Fencress tugged at her cowl, wondering just what 'help' Karnag had in mind. She was by no means a squeamish sort, but didn't fancy etching bloody notes into the skin of the dead, chopping bodies into tiny pieces or chatting with the corpses of witches. She'd seen Karnag do all those things and wagered his current task would entail something similar.

She looked to him, his hard gaze still affixed to the battlefield, and wondered how long she'd remain at his side. Her resolve was waning, she knew, and every day there seemed less a chance of saving her old friend. She worried whatever had been left of him after they'd killed the Lector had since drained away, bit by bit, and now was forever gone.

Karnag chuckled. "These fools plot and plan even now though they have no measure of the menace awaiting them, no notion of the fate they face. They, and their so-called Spider King, fail to understand I have become death. That is precisely what they will find when they find me."

Fencress stirred. Night still hung upon the sky and Karnag had yet to rouse her but sleep had been fleeting at best. She sighed, stood, and drew her cloak and weapons about her.

The night seemed eerily quiet, the battle below distant and muted. The sound of Paddyn's snores rose and fell, though this night he and Drenj had chosen to camp well down the opposite side of the hill.

Far enough from Karnag to be free of his presence, but close enough that odds are he can still protect them.

Perhaps a smart bet.

She straightened and her eyes found him. Karnag, back to her, remained seated just where he'd been. Now, though, he held *Gravemaker* at his side, its point pressed into the ground and his arm raised overhead to grasp its hilt. The dirty blade shone crimson in the moonlight.

"Fencress Fallcrow," he said, gaze not straying from the battlefield. "You need not yet arise. They are coming, though there is still time for rest."

"Forgive me, Karnag. I've not slept well, nor much for that matter."

Karnag pulled his sword from the dirt and laid it across his lap. "Then you may sit."

Lovely, Fencress thought, though she moved to the highlander's side and sank to a seat. She looked to him, his eyes affixed to the field below. "What foes do we face?" she asked.

"None that will not be overcome," Karnag said, no trace of uncertainty upon his voice. "Thaydorne sends me his so-called best, his so-called heroes. They will be accompanied by Necrists, though their workings are known to me now."

Fencress tucked black hair within her black cowl. "Necrists?"

"Followers of Yrghul the Lord of Nightmares, and now allies of Thaydorne. I have mastered dark truths they only fumble at." He fell quiet for a moment, eyes closed. "All will perish."

"You have changed much, Karnag. I…" She thought of saying more but thought better of it.

Karnag produced a rag and set about cleaning his sword. "You worry, Fencress, but my blade will never be brandished against you. You are my friend and will always be."

Fencress looked to him and wanted to say more. She wanted to talk of feelings of friendship, of loyalty and unbreakable bonds and other such sentimental nonsense.

But it felt false.

Worse, it felt *dead*.

Karnag tossed the rag aside. Fencress noticed the cloth was darkened with blood, then saw Karnag's hand deeply cut and bleeding. Karnag, though, paid no regard.

"They come," Karnag said. "An hour from now,

Thaydorne's captains will arrive to face me. Much blood will run upon this hillside."

"Should I wake Paddyn and Drenj?"

"Only if you'd prefer they die."

Dawn drew a hint of purple upon the far horizon. Fencress looked to it then to Karnag. The highlander had risen, standing with sword low a dozen yards down the hillside and uttering words Fencress could barely hear. Words that sounded sharp and broken and chilled her to the core.

He paused his chant and stiffened. He rolled his head and stretched his limbs.

Fencress squeezed the hilts of her twin blades then walked toward him.

"They come," Karnag said, shoving the point of his massive sword into the ground. "Thirteen is their number. Seven captains of the Spider King and six Necrists in their wake."

She came to stand at his side. "Seven men and six witches, then."

Karnag nodded. "Your blades will be needed." He turned to her and his eyes seemed suddenly different, fuller, brighter and kinder, somehow. "But after this day, Fencress, you will take your leave of me. You are free."

She looked to him for a moment, uncertain. There was finality in his words, it seemed. It sounded as though he'd given permission to set aside the obligations of friendship, to unravel the bonds between them. She knotted her brow, struck by conflicting emotions. There was relief, certainly. But with it, she felt regret.

She drew a breath. "You have my help this day, Karnag."

She could think of no more words than those.

"After today," Karnag continued, "I will challenge Thaydorne himself. That is a battle I insist upon fighting myself and myself alone. He shall fall by my hand and no other."

Fencress looked to him. "This is our last scrap, then, Karnag? Our last fight?"

Karnag said nothing, eyes fixed now upon the slope below. "They come."

She tugged at her cowl, drawing it tight. *Then this is the end of it.*

She followed his gaze down the stretch of the hillside and to the darkened field beyond.

"You see them?" he said. "There, moving aside that fallen horse."

Fencress peered long and hard but discerned nothing. Karnag pointed, jabbing a finger toward something amidst the shadows and shattered carnage.

And then she saw them.

Shadows *deeper* than shadows. Figures warping the black of night to cloak themselves.

"The six witches you spoke of?"

Karnag sniffed. "Necrists. Necrists working the dark to hide Thaydorne's warriors though they cannot hide them from me. Not since I discovered their secrets. Now they will learn I am death and the darkness after. I am the fear of the night." He straightened, his frayed braids a messy veil upon his face. "Let them come."

Fencress squeezed the handles of her twin blades hard enough that her fingers ached.

"Ready yourself, Fencress. Ready your blades and prepare yourself for the horrors you will witness. These will not be natural things to mortal eyes."

She glanced to him, wondering if what she'd see could compare to what Karnag had become. She wagered odds were she'd seen the worst. Whatever came would certainly seem a reprieve. A faint smirk twisted her lips. "Let them come, indeed."

Karnag looked to her, eyes dead as ever in the pre-dawn light. "They are near."

Fencress looked down the hill and saw them. Darkness disturbed by something darker, a blacker black amidst the night.

Karnag tugged *Gravemaker* from the dirt. "They conceal nothing," he growled, tapping the great blade upon an open hand striped with scabs and fresh blood. "Mine is the vision that beholds all things. All are revealed before me."

There came then a strange sound upon the air, a sound that struck Fencress like the buzz of many insects within a roomful of madly ticking clocks. There seemed an anger to it, a spiteful tone that caused her skin to prickle. She studied the hillside, pulling her cloak about her shoulders.

"The Necrists cast their spells," said Karnag, his voice low. "They cast spells begging Yrghul for protection and for strength. But they have learned little and have forgotten much more... These enchantments are pale imitations of the potencies of the dead gods, and I shall tear through them like fire through parchment."

The mass of shadow gathered at the base of the hill, writhing and twisting together. Thick tendrils of black stretched outward and upward along the slope. Up they came, searching like fingers.

Fencress drew her blades, studying the approaching shadow. *Can such things be cleaved or cut?* She found she'd retreated a step behind Karnag.

Karnag drew in a great breath, his torso swelling as though he sucked in the whole of the night. He lowered *Gravemaker* to his side and looked to Fencress. "Be ready. You will have a moment to slay the first warrior and then others. You must seize those chances for I must focus upon the Necrists and the things beneath."

She looked askance at him then nodded.

The tendrils writhed closer.

Fencress held her twin swords before her, moving backward on soft feet. Terror—a thing she'd not felt often—shook her.

"*K'Sharvukkam!*" Karnag screamed, expelling what seemed all the air within him. Black smoke curled from his mouth as many echoes of his shout resounded. A pale glow rose, seeming to emanate from somewhere above Karnag and spreading to just beyond the foes below.

The shadows fled. They retreated from the hillside and then from the attackers. A circle of robed witches—*Necrists*, as Karnag called them—stood surprised and apparently helpless, ugly faces full of stitches jerking about and hands twitching feebly. Their mouths moved but any sound seemed strangled within their throats.

In their center, though, stood others. Hard men, towering figures hefting many vicious weapons. These looked unlike most of the young, angled Arranese they'd encountered thus far. These were veteran killers, scarred and steely-eyed and seemingly all as versed in death as Fencress and her company.

All save Karnag, that is.

"Come!" roared Karnag. He swept *Gravemaker* overhead and kept it poised there, an executioner's axe for any necks that came near. "Come!"

The last word seemed an unnerving bellow, thundering so loudly across the hills and the field below Fencress wondered whether Karnag's lungs or something far deeper propelled it. The ground shivered beneath them, and the Arranese looked nervously to their Necrist escorts.

Karnag wound *Gravemaker* in a wide circle. "Come!"

The Arranese warrior at the fore—a massive, broad-shouldered man crisscrossed with leather straps and holding vicious axes in both hands—spat and cursed to his brethren. He began ascending the hill. The rest of the Arranese and their Necrist companions cowered behind.

Karnag laughed, an unsettling, choppy growl. "You, Hazzak? You lead this sad company?"

The warrior stared to Karnag with puzzled eyes. He spat once more and whipped his axes about, pulling the blade of one across a forearm. He pressed a thumb against the welling wound then drew bloody streaks beneath his eyes. "The Spider King has sent us to kill you," he said in his sharp accent, "and this we will do."

Karnag laughed again. "You, Hazzak, whose very father was among those your so-called Spider King slaughtered?

Whose father's bones helped build his throne? Ha! Very well. Let your bones be among the many to build mine."

The warrior slowed, his steps halting. "You speak from ignorance," he said after a moment. "You know nothing of such things. You know nothing of me or my father."

Karnag thrust his sword-arm forward, pointing the blade at Hazzak. "I behold *all* things, their beginnings and most of all their ends. Come now and embrace yours. Come now and join your coward of a father in the old hells."

Hazzak's face snarled to an angry knot. "You dare say such?" He glared at his companions. "I will slay this infidel myself!" He bolted up the slope, pace quickening as he approached. He was an even larger man than he'd appeared at the hill's bottom, standing nearly a full head taller than Karnag. He brandished his axes and raised them as he neared.

Karnag trained *Gravemaker* toward the rushing warrior and sank, knees bending. He then twisted the blade to his side, face stoic as the tomb.

The warrior charged at Karnag, whipping his axes about with great fury. Karnag, though, bent and bowed and parried, deftly avoiding every blow. *Gravemaker* rang as the twin axes glanced off it.

Karnag worked his sword—lazily, it seemed—as he turned aside the onslaught. He appeared calm, disturbingly so, with eyes focused upon the Necrists at the base of the hill. His mouth moved though Fencress could hear no words.

Hazzak continued his assault. He heaved his axes,

raising them and throwing them down again and again while roaring some guttural noise.

Karnag slipped from side to side and twisted about, avoiding every strike. He took several steps backward, pulling even with Fencress. He chanted *something*, a low mumble Fencress could just hear amidst the sweeping sound of weapons and the cry of the Arranese.

Prophecy? Witchery?

The Arranese brute pressed on, swinging his axes and pressing against Karnag as the highlander retreated. The warrior's blows fell dangerously close to their mark, mere inches from Karnag's gut and sides and neck. Karnag's parries drove him aside, though, to just near Fencress.

She saw her opening and shot forward, shoving her twin blades toward the fleshy parts of the man's side.

The swords found their targets, driving into the meat between the warrior's ribs and beneath his underarm. He gasped and stumbled, slowly pulling free of the blades and leaving spouting wounds in their places. He turned to Fencress for an instant, clearly stunned. He began to collapse and, as his did, Karnag reached outward to seize the man by his knot of hair.

"*I have become death!*" Karnag boomed. His hand flexed upon the man's hair then yanked upward with a great *crack*. The body slumped to the ground, separated from the head Karnag now hoisted before him.

The Arranese and their Necrist companions seemed dumbfounded, shrinking and silent.

"Come and find your ending!" Karnag threatened, brandishing the head before him. He drew back his arm then heaved it forward, hurling the disembodied head toward the gathered foes below. The head wobbled and spun as it soared, spilling gore in all directions.

The Arranese scattered, though Hazzak's skull still managed to smack one of the warriors square in the face. The man—a thick fellow with ears pierced by many ringlets—teetered back, swiping hands against a face spattered with blood and fleshy bits.

"Take Hazzak to your Spider King," Karnag taunted. "Take him now, lest I take *all* your heads. Every one of them. You have this last choice, the last you may ever make."

Fencress looked to Karnag. His eyes were trained upon the group below and his mouth moved and mumbled once more.

"*Karnag...*" she whispered.

He regarded only the foes.

The Arranese seemed to gather themselves, faces flushed with rage. "Take him!" roared the man with the bloodied face.

"Ha!" Karnag snorted. "Your fate is foretold, then."

The warriors charged as one. Six vicious Arranese tore up the slope, hoisting curved swords and long spears and wicked axes ready for violence. Behind them the Necrist witches seemed again able to work their magic, mouths chattering and hands gathering shadows. Darkness swelled about them, moving upward to mingle amidst the rush of warriors.

Karnag laughed a roaring laugh. He whipped *Gravemaker* about as though the blade were weightless. He steadied his feet then thrust the sword's point toward the oncoming foes. He shut his eyes for an instant then smiled. "The *Gravemaker* sings again, and now your master will hear its song at last! Listen to my song, Thaydorne!"

Footfalls thudded up the hillside and the Arranese screamed in fury.

They came then upon Karnag and the clash of weapons grew to a maddening cacophony. Karnag slithered between many blows, moving and dodging in ways that seemed inhuman. His sword, too, appeared unnaturally fast, fending away strike after rapid strike.

Fencress moved along the edge of the combat. The Arranese pressed upon Karnag but the highlander's parries had turned to strikes, piercing and slashing and taking parts and pieces from his attackers. Several staggered away grasping deep, weeping wounds.

She knew to take advantage. She slipped about just as she'd done many times when working with Karnag, thrusting and turning and dancing about the stumbling wounded, soft on her feet with hands swift as murder. They fell about her, clumsy and clutching grave injuries. She watched them fall and readied herself once more, shaking blood from her blades.

She watched as Karnag wrestled with the last few Arranese. He roared and another limped away, a dumb look on his face with *Gravemaker* stuck in his chest.

Karnag seemed to pay no heed to his wayward sword, working his hands like weapons upon his foes. All about him curled swelling tendrils of shadow.

Fencress stared down along the length of the shadows—down the hillside—and saw the witches concocting their horrors in earnest once more. They worked the night like weavers upon a loom, deft hands spinning and twisting as though drawing the dark toward them.

"*I am death!*" Karnag roared, then threw the two remaining Arranese from him. "I am the light and the darkness! *K'Sharvukkam!*"

They tumbled away, bleeding and lame, limping like beaten dogs. One had lost his arms, another his nose and the better part of his jaw. The shadows, too, receded, falling from the hill like the outgoing tide.

Karnag straightened, many wounds crossing his form though he seemed to notice them not. In bloodied hands he held the arm of one Arranese and the jawbone of the other. "I have taken these from you, but I must take more to form the verses of my song. Whose verse will first be heard by your so-called Spider King? Whose ending will be first to reach his ears?"

The wounded Arranese faltered across the hilltop, vainly attempting to flee their executioner. Karnag, though, shoved them down, pinning them to the earth with hands still clutching their disembodied parts. He held them there, side by side, as they bled and moaned and croaked for mercy.

There would be none.

He tossed aside the parts then wound blood-slicked hands about the necks of the two warriors. "More verses," he growled. "More verses for my song." An awful gurgling followed.

"No!" wheezed the armless man.

Two quick snaps sounded. Fencress looked to see Karnag tearing the heads from their bodies, parts of the spines still dangling from them. Karnag laughed and thunder above.

"There," Karnag grated, a sick grin on his face as he cast aside the heads. "Thaydorne has heard. He has heard a distant dirge, a mournful cry of death. He has heard this song but disbelieves its message. Only through *their* demise will he understand…" He gazed toward the gathered Necrists and his smile widened all the more. "Watch as they try to conquer me. Watch as they fail and watch as they die."

Once again the Necrists' chattering filled the air. Fencress stared to them, the black-robed witches with heads made of wriggling flesh and unsightly stitches. Their black eyes twitched and glared, reflecting terrible rage and an abject madness. They conjured the shadows once more and darkness swirled and swelled about them.

But shadows moved about Karnag as well, shadows that drifted from the heads he held and wafted from the corpses nearby. As they neared they coiled about him, encircling his form for a moment before settling upon and darkening his many wounds.

"Karnag…" Fencress whispered. She rubbed at her eyes, wondering if they deceived her.

The images remained. The shadows appeared to be knitting together Karnag's bloodied rents, seeping within the wounds then drawing them shut. In their place they left stitches, black and gnarled.

Fencress winced and watched as her old friend strode toward one of the dead Arranese and retrieved *Gravemaker*. He seemed to admire the red slick of blood upon the blade, eyes again dead. He turned his gaze to the Necrists and Fencress eased away, retreating up the hill.

The Necrists beneath worked furiously, forming great billows of shadow that writhed about. Their faces—grotesque things of patchwork flesh—were only occasionally visible in the inky dark they summoned. Then, at once, they screamed, the sound a shrill cry that pained Fencress's ears. Black tongues flailed in their wailing mouths and their outstretched hands twitched and their flesh wriggled.

Their shadows wound into great tentacles and whipped up the slope, slithering through and within and between the remnants of the dead Arranese.

Karnag laughed. "Bring your darkness!" he snarled through a gnash of dirty teeth.

The tendrils wound up and up and then met him, twirling and twisting around his body and wrapping him in a shroud darker than night.

Though only for a moment.

"*Sharvukam khul araga!*" Karnag screamed, striding forward. He sloughed away the shadows, unhindered.

He stared toward the witches and lowered his sword to the ground, shadows twitching about him like wounded things. "There are powers you've forgotten. Worse, there are *places*…" He tilted his head to a side and giggled. "Do you not know why I stand *here?* Why I chose this from so many places I could have confronted you?" He sucked in a deep breath. "*Do you not know!*"

The Necrists looked to each other in apparent confusion and their shadows shrank.

Karnag laughed again. He stepped about, snatching

the disembodied parts of the dead Arranese and tossing them down the hill in a slow, haphazard way. "Have them!" he cackled. "Have your mighty escort! Perhaps they can still protect you!"

The Necrists whispered and glanced about then resumed their chant. They glared at Karnag with mad, obsidian eyes and soon the darkness they conjured seemed an impenetrable wall.

"Good," Karnag chuckled. "You will bear witness, then. You will bear witness as I remind you what lurks in the true darks of this world. You will bear witness as I remind you of the old hells left by the Elder God, the ruins left by the *Ehlohir Allumahr*."

The summoned shadows of the Necrists rushed up the slope once again.

Karnag threw his arms outward as though to embrace the darkness. He strode farther down the hill, into the wave of shadow. It broke against him and wilted to his sides and his laughter sounded all the louder.

"I am your ending," he said in the gravest of tones. "On this day, Thaydorne will hear the last of your mortal pleas. Sing them loudly so he may hear, else your deaths will pass unmarked."

The Necrists wailed and shook, bodies quivering so fast they became blurs to the eye. It seemed to Fencress they were desperate. Frightened, even. Their mad chanting broke with stutters and stammers and their gathered mass of shadows twitched almost as much as they did.

Karnag slammed *Gravemaker's* point into the earth and began a new chant of his own, hands working as though trying to pull something from the ground beneath.

Fencress listened, keen ears finding Karnag's words amidst the din of the Necrists below.

"*Yahe cradus a rasham y despocha… Yahe cradus a rasham y despocha…*"

Over and again he said the words, hands and sinews straining as he seemed to will the depths of the ground upward.

Fencress took another step back. *What witchery do you work, Karnag?*

The earth groaned and shifted and shook, feeling as though it were collapsing beneath Fencress's feet. She stumbled and nearly fell.

A yelp sounded behind her and she glanced back to see the heads of Drenj and Paddyn peeking just beyond the crest. Both looked on with eyes agape.

Karnag's words grew louder and Fencress stared to him once more, feeling her curiosity dangerous but undeniable. She crept closer and watched as Karnag worked his sorcery. His muscles tensed, veins bulging from his neck as though he struggled to hoist a heavy thing.

A great rumble sounded and the earth shook again.

She saw then a fissure spreading from *Gravemaker's* point. The rift shivered down the slope toward the Necrists, widening as it did. Quickly it grew to a chasm, broad and jagged, and the ground against its edges tumbled into its deepening depths.

Then, abruptly, it stopped.

The Necrists fell silent.

A reddish light emanated from the hole, accompanied by a hideous moan that sounded anything but human.

The woeful cry grew louder and the chasm's light

dimmed, leaving only the pale luminescence Karnag had summoned. A cold wind rushed from the abyss, and upon feeling it Fencress grew fearful. She tugged her cowl tight and retreated another few steps.

The Necrists staggered back as well, clutching each other and staring to the void. Only Karnag held his ground, hands before him like he welcomed whatever had been trapped beneath the world.

Then *something* emerged from the chasm. It seemed a specter, a wraith, colored and shaped like the elongated cast of a man's shadow in the afternoon sun. It reached ethereal arms upward, clawing long fingers at the sky as though it could grab it.

Another wraith ascended to its side. Then others still.

At last a total of six figures had risen from the chasm's depths, tall and narrow and almost featureless things. They swayed about, their lanky, separate forms difficult to distinguish and seeming at times to merge. They appeared only sketches of darkness, though upon whatever heads they had there formed hollow eyes and sad grimaces. The expressions were perhaps no more than gaps in the darkness, though it seemed to Fencress their faces affixed to Karnag.

The wraiths came closer to him and their sad groans swelled. Their mouths drooped and within them Fencress swore she could see glimpses of countless other spirits, distant and ghost-like faces with empty eyes and reaching hands trying to climb to the world above.

She shrank back, harrowed by whatever Karnag had called from the deep. Her hands gripped her blades though she wagered they'd prove no use at all against such terrors. These seemed things forged by the darkest and foulest forces imaginable. Not the evils of men, but the darker evils of dead gods.

The Necrists beyond them—still visible through the spectral bodies—appeared dumbfounded, their ugly, stitched faces slack and their black eyes wide. Hands shook but seemed incapable of commanding the shadows.

"*Yahe cradus*," said Karnag.

The wraiths' moans softened, sounding now like the distant wail of the wind.

Karnag drew a finger toward the Necrists. "*Despocha Necrista.*"

The wraiths' mouths turned to ghastly grins. They nodded and spun toward the Necrists. Their long arms and fingers of darkness lashed toward the witches, wispy forms swelling as they drew near their prey.

"More verses," Karnag grated. "Sing loudly, so he may hear. Tell Thaydorne the pain of his ending!"

Dark robes and pale flesh were rent asunder. With hideous swiftness the wraiths took the Necrists into the depths of the chasm.

But they did so bit by bit. The arm of one Necrist, half the skull of another, the odd leg, and on and on. Black blood spouted and flowed. Those witches who still had their tongues cried out, voicing piercing howls that told of the worst of agony. The wraiths, too, cried their sad cry, joining an awful chorus that sounded across the hilltop and beyond.

And above it all rang Karnag's laughter.

Fencress rushed up the hill and down the opposite slope.

Paddyn and Drenj crouched just beyond, both wide-eyed with trembling hands upon their weapons.

Paddyn looked at her, slack-jawed. "What the fuck!"

"Get up," Fencress commanded, tugging tight her cowl with a trembling hand. "Get up and make ready to leave this place. We're free of him but must leave as quickly as we can."

Another roar sounded behind them. Fencress resisted the urge to glance back.

"B-but…" stammered Drenj. "Demons… Demons! We'll all be slain!"

"Only if we stay here, you fool!" Fencress snapped. "Get your asses up and let's get away from here!" She thrust out a gloved hand and Paddyn found it and she tugged him upward. She threw the other toward Drenj, but after a moment of his inaction she pinched his ear and yanked it until the rest of him followed. He squealed when he stood, and she slapped him for it.

Drenj spat. "How dare—"

"Get moving," Fencress growled, her eyes narrowing.

Drenj looked to her, his lower lip quavering and eyes blinking rapidly as though trying to hold their tears.

Fencress held his gaze and remembered something Karnag—the *old* Karnag—had told her long ago. "Never allow fear to be the thing that kills you," she said. "There are plenty more dangers worse than that, but if your fear is the one worrying you most it'll get you before any of the others."

Drenj nodded and looked away.

"I've already packed most things up," said Paddyn,

pointing toward the horses tied to a tree down the hillside opposite Karnag.

"Good work, Paddyn," Fencress said. She quickly fetched what things were still at her campsite nearby then jogged down the slope. "Let's go, boys."

"Where?" called Paddyn.

Fencress neared the horses and shook her head. "Away from here. We'll find a quiet inn and hide out for a few days, at least until the war makes its way farther north. Then I'd wager Riverweave would make a decent stop. There's certain to be plunder aplenty after all that chaos, as well as word of how the war's going and what's happening elsewhere."

"And from there?" asked Drenj.

"If we hear it's not too dangerous for our liking then perhaps we can start making our way home. Home to Raven's Roost."

"I'd like that," said Drenj, his voice weak. "I'd like that much."

Fencress looked to both the young men, seeing fear in their eyes. "I can't make promises but chances are whatever we find will send us heading far from the fighting." She pulled from her pocket the pair of fine dice she swiped in Shank's Hollow, tossed them upward then snatched them from the air in a gloved fist. "And you know how I feel about chance."

25
HOMECOMING

GAMGHAST LOOKED TO the small crowd gathered in the great hall of the Bastion. Several he knew to be part of Alamis's entourage, others seemed minor nobles or wealthy citizens judging from their finery. All stood with eyes narrow and expressions dour, obviously displeased by the homecoming before them.

"Who dares?" demanded Tannin, sword raised as he stood before the gathering. "Who among you dares to challenge your queen? Who questions her right to rule?"

"Guards!" howled one at the fore, a man Gamghast recognized. A smaller man in a puffy, yellow shirt that neatly matched his puffy face and jaundiced eyes. "Guards! We have traitors within the great hall! To arms!"

Gamghast remembered him. *Sir Edren. The nobleman who'd threatened to skewer Tannin 'like a pig.'*

The ring of weapons echoed from the distant reaches of the palace. Sir Edren's suspicious look changed to one of smug satisfaction. He began rocking on his heels and placed a hand on the decorated hilt of a sword slung upon his hip.

Tannin took a stride forward. "Sir Edren," he growled, "I'll warn you but once. Alamis is dead. Your allies are few and justice will be severe for any who proclaim treason. Stand down. Stand down *now*."

Edren shook his head. "Rune's king has died and Rune has moved on. The people of Rune long ago wearied of old traditions and forgotten faiths. Sovereign Alamis was our rightful leader, and the only treason that's been committed is your murder of the man."

Queen Reyis moved by Gamghast and toward Tannin.

"*My queen!*" Gamghast hissed.

She proceeded onward and soon stood at Tannin's side. "Rune *has* a king," she said with a voice clear and true. "Rune has a king, and by law so long as I carry the heir the crown is mine and mine alone. Stand down, just as Tannin said. Leave this place now, or be led out in chains."

The sound of many boots resounded from the passageways feeding the hall.

Gamghast darted his gaze about. Tannin had managed to summon a few dozen loyal soldiers, all of whom gathered near with weapons at the ready. But if the guards of the Bastion remained loyal to Alamis and his followers, Gamghast knew Tannin's men would be vastly outnumbered.

He scowled then quietly rehearsed the divine words of destruction he'd used in the Grand Court of Magistrate Examiners. He did not desire bloodshed unless no other option remained, but this seemed such a circumstance. He patted his robes and realized he'd not the quicksilver the spell required. He cursed beneath his breath.

The sound of hard footfalls grew louder and the jingle of moving armor accompanied it. Gamghast tried to see something through the gathering but could not. He squeezed his eyes shut for an instant and muttered a prayer.

Sweet Illienne please protect those righteous and true to your cause...

"Stand down," Tannin demanded once more.

Sir Edren strode about, his gait a swagger. He shook his head again. "Rune has moved on. Those who've realized that are making ready for a new order of things. An order that needs no king, and certainly needs no queen."

"Stand down," Tannin repeated. "I'll not ask again."

Sir Edren snorted. "You and your so-called queen will never make it out of here alive. There are four hundred guards in this castle, and it sounds to me at least half of them are headed this way."

"They'll not arrive before I've dealt with you."

"You'd not dare."

Tannin took another stride forward and leveled his blade toward Sir Edren.

"Tannin!" shouted Queen Reyis.

Tannin stood still, frozen as a statue with sword poised before him.

Sir Edren glanced to the knot of nobles behind him then back to Tannin. "Mind your leash, dog," he said through a chuckle.

Queen Reyis drew in a deep breath. She pressed

hands against the swell of her stomach and straightened. "Tannin, take his head."

Tannin moved swiftly, a whirlwind to behold. He thrust forward and swept his blade in a tight arc not once but twice across Sir Edren's throat. The nobleman gasped silently, eyes wandering the room then rolling toward the ceiling and the back of his skull. He collapsed at Tannin's feet and as he did his head tumbled from his shoulders. A great crimson pool spread from the wound.

A horrified gasp rose from many, Gamghast among them.

"Who else?" said Queen Reyis, her voice a clarion call. "Who else among you?"

Those remaining retreated many steps, beholding Edren's decapitated corpse in abject terror. They clutched each other, stammering as they seemed unable to make sense of their predicament.

Tannin stood firm as a bulwark before them, between the nobles and the queen and with his blade poised dangerously. "*None* dares challenge the queen's right of rule in this place. None!"

Soon the hall thundered with the sound of heavy footfalls. Gamghast strained to see though the crowd and the dim chamber beyond. There were glimmers, reflections of many candles and torches. Weapons and armor, he knew. It seemed more than a hundred soldiers poured into the hall.

Tannin bent to wipe his blade on Sir Edren's puffy shirt, then rose and turned to Queen Reyis. "Alamis is dead, my queen, and Rune's soldiers are keenly aware of the losses suffered at the front. We need fear nothing from these guards."

"I pray you're right," Gamghast whispered to himself, patting the wisps of his beard with a trembling hand. *Sweet Illienne please spare your loyal servant and all those who act for the greater good of your realm.*

The mass of soldiers rattled to a stop. "What happens here?" came a gruff shout.

"Treason!" exclaimed Tannin, turning back toward the crowd.

A great murmur arose from the gathered nobles.

"Treason?" cried one.

"These *traitors* murdered Sovereign Alamis!" exclaimed another, a tall man with an upturned nose. "Seize them!"

Tannin stood firm, sword gripped at his side. "Who commands the Bastion's Guard" he shouted. "Captain Belwyn?"

"Aye," came an answer from the soldiers at the hall's far end. "Sergeant Tannin?"

Tannin nodded then sheathed his sword. "Aye. This mob has threatened the queen's life and denies her authority here in her very home."

The nobles traded what appeared nervous glances.

"Traitors!" shouted the tall noble. "This man and his company are traitors! We—several of us—witnessed them slaughter Alamis and his personal guard! We *demand* their arrest, and the Bastion's Guard is bound to obey!"

"Stay precisely where you are, traitors," echoed Captain Belwyn's voice, "and do not dare draw arms."

The tall noble raised his chin. "Justice, at last."

"Seize them," commanded the captain.

The clatter of hard-heeled boots followed. Soon many armored soldiers pierced the crowd of nobles, hefting halberds and swords.

Gamghast braced himself against his staff and swiped a bent hand across the wisps of his beard. He thought again of the spells he'd learned and wondered what sort of divine aid he could summon.

"Against the walls with them!" shouted Captain Belwyn.

Sweet Illienne please spare your loyal servant! Gamghast gripped his staff and made ready to call a blinding light.

"Against the walls!" commanded the captain once more.

"How dare you!" complained the tall noble. "Have you any—"

His words were cut short by the butt of a halberd against his belly.

Gamghast's eyes widened and he looked to Queen Reyis. She stood near, straight and proud, hands caressing the fullness of her pregnancy. Beside her loomed Tannin, weapon at the ready and the threat of danger upon his one-eyed face. The soldier's features seemed to ease, though, as the castle guard manhandled more and more of the nobles and pressed them to the hall's edges. Soon all had been forced aside by bullying soldiers and the chamber ahead cleared.

"My queen," Captain Belwyn said, emerging from the hall's edge to stand before them. He bowed. "It is a fine and blessed thing to have you and the proper heir to the Bastion home at last. Welcome, and may the dead gods never allow another to deny you entry again."

Queen Reyis slammed a fist against the wall. "They will pay for this," she said in a low, level tone. "They will pay for this with all they hold dear."

Gamghast took a step to stand beside her, just inside the royal bedchamber. It was an opulent room, all purple pillows and plush chairs and ornate tapestries, though the odor within was most foul. At the chamber's far end stood a bed, upon which lay High King Deragol. His thin, rotting corpse had been stretched to the bed's four posts, gray and emaciated. A crude valve had been fitted into the High King's left side and a bowl of congealed blood rested beside it.

"Damn them," Reyis said, seeming to suppress a gag. "Damn them all to the old hells."

Gamghast pressed a hand to his beard and swallowed hard. This was a desecration Rune had not witnessed in centuries. "Alamis and the Necrists have defiled your husband as well as this place."

"They will pay," Reyis said through gritted teeth. "Tannin," she said, turning her head, "gather but a few soldiers and take with you his body. Build a small pyre in the gardens and prepare to set fire to it this night."

"It shall be done," Tannin said with a sharp bow.

"My queen," Gamghast said, pressing nearer. "He should be buried in the manner of his forefathers."

"No," she breathed, shaking her head. "He will be burned. His corpse will not rest in the ground in this abominable state."

"My queen?" asked Gamghast.

"Burned and then mourned quietly," she said, her

voice firm. "I'll not have my husband's last years be the subject of derision or ridicule. I'll not have his funeral be an opportunity for traitors or the disheartened to cast blame upon him for the war or mock the madness that afflicted him in his final years. No. We will mourn him quietly, and let him pass to the heavens of the Elder God."

Gamghast approached the body. The High King seemed a ghastly horror, the smell awful. The corpse appeared withered and ruined, the skin wrinkled and blanched as though drained of all the fluids within it. The eyes, the haunting eyes, stared wide at the ceiling, lids peeled from them such that they seemed to behold only terror.

"We will honor him quietly," Reyis said again. "Then we prepare to take vengeance upon all the enemies of Rune."

Zandrachus Bale gazed out upon the luminous cavern, the Sacred Place beneath the dead city of Cirak. It was as brilliant and beautiful as he remembered, all lush greenery and incandescent walls and sparkling mist thrown from the tumble of its waterfall. Compared to the desolate steppes of Arranan he'd spent the last weeks traversing, it seemed a paradise.

He sighed.

A paradise but for the purpose that's brought us here.

"It's alright, Bale," whispered Lorra, gripping his shoulder. "Your voice will be heard, and will be as strong as any of theirs."

Theirs.

He glanced just ahead, to the metallic forms of

Kressan and Sienne setting off hand in hand toward the cavern's distant end.

He waited a moment before moving to follow them. As much as the Sentinels had fascinated him in his studies, he did not particularly enjoy their company. That, and he remained troubled by their reluctance to commit to Rune's defense. They'd voiced anger, but there seemed in that no sense of loyalty.

"She's still here," said Lorra, easing him ahead.

Bale looked onward, studying the white pillars of the pavilion. In their midst he could see Lyan, tall and golden and menacing. Near her were three other figures, smaller and apparently more *human*.

"Who are they?" asked Lorra, pointing.

Bale shook his head. "I don't know," he said, squinting to sharpen his vision. "There's one clad in a green cloak. A Variden, perhaps?"

They walked on, Bale keeping them half a dozen or so yards behind the twin Sentinels on the winding, white-washed path toward the pavilion. As he looked ahead to Lyan his heart trembled and his feet felt like stones. He felt her black eyes upon him.

I am too weak an instrument.

Lorra pressed his elbow, moving him along. "I'm here with you, Bale, and we'll not be afraid of them. Remember, they needed *you* to save them."

Her hand wound into his and the feeling of it soothed him. He tugged in a breath and quickened his pace. He resolved to put aside his weaknesses—cowardice most of all—and tackle the task at hand.

The fate of Rune and all he held dear demanded it.

"*Zandrachus Bale*," came the disembodied voice of Lyan the Just. As before, it sounded inside his head rather than his ears.

Bale's eyes joined those of the Sentinel, statuesque at the pavilion's center. Only a white shift covered her towering form. That and the giant, gold sword strapped to her thigh.

"*You have summoned my sisters*," she continued. "*For this I am grateful. I've learned your task proved more troubling than I anticipated, and for that you have my apologies.*"

"You are welcome," Bale mumbled, bowing slightly as he walked.

Lyan did not reply, instead descending the pavilion to meet Sienne and Kressan. The three Sentinels joined in a brief embrace then moved within the circular structure's pillars, sharing many whispered words between them.

Bale's stride slowed once more and only after the space of several moments did he and Lorra begin to ascend the stairs of the pavilion. He squeezed Lorra's hand and in return she squeezed his all the more, taking the lead. He glanced to her sharp features, marveling for an instant how she remained so fearless in the company of demigods.

She looked back to him, her sea-green eyes finding his own, and she smiled. He smiled in return and for an instant felt weightless, moving up the pavilion with ease and prepared to address the Sentinels as Castor's proxy.

And then Lyan shook. Just ahead of them, in the pavilion's center, Lyan shook and the pavilion shook with her. Her every tendon and thew seemed to tense and flex, golden and bulging and appearing ready to burst from her skin. Her obsidian eyes stared upward and her face twisted with a snarl.

"Thaydorne!" she roared, the sound of it jolting the whole of the cavern. She unsheathed her sword, its long blade scraping from its scabbard.

Sienne and Kressan withdrew from her. The three humans retreated as well, moving to the pavilion's edge. Bale gripped Lorra's hand with all the strength in his own.

"Thaydorne!" she raged again, screaming toward the far ceiling of the chamber. "Betrayer!"

She drew back her sword in a wide arc then rushed to a pillar in a single, great stride. She swept the blade and the sword slammed into the stone. With a terrible shrieking sound and a shower of sparks, the stone was cleaved asunder.

Lyan stepped away as the top half of the pillar toppled and crashed against the pavilion floor. The massive cylinder rolled back and forth for a moment, revealing the shattered stone beneath it, before settling in the depression it had formed.

"*Thaydorne?*" hissed the green-cloaked man, tall with wary eyes and a head crowned by receding, gray hair. He took a stride toward the pavilion's center, a hand lashed around the Coda on his opposite arm.

Lyan's chest heaved and she regarded him with narrow eyes. "I have just learned of this, Andrill of the Variden. I have just learned of this and I'm angered, for we have been betrayed. Betrayed by one of our own…" She dropped her sword and the weapon fell with a loud *clang*. She slumped slightly, flexing her fingers and shaking her arms.

"Thaydorne?" the Variden Andrill asked again. "How can this be?"

Lyan looked to him, her lower lip shaking. "My own sisters—*his* sisters!—were captured and tortured by him when they discovered this."

Gold-skinned Kressan nodded and moved near Lyan, looking small and frail beside her. "It is true. Thaydorne is Arranan's Spider King, and my sister Sienne and I discovered his intent to draw Yrghul's power from the Godswell. When we did, he nailed us to horrible spikes and bled us for months into the Necrists' cauldron."

Lyan scowled, straightening to her full height several heads taller than them all. "He has betrayed us most of all, Andrill of the Variden."

The two other humans came beside the Variden, faces grim. One was a fine-featured Harkanian woman, black-skinned and draped in a robe of yellow linen. Her companion appeared to be a brute from somewhere near the Waters of World's End, broad-shouldered and foul-faced and clad in slick, silver furs.

"You must not abide this," growled the man in furs. "Pastine's last disciples will not."

"No," Lyan said loudly. "No, I will *not* abide this. Justice demands Thaydorne be dealt with and destroyed if necessary. He and all the minions of Yrghul who've granted their aid. Ready yourselves, followers of Illienne the Light Eternal, for at last we return to Rune."

26
BLOOD TO HEAL
THE WOUNDS

LANNICK SKULKED ALONG the side of a muddy street, prized sword drawn. Though night had fallen upon Riverweave, fires blazed in many places, lighting the canals, shacks and shanties and playing tricks with shadows. He hissed more than once, mistaking the shifting dark for oncoming soldiers.

Or Necrists.

Shouts rang from many places, cries of alarm and groans of the desperate. There came the shuffle of movement, too, with figures dashing about the tight streets.

Lannick kept close to Arleigh, Cudgen and Ogrund. The four of them had slipped within the city together, among the very last of the deserter army to enter. They'd travelled upon a rickety skiff that drew little notice from the flood of refugees upon the river, and the only soldiers they'd encountered had been those dashing toward

Riverweave's southern edge. From the whispers and cries he'd heard, Lannick learned the enemy approached the city's south gates, assailing Rune with all the subtlety of a battering ram.

He shook his head. He reckoned Rune could—and should—win this war. Considering the might of Rune's forces, General Fane *had* to be losing the fight through the foulest of intents, and the most important step in turning things around was removing him from command.

Lannick dearly hoped he'd be able to deliver the final, killing blow. The general had committed the worst of atrocities upon him, and had left the deepest of scars upon his soul.

Those scars still ached, and Lannick knew he needed blood to heal the wounds.

"*Keep your edges sharp, lad,*" he remembered Brugan saying.

He dragged in a long breath and squeezed his damaged hand to a fist.

"Ahead," whispered Arleigh Lay, his chainmail concealed beneath moth-eaten blankets. "More soldiers."

"Ours?" hissed Cudgen Ashworn, taking his longbow from his shoulder.

Arleigh brandished his dagger, the long blade glimmering from nearby firelight. "Can't tell. Maybe not." He leaned into the cross-street, peering round the corner, then motioned back with the stump of his other arm. "Stay silent and stay still."

They waited long moments, pressed against a building of splintering wood beneath a thatch of knitted reeds.

Sounds were difficult to distinguish as havoc ruled the city and distorted perceptions.

"More regulars," Arleigh said. "Or… These might be ours. I think I recognize one from the deserters' camp."

"Keep quiet," whispered Lannick, trying to focus. "We know the bastards who caused our troubles made camp with Black Jon as well. General Fane is the worst sort of deceiver, and his Scarlet Swords are just as vile."

"True enough," said Cudgen, drawing an arrow and fitting it to his bow.

They remained still, watching a knot of soldiers pass through the intersection before them. This group, too, draped themselves in rags or heavy cloaks and wore wary expressions. Lannick reckoned they shared their purpose, though he thought it better to remain silent.

As they vanished from view Arleigh gestured ahead. "Let's move."

"Wait," said Ogrund in his gravelly voice, grabbing Lannick's shoulder. "I need a word with you. There is news you must hear, grave news. General Fane may possess an Auruch. Worse, Thaydorne is the so-called Spider King. It is he who leads the Arranese."

Lannick glanced to Ogrund, surprised but focused upon his task. "I care not for dead gods or their doings or what trinkets they left behind. I need to kill the general, no matter what."

"Dammit," spat Arleigh. "We need to move while there are few eyes about!"

Ogrund looked to Lannick. "You must be mindful of the greater forces at work in these things."

Lannick glared to the man. "Vengeance, first of all."

Ogrund studied him impassively. "Move, then."

They set out across the muck-filled intersection. Lannick glanced up and down the wider cross-street as they did, spying a number of blazing fires and countless slumped figures that seemed disabled, diseased, or dead.

"How far?" Cudgen asked, easing his arrow from his bowstring.

Arleigh shook his head. "I don't know. A vacant storehouse at the city's center, Black Jon said. Near the governor's mansion. No doubt a fuck of a lot easier to find when it's not nighttime or wartime."

Ogrund strode forward. "I'm familiar with this place. One of my order patrolled Riverweave after learning of General Fane's affiliations with the Necrists. The mansion is due east, and the storehouse a mere ten blocks south of it."

Arleigh looked back with a sneer. "Like I said, you're more useful than I'd thought. East it is."

They walked hurriedly though not overly fast. Lannick so wanted to run, to race to that moment he hoped awaited him, but knew it best to appear more like worried denizens of the city than soldiers charging to war. He shifted his jaw and gripped the handle of his blade.

Soon. So very soon.

They followed Ogrund now, the Variden leading them down an avenue lined on one side by a canal and countless colorful structures on the other. This street, at least, hadn't yet been set ablaze, and they passed taverns, guildhalls and craftsmen's shops all seemingly abandoned. Lannick reckoned the city—known as a bustling hub for merchants and mingling cultures—would be vibrant even at this late hour but for the war threatening to consume it whole.

Just then a group of men dashed from an alleyway not more than a dozen yards ahead. Lannick and the others crouched low and readied their weapons. The group—four figures—spotted them and brandished their steel.

"Careful," said Lannick as much to himself as his companions. "We're at war," he said, voice swelling. "We'd all do best not to kill the wrong folks. Identify yourselves."

Three of the men kept their weapons poised before them, hands shaking with what Lannick knew to be nerves. The fourth—a thickly-built sort—lowered his sword and strode forward. "We're soldiers fighting for Rune, of course," he said with a gruff voice. "You?"

Lannick found the voice familiar, and in the flickering dark could make out a square face beneath a bristle of brown hair. "Sergeant Kaldare?"

The man said nothing and kept still. The soldiers behind him traded whispers and held their blades tight.

Lannick sheathed his sword, swallowed hard, and took a step toward the man. "I reckon we're headed the same way, Sergeant. And we both want the same bastard stuck on the points of our swords."

The man took another stride forward. "Captain deVeers?" the man—Kaldare—chuckled. "Back from the dead again? Happy to see it."

Lannick smirked and clasped the man on the shoulder. "Time to put someone else in the grave."

Riverweave grew ever more chaotic as they approached its center. Shouts and the crackle of fires tearing through homes. Desperate folk screaming as they threw water from the canals to douse the flames.

There came too the sound of steel against steel. It seemed at least some of the Arranese had breached the city. Lannick caught glimpses of flaming arrows streaking through the sky as well as red-cloaked soldiers racing ahead.

"Those soldiers aren't ours," Lannick said. "Those are Scarlet Swords."

"Fane's bastards," growled Arleigh Lay.

Riverweave's narrow streets frustrated his view but Lannick could see the low edge of the night held a glow not far away. It appeared brighter than the cast of the other fires, as though a massive blaze had been set beneath.

Lannick pointed. "Ogrund, could that be the storehouse?"

The Variden drew aside him, holding his Coda. "It's in the direction, though difficult to say if it's the location."

Lannick felt a hollow in his gut. "I fear that's our army."

"Under attack?" asked Cudgen Ashworn. "From Arranese or Fane's men?"

Lannick nodded. "Either way, it's Fane's doing. He's either allowed the enemy to assail our men or he's ordered his own attack. We'd best hurry."

They doubled their pace. Their weapons rattled and their armor hissed but they could afford caution no longer.

The crowd thickened, folk fleeing this way and that. Their pace slowed as they weaved and squeezed through the masses. Huddled people, laden wagons and scrawny livestock all wandered in their way.

Arleigh pressed ahead, swinging his handless arm through the tide. "Move, for fuck's sake!"

Finally, after many frustrated moments, they came to a wide intersection, the narrow street meeting a broad avenue split by a canal. They gathered themselves and looked about.

"Dead gods!" cursed Sergeant Kaldare, thrusting a finger toward the water.

Lannick followed Kaldare's gaze to see a cluster of three wooden skiffs jammed against the supports of a gangway, knocking together upon the canal's flow. Atop the rafts slumped soldiers riddled with many arrows.

"Fuck!" barked Arleigh Lay. "Hanner?"

Hanner Hale's barrel-chested corpse splayed over smaller bodies beneath it, the dead man pierced by arrows. His mouth rested agape, blood dripping from it to stain his salt-and-pepper beard.

"Our men…" uttered Kaldare. "Dead gods. Could it be deMond was right? An army broken into so many pieces can't win?"

Lannick glanced to him. Kaldare seemed to have said the words without accusation, though they stung Lannick all the same. He squeezed the hilt of his sword. "We'll win this fight. I swear it."

Fires blazed all about and the clamor of combat sang upon the searing air. Lannick swept sweat from his brow with a bandaged hand and charged ahead, leading his companions toward whatever raged beyond.

A battle? A massacre?

He cursed himself for getting captured, for being delayed. And most of all for underestimating General Fane. He should have known Fane would learn of their coming, and that he'd have a plan for dealing with them.

The general was mad and arrogant and utterly devoid of morality, but he was no fool.

The road turned and broadened and the crowds thinned. Just there, visible in the fires that lit the night and not more than a dozen yards away, loomed a clutch of red-cloaked soldiers. They pressed swords against a man, the last of what appeared to have been a half-dozen soldiers from the deserter army. They thrust, and the man slipped from the blades to rest upon a heap of dead comrades beneath him.

"Fucking Scarlet Swords!" growled Arleigh, his long dagger held crossways before him.

The Swordsmen—five in number—spun about and raised blood-stained weapons. "More traitors," grunted one.

"More *dead* traitors," laughed another.

Lannick and his companions stood firm, wary. Lannick eased his grip on his sword then tightened it. He drew a steady breath.

Keep your edges sharp, lad.

The Scarlet Swords stretched across the road's width, each big and menacing with eyes hungry for violence.

Lannick was happy to give it to them. He moved to the fore of his men, hatred swelling in his heart. "The general will die upon our swords, as will all those loyal to him. I am Captain Lannick deVeers, Protector of Ironmoor, and I swear this to be true."

The lead Swordsman, a broad-shouldered man with an unruly beard, cracked his neck and swayed his sword. "This rotten turd again? Last I saw him he was at the brig in Ironmoor, whining from the quarterstaff I'd smacked against his head and the boot Keln kicked against his chin. Let's give this drunk the death he deserves."

The Swordsmen charged as one.

Lannick ripped away the rags covering his cloak and armor with his injured hand—wincing—and held the bundle at his side, preparing to throw. "Do the same," he hissed. "Throw the tatters as they near."

He shifted his weight upon his feet, making ready to move amidst the coming rush of bodies.

A bowstring hummed behind him and there came the *thunk* of an arrow slamming into the chest of a Swordsman. The Scarlet Sword farthest to the right clutched his wound, stumbled and fell.

The remaining Swordsmen closed the distance, snarling and shouting and raising their blades.

Yards shrank to feet.

"Now!" Lannick roared, wheeling his arm to cast the rags forward.

Lannick hurled the robes, the ratty cloth spreading like a fisherman's net. His men did the same. The rags tangled weapons, providing just enough distraction to take advantage.

The man before Lannick—the lead Swordsman—cursed as the rags wrapped about his sword. He slowed his stride, sweeping the steel uselessly about.

Lannick seized his moment. He dodged aside the Swordsman then shoved his blade toward the space just above the man's hip. The chainmail armor offered resistance but Lannick pressed the sword through, through the tight links to the kidney, the liver, the guts.

The Scarlet Sword howled. Lannick's hand shook as

the hilt was yanked away from it, the weapon scraping as the Swordsman tumbled to the ground.

Lannick whipped his head about and spied the sword left by the man Cudgen had dropped. He snatched it then looked to the scuffle behind him.

The remaining Scarlet Swords battled his men. Arleigh wrestled with one, though he'd twisted his dagger near the Swordsman's throat and seemed poised to finish him. Kaldare and two of his men struggled with another, a brute with a battle-axe. The third Swordsman withdrew from a dead soldier—the last in Kaldare's company—and began moving toward Cudgen.

Where's Ogrund?

He shook his head and eyed the Swordsman closest— the big fellow squared against Kaldare and his soldiers. Lannick moved, readying the dead soldier's weapon.

Just then the burly Swordsman dodged the sweep of Kaldare's sword, lunging back as he did. He slammed into Lannick and nearly knocked him to the ground.

Lannick staggered. He stumbled then tripped over one of the bodies and spilled onto the sloppy street. He cursed then pushed himself upward, eyes trained to the axe-wielding Swordsman again facing Sergeant Kaldare and his soldiers. The Swordsman wheeled his axe backward with a roar and charged.

Lannick pressed ahead but was too far away. The Swordsman brought his axe round, cleaving it into one of Kaldare's men, a red-faced recruit by the looks of him. The axe tore through mail, bone and flesh, and the soldier crumbled with an awful wheeze. He slid off the axe head and dropped to Kaldare's feet with a squelch and splash of muck.

Lannick gritted his teeth and moved forward. The brute readied his axe and attacked. Kaldare and the young soldier alongside him just managed to dodge the blade's sweep, retreating behind the corpse of their companion. The Swordsman pursued, swinging the weapon once more.

"Gah!"

Lannick looked to see Arleigh drop to the muddy street, a Scarlet Swordsman beneath him. Arleigh's hand squeezed about the hilt of his dagger, the point of it stuck in the throat of the Scarlet Sword. Arleigh growled and twisted the knife and the Swordsman gurgled.

"Fucking bastard!" Arleigh screamed in the man's face. Lannick saw then Arleigh had been wounded again, his bandaged brow soaked anew with blood.

Lannick turned again to Kaldare and the axe-wielding Swordsman bearing down upon him and the young soldier. They were close, Kaldare waving steel and forcing the Swordsman to retreat a few steps. The man's crimson cloak whirled just before Lannick.

There'd been a time, Lannick knew, when he would have considered a knife in the back a dishonorable, cowardly thing. Such notions, though, had since been stripped away by the deepest of losses. Now he cared not at all for the righteousness of his means. He cared only for the righteousness of the ends he meant to achieve.

Fuck everything else. Fuck Fane and his Scarlet Swords.

Lannick roared as he slammed his blade into the back of the Swordsman's neck, the point driving through spine and throat and spraying gore across the street and soldiers beyond. The body slumped to the ground, and Lannick yanked away the sword.

For a moment he stood, his whole body clenched and hatred coursing though him.

"Captain!"

The shout came from Arleigh. Lannick looked to see Arleigh pressing away from the dead Swordsman beneath him to run toward Cudgen.

Lannick raced ahead, Kaldare quickly coming alongside.

Cudgen had retreated down the road. He was wounded, limping back and clutching his side. He'd lost his bow and held now a sword with a trembling hand.

The Scarlet Swordsman loomed before the man. He laughed, shoulders shaking. He struck with what seemed only a slight effort, but Cudgen barely managed to ward away the blow. Closer the Swordsman came, swaying his weapon and his laughter growing loud.

Lannick and Arleigh rushed onward, Kaldare and his young soldier close behind.

The Swordsman, a burly lad with a sly look, seemed to sense their approach, turning and pointing his blade with a grin. "You old shits? Who are you to challenge the general during wartime? Death is the punishment for treason, you know, and I'm happy to administer the sentence." He flipped his sword then caught and readied it once more. "Come."

Lannick neared the man, slowing and leveling his blade. "Just as I said, the general dies. The general and all his dogs."

The Swordsman sprang forward, slashing his blade.

Lannick leaned and lurched and parried. He avoided the brunt of the assault though a strike he deflected dug into his forearm, chewing through chainmail and ripping the flesh.

The man was strong but Lannick had dealt with strong men before. He moved and parried, feet light, and weathered the storm. Soon the Swordsman's attack slowed, his sword seeming heavier in his hand.

Lannick moved in, working his blade about the Swordsman's head so the man would have to lift his own. The Swordsman seemed tired and the effort appeared to tax him. Lannick pressed on, their blades clashing and clanging.

Just then a figure flashed between them. Arleigh charged and buried his long dagger in the Swordsman's back. The two toppled over together, the Scarlet Sword twitching as Arleigh worked the blade near the heart.

Arleigh grunted. "That's how we do it," he said, wiping gore and gristle from his hands and face. "These fucking soldiers always expect to fight the foe in front of them, but never sense the knife in the back until its already there." He chuckled grimly and stood. "Cudgen, you alright?"

Cudgen limped to retrieve his bow. "Bastard broke a couple of my ribs, maybe, and sliced my leg but not too deep. Nothing that'll keep me from putting an arrow in the heart of our dear general."

Lannick's chest still heaved from effort and his head still hummed from the clash. He staggered to the Swordsman he'd felled earlier and yanked his prized weapon from the soldier's side. He looked about, realizing he remained troubled by something else. "Where's Ogrund?"

Arleigh and Kaldare came to stand aside him, eyes

scanning the street. Lannick turned but found no trace of the Variden in the flickering firelight.

Arleigh spat. "Fucker abandons us just as I start thinking he can help?"

"I do my part as always, Arleigh," came Ogrund's grumble. Soon the stout man emerged from an alleyway, sheathing a blade that glowed a faint green. Black blood stained his cloak.

Lannick stared to the Variden and swallowed. "Necrists."

Ogrund nodded. "The general's Scarlet Swords aren't the only threat stalking this city. Three Necrists tracked us, and now all three lie dead in that alley. What is more, the governor's mansion is near, and I sense the presence of many Necrists within. The general is *there*, Lannick, and it is not just soldiers who guard him. Soldiers and things far worse."

Lannick peered down the street toward the flickering chaos beyond. "What did you say, Arleigh? That soldiers expect the fight in front of them but not the knife in the back?"

"Something like that," said Arleigh. "But either way, damned right."

Lannick nodded. "Well right now I reckon most soldiers not battling the Arranese are engaging Black Jon's army. Fane likely sent many of his men—even some of those in his personal guard—to vanquish the 'traitors' at his doorstep."

Kaldare shuffled beside him, his surviving soldier in tow. "I suppose that's true, Captain, but what is it you're suggesting?"

Lannick tugged in a breath, hoping he was making

the right decision, hoping years and years of drink hadn't dulled those instincts he'd once possessed. "The six of us likely wouldn't tip the balance in whatever combat is taking place ahead. But now, while it's happening, the general's defenses may well be at their weakest. If we could manage our way into the mansion…" His voice trailed away and he gripped his sword.

Can vengeance be so close?

Kaldare looked to him. "We're soldiers, Captain. More, we're leaders. We shouldn't abandon our men."

Lannick squeezed the blade all the tighter. "I'll not tell you what to do, Sergeant, but I'm here to kill General Fane. I'm here for that most of all."

"You're right, Lannick," said Ogrund, taking a stride closer. "Our best chance might well be now, or rather near to now. We should take cover and hide until morning. Then we can enter the mansion after the sun breaks the darkness and the Necrists' power wanes."

Lannick placed his wounded hand upon the Variden's shoulder. "Let's do this, Ogrund."

"With you, Captain," said Arleigh. Cudgen the same just after.

Kaldare stood silently for a moment before shaking his head and smacking his fists together. "I've just lost two good lads at the hands of Fane's Scarlet Swords, and those are only the most recent of that man's crimes. I'm with you, Captain. If now is our best chance, we must seize it. Let's kill the general."

27
AN UNHOLY END

THE BATTLEFIELD BELOW had all but emptied, Rune's soldiers having retreated behind the scant cover of Riverweave's walls with the horde of Arranese warriors crashing against them. Reeds and grasses lay bent and blood-stained.

All were gone now. All but the mangled mass of the dead and their reek upon the sea's breeze.

Prefect Lavris Kreer stood in the stirrups of his white steed, a thin hand shielding his eyes from the sun just breaking the distant horizon of the Sullen Sea. "My Variden companions," he said, "certainly your young eyes are keener than mine. The seeking stone holds to the field, though I see nothing."

Wil eased forward in his saddle, the leather creaking. "Naught but carnage as far as I can tell. You're certain the highlander could not have corrupted the stone? That he could not have worked Castor's spirit to deceive you?"

Kreer stiffened, thoughts drifting to the highlander's

certain deception with the Spell of Remembrance. *No*, he thought. *I would sense—I would know—such a perversion of the Old Faith.*

"Prefect?" Wil asked. "Could he not do this?"

"The highlander may be prone to deception, but the powers I employ far predate that barbarian's theft of the spirit and do not rely upon a human medium. These powers derive from Illienne herself, and, as such, are beyond corruption."

Wil looked to him, brow cocked. "Beyond corruption? And yet we've now learned it is Thaydorne himself who is the so-called Spider King, that it is a Sentinel who lays siege to Rune. Thaydorne, too, draws his power from Illienne, yet it's clear he's corrupted by ambition, the Necrists, and Yrghul's wickedness."

Kreer stretched a long finger upward. "I have yet to accept the truth of this *rumor*," he chided. He then raised a second finger. "More, the Sentinels were human once, and thus carry with them human failings. Only the elder powers, the elder prayers of the Old Faith, can be trusted."

"This rumor is truth, Prefect," said Wil, eyes narrowing. "What I've learned from my brother Andrill is beyond question. Through my Coda I learned this truth from Andrill, and through his ears I heard this truth from the mouths of the Sentinels themselves, from—"

"Listen!" hissed Stendall, the tall and lanky Variden turning his horse southward. "Be quiet and listen!"

Drums. The low thunder of drums like a heart's beat upon the air.

"Where, Stendall?" said Wil, easing his steed a few strides ahead. "My ears can't discern the direction."

Stendall gestured southeast.

Prefect Kreer sat tall in his saddle. "Wait. We must simply wait. The drums signal the arrival of the Spider King and his coming clash with the highlander. If the Spider King is Thaydorne as you claim, then either these two will conspire or one of them will meet an unholy end."

Wil grunted. "And if it's Castor who meets that end? What then?"

Kreer's lips tilted. "When the body is broken the soul will be set free. Another vessel shall be filled."

"Wil," Stendall said, guiding his horse a few strides down the slope. "Wil, I see him. There, amongst the corpses."

Prefect Kreer peered beyond his Variden associates but could see little in the morning sun. "Lund?" he called to the freckly acolyte just behind him. "Can you see this? The stone does point that way."

"I'm not sure, Prefect," said Acolyte Lund, shuffling beneath his brown robes. "There are so many bodies and it's… There… There?"

Stendall nodded. "He's waiting. He's waiting for Thaydorne. Just listen."

Kreer straightened and squinted, staring down the slope. Low upon the breeze and the thumping of drums he heard it. A guttural, harsh sound, a language from the darkest and most vile of places.

From Yrghul himself.

Kreer sniffed in a breath through his long nose. "The spirit must be freed…" he said. "The highlander speaks blasphemy, the words of the Lord of Nightmares. Castor would never give voice to such lies."

Wil eased his horse near. "My brother Merek knew this

to be true and I've no cause to disagree. No Sentinel loyal to Rune and the Light Eternal would commit the atrocities this man has so wantonly perpetrated. I must agree with you, Prefect. He possesses a bloodlust that betrays a wicked nature."

Kreer looked to the man. "Precisely, Variden. Precisely."

The prefect returned his eyes to the battlefield, seeing now the highlander standing not a hundred yards away, down the steep slope and amidst a pile of broken bodies. The broad man was clad in stained leather, black hair flailing in the breeze. At his side he held a massive blade and his gaze was affixed to the southeast.

To the drums. To the Spider King.

"Thaydorne!" the highlander screamed, his voice a jarring commandment. "It is your time, a time foretold by fate! Come!"

The drums sounded louder and at last Kreer could see movement farther down the field. There, perhaps a league nearer the sea, moved figures, several dozen with weapons glittering in the waxing sunlight.

"Prefect," said Wil. "You and your acolyte should come closer. Stendall and I can conceal us, and I fear such concealment is quickly becoming necessary. Those upon the field are not friendly to the likes of us, no matter what you think of Castor's spirit."

Kreer held still for a moment, peering down to the highlander. *Castor,* he prayed, *should you depart the blasphemer's corpse, fill my body and I swear I will serve with all the dignity and wisdom you deserve.*

He closed his eyes and tilted his face to the sun, feeling its warmth.

Sweet Illienne, I am but a vessel waiting to be filled.

"Prefect," Wil said again. "The enemy is near."

Kreer nodded and pulled the reins, guiding his white steed toward the Variden. Lund clumsily did the same with his dray mare.

Wil clasped the black iron Coda upon his wrist and his companion Stendall did also. Both muttered word upon word. Elder words, the words of true, divine spellcraft gifted by Illienne herself.

Kreer recognized the rudiments of the language, of course, though he knew not how the Variden gave force to the phrases. Each of the Sentinels and their followers possessed and guarded over their own powers, and Kreer knew the disciples of Valis wielded some of Illienne's most potent abilities.

His mouth pinched to a scowl, but he quickly swept aside any sense of jealousy. Soon, he knew, he alone would hold the spirit of Castor, the spirit of an eternal Sentinel. The Variden would remain mere fractions of their master, mere hints of his divinity.

"Stay close, Prefect," whispered Wil. "For now we will seem no more than brush and branches to the highlander, the Spider King, and the Spider King's entourage. Wander not, though, lest you be revealed."

Kreer glanced to Wil then steadied himself, training his eyes again upon the field.

"Thaydorne!" bellowed the savage once more.

Kreer gritted his teeth, knowing in the depths of his soul the highlander should have been slain at the Abbey long ago. Castor's spirit had been stolen and defiled, the desecration becoming worse with every passing day.

He so *despised* this barbarian. He so loathed him for the prize he had stolen, the sacred spirit he'd taken for himself.

"I will kill him myself!" he blurted.

Wil turned to him. "No, Prefect!" he hissed. "This highlander is more powerful than any one of us. He's proven that already, at your Abbey, and has clearly grown in strength since then. We must not be rash. We must take greater care than we ever have, for it is clear the stakes are at their greatest."

Kreer sniffed and swallowed, then settled upon his horse. "We are concealed?"

"Our forms are hidden, but not the sounds we make. Silence is vital, Prefect."

"Very well," Kreer said quietly. "May Illienne protect us all."

The drums thundered all the louder as the newcomers approached. Dozens of ornamented Arranese both mounted and on foot picked their way through the field of broken corpses, drummers at their fore. In the center of the Arranese strode a hulking man, standing several heads taller than any about him and his skin stained gold.

Kreer drew a sharp breath, knowing now the Variden's rumor had to be true. This so-called Spider King was no mere mortal. "Thaydorne..." he murmured.

"Prefect," whispered Wil. "Look at those in his tow."

Kreer scowled, spotting a number of figures in cowls and robes of black, flesh concealed from the rising sun. "Necrists. Are you certain they won't be able to see us, to see through your illusion?"

Wil shook his head. "Not in so small a number. Only

a great many working together would be able to pierce the veil we've woven."

The Spider King and his entourage moved onward, closer and closer still to the highlander. They came to within fifty feet of the highlander awaiting them, the savage's great blade weaving through the morning air as though beckoning a fight.

"This is no meeting of allies," whispered Kreer. "One of these Sentinels will fall this day."

Wil nodded. "We witness a momentous and terrible thing."

Kreer knitted his hands together and prayed once more to receive Castor's spirit. *Sweet Illienne, your humble servant stands ready.*

"Thaydorne!" The highlander's roar seemed unnaturally loud, the very earth quaking beneath them all.

The drums faltered.

The field was still for a time, everything pausing for the span of several breaths.

Then the enormous, gold-skinned Thaydorne moved forward, pressing the decorated warriors aside like children. "And so I behold the truth with my own eyes," he boomed. "The fabled Gravemaker is none other than my brother Castor, wearing yet another face and hiding within yet another mortal's body. You dare *confront* me, Castor? Here, before my chieftains? You choose an odd and unfortunate occasion for your embarrassment, my brother."

"Come," said the highlander. "It is the anointed time, the time the mighty Thaydorne meets his fate."

Thaydorne passed his drummers then slowed. He looked to the highlander with a curious gaze. "You have no gift for combat, Castor, and no divine blessing to aid you against me. *I* am the soldier and *you* the scholar. You have challenged me and slain those in my charge, but because of our kinship I offer my forgiveness. I will forgive you should you but join me against the kingdom that banished us. Join me, and together we will seize what was stolen from us a thousand years ago. All that and much, much more."

The highlander stood unmoved, sword still swaying.

Thaydorne's face, a handsome, golden visage beneath a hairless head striped by many black lines, twisted to a snarl. "Have you lost your ears, Castor? You have slaughtered my champions, some of my best. You have issued *threats*! Yet you are no match for me, Castor. Not in combat, no matter what mortal form you occupy. How *dare* you do this!" His whole body seemed to tremble with anger.

The highlander laughed. He laughed and he lowered his sword, though only slightly. "You fail to understand, Thaydorne. I am not Castor. I am more. I am the Gravemaker. I am the wielder of light and darkness and the death between. It is you who must yield, and you have but this one chance."

Thaydorne took long strides about a knot of corpses and came to stand within mere yards of the highlander. "You challenge me?" he snarled, unsheathing the monstrous blade strapped to his back.

Kreer looked upon it with eyes wide. *Ealyr Rigellus. Heaven's Reaper, the very sword said to have struck down Yrghul the Lord of Nightmares.*

Thaydorne leveled the weapon toward the highlander. "For all your wisdom, Castor, you have proven yourself a fool. I urge you once more not to do this, my brother."

The highlander raised his sword. "I am not Castor. I am more. You must know, Thaydorne, that Yrghul summons but one son. He summons me, and this day you will learn why. Bring your strength. Bring your steel. No matter. You shall be destroyed and desecrated all the same."

Thaydorne's chieftains dashed ahead, coming to stand alongside the colossus and rattling weapons. His Necrist companions remained hunched together at the rear, hissing their dark words.

"No," Thaydorne commanded. He swept his blade and it hissed in the air as he did. His massive form seemed made entirely of muscle. "I need not rely on any man's help. I need not rely on sorcery. I possess *divine* strength, *divine* fortitude. I will tear apart this perversion with my hands and my blade. Mine alone." He threw his golden arms outward. "Make my arena."

The Arranese chieftains—ornamented warriors with painted faces—moved as one, rushing to ring the two Sentinels and the many corpses between them. Once the wide circle was complete the drums rumbled anew.

"We battle now, Castor," said Thaydorne. "The time for mercy has ended. I fear you will feel pain at your death, my brother. Great, great pain. And I apologize for none of it."

Karnag Mak Ragg beheld the foe before him. This golden giant, this Sentinel, wielded his blade with a force and quickness Karnag had never felt nor seen. Thaydorne cleaved the air, sweeping the blade down and up and across with a speed that nearly blinded and a strength that shook the earth.

Yet Karnag knew the weapon's path before Thaydorne's arm guided it thus.

The Sentinel was strong. He was quick.

Karnag, though, perceived all before it happened. He moved and weaved with a new elusiveness he'd stolen from the shadows. The Sentinel's sword came close again and again, near enough that Karnag could feel the whip of hot air upon his skin.

But the blade did not find flesh.

Thaydorne possessed immense strength, but Karnag ever remained a fraction of an instant ahead. The great Sentinel struck and struck once more the corpses tangled upon the field, their bones shattering and bodies bursting in showers of gore.

The strikes came swiftly and Thaydorne's sword howled as it brushed near. Karnag contorted and evaded and parried, though he could find no room to attack.

But he had embraced his prescience. He had mastered it. And with the knowledge he'd taken from the Necrists, he'd mastered the dark magics as well. He beheld things yet to be and the shadows lurking between.

More, he beheld those things through the eyes of a killer.

He waited for his moment.

He waited with the patience of the greatest slayer the world would ever know.

There.

Thaydorne's foot smashed into the guts of a fallen Arranese—one of his own so-called champions—and for an instant it snagged in the ribcage.

Now.

Karnag ripped *Gravemaker* toward the Sentinel with great rage. The sword found home, slicing into Thaydorne's side.

Thaydorne stiffened and tensed for a moment, time enough for Karnag to yank the blade free of the giant's body.

But the Sentinel did not falter. Not for long. Thaydorne shook off the wound and renewed his assault, pressing upon Karnag with fury and flashing steel. He roared, his golden face set with wrath and his voice like thunder.

The Sentinel's attacks came quickly. So quickly they narrowed that span of foresight Karnag beheld, so quickly he could not react to them in time.

Heaven's Reaper drove into his thigh, shearing through leather and skin and sinew. Karnag managed to slither away just before the blade broke bone.

He cried out and lurched back, feet finding thin spaces among the many dead. He felt the shadows working within him, mending the wound. The pain, though, remained. A searing pain that weakened and distracted him.

"I am stronger than you!" screamed Thaydorne, gold and massive and menacing before him. "I am faster!"

Another sweep of the fabled blade. Karnag managed to avoid it, but only barely.

"I am a *god* among men!" Thaydorne roared. "What are you?"

The blade came too close again, biting into Karnag's hip.

"Gah!" Karnag spat. He retreated, squared to his enemy, then wheeled his weapon about. He willed his mind to disregard the pain and focus upon those moments *between* moments. Upon those small, almost indiscernible details written on the atlas of fate.

There, again.

"I am a god!" shouted Thaydorne.

Thaydorne gloated before him and Karnag lunged, driving the point of his blade into the giant's sword-arm.

The Sentinel gasped and nearly dropped his weapon. His arm bled like that of any mortal and his blade twitched in a hand that seemed to struggle to grasp it.

Karnag smiled. "I am death."

Thaydorne's brow bent and worry crept across his face. "Castor, you cannot—"

Karnag leapt ahead, roaring, and swept *Gravemaker* before him. The sword ripped through Thaydorne's abdomen, a torrent of blood following it. "I am death!"

The Sentinel staggered but did not fall. He withdrew several strides beyond the reach of Karnag's sword and looked to him with eyes wide. His hand clutched his belly, blood flowing freely through his fingers, then glanced to the huddled Necrists cowering outside the ring.

"How?" Thaydorne croaked.

Karnag gnashed his teeth, *Gravemaker* poised before him. "You do not listen, Thaydorne," he grated. "You do not *learn*. I am not Castor. I am more!"

Karnag witnessed the coming instant, the briefest opportunity. Shock still rattled Thaydorne and his good hand still struggled to contain his innards. He would not be able to evade the strike.

Karnag charged toward his foe. He dashed aside the giant then whirled about, shrieking and swinging *Gravemaker* low. The blade tore through the tendon just above Thaydorne's heel and the Sentinel dropped to his knees with a heavy thud.

Karnag wheeled round once more, whipping the sword with a terrible strength all his own.

The steel ripped through Thaydorne's throat and the Sentinel's golden head fell from his golden body in a tumble of blood and gristle.

Silence.

The whole of the gathering seemed to inhale and Karnag reveled in it. He grasped with both hands Thaydorne's severed head, all golden and striated by black stitches.

He lifted the head above him and turned slowly about, looking to the decorated Arranese whose painted faces sagged with drooping mouths. "*This* is your Spider King, and *this* is his end!" He heaved the head toward that edge of the circle nearest the lurking Necrists.

The Necrists chittered for an instant, but then fell quiet.

"You dare not," Karnag snarled, black tendrils escaping his mouth.

The Arranese stood in dumbfounded silence, gazes affixed to Thaydorne's disembodied head. The skull still listed to and fro upon the field, eyes wide like those of a slaughtered cow.

Karnag saw this and he laughed. He rounded the circle and laughed all the more, spittle spraying from his mouth as he cackled. "You thought *him* a god?"

They dared not answer him.

"He promised you *conquest*. He promised you deliverance and he promised eternity. But he cannot deliver these things. He cannot deliver these because he was from the beginning deceived—he was unsuited. He thought he was summoned as the chosen of Yrghul, but Yrghul chose but one son. *I* am the chosen son, and it is I alone who can lead you to eternity. It is I alone who can destroy Rune!"

The Arranese swayed and shifted and the Necrists whispered.

Karnag threw his arms outward, Thaydorne's blood dripping from them. "It is I alone! Follow me now, and together we will take the whole of the world and the whole of the heavens above!"

A murmur arose.

The Arranese chieftains moved forward, tightening the circle they'd formed. Karnag stood tall in their midst and as they neared him they bowed low.

"We follow strength, my lord," said one of the bowing Arranese. "We are humbled in your presence."

"Rise," Karnag said.

The chieftains did so, haltingly. Fear stained their eyes.

"And you?" Karnag roared, pointing *Gravemaker* toward the huddle of Necrists beyond the circle.

The necromancers stood only for a moment before prostrating themselves upon the plain.

Karnag reveled in it all, sucking in the death-tainted air.

Then, though, he remembered the eyes upon him, the spies who dared watch him *become*.

He wheeled toward the hillock, toward his old pupils. Toward the aged prefect and the bumbling acolyte. The fools who thought they'd hidden from him.

He leveled *Gravemaker* and laughed. "You? You dare think you can capture what is mine to possess? Come, then! Come!"

Two green-cloaked Variden appeared and yanked away the prefect and acolyte, their petty illusion spoiled. The four hurriedly mounted horses and galloped over the hillcrest and away.

Karnag smiled at this.

Those men would warn others.

Together, they would spread Karnag's tale.

Together, they would spread news of his deeds, and all who heard it would *fear*.

28
OLD SCORES

LANNICK STOOD AT the window of the abandoned merchant's shop, looking out from the barren second floor to the streets below. The sun had risen to near midday and reflected off many puddles of water and blood. Smoke seemed to rise from everywhere and the air carried the ring of combat and the stink of the dead.

The streets just below, though, were empty save for the occasional soldier charging toward the battle or a group of them hauling away an injured comrade.

"Black Jon's holding his own!" blurted Private Yurick, the last of Kaldare's men. He was a burly, exuberant and red-haired youth who'd taken a liking to the Scarlet Sword's axe that had felled his companion. He hefted the weapon now, shaking it toward the window.

"Let's hope so," Lannick said with a smirk. "Rune needs Black Jon and all his men."

Ogrund grunted from behind them in the small room.

"More than you know. I've just learned the enemy is far more dangerous than we expected. We war against *eternal* forces, Lannick. These are grave moments, and never has so much depended upon us."

Lannick turned to his Variden companion. "Then we *must* kill the general. We must focus on that now. On that above all things. All those other troubles will be waiting for us when we're done."

Ogrund nodded slightly, eyes narrow as ever. "I am with you, Lannick. But remember also what I said. Our comrade Alisa learned the general bargained with the Necrists for an Auruch. We have no idea what powers he may command. We must take care."

Lannick clenched his crackling jaw. "Fane dies this day."

"Then what the fuck are we waiting for?" sneered Arleigh Lay. He scraped his dagger across a whetstone and wore fresh bandages about his forehead and mess of black hair. He snorted. "Let's kill the bastard."

"Fucking agreed," muttered Cudgen Ashworn through a cough, a wince and a hand pressed against his side. "We've old scores to settle. Each and every one of us."

Lannick turned back to the window, a smile finding his face. He looked to the governor's mansion two blocks distant, its white walls and red-shingled roof bright beneath the sun. He squeezed a hand about his sword. "Ogrund?"

The squint-eyed Variden pressed close to the window, appearing to study the sky and then the nearby mansion. "Yes," he said in his gravelly voice. "Now is the time."

They splashed across the street, cloaks hunched high on

their shoulders. The nearest structure, a tall building with heavy eaves and boarded windows, provided cover.

"The streets are nearly empty," said Arleigh. "We're safe for now."

Lannick peered round the corner, down a narrow alley that emptied near the mansion. "There don't seem to be eyes on us yet." He tugged in a breath and pulled his sword free of its scabbard. "Let's go."

They rushed through the alleyway and the refuse crowding it.

Then footsteps.

They stopped short of the alley's mouth, listening.

"Come close," hissed Ogrund. He clutched a Coda that now glowed a pale green.

Lannick drew near to the Variden, knowing the man meant to conceal them from whoever moved beyond.

Scarlet Swords—a half-dozen of them—trotted along the street. "Fane's losing the city," grumbled one. "His own soldiers are turning against him!"

Lannick felt his heart leap. "This is our chance," he whispered.

The Scarlet Swords moved on, the sounds of their steps fading. Soon the street seemed quiet and unoccupied, the only noise that of the battle raging in the distance.

"Now," said Lannick. "We go now."

"Remain close to me," said Ogrund. "So long as you do we'll appear no more than a huddle of refugees to any onlookers. Wander too far, though, and you'll be revealed to their eyes."

Kaldare looked to the Variden with a cocked brow. "You can do such things?"

"Trust him," said Lannick, "and do just as he says."

Arleigh snorted. "Once again, this fellow's more useful than I'd thought."

They slipped from the alley, moving across and up the wide thoroughfare. There, a mere fifty feet away, stood the governor's mansion, a tall, two-storied structure of white wood agleam in the sunlight. A smattering of red-sashed soldiers wandered the fenced grounds and a couple of Scarlet Swords leaned against tall columns lining the home's facade.

"Let's move past," whispered Lannick. "Move past the mansion and take in everything you see. We need to find our best way in."

They walked in a tight group, hands squeezed about weapons and eyes affixed to the mansion and the foes loitering about it.

"Stay close, lads," Lannick whispered. "Stay quiet."

They crept along, most glancing nervously to Fane's guards then hiding their eyes. Lannick, though, knew the power Ogrund worked and scrutinized the mansion's every angle, window and door. It was a massive structure with lush gardens, the whole of it standing behind a tall fence of wrought iron. The home had numerous entrances and exits, and there didn't seem nearly enough men to maintain an adequate watch.

"There," he whispered, pointing toward the rear of the building as it came into view.

A single Scarlet Sword slumped upon a bench, stoop-shouldered with a bottle of wine beside him. He looked blearily about, seemingly untroubled by the combat raging not far away.

Lannick looked to Cudgen Ashworn. "Can you take him out from here? Silence him with a single arrow?"

Cudgen stared about. "Get me a better angle," he said quietly. "Then I'll skewer the son of a bitch."

They walked to the intersection just ahead then turned to move along the rear of the property. The Scarlet Sword glanced to them but briefly, returning his attention to his wine.

"Here's a good spot," said Cudgen.

"Quickly," whispered Lannick. "Ogrund's concealed us, but we'll look suspicious if we linger."

Cudgen drew an arrow from his quiver. "I'll not take long." He fitted the shaft to his bowstring and drew, groaning as he did. "Damned ribs," he hissed.

Lannick leaned near him. "Can you do it? If the soldier cries out we'll have trouble."

Cudgen sniffed and nodded his thin face. His hands shook but then steadied. "No one's robbing me of this."

He let fly and the arrow plunged into the Scarlet Sword's gullet with a *thud*. The wide-eyed, red-cloaked soldier collapsed from the bench, rolling into a bed of flowers with soft rustle.

Cudgen grunted. "No one."

"Let's go," Lannick said, pointing toward a nearby doorway of the mansion. "The other soldiers are elsewhere for now."

They bolted forward, pouring through the gate and across the grounds. Lannick leapt over the fallen Scarlet Sword and pressed toward the entrance. The door gave way with a sharp shove and in moments he and his companions had squeezed their way inside the mansion.

He felt the chill immediately.

"Ogrund…" he whispered.

"I sense it, Lannick. I sense there may be a good number of them. We must take care."

Lannick clenched his blade all the tighter and sidled down the short hallway before them.

Soon they came to a chamber, a larder seemingly intended for fresh stores of bread and produce. Now, though, withered vegetables drooped in wet sacks and loaves of molded bread wilted upon the shelves. All of it reeked of decay.

A door stood at the chamber's far end and Lannick eased it open. The room beyond—a kitchen striped with ribbons of light from shuttered windows—appeared unoccupied by anything but stench. A cauldron of fetid stew hung within a fireplace, and atop a counter rested a rotting hunk of meat swarming with flies and maggots.

"Kindling," Lannick said through a grimace as he gestured to the hearth. Against the bricks stood a low, neat stack of sticks and firewood. "Everyone grab some."

The men did as ordered, each taking a handful of dry wood. If there were as many Necrists as Ogrund suspected, they'd need flames.

Lannick led them onward, across creaky wooden floors that complained far too much for comfort. They moved into a great parlor filled with plush chairs, tapestries, and tall windows veiled by heavy curtains. An eerie quiet smothered everything.

Ogrund clasped Lannick's shoulder. "There."

Lannick turned to see a winding staircase near the front door to the mansion. He nodded. "Quietly."

They tiptoed up the stairs but the wood groaned as though they trudged. Their chainmail hissed and their weapons rattled. It seemed all too loud to Lannick's ears, especially with shadows lurking in every space unlit by the thin striations of sunlight.

He stared toward a second floor engulfed in darkness. "It's too quiet, too empty... He must know we're here."

Ogrund nodded. "Or *they* do."

Lannick ascended, trying to remain soft on his feet but the wood complained all the same. He held his sword before him and his bandaged hand drifted to his Coda. He wondered whether it'd prove wise to chance this endeavor without it. He clenched his teeth then resigned himself to the inevitable.

I'll need it.

They pressed on. The stairs led to a long hallway. Only scant light penetrated the corridor from the rooms that lined it, all the doors splintered in places. The air became ever colder.

Lannick paused to peer through cracks in the doorways. A library. Two bedrooms. Spaces lit by thin rays of sunlight but all empty.

"Where is he?" asked Arleigh.

Ogrund pointed a finger toward the ceiling. "I'd reckon there, in the attic. He and his council of Necrists."

Lannick stared ahead. After a moment he shook his head. *To the old hells with it.* With his wounded hand he pried open the lacquered box holding his Coda then slipped the hand through. He twisted his wrist and the cool iron closed about it.

Many images and many thoughts crowded his head, just

as he knew they would. He'd readied himself, though, and focused on the task at hand. On the person—the vicious murderer—who awaited him just ahead. On his dead family. On the last decade stolen from him.

On vengeance.

The thoughts and images faded. He sucked in a steadying breath then led his companions down the hallway. Then down another and another again.

They came to the base of another stairwell, the chill intensifying as though the cold cascaded from the ceiling. Lannick caressed his Coda. "He *is* there," he whispered. "Waiting for us. Light the firewood. We'll use it as torches, then as weapons when the times comes."

Kaldare grunted. "But we'll forfeit any element of surprise. If the whole of this place is as dark as this, he'll perceive our approach long before we get near."

Lannick, scowling, peered toward the darkness above. "It matters not. He and his Necrists know we're coming."

They moved upward, carefully and with weapons and torches before them. Lannick couldn't be certain, but thought he heard a faint chittering upon the air. No doubt the Necrists were working their sorcery. And no doubt General Fane played some part in it all.

"Captain," whispered Arleigh. "We should just set fire to the whole fucking place. Let the flames sort these bastards out."

Ogrund grunted. "No. The Necrists could still escape through their shadowpaths. So long as they can find or form a line of shadows, they—and the general—can escape."

Lannick nodded. "We'll need to face him. We need to make certain he dies."

The tight stairwell wound to a door, heavy and shut before them. Lannick tried the knob, gently, but it was locked from within. He leaned close, trying to hear some hint of what awaited them. There were indeed chitters and slithering sounds. Necrists' voices, distant and fading.

The air's chill felt as though it faded as well.

"Ogrund?" Lannick hissed.

The Variden's narrow eyes widened. "Hurry!"

Lannick reared then smashed the door with a shoulder. The wood did not bend. He slammed his shoulder again. The wood did not give, but just then a faint *click* sounded.

He tried the knob again and the door yielded. He paused. "It's unlocked?"

"Go!" barked Ogrund.

They charged through.

The room, though, appeared empty of any foes. It was a tall, raftered attic strewn with tables and chairs haphazardly arranged. Its few, narrow windows were covered by boards and curtains of black, and no sunlight wandered within the dark. The room stank of pitch and the floors sucked at their feet.

They moved forward, staring up to the blackened beams. Their torches lit most of the space but shadows danced all about.

"They're gone," Lannick said. "Either they escaped, or were never here."

Ogrund strode on, holding his torch firmly before him. "They were here, an instant ago. I sense a shadowpath has just closed. There…" He pointed toward what seemed the darkest corner of the room. "They left through a portal there."

The room's door—the one they'd just entered—slammed shut. There came a clatter from beyond it.

Then hammers. Heavy hammers pounded from the other side.

Worse, smoke arose. A foul, black smoke from the floor beneath.

"Fire!" screamed Arleigh Lay. "Fuckers did just what we should have!"

A sweltering heat smothered them. Flames began licking their way through the floorboards.

"Dead gods!" cursed Lannick. He dashed to the door and smacked a shoulder against it.

The door wouldn't give.

He kicked it once and again and still nothing.

"Help me!" he shouted.

Kaldare rushed near. He slammed the door but to no avail. "Private Yurick!" he barked.

Kaldare's soldier bounded across floorboards that shuddered beneath his big form. After a signal from the sergeant the youth smashed the door with a shoulder that struck like a sledge. The wood splintered in places but remained unmoved.

Fire snapped and cracked and heat seared Lannick's lungs. The floor groaned and a corner of it fell away and into the fire below.

"Hurry, Lannick!" cried Ogrund.

"Try your axe, lad!" Kaldare said, taking a stride back. Lannick retreated as well.

Yurick swept his axe round then brought it forth. He

cleaved the heavy planks and the whole of them shook. He struck again and the wood gave way.

But more planks had been nailed in place beyond.

Yurick turned to Kaldare, his youthful face puzzled and his red eyebrows knitting.

"Dead gods, boy!" shouted Kaldare. "Keep at it!"

Lannick looked behind. Arleigh and Cudgen pressed close. Ogrund, though, stood at the room's far end, his Coda shining green. He stood near where the floorboards had collapsed, staring to the fire and the level below. Boards began giving way beneath him and he danced back.

Flames erupted through the breach and the planks beside it glowed like cinders.

"Ogrund!" Lannick screamed.

"I see them," he grated. "There, on the first floor. The Necrists and General Fane."

Fane.

Lannick slipped across the groaning boards to stand beside the Variden. His skin burned beneath his chainmail and sweat dripped from his brow. But his eyes widened and he dared not move away from the fires sweeping near.

There, through gaping, fiery maws in the mansion's floors, *he* stood. He stood in his red surcoat with gilded rapier in hand. He stood immobile, staring upward to them.

And his scarred face stretched with a smile.

"Fane!" Lannick screamed over the inferno's roar. Hate filled his heart and he glowered at the man. "It ends this day!"

General Fane remained still, smiling. Almost serene. Then he beckoned with a gloved hand. "It does indeed," he called, his voice rising just above the sound of the snapping flames. His smile widened, then he strode from view. At least a half-dozen robed Necrists shuffled in his wake.

Lannick whirled about. Flames engulfed the room. Arleigh and Cudgen pressed against the far wall as Yurick worked his axe and Kaldare barked desperate orders.

More gaps opened in the floor between them and the rafters had caught fire as well.

Lannick knew they were trapped. All of them were doomed if he didn't do something. He gnashed his teeth and squeezed the hilt of his sword. "Ogrund!"

Ogrund looked downward. "Remove your armor. That will lighten you, and then we can use Valis's power to get you below. I'll remain here to help your friends."

Lannick glanced to his companions squeezed against the room's edges, to Arleigh and Cudgen most of all. "N-no," he coughed, throat raw from the smoke. "I should—"

"Get below, Lannick!" urged Ogrund. "We need to get you below or we'll lose him!"

Lannick drew aside his green cloak then pulled away his heavy coat of mail. His padded shirt beneath was sticky with sweat but far less stifling than the armor. He returned his cloak to his shoulders and focused on the power of his Coda. "Ready."

"There," Ogrund said, pointing to a span of floorboards twenty or so feet down a corridor on the level beneath them. "That wood will hold. From there, find your way to the ground floor and to the general."

Lannick held his Coda and understood.

"We'll find you, Lannick. Just keep your Coda upon your arm."

Lannick moved back a few soft steps then charged

toward the widening, fiery hole, clasping Ogrund's hand as he did. He felt Ogrund tug then release him, altering his trajectory just enough as he dove toward the floor below.

Through smoke and fire he fell. With his Coda's divine gifts he found the edge of a doorframe and shoved hands against it, propelling himself farther along the hallway and toward its opposite side. He angled in midair so that his boots pressed against the far wall. He leapt onward, just enough to propel himself to the square of planks untouched by the flames.

"Go!" Ogrund shouted from above.

Lannick looked to his old comrade.

"Do this, Lannick," Ogrund said. "Do this for all of Rune."

Lannick nodded then dashed down the hall.

Lannick darted onward, feet finding the firm wood between the flames. Those spaces were few, though, and the whole house snapped and shook and seemed ready to collapse. Fires blazed all about, hungrily consuming floorboards and walls. The crackle and roar deafened him.

Most of the stairwell from the second floor to the first remained intact. Lannick danced downward, hand balancing upon the railing and steps nimble with the power of his Coda.

The flames hadn't yet devastated this level of the home, but smoke swelled throughout. Lannick's eyes burned and he blinked away tears. After a moment he studied what remained of the mansion, seeing only dark silhouettes of fineries and furnishings and a thin, vertical thread of light ahead of him.

Despite the heat he felt again the chill of the Necrists. They weren't far. Possibly somewhere within the mansion, possibly somewhere just without.

He drew his sword and looked again to the light, to the mansion's main entry.

He reckoned the front door stood ajar, something he'd not seen when they'd entered the place. He crept forward, eyes darting about the dark but finding nothing. The fire's fury sounded loudly but there were harsh sounds from outside as well.

He clenched his jaw and came to the door. Drawing a breath of the cleaner air, he peeked through the crack.

Beyond, a battle raged, the writhing edges of it not more than a few blocks distant. What seemed more than a thousand soldiers crowded wide streets and tight bridges, steel clashing and shining beneath the afternoon sun. Many soldiers with red sashes fought alongside many more wearing the black stripe, all pressing against a diminishing force of Scarlet Swords and soldiers in their charge.

Black Jon's done it...

He smiled crookedly.

But he knew there was still the matter of the man.

Still the matter of vengeance.

He chanced opening the door just wider. He looked about the mansion's manicured gardens for some sign of the general but could see none.

"*Where are you?*" he whispered. He suspected once the general caught sight of the battle he'd plan to get far away, perhaps on a fast ship waiting in Riverweave's harbor.

He eased the door wider, wondering if Fane and his Necrists stood in stunned silence just outside his narrow view.

The cold feel of the Necrists' presence slithered down his spine.

They are very close...

Then came a cold, crushing sensation around his chest.

Icy coils seized him. The darkness wrapped about his arms and legs and torso. The tendrils bit and squeezed his flesh. They ripped him from the doorway and back to the room's black interior.

"No!" Lannick screamed, struggling against the shadowy bonds. The tendrils spun him about and held him before his foes.

In the swirling smoke six Necrists grinned at him, their pale, patchwork faces writhing against gnarled stitches of black. Among them hunched a misshapen Shodafayn dwarf, and just behind stood General Fane. Fane wore a smug, sick look upon his scarred face, black eyes twitching madly.

"It ends this day," Fane said. "Just as you said, Captain deVeers."

The tendrils wound tighter and Lannick felt his bones creak and crack. He winced, he wheezed, but tore his thoughts from the pain to the power of his Coda.

"No!" he roared again.

Six Necrists was a fearsome number for one Variden to handle—but Necric powers were weakest when the sun wound overhead. Lannick worked his will with his Coda and forced away the black tendrils just enough to free his sword-arm.

His sword dripped now with green fire and Lannick hacked against the cold bindings that seized him. It felt as though the shadows had physical form, resisting the blade. He cleaved again and again, his sword slowly carving through those swirls of deepest darkness.

At last the black tentacles twitched and wheeled away. They retreated and diminished and Lannick fell to the mansion's floor.

He smacked against the hilt of his sword—just enough to tweak the old wound to his ribs—but quickly regained his footing.

"Seize him!" shrieked Fane.

Lannick darted back several strides, Coda aglow and eyes straining to find the Necrists. The fires flared about the room, licking the walls and roiling against the ceiling. The thick smoke made it difficult to see much of anything and the Necrists' chittering grew ever louder. Lannick rubbed at his eyes but could discern little of his foes.

A whip of shadow lashed at him from the darkness, searing his side. He buckled for an instant only to be thrashed by another. He buckled again, dropping to a knee as he flailed his sword and blindly tried to strike his enemies in the smoke-filled blackness.

Fane laughed, somewhere. Lannick's eyes darted toward the sound, but so much smoke and shadow choked the room it was impossible to locate anything.

The shadows seized him once more. Their cold forms wrapped about his chest and held him down, keeping him upon his knees and against the floorboards. He worked against the bonds but could not stand or break loose.

There came the sound of boots upon wood. *Click, click, click.* Lannick clutched his sword with white knuckles, hoping to free himself for the briefest of moments. Just long enough to kill the man who tormented him still.

"You humiliated me at Pryam's Bay," Fane scolded. "You humiliated me and I *broke* you. I *did* break you. I ordered my men to kill your family. And then? Then your arrogance and your betrayal of the High King's banishment were grounds for execution. But he pardoned you. I honored that pardon, Lannick. You were a broken man, and for years I respected the High King's edict, permitting you to wallow in your grief." Fane sucked in a breath. "But then you defiled my daughter…"

Lannick turned his head upward to the general with a scowl. "I saved her life, Fane."

General Fane smiled. "Did you? She's dead, now. Dead and in many pieces. When they failed to capture you at Vandyl's keep, the Necrists came for her after all. Her and her sister."

Lannick struggled against the tendrils of shadow but could move little. "You sick bastard…"

Fane laughed, a clipped, rapid laugh that grated against the ears. He caressed a rounded object in his hand. "Power has a price, Lannick."

"Y-your Auruch," Lannick coughed from the smoke. "You traded her for an Auruch."

Fane looked away. "Her, and much, much more…. But as I said, power has a price." He drew his rapier, steel sliding from the scabbard with a hiss. "I listened to you, you know. I listened to you work to defeat me. I listened to you plead to Thane Vandyl, which is why I have assassins disposing of the man even now."

"You bastard," Lannick cursed.

Fane sniffed. "I listened to your talk at the deserters' encampment and I listened as loyal Harl encased you in a coffin and I heard you cry out in agony. Through the ears of my Auruch I've listened to *many* voices, Lannick—I've listened to whatever voices in this realm I desired to hear, and I've learned much. Your death, however, is something I'll gladly witness with my *eyes*."

More tendrils wound about Lannick, frigid and painful. They pulled him from the floor and dragged him upward. He twisted and fought against the grasp but his efforts were in vain.

Fane pressed his rapier forward, forcing Lannick's chin upward with the blade. "Keep your edges sharp, lad," he grinned. "Your dear friend said that, yes? The one the Necrists butchered?"

Lannick snarled. "You coward! You won't face me without your Necrists or Scarlet Swords. Too much a coward to face me alone!"

"I'd wanted you to die in the fire, and you will. It seems fitting. I'd intended you to burn in the attic, but this will prove all the more satisfying. This way you can bleed upon my blade before the fires consume you."

Lannick struggled, jerking and kicking. But his sword-arm remained pinned to his side and in the pain and confusion he found it difficult to narrow his thoughts to his Coda. Worse, the whole mansion seemed on the verge of collapse, flames devouring wood that groaned and bent and burned.

Horrid screams came from above.

Fane smirked. "I fear the fire is taking your friends."

Lannick growled, then spat in Fane's face.

Fane swiped away the spittle with a gloved hand then sniffed sharply. In an instant his steel whistled as he whipped back then jabbed his rapier into Lannick's gut. He withdrew the blade as quickly as he'd thrust it, then regarded Lannick with black, twitching eyes.

Lannick gasped, wanting to slump to the floor but the shadowy bindings held him fast. An awful pressure filled his abdomen, a great, pulsing pain. Hot blood pumped from the wound and soaked his shirt. He tried to cry out but his voice emerged soft and pathetic.

Fane's eyes narrowed and he came closer. "It hurts? Just wait for the flames."

Something snapped overhead. Fane looked about and seemed to study the blaze. He turned to the Necrists. "It's time we leave. Create your path."

Lannick felt the icy bonds slip away and he flopped to the floor.

The pain was terrible.

His sword fell from his hand. He ignored the clatter, though, clutching the welling wound in his gut. He sucked in a breath then twisted to see the silhouette of the stunted Shodafayn waddling toward a far corner of the room and the Necrists following it.

Fane, though, remained. "Bleed, Lannick," he laughed, nudging Lannick's forehead with the toe of his boot. "Once again, you are left with only that." He spun on a heel and took a step toward the room's opposite end. "Bleed, for it's all you've done for a decade now, all you've done since you dared challenge me. And now you will bleed and then burn." He walked on.

Lannick drew a trembling, bloody hand from his wound and clutched his Coda. He swooned and hurt profoundly but with what was left of him he willed his mind to the instrument. He could not allow this moment—*this moment*—to escape him.

After an instant a surge, a divine surge, filled him. He reached for his prized sword and pushed himself to a knee.

"Fane!" he spat through a cough. He drew deep upon the power of his Coda, his mind finding potencies he'd all but forgotten. He struggled then rose to stand and steadied his sword before him. "Fane! The same coward who would've lost the battle of Pryam's Bay but for me and my men, who then tried to destroy all those who outshone him! You are the worst and weakest of all."

Fane whirled about, rapier in hand. "You'd like to bleed more, Lannick? You'd like to bleed more before you burn?" He snorted then strode back toward Lannick, twirling his blade before assuming a precise fencing stance. "Very well."

Lannick focused all he could upon the Coda, knowing he'd not be able to stand without it. He absorbed its power and his limbs tingled. Green flames again poured across his sword.

Fane lunged. Lannick swiftly parried, sending the strike wide. He winced, though, as the pounding pain seared his guts anew with the movement. Worse, the pain pulled his thoughts from his Coda.

The general whipped his blade about and lunged again. Lannick dodged but the sharp steel pierced flesh near his hip. The blade whipped about once more and Lannick felt the weapon slice his cheek.

Fane laughed his staccato laugh.

The sound of it burned Lannick—burned him more than all the blazes about them. Rage erupted within and he swung his blade toward the general with all the fury he possessed.

Fane, though, seemed to expect it. He clipped the blade just enough with his rapier, warding it harmlessly away. The effort left Lannick twisted about and Fane drove the point of his sword into the meat of Lannick's shoulder.

Lannick staggered back but Fane closed in, swiping and darting and feinting with confounding speed and precision.

Lannick chanced a glance behind, seeing the mansion's front door only a few yards away. *If I could just draw the general outside, if I could just have him witness his defeat...*

Just then the ceiling cracked. The floors above groaned and the wood snapped and shattered. Fiery timbers tumbled into the room, forming many blazing barricades. Lannick turned to see the door blocked now by a wall of wood and flame.

Heavy thuds sounded at the far end of the room. "Fuck!" came a shout.

Lannick peered through the smoke and flame before feeling a hard smack against his already bloodied shoulder— a burning floorboard from the ceiling. He staggered and fell to his knees, reckoning the whole house was coming down upon them.

Fane paused his assault, turning to stare about the chaos. Then he returned his black eyes to Lannick. He thrust his rapier forward, just beneath Lannick's chin.

Lannick had not the strength to repel it, instead looking to the general and feeling any chance of revenge and redemption bleed away.

The fires roared and the wood cracked and snapped and groaned. Screams from elsewhere in the house.

Fane sniffed. "In no arena could you best me," he crowed over the din. "I will always be your better, and today I will be your end. I took your fame, your family, and your hope. Now, we finish this sad dance."

Lannick's hands shook and his heart stuttered. He coughed and dropped his sword and clasped his Coda once more. "*Ogrund?*" he voiced within, stretching thoughts through the dull iron's divine gifts.

No answer came.

But as Lannick grasped the Coda he beheld a muddled vision: a shifting, obscure view through Ogrund's eyes. He could see his Variden companion's blade thrashing against retreating Necrists in some corner of the mansion. Arleigh Lay and Kaldare battled beside him, swinging shafts of flaming timber toward the enemy. And there, beneath them, the gutted corpse of the Shodafayn.

Lannick released the Coda and found his blade once more. He smiled. "Your Necrists are being slaughtered, Fane. Their Shodafayn is dead. The fire will take us both."

"No," said Fane, blinking.

A horrid shriek sounded—a Necrist dying.

"No!" screamed Fane. He turned, withdrawing his blade from Lannick's throat and brandishing it toward the blazes beyond.

Lannick swooned from the deep wound in his belly, in his shoulder, near his hip. His eyes blurred and the thickening smoke seared and choked the lungs.

But he drew upon all the power of his Coda and all the depths of his grief.

And he rose.

Fane stood just before him, back turned as he seemed to search for his Necrist allies.

Lannick plunged his blade into the general's back, just beneath the neck. The man tensed and twitched then sank to the floor, sliding off Lannick's blade as he did.

Lannick looked upon Fane's corpse, emotion welling within him. Tears filled his eyes and he fell again to his knees.

He coughed, pressed a hand to his abdomen, then slumped to the floorboards.

Lannick felt himself hoisted and jostled by ungentle hands. His head listed about and his toes dragged across the ground. He sensed sunlight upon him.

"Get clear!" shouted a gruff voice. "Get fucking clear!"

Lannick forced open his eyes. All the city burned and panicked soldiers ran everywhere. The streets were chaos.

"They've toppled the walls!" shouted one red-sashed soldier charging near. "The Arranese have breached the city!"

Lannick rolled his head from side to side. He saw Arleigh and Kaldare hefting him along, soot-covered faces scowling. Cudgen and Kaldare's man Yurick flanked them.

"Og…" Lannick breathed. "Ogrund?"

"Head north!" barked Kaldare. "North! This city is lost!"

"Ogrund?" Lannick wheezed with scalded lungs.

Arleigh looked to him. "Ogrund died getting us free of that furnace. He died saving you."

29
A NEW BEGINNING

FENCRESS FALLCROW FLICKED the reins of her horse, grimacing against the morning gloom. Riverweave appeared a mess of smoldering embers and steaming stink, and she didn't fancy lingering any longer than necessary.

"Look all about, boys," she said. "The whole city's been burned to the ground, but this place always held plenty of riches. Thieves have far keener eyes than soldiers so I wager we'll chance upon some overlooked loot. Perhaps more than enough to make a new beginning for ourselves when we return to Raven's Roost."

Drenj rubbed at his dark eyes and looked about the wreckage, lips trembling and nerves very clearly frayed. "You're certain they're gone?"

Fencress tugged at her cowl and stared northward. Dead bodies, hot ashes, and the burned-out bones of buildings seemed all that was left of Riverweave. "Long gone," she nodded. "The Arranese are making quick work of Rune's army, and I reckon all Rune's nobles will be bending knees to that Spider King by the time this is over. Which is why we should grab what we can and get clear of here. Lickety-split, nice and quick."

"Bending knees to the Spider King, unless…" said Paddyn, voice whistling though his missing tooth. "Unless Karnag defeated him. Like he said he would."

Fencress frowned and thought on things. "Well, if Karnag's bested that giant bastard then he's likely leading the Arranese army or terrorizing it. Either way, he'll not be prowling about all this rubbish and ruin."

Drenj sniffed. "The place is a grave, Fencress. Just the sort of thing Karnag enjoys."

"Karnag digs new graves," she said. "He doesn't loiter about old ones. Let's move along."

Many of the city's bridges had been turned to ash, though there were still enough standing to allow them to work their way ahead. They moved farther into the city, slowly, and found the whole place a wasteland.

Fencress spied some signs of life—sad signs, but signs nonetheless—as they moved deeper into the devastation. Plenty of wounded soldiers struggling about or slumping against slain comrades. Grubby bandits hunching near the dead and picking them clean of their valuables. Desperate folk wandering wide-eyed like they'd lost everything and had no idea how to begin starting over.

And, in between, stinking canals crammed with corpses.

Fencress shook her head. "The glory of war, boys. Or rather, the shitty side of war the nobles pretend doesn't exist. Folk left dead or destitute for riches and rewards they'll never share." She looked about and shook her head once more.

"There," called Paddyn, slipping off his horse to move knee-deep in the scraps of a burned home. "Ah," he said after a moment. "A purse with a few silver crowns is all."

"A shame," said Fencress. "That looked like a big house, and big houses usually mean big scores. How much have we found?"

Paddyn looked to the coins in his hand then began counting on his fingers. "Maybe thirty silver crowns? Give or take?"

"Get back on your horse," Fencress said. "We should keep moving. We'll get closer to the city's center, where I recall the fat merchants have their fat mansions. I wager we'll find something there."

Someone screamed nearby. "My child!" a woman shrieked. "My child!"

"I don't like this, Fencress," said Drenj, eyes darting about. "We've found nothing of value beyond a handful of coin. We should head home now that we finally have a chance. We should leave this place."

Fencress pulled away her cowl and shook black hair slicked with sweat. The air was steamy and smelled of death. She very nearly agreed to Drenj's suggestion but felt certain they'd come upon something.

Perhaps something just ahead.

She pulled her cowl back over her head and stared to her companions. "I'll not have our journey here be for naught. Just give it a bit longer. Then we'll get clear."

They moved onward, swaying as their mounts searched for footing amidst the carnage. The place felt a faint ghost of the bustling bazaar Fencress remembered from her last visit not too many years before. Now it seemed all filth and flotsam.

"I can't manage this, Fencress," said Drenj, shivering. "I can't stomach all this death, not any longer and not any more."

Fencress looked to the Khaldisian. The lad's eyes twitched and he mumbled beneath his breath. She eased her horse closer and clasped his shoulder with a gloved hand. "Just a while longer, my friend," she said. "Just endure this a while longer and we'll leave."

After a time, they came upon what appeared to have been a row of artisans' shops, reduced now to broken frames littered with fineries turned to blackened rags. A dozen yards ahead a group of scavengers rummaged through the remains of a potter's shop, inspecting and discarding vases and bowls, the clay shattering in the street beside them.

"There's something," whistled Paddyn. He leapt from his horse and ambled across ash and cinders toward the remnants of a tiny store. *The Gilded Garments*, read the cockeyed sign peeking from the wreckage. Paddyn reached into a pile and drew something upward, giggling with glee.

"There!" he said, holding an iron box with its lid open. The box was filled with perhaps two-dozen gold crowns. "Gold!"

Fencress straightened and beheld the scavengers with a narrow gaze, sliding her twin swords halfway from their scabbards. One looked to them with eyes agog until he spied Fencress's weapons.

Paddyn handed over the gold, a silly smile splashed on his face.

"Well done, Paddyn," Fencress said quietly, "but discretion is a thief's best friend. Keep your mouth shut when you happen upon a real score."

"Sorry, Fencress," said Paddyn. "Excited is all."

"It's alright, lad," she said, easing her weapons back inside their scabbards. "Just remember, the folk who come to the battlefield after the fighting are often worse than those who did the fighting in the first place."

They rode past the scavengers and beyond the shops to an area of the city with broader streets and swaths of ruined timbers tucked within grounds of trampled grass. These seemed the great husks of burned-out manors, perhaps the largest homes in the city.

"This, boys," Fencress said with a smirk, "is where we'll make this venture worth our while."

Paddyn pointed a finger toward a massive stack of cinders and ash inside a fenced garden. "That seems the biggest one. And no bandits about it, either."

"Let's go," said Fencress, tugging her gloves tight on her hands.

"P-please," sputtered Drenj. "We should leave." Again he seemed to talk to himself, mouth moving and head shaking.

"Not yet," said Fencress firmly, looking toward the ruins. She forged ahead, nudging her horse along a wider street cluttered with fewer corpses and little debris.

They guided their mounts though an open gate of wrought iron then into the gardens, a mess of bent and broken flowers and flattened grass surrounding a mountain of blackened ruin.

Fencress slid off her horse. "Come on, boys," she said with a wink. "We'll loot this spot then leave for Raven's Roost all the richer."

Paddyn followed suit, Drenj a long moment after.

Paddyn rushed ahead. "A fallen chandelier! And all of it silver!"

"Remember, Paddyn," said Fencress, pressing a gloved finger to her lips. "Discretion."

"Right, right," whispered the youth, admiring the tangle of metal.

Drenj tiptoed past Fencress toward the remains of a staircase, the boards toppled and burned. The Khaldisian looked down and rooted about, seeming to mumble all the while.

"Drenj, my friend?" Fencress called.

Drenj shooed a thin hand. "I... I can hear them," he said, voice just above a whisper. He pulled something away from the rubble. Then he hunched over and wept. "I can hear them..."

Fencress looked to him, brow cocked and worry on her mind.

But then something drew her gaze.

Something near the center of the wreckage, just beside a pile of fallen bricks.

Something that called to her, something that did more than just catch the eye.

She pulled tight her cowl and stared. It appeared a trifle at this distance, a curved piece of black amidst a mess of burned things.

Yet call to her it did.

She walked closer, studying the object.

A bracelet of dark iron, unclasped and open. She stared upon it, and it beckoned.

She stood just before it and recognized it as the same sort of sorcerous instrument Merek wore, the same sort of thing Merek used to capture Karnag.

Yet, again, it called to her.

She sucked in a long breath, looking at the black metal and noticing how it seemed to reflect none of the light about. She stooped, pulled the glove off her hand, then retrieved it from the ashes.

The iron felt cool. Cold, even.

She drew it close to her other wrist, knowing somehow it was *meant* to fit there. Closer still, then the iron snapped shut about her arm.

A cataract of images and voices crashed within her head. She fell to a knee, hands bracing her skull and trying to keep it in a single piece.

"No!" she screamed.

Countless voices not her own, countless visions she'd never seen with her own eyes. A war between gods. Immortal warriors—Sentinels—defeating the vile god Yrghul as the gods fell to oblivion. A terrible betrayal, then a terrible sacrifice as a Sentinel poured his power and blood into the metal objects—the Codas.

And after, a tireless vigil against the ever-present dark.

Fencress wrapped a hand about the Coda, the object glowing a dull green. She heard the voices, beheld the visions.

And one thing above all troubled her.

"Karnag…" she whispered. "What have you done?"

NEXT IN THE SEQUENCE:
THE CONCLUSION OF THE TRILOGY

THE RUIN OF HEROES

A REQUIEM FOR HEROES, BOOK THREE

COMING SOON.

www.ingramcontent.com/pod-product-compliance
Lightning Source LLC
Chambersburg PA
CBHW021836010726
47493CB00005B/1415